D1384724

GUMSHOE
ON THE LOOSE

Also by Rob Leininger

The Mortimer Angel Series
Gumshoe for Two
Gumshoe

Other Novels
Richter Ten
Sunspot
Killing Suki Flood
Maxwell's Deamon
January Cold Kill
Olongapo Liberty

GUMSHOE
ON THE LOOSE

A MORTIMER ANGEL NOVEL

ROB LEININGER

OCEANVIEW PUBLISHING
SARASOTA, FLORIDA

ISBN 978-1-60809-274-1

Published in the United States of America by Oceanview Publishing
Sarasota, Florida
www.oceanviewpub.com

10 9 8 7 6 5 4 3 2 1

PRINTED IN THE UNITED STATES OF AMERICA

For my wife, Pat,
who puts up with a lot.
A lot.

ACKNOWLEDGMENTS

This novel wouldn't exist without the dedication and expertise of the Oceanview Publishing team: Pat and Bob Gussin, Lee Randall, Emily Baar, Lisa Daily, and others. Many thanks to all of you.

Thanks also to my "readers," Tracy Ellis, Madelon Martin, and my wife, Pat, for making it appear as if I know what I'm doing.

And a special thanks to fellow writer and best-selling author John Lescroart for his unflagging support, for making me smile with almost-daily e-mails, for believing in the Gumshoe series, and for his gift to the world of the Dismas Hardy novels.

GUMSHOE
ON THE LOOSE

CHAPTER ONE

I AM A murderer.

Technically speaking.

One of these days I'll have to look up the applicable statutes to get a better handle on that, see if there's any wiggle room, but I don't think the wording offers much in the way of latitude when you remove someone from this earth with malice aforethought—so, yeah . . . technically I committed a good-sized felony, not that I'm about to give myself up. On the other hand, the Bible says something about an eye for an eye, and it was written centuries before the Nevada Revised Statutes, so I think I'll be okay during check-in at the Pearly Gates. If not, I'll have Maude Clary—Ma—for company in the other place.

Saturday evening I was sitting at the bar in the Green Room in Reno's Golden Goose casino with Ma to my left and Holiday to my right, so I had the only two women in the place all to myself, a situation with cosmic underpinnings. As a gumshoe, a PI, albeit in training, women have flocked to me like pigeons to a statue. I had no control over that. I didn't encourage it. There wasn't a damn thing I could do about it—not that I wanted to, since it put a little extra spring in my step. Ma was my new mentor and boss, sixty-two years old. She could drink me under the table any day of the week, not that we ever gave it a try. And Holiday, perched beside me, was a hell of a sight, twenty-five years old, a gorgeous girl with three inches of tight tummy showing, and enough pneumatic cleavage to cause a riot.

Pneumatic? I know from experience that if you remove the inner tube from a bicycle tire and pump it up for a while, it gets big and firm. I did this when I was twelve. I kept pumping and it eventually popped, made a hearty bang—the bicycle tire, just to be clear. But I'm older now and more worldly, able to compare over-inflated bicycle tires to other things. In life, this is called growth and sophistication.

"Don't look now, but you're getting more than your share of attention," I said to Holiday, referring to three college-age guys at the far end of the bar, drooling in her direction.

She gave them a cursory look. "Yep."

"I said, 'Don't look.'"

"I heard you. In case you didn't know, 'Don't look' means, *'Hey, look.'* Also, Mort . . ."

"What?"

"In bars, you're *still* impossible to talk to. Other places, too, like in cars, restaurants, airports, but bars are the worst."

"Anyway, kiddo, nice big smile at the lads. It's likely they're athletes. They've got a team salivation thing going. I think the guy in the Eddie Bauer polo shirt is in the lead."

"Uh-huh."

"You don't sound impressed. This is your thing, remember?"

"Not like it was before. I mean, it's okay, but it doesn't have the kick it used to. Right now, it's practically gone."

"Sorry about that."

"Don't be. What I've got with you is a lot better."

"Okay, then, I'm *not* sorry."

Ma lit a cigarette and blew a cloud of carcinogens toward the ceiling. "You two oughta get a room."

Holiday gave me a look. "Not the worst idea ever."

"Can't. This is Saturday."

"Rules were meant to be broken."

"If you break rules, you have no rules."

"Spoilsport."

The trio of hopefuls looked like poli-sci grad students, early to midtwenties, preppy in a modern-era way, shooting me dirty looks, no doubt wondering what a girl like Holiday was doing with an old coot like me, forty-two years old. At their age, I would've done the same. They would have stared bug-eyed at us if they knew what redlined her engine.

The television above the bar was tuned to a local station. News at Eleven came up on Channel Four. First up, no surprise, was the ongoing story of Jo-X's disappearance. Jonnie Xenon was Nevada's very own "gangsta" rapper, an opportunistic, foul-mouthed piece of shinola, twenty-four years old, who had taken advantage of all the flaws and loopholes in the First Amendment to make millions while encouraging kids to kill their parents and rape their hoes—a ho being pretty much any female in the vicinity who still had a pulse, not that a pulse was an absolute requirement according to Jo-X. He was pulling in something like five or six million a year, another reason I didn't like the guy, but not the main one.

"Just look at that fuckin' moron," Ma said, blowing an angry cloud of virulent green smoke at the TV—green due to the track lighting that helped to give the Green Room its name. "I know a mineshaft he could get dumped down if someone wanted to get rid of the body."

"They might've filled it in after getting Reinhart out," I said. Presidential hopeful Senator Reinhart and three others had been removed from a remote mineshaft in northern Nevada last year. Ma and I had found the person who'd murdered them, but the FBI and local police didn't know that, still didn't have a clue.

"Hope not." Ma stared at a clip of Jonnie-X onstage, gutter rapping, every third word bleeped out to get his act past the applicable FCC regulations. "Be a shame not to have a mineshaft when you need one."

Maude Clary was a battle-axe, five foot four. At last weigh-in she tipped the scale at a hundred eighty-five pounds. My estimate. The actual number was a state secret. Her hair was going gray, but she refused to color it. She was my boss and also my accomplice in that malice aforethought business that took place in Paris, France, last October, eight months ago.

Holiday, on the other hand, was five-eight, slender, a hundred twenty-six pounds, and about as beautiful and curvaceous as a girl can get. She had frizzy light blond hair in a tousled bedroom style, three inches off her shoulders. She'd also flown to France and had played a minor part in the untimely and well-deserved death of Julia Reinhart, Senator Harry Reinhart's trophy wife. Julia had crushed his skull with a length of iron pipe and dumped the carcass down that mineshaft, something that would give rich old farts with trophy wives a reason to rethink that decision—if they'd known she was the one who'd killed him.

Julia also murdered my fiancée, Jeri DiFrazzia, which still caused me to jolt awake at night with a heart so heavy and black I stayed awake for hours. So, the three of us, Ma, Holiday, and I, were close, sharing the secret pleasure of having sent Julia on a one-way trip down the river Styx from her luxury Paris hotel suite.

Which, of course, made me and Ma murderers and Holiday an accomplice, not that we were losing sleep over it.

Holiday's real name was Sarah Dellario, Holiday being something of a "stage" name, no longer used now that she wasn't making the rounds of bars pretending to be a hooker while she searched for her sister, Allie—also murdered by Julia Reinhart.

Holiday and I had been seeing each other in a quasi-informal manner, probably not understandable to outside observers if there had been outside observers. It didn't involve aerobic activity, but we sometimes ended up soapy in a shower so it was a great way to get clean. For historical and sentimental reasons, this took place on Tuesdays and was a weekly morale booster for both of us even if Ma gave us a lot of good-natured flack about it.

On the other hand, Sarah—Holiday's alter-ego—was a civil engineering student at the University of Nevada in Reno, with a three-point-eight-five grade point average, able to concentrate for hours on end on things like structural dynamics, eigenvectors, and unholy arcane shit like that. She knew a hell of a lot more math than I did, elementary calculus being not only an oxymoron but something she thought of as a no-brainer. I liked both sides of her, but was able to converse better with "Holiday," as less math was involved.

"While I'm gone," Ma said to me, pointing the last two inches of her cigarette at the TV at a clip of Jo-X entering a limo with his latest arm candy, Celine, "you oughta find that dimwit."

"Who? Celine?"

Ma skewered me with a look. "*Jo-X*, boyo."

"I'll get right on that."

"It's what you do, God only knows how." She paused for a moment, then said, "Just so you know, if you *do* come across that rancid sonofabitch and cause another one of your uproars, you're fired."

"Okay, then, I won't get right on it, even though that would put Clary Investigations on the map and be fantastic for business. You could up your rate to two hundred an hour, get even more high-end business. By the way, when are we going to make that Clary & Angel Investigations?"

Which, I thought, made sense. My name is Mort Angel. My birth certificate has me as Mortimer Angel—which is wrong and my mother's fault since—obviously—her handwriting was as bad forty-two years ago as it is now. I don't know what clown thought that squiggle or flourish she'd put at the end of Mort was "imer," but all sorts of legal crud ended up in the name Mortimer Burris Angel, which is how I have to sign documents when the IRS gets picky and tight-assed. And, having worked as a field agent for the IRS for sixteen years, I can say picky, tight-assed, and humorless doesn't begin to cover it. Criminal, however, does. Because I discovered I had a soul, I had to crawl out of that sewer, not that I harbor any resentment. Any place that puts you in touch with your soul can't be all bad.

Ma looked up at the ceiling. "Well, now, lemme see—what's the weather like in hell today? How close *is* it to freezin' over?"

Holiday laughed softly, then put a hand on my arm. A very nice hand it was, too.

So . . . Jonnie Xenon had disappeared without a trace. Good deal. He'd missed a concert in Seattle and hadn't been seen in five days—five endless, heartbreaking days that had millions of throbbing little hearts devastated, dying in little teenaged chests. I imagined tens of thousands of fourteen-year-old girls crumpled in their beds, unable to eat, crying their eyes out at the loss. Such is the nature of our world in which a sociopath like Jo-X can become a teenager's love object—in which perception trumps reality, even for so-called adults to the point that politicians can lie their way into office then do as they damn well please. Jonnie Xenon had become Jo-X in the brave new patois of the rich and famous that gave us JLo, A-Rod, and Kim K. It didn't always pan out, however. Barack Obama would have been B-Ob, or BOb, which would obviously have become "Bob," which lacked the requisite pizazz—Bob being a neighbor who forgets to return borrowed tools and shrugs when you tell him his dog craps in your front yard.

Jo-X was six-five, a hundred and sixty-four pounds, looked like a two-by-four with limbs. Onstage he was bare-chested, glinting with body piercings, blond hair whirled in a blender—a stringy punk with a sunken chest and a mouth so foul Clorox wouldn't get the stench out, although I'd be willing to give it a try. A hundred million adults in the country wished him ill, so I think Ma was wrong about firing me if I came across him—which wasn't going to happen. But if I did, it would be because he was dead, since that's my MO, even though it has never been my fault, at least not in the state of Nevada. I wasn't the one who decapitated Reno's mayor and district attorney last summer, nor did I chop off the hand of our lying senator, Harry Reinhart, and FedEx it to myself, then chuck him down a mineshaft, all of which are other stories. Good ones, too, as far as they go.

Anyway, Maude Clary was my new boss. I was working on my ten thousand hours of training to become an actual PI, not a PI-in-training, which is what I've been for the better part of a year. She and I get along well even though she has a poster of me on the wall of her office in which I'm standing with a smiley grimace on my face, wearing nothing at all but a little red body paint on my . . . body that looks more or less like a lumpy jock strap, at least from a distance. Body paint, by the way, that Holiday brushed on that critical region a few minutes before she and I participated in San Francisco's World Naked Bike Ride in March, three months ago—over fifteen hundred nude or seminude people riding bicycles through the streets in what was theoretically a protest, but was actually a happy, smiling bunch of people who wanted to ride naked through the streets. The slogan for the WNBR is "As bare as you dare," which pretty much tells the story of how and why. Ma took the picture from the sidelines and turned it into an eleven-by-seventeen laminated poster. She keeps it hidden behind another poster that she can swing out of the way on a little hinge arrangement whenever she needs a laugh or to remind me of who's the boss in the place.

"Check this out, Mort," she'll say, then *voila*! there I am, in the buff except for that body paint, listening to her cackle. If she wasn't twenty years older than me, I'd beat the tar out of her. Thing is, I'm six-four, two hundred eight pounds—pretty much all muscle after digging six hundred fence post holes in Australia in four and a half months during a "summer down under"—so getting a jury to see my side of things would be tough. Worse, to explain roughing her up I would have to make that poster exhibit número uno in my defense, so . . . forget it.

Jo-X's disappearance was wrapping up on the television. His latest girlfriend, "Celine," mysterious, tall, beautiful, with skin so smooth and dark it was like fine obsidian, was also missing. She was just Celine—a one-namer like Cher and Madonna. I had no particular opinion about Celine other than typical male awe at her wardrobe and the size of her breasts, and disgust at her taste in boyfriends, but Jo-X's disappearance was the best news I'd heard in a long time. Even better if he remained forever among those never heard from again.

"Ladies' room?" Ma said to Holiday, sliding off her barstool.

"Sure."

Off they went. I don't know what women do in there, but they often go in pairs. Possibly a woman alone risks mugging. More likely, they talk about the guys they leave behind, then have to fix their mascara once they're finished laughing. I'll have to ask. All I know is that I've never said, "Yo, Earl, want to go to the men's room with me?" If I did—and, worse, if Earl took me up on it—we'd arrive back to a pair of empty chairs.

But tonight, I stayed when they left, as I generally do, and this time it paid off. An incredibly beautiful black girl came in the door ten seconds after Ma and Holiday went out, looked around, then came over and settled onto the pre-warmed barstool to my right.

Which figured.

As a field agent for the IRS, one of Uncle Sam's goons, women had avoided me as if I had signs of late-stage bubonic plague—not a big surprise since the IRS has a reputation for ruthlessness and a tool with which lawless administrations go after political enemies. On a more daily basis, Internal Revenue is used as an instrument of domestic terror. But a year ago I'd quit the IRS to become a PI, a gumshoe, and my life changed overnight—literally. Arriving home the night before my first day on the job, I discovered a naked blond in my bed. Friendly one, too. Now this sort of thing—the girl wandering into the Green Room and taking a stool next to mine—had become routine. I'd become a babe magnet à la Mike Hammer. Better than, actually.

The girl, probably not two years into her twenties, turned to me and said, "Mr. Angel?"

Damn—magnet theory right out the window. "I hope that was just a lucky guess, kiddo."

"Hardly. My dad doesn't like you. He says you're a maverick and unprofessional. But, I think, maybe . . . that's what I need."

CHAPTER TWO

A MAVERICK. I liked that. *And* unprofessional, so I was two for two. I didn't know her dad from Bill Cosby, but that maverick thing was just great. I could see putting that on a pebbled window on my noir office door in a dim hallway—a door with a bullet hole or two in it for the feng shui. Or . . .

"I should have a sign in front of my office with a bullet hole in it," I said. "Mort Angel, Maverick PI."

Her smile looked a little green, and I didn't think it was from the lighting. Her skin was a creamy shade of walnut. She was Halle Berry black, maybe one shade lighter, and every bit as beautiful, but taller. I figured her for five-eight, five-nine, with a body that would leave nothing but heartbreak and dreams in her wake. A scent of lilac came off her, so subtle it might have been my imagination.

"Wouldn't that be Mortimer Angel, Maverick PI?"

"Mortimer? Don't know anyone by that name," I said. "Sounds like it'd have to be a birth certificate error. There was a Snerd by that name, but he was a dummy."

"You're a maverick, but not a Mortimer?"

"Right."

"So, all that hoopla on the news last year was wrong?"

"Right."

"Right it was wrong—or wrong it was right?"

"Well, I didn't say wrong, so it couldn't have been the latter, but you sound a lot like me when I want to be annoying."

She offered up a half-smile. "It's a knack."

"Spooky. I've got a lot of cool knacks, too, but I would find it very annoying if you're as annoying as me. Buy you a drink?"

The girl slid off the stool. She hadn't been there one full minute and already she was starting to attract attention, as gorgeous girls do. More heavy breathing was coming from the three losers at the end of the bar. She looked at them, then back at me. "I can't stay. I mean, now's not a good time. Those guys are ogling, and it's likely the two women you were with will be back soon. Do you have a card? Like a business card?"

I did. Proudly, I got one out of my wallet. It said Mort Angel, Private Investigator, Clary Investigations. I made a mental note to change that to "Maverick PI" as soon as possible and have another five hundred cards printed up.

She wrote a number on the back as the bartender, Patrick O'Roarke, eased closer to get in on the action. "Call me," she said. "Tomorrow morning right at ten."

"Right at?"

"Ten. I'll have my phone on, waiting." She turned to go.

"Hey, hold on a minute, Buttercup."

"What?"

"For starters, who's your dad? The guy who doesn't like me?"

"Tomorrow, Mortimer. I can't talk here." She cast an eye at O'Roarke, who was hovering, giving her an admiring male look.

"Mort. At least tell me your name."

"Danya."

She walked away. I watched her go. I had to—just one of those things that can't be helped, at least not without special drugs and a lobotomy. The dress was short and tight and she was slender, model perfect, hips like a dancer, legs long and shapely. The weird thing, though, was that I hadn't gotten a vibe of sexual tension from her, no estrogen mist trying to pull me in. She was a hell of a sight, but that was all. Strange. Maybe my PI aura was on the fritz and this was the first sign of its going dark.

"Man," O'Roarke said, voice brimming with awe. "I gotta get me a PI license."

"Or a lobotomy," I said.

"Yeah, that'd do it. Have to be a good one though, not one of those do-it-yourself lobotomies."

* * *

Holiday and Maude Clary came back as Danya was leaving. Holiday slid onto the once-again-vacated barstool. "Wow! Who was that?"

"Danya."

"Danya who?"

"Wish I knew." I looked at the back of my card. All she'd left was a number. I stuck it in my wallet. Twenty-six years ago, it would have been right next to a never-to-be-used condom.

"You don't know her, huh?"

"Nope."

"She just sidled in and sat down next to you?"

"Sidled? I'm not sure. How about you demo that for me and I'll let you know."

"She was real pretty, Mort."

"Uh-huh. How do you know she sat next to me? She leave a ring of fire on the barstool?"

"Close. It's that smoldering envy in O'Roarke's eyes."

I gave O'Roarke a look, and he grinned and moved away.

"So, what'd she want?" Holiday asked.

"A phone call. At ten tomorrow morning."

She smiled easily. "You gonna do that?" Like Jeri before her, Holiday wasn't the jealous type. It had taken me quite a while to come to grips with that, but eventually I'd had to admit that she had no intention of staking a claim on my hide. Whatever we had wasn't destined to be forever.

"Don't know yet," I said.

On the stool to my left, Ma said, "We're between cases. Might be business we could use."

"Anything's possible."

"Yeah, well, if it's business, it's *my* business, so don't scare her off."

"Scare her off? A big old pussycat like me? I don't know how you come up with off-the-wall stuff like that, Ma."

"Like I said, don't scare her off."

Holiday took my hand again. "Yeah, don't scare her off. Just remember I get you on Tuesdays."

I put an arm around her waist and gave her a squeeze. "Not the kind of thing that slips my mind, woman."

Ma stared at us. "You two don't quit horsing around, I'm gonna unroll a fire hose or call 911."

"Settle down, Ma," I said.

"Right. *Me* settle down." She knocked an empty glass against the bar. "Hit me again, Pat, you doll, you," she said to O'Roarke. She gave me a look. "That Danya girl . . . whatever she wants, don't go makin' headlines again, boyo. She looked like the type."

"What type is that?"

"Beautiful, busty, slinky, trouble."

"I've learned not to trust that sort of thing, Ma."

"Yeah? Why's that?"

"Holiday here. It's her fault. She's beautiful, busty, slinky, pretended to be a hooker last year, which is sort of like trouble, and turned out to be an engineering student with an IQ off the charts. I've got Danya pegged as a nuclear physicist."

"Possible," Ma replied. "But I play the odds, so I'm not thinking physicist. With me off to Memphis on Amtrak tomorrow morning, I don't want to see you in the news by the time I get there, which won't be for two and a half days."

"Check your cell phone on the way, Ma. Maybe you won't have to wait that long."

Holiday laughed, then she slid off the barstool and took my hand. "I wonder if we could make an exception to . . . to Tuesday."

"An exception?"

"Yes. Like . . . tonight. Call it a Special."

"Well, I don't know. It's only Saturday. I'll have to check my appointment calendar, see what I've got going."

"Uh-huh. Lots of things to do between now and tomorrow morning. Maybe you could cancel something."

"Life is a whirlwind of responsibilities and obligations."

"I'm glad you understand that. Which means we should go."

"Yeah? Where to, and do what?"

Her eyes sparkled. "I want to . . . show you something."

Ma laughed. "You two. Just don't forget you're gonna drive me to the station tomorrow, Mort. Train leaves at seven fifty, so you better come by the house by seven, if you can get on your feet that early."

Ma was headed to Memphis to visit her kid, Taryn Curtis, thirty-six years old, married, two kids about to become teenagers. Taryn was in real estate, working on her second million dollars. Ma was going to be gone for two weeks.

"I'll be there," I said.

"Make sure he's up and on time," Ma said to Holiday.

"I'll get him up, Ma. Give me half an hour."

Ma waved us away.

* * *

We went to Holiday's apartment, which was a ten-minute walk from the university. In April, I'd sold the Ralston Street house and bought Jeri's place on Washington Street between First and Second, half a mile west of downtown Reno. Her brother, Ron DiFrazzia, sold it to me. Giving up the house on Ralston Street felt weird. I'd lived there all my life except for a seven-year period when I'd rented it out after Dallas and I had been married for three years and moved into something bigger. After the divorce, I moved back in.

But things were different now. It was taking me a while to adjust to it, all my stuff in the large, well-maintained, two-story house Jeri had owned. The house on Ralston now belonged to a couple in their twenties with a year-old baby. Now I had a house with elbow room—and a home gym, which I used frequently, religiously, in fact. I could do twice as many chin-ups as I could in college. After digging post holes when I was recovering in Borroloola, Australia—recovering from Jeri's murder—I was in better shape than I'd ever been. No point in letting it go to seed. I'd done roughly ten million foot-pounds of work digging those holes in tough red earth. According to Holiday, I had a *Thunder Down Under* look. Who was I to argue with that?

She opened the door to her apartment and we went in. "How about a shower?" she said, unbuttoning her blouse.

Again—who was I to argue with that?

* * *

At the Amtrak station at seven twenty the next morning, Maude Clary and I sat in the waiting room downstairs. The tracks were thirty-three feet below ground level in "The Trench," a 265-million-dollar rectangle of ugly concrete that ran east–west through the heart of Reno's gambling district and was still causing untold financial trouble for the city. Even paying the interest on the loan was a headache. The Trench was an enduring monument to the hubris of elected officials who'd rammed the project through, even though sixty-five percent of the voters had opposed it. And, of course the voters were right, and the officials were wrong, but since when was that a surprise? And since when did voters—your basic know-nothing citizens—have the right to tell brilliant, infallible elected officials what they wanted or what made sense?

At seven thirty-five, the train pulled in. Minutes later, Ma and I went aboard, and I helped her get her luggage settled in a sleeper car.

"That Danya girl," Ma began, then stopped.

"Yup," I prompted.

She stared at me for a moment, then sighed, as women often do around me. "Lemme know what she says. We'll see if it's anything we want to get involved in."

"Will do."

"She was one god-awful beautiful girl, boyo."

"She was? I don't notice stuff like that."

Ma punched my chest. "Don't let that spin you around."

"Me? Spun around by a dame? You kiddin'?"

Ma shook her head. "Jesus."

"I've got Sarah," I said. Sarah, Holiday—Ma and I called her either or both.

"Right. She's god-awful gorgeous, too." Ma patted the bed she would be sleeping on the next two nights. "This thing's kinda hard. Hope I sleep okay." She turned and faced me. "What we do, Mort, is we investigate stuff. So, see what this Danya girl wants, but don't do nothing 'til I give you the go-ahead."

"You're the boss, boss."

"Damn right." She gave me a look. "You've got my number. Keep me in the loop all the way. If this girl's gonna be trouble, we don't touch it."

"In the loop. Got it."

About then a guy came by and told me to get off the train or buy a ticket, they were leaving in five minutes. I kissed Ma on the cheek before I left, then watched and waved to her from beside the tracks as the train pulled away.

* * *

Right on time at ten a.m., sitting in my Toyota Tercel in the parking lot of an IHOP after breakfast, I phoned the number Danya had given me. The Toyota was a vintage piece of shit twenty-some years old that I couldn't get rid of—not after selling the Ralston house. I get attached to the past in strange ways. Maybe it was that the side mirror of the Tercel howls when the car reaches sixty miles an hour. If I got a new set of wheels, it probably wouldn't do that unless I gave it a mirror transplant.

Danya didn't answer. The call went to voice mail—a generic message that gave me no information. I checked the number, tried again. Nothing. I left a message that I'd called as requested, then put the car in gear and took off.

Women. Easy come, easy go. Danya wasn't going to be a bit of trouble, so Ma could rest easy.

I was rolling north on Kietzke Lane doing forty miles an hour when my cell phone rang. I picked it up and answered it—illegally. I had a hands-free headset somewhere. Maybe in the glove compartment or under a front seat. I wasn't on the best of terms with the Reno police department, in particular, a detective named Russell Fairchild, whom I'd embarrassed last summer by solving his big case for him—finding the two women who had decapitated Reno's mayor and district attorney. Oddly enough, when Senator Harry Reinhart's right hand had been shipped to me via FedEx two months later, which was a big breakthrough in that missing-person case—that still hadn't patched things up with him. Fairchild was a hard man to please.

"Mort," I said.

"Mr. Angel? Mortimer?" A woman's voice.

"Wrong number, kiddo. I don't know any Mortimers."

"I mean . . . Mort."

"Speaking. Is this Danya?"

"Yes."

Sometimes new relationships are like this. Awkward before they blossom. But I had a nice three-dimensional image of her in my head, the way she'd filled out that dress the night before.

"Okay," I said. "What's up?"

"I . . . well, last night I was going to have you come over to my place today, my house, so we could talk. In private."

She got that far, then stalled.

"I hear a 'but' in there. You were *going* to have me drop by."

"*But* . . . there's a guy snooping around my house. I don't know what he wants, and . . . he looks kind of creepy. Right now I can't . . . can't . . ." Her voice drifted off.

"A guy?" I was suddenly on high alert, which is what gumshoes like me are known for. Damsels in distress and all that. In the IRS we took damsels for all they were worth, young, old, didn't matter. Things had changed since King Arthur's day.

"I was in the kitchen," Danya said. "I looked toward the front of the house and saw him peering in a living room window. I went out the back and over our back fence. My car was parked on the street. I . . . well, I took off. I can't talk to anyone right now. Except for you, I mean. Anyway, I'm pretty sure I forgot to lock the back door when I went out, so now I don't know what to do."

"Call the police."

"I can't do that."

Okay, *that* was fishy, but being a sensitive guy I didn't tell her that. Last night she'd wanted a maverick PI, which was also fishy, but fishy was a big part of my growing repertoire as a PI. And that maverick thing really had me going. I wanted to explore it further—which meant I might not live to see fifty, but . . .

"Am I on the payroll yet, kiddo?" I asked.

"We'll have to talk about that later. Right now, there's that guy skulking around."

Skulking. The plot and the prose was thickening.

"What's the address?" I asked. "I'll come check it out."

Exactly as if I hadn't learned a goddamn thing last year, having almost been murdered twice in less than three months, but in the category of slow learners I reign supreme. Or . . . it might've been that Hammer-Magnum-PI thing—getting tangled up with stunning women. Now that I was a gumshoe, I attracted them like white cat fur to a black wool suit.

She gave me a street address on Elmcrest Drive in northwest Reno. "Hang tight," I said. "Where are you now?"

"I . . . well, I'd rather not say. I mean, I don't know what's going on right now, and there's that creepy-looking guy."

Still fishy. Perfect.

"Keep your phone on," I said. "I'll be in touch."

I hit the interstate, I-80, and took the Toyota up to yodeling speed—sixty miles an hour. At that velocity, the side mirror sounds a lot like Madonna. Jeri's house—mine now—was more or less on the way, so I got off the freeway at Keystone, swung by and got a .357 Magnum revolver, stuck it in a shoulder holster and covered it with a dark-blue windbreaker, then continued north and west on surface streets—up West Seventh, right on Stoker, left on Elmcrest, a residential street that meandered up into the foothills, and started checking house numbers.

The house was set back about twelve yards from the street, dark beneath good-sized elms. A driveway went along the west side of the single-story house, ending at an unattached garage in back that had a slight lean to the left. The house itself was an older ranch-style affair, gloomy-looking with brown siding and dark-green trim. A gutter was loose in front, awkwardly wired to an eave. The lawn was patches of grass struggling to survive, but most of it had given up long ago. Reno was in the midst of yet another drought. With population growth out of control, lawns were becoming a thing of the past. It didn't look like the kind of place I'd expect a girl like Danya to live in, as beautiful and intelligent as she was. Which was a kind of prejudice, I know, but there it was all the same. The house didn't seem to fit her.

I drove by slowly, didn't see a creep hanging around, peering in windows. That didn't mean there hadn't been one. I parked two houses up the street and walked back, loosening the gun in its holster, keeping it out of sight under the windbreaker.

The neighborhood was quiet, no kids running around. Maybe they were still in bed. It was the end of the last week of June. School was out for the summer, but no kids? Maybe all their electronic shit was keeping them indoors and obese. No cars were moving on the street. About that time, it occurred to me

that Danya had said "our" back fence. *Our?* A slip of the tongue?
A live-in boyfriend? I turned left and ambled up the driveway
beside the house with a faint chill humming in my spine, keeping my eyes on the house and its windows, flicking them to the
backyard and the canted garage every few seconds. Last year
I'd done something like this—twice—and both times I'd come
across murderous psychos.

I rounded the corner at the rear of the house, and goddamn if
there wasn't a creep coming out the back door. At least I thought
it was a creep, but the species has so many faces that this was
only a guess on my part. Until, that is, a sneaky, startled look
gave him away.

"Hey!" I yelled, to see what would happen.

The guy jumped off a low back porch and ran—so, yep, creep.

I took off after him, eight yards behind when he darted around
the far corner of the house, headed for the street, camera on a
strap banging against his hip, and found a fence with a locked
gate in his path. He was hiking himself over when I caught his
belt and hauled him back, threw him against a garbage can, hard.
He bounced off the can, spun, and landed on the ground half
buried in a shrub. The garbage can fell over, dumped orange
peels, coffee grounds, soiled paper towels, and other crud onto a
concrete walkway.

"Hey, don't . . . don't do nothin' you'll regret, man," said the
creep, holding his hands out defensively.

"So far so good," I replied. "Who the fuck are you?"

"*Celebrity News.*"

Celebrity News? The only thing that came to mind was a sleazy
tabloid that wouldn't make decent toilet paper. Which didn't
make a bit of sense—but being a gumshoe, I thought it might be
a clue. To what, I didn't know. Things were still fishy.

"What's your name?" I asked, glowering at him as if I owned the place. He rolled out of the shrub and hiked himself backward until he was sitting on the ground against the side of the house. If he worked for the *News*, he might be leaving an oil slick on the siding. I would have to check that later.

"Bill," he said. His camera was on the ground. He picked it up and held it protectively in his lap.

"Bill who?"

"Hogan. Bill Hogan. I'm an investigative reporter."

"A reporter?"

"Yeah." He glowered at me. "Investigative."

"For *Celebrity News*? The tabloid."

"News magazine. Yeah."

"Tabloid. Means you're a Gutter Press investigator."

"If you say."

I let that sink in for a few. Son of a bitch was going to give us genuine investigators a bad name.

"Wallet," I said.

"Huh?"

"Your wallet. Let's see it."

"Got a warrant?"

"Trust me, dimwit. My warrant leaves scar tissue, so you don't *want* to see it." I kicked his foot and put enough steel in my voice to make a lug wrench.

The steel thing worked because he dug in his jeans and tossed his wallet to me. I pulled out a driver's license. Vincent Ignacio. And half a dozen business cards for *Celebrity News*, also in the name of Vince Ignacio. Fucking things actually said Investigative Reporter. I kept one of the cards.

"Looks like you stole Vince's wallet, Bill. Maybe I should get the police over here, get you into some of those polymer flexi-cuffs, see if the *News* likes you enough to make your bail."

"Shit," he said, leaning back, giving up. "Okay, so I'm Vince Ignacio. So what?"

"There isn't any 'what,' Vinny. There's only truth, justice, and the American Way. I didn't think the *News* had reporters. I thought they just made shit up, like with a dartboard."

Maybe my voice had gone a bit soft because he smiled, sort of, and said, "They do, mostly. Space alien stuff, Loch Ness, Yetis seen dragging a moose down Main Street in a remote town in Maine. Sometimes we go after a real story, get it on the front page to get some credibility."

"And you think there's a real story here, at my place?"

"Shanna Hayes? *Hell* yeah. You kidding?"

Shanna Hayes. Didn't ring any bells with me, but now was not the time to hesitate and give this scrawny little weasel a toehold. But that last comment made me wonder.

"What about her?" I asked, giving the weasel a toehold big enough to launch him onto the roof of the house.

He gave me a long look, digging in with his eyes, evaluating, detecting ignorance, the investigative creep. "You don't know? How well do you know Shanna, anyway? Like you once saw her across a parking lot and almost said hi?"

So, he wasn't stupid. Time to roust the sonofabitch. I grabbed the front of his shirt and lifted him off the ground. He was maybe twenty-six years old and a spindly little shitbird, five-six, a hundred forty pounds in wet clothes. His hair was stringy, over his ears, nose big and pointy, lips thin, eyes close together, and he had acne scars on his cheeks. I didn't like the guy. Danya said he looked creepy, and I didn't disagree.

"Shanna and I are engaged, asshole," I said, putting my nose two inches from his. "That's how well I know her."

He laughed. "Yeah, right. Means you don't know nothin' about her. Anyway, she's so far outta your league, dude—"

When someone ten inches shorter and seventy pounds lighter laughs in your face, you know you've stepped in it. How deep, you don't know, but once you've got a bluff going you've got to keep at it or die, so I slammed him up against the side of the house hard enough to make his teeth click and his eyes snap open.

"You saying she's dumb, man, marrying me?" I snarled. "That what you're saying?"

Sensing that death might be closer than he'd thought, he said, "No no no, *hey*—"

I wasn't sure how much longer I could keep this going. I had the feeling I'd already blown it, so I popped the SD card out of his camera and put it in a pocket. "Mind if I keep this? Shanna's into photography. Might see something she likes, get it framed." I didn't wait for an answer. I hauled him around the back of the house to the driveway and out to the street. I wanted to know more about this Shanna he was after, and why he was after her, but anything I asked would only make things worse.

"Hit the road," I said in Mike Hammer's voice. In fact, I didn't know what Hammer sounded like—which would be Biff Elliot in *I, The Jury*, then Ralph Meeker in *Kiss Me Deadly*—so I winged it. It must've worked, because Ignacio hustled across the street and into a red Chevy Cruze. I caught the license plate as he took off. It was a rental, which figured. His business card was from Chicago, home of tabloid journalism and tabloid politics. I watched as he sped down the street and turned right at the first opportunity.

Which left me with only one of two possibilities. I could get the hell out of there and go have a beer even though it wasn't yet noon, or I could stick around and apply recently acquired detection skills to the place before calling Danya—very likely the aforementioned Shanna Hayes who was "so far outta my league, dude" that it was cause for unbridled laughter.

So, of course, I chose the course most likely to get me back into the national spotlight.

I've only got a few real knacks, but that's one of them.

* * *

First a quick tour of the backyard, which was dry grass, crumbling brickwork around a long-defunct garden, and the garage, which was emitting a funky smell, like moldering grass clippings. The yard was enclosed by a six-foot fence of warped planks, gray and splintery from years of exposure to sun and rain. An ancient dilapidated doghouse was up against the back fence, no dog. And that was about it. Not much going on back there.

Then to the house. As Danya had thought, the back door was unlocked. More than unlocked—Ignacio's exit had left it wide open. Which meant I could enter without breaking.

I stuck my head inside. "Shanna?" I called out loudly. "Anyone home?" My reward was a deep, dead silence—which gave me my second chill of the morning. With my luck, I would go in and find Shanna, all right, strangled or bludgeoned, and Vince on his way out of town, having ditched a stolen rental car, grinning because his real name was Ted Bundy or John Wayne Gacy, something like that. At least I hadn't touched the doorknob and left prints.

With my gun out, very likely leaving a trail of hair and fibers, I eased into the house, into a kitchen with windows facing the backyard. Nothing was obviously out of place, no blood or appliances on the floor, so I figured there hadn't been a fight in there. Still calling for Shanna, I crept down a hallway toward the living room and the front door. Halfway down, it branched to the right, toward two bedrooms and a bath at the far end. I took a quick look in the living room, empty, a glance out at the street, nothing moving out there, then went back to the bedrooms. The one on the left was smaller and full of girls' things. The one on the right was the master bedroom with a walk-in closet, also full of girls' things. The room had a king-size four-poster bed with a royal blue comforter and matching pillow covers.

"Who the hell are you?"

I whirled. The girl was wearing exercise clothes—red nylon shorts and a seriously overloaded gray halter top, bare midriff, a belly button ring that was half-inch gold handcuffs studded with diamonds or cubic zirconia or maybe even moissanite—hard to tell which from ten feet away. She was a vision; tanned, lean, tall, strawberry blond, covered with a light glaze of sweat, and she had a kitchen knife in one hand with a gleaming eight-inch blade.

Perfect.

CHAPTER THREE

SHE KEPT THE knife on me, so to speak. At least it was pointed at my chest. "Are you, uh, Mortimer?" she asked, wary, eyes narrow, mouth tight, still a little out of breath. I figured she'd just returned from a run—one of my myriad deductive skills bubbling up. It also explained why no car had pulled into the driveway at the west side of the house, which I might've heard.

Her question also told me I was expected, which meant there was a good chance she wouldn't charge across the room and skewer me before I could answer. "Almost," I said.

She lifted the knife another inch. Evidently no one had told her not to bring a knife to a gunfight. My revolver was still in my hand, hanging at my side.

"Almost? What the fuck does that mean?" She backed away a step.

"Language, kiddo. And the name is Mort, not Mortimer."

That slowed her down, got her brain going again.

"Mr. Angel?"

Man, these people were hard to train. Mister? Well, I guess I was to this girl, twenty years old, give or take, and gorgeous. The word "buxom," if applied to her, would have been a world-class understatement. "Mister," however, put me out there at arm's length and in a different generation—farther away than I wanted to be—no disrespect to Holiday. But the thought blew through my head that this PI thing—beautiful girls cascading around like confetti at a New Year's party—was still right on track. Sixteen years with the IRS, a thousand field audits, and I'd never seen a girl like this.

I stuck my gun back in its holster. "That's me. Or I. Not sure about the grammar, kiddo, so you'll have to make allowances."

She smiled, sort of, still a bit uncertain. "Danya said she talked to you last night."

"Yes, she did."

"Mind telling me where and when that was?"

I lifted an eyebrow. "That sounds like a test."

"You got it." She still hadn't put the knife down.

"Good for you. Can't be too careful these days, what with a world full of terrorists and politicians. I saw Danya in the Green Room at the Golden Goose. About eleven fifteen last night."

Her smile illuminated the room. She put the knife on top of a dresser near the door, came over, and shook my hand—a good firm shake, about like she'd shake the hand of an insurance agent right after signing up for term life. "Hi. I'm Shanna."

"Hayes."

A flicker of distrust again. Her smile dimmed slightly. "How do you know? Danya wouldn't't've said."

"Vince Ignacio told me."

"Who?"

"Guy called Vince. Probably calls himself Vinny. I chased him out of here eight or ten minutes ago. Him and his camera."

"I don't know any Vince or Vinny."

"Short rat-faced guy with bad hair? In his mid- to late-twenties. A reporter for *Celebrity News*. He was in the house, snooping around. Just coming out the back door when I showed up."

She sagged. "Sonofabitch, goddamnit, fuck."

That pretty much covered all of life's most useful words. Maybe she'd done a stint in the Navy.

"Where's Danya?" she asked.

"Dunno."

"Seriously? She was here when I left. She didn't say she was going anywhere."

"Where's your phone? You two don't keep in touch?"

"Right here. What's left of it." She got an iPhone off the dresser top, or half of an iPhone, shedding pieces. "Yesterday I dropped it in a Raley's parking lot and some guy ran over it with a pickup truck."

"That'll do it." I looked around the room, trying not to stare at her top because the phrase "dirty old man" was circulating up there in the rafters. Thing is, a jog bra can only hold so much, and hers was about maxed out.

"I called Danya at ten like she asked," I said. "Got no answer. Twice. I left a message. Then she called back, said there was a creep looking in the windows here, so she went out the back and got lost. Didn't say why, or why she didn't call 911 to get the police out here to save the day—"

"Well, fuck." For a moment, Shanna stared at the floor. "I guess this was bound to happen, or could've happened. Maybe I should've, I don't know, done something..."

She'd lost me. "What was bound to happen?" I asked.

She didn't answer. She held out a hand. "Can I borrow your phone? I've got to talk to her."

I handed it to her. She dialed, listened for a moment, gave it back to me, shook her head. "Voice mail."

"She do that a lot?"

"Not if she knows it's me. She might not answer if she didn't recognize the number, which I guess she wouldn't."

"Now what? Know where she'd go?"

Again, she didn't answer. She plucked at her halter top, which had a damp V in the cleavage and dark spots beneath her armpits. "I ran down to the gym, that's three miles, worked out, then ran back. Mind if I get out of this? I need a shower like crazy."

"Do I look retarded?"

Her eyes narrowed to slits. "I didn't mean to put it that way or imply anything, Mr. Angel. Go wait in the living room or something while I get cleaned up. How's that?"

Mr. Angel? Shit. "Exactly what I was thinking."

"I'm sure. Good-bye." She shooed me out.

I went into the living room with stupid thoughts circling in my head. Shanna Hayes had a figure that would stop traffic. Bouncing along the sidewalks between here and whatever gym she belonged to, which is what she would do—bouncing, that is—I thought RPD would classify her as an attractive nuisance and put an end to it to keep the number of fender benders under control. Ignacio had told me I wasn't in her league, and from his perspective that was about right. She was six feet tall, with short spiky blond hair accented with a fluorescent pink streak on the left side, slender and leggy, terrific skin, beautiful, with the kind of figure that ends up on the covers of magazines and makes millions of high school girls feel perfectly and permanently inadequate.

I peered out the windows again. Still nothing was going on out there in the street. I wasn't sure why I thought there might be, but Ignacio's presence had me worried. I had the feeling things weren't as they seemed around here.

Which is when my phone rang.

I checked the number, then said, "Hola, Danya. So nice of you to check in."

"You just phoned," she said tersely. "What do you want?"

"Do you want a complete list or just the top two items?"

"Don't be funny. What do you want?"

"For starters, how about telling me where the hell you are. We had a date."

"I'm . . . around. Where're you?"

"Your place. I chased the *Celebrity News* creep away."

Silence. Then: "*Celebrity News?*"

"Uh-huh. I take it you weren't expecting publicity or a photo op with a nationally distributed tabloid."

"Oh, my God. I, uh . . . is anyone else there?"

My gumshoe training kicked in. "Like who, kiddo?"

"Well, *anyone.*"

"Maybe blond? About six feet tall? Figure not too awful?"

"Oh geez. Let me talk to her."

"She's in the shower. I got chased into the other room. And I don't know if she's still got that knife with her."

"Knife . . . ?"

"Bit of a long story. Thing is, right now I'm not welcome in the shower—uh, the bathroom. And my health insurance doesn't cover avoidable knife wounds."

"Tell her you're coming in anyway. Or something. Tell her it's me. I've got to talk to her. Give her your phone, like *right now*!"

Lot of excitement there, not that I needed to be told twice to pop into the bathroom to give Shanna the phone. Of course, to avoid a reverse *Psycho* scene in which the girl in the shower with a knife attacks the guy in the bathroom—not an easy thing to explain, if it came to that—this would require some finesse. But, no problem. Having tracked down mom-and-pop tax dodgers for the IRS for sixteen years, I was all about finesse.

I went down the hallway and stood outside the bathroom door, which was open six or eight inches, not a bad sign.

"Hey!" I yelled. "I'm comin' in, that all right?"

"*No!* Stay the hell out!"

"Danya's on the phone. Says she wants to talk to you."

"*Gimme it!*"

Good enough. I pushed the door open. Shanna had the shower door open, one well-muscled sudsy leg already out the door, a loofa in one hand, the other hand trying to grab the phone, and damn if the shower wasn't one of those clear glass jobs, none of that pebbled stuff that leaves you uncertain about what's behind it. Her handcuff-motif belly button ring glittered nicely in the light. The rest of her was simply panoramic.

"Don't get my phone wet," I said.

She grabbed it. "Get out."

Brusque kid. And wet. But the seamless tan from head to toe looked good on her, and the hot-pink toenail polish.

I got out, taking with me a sight that would stick with me for a good long time. You wake up in the morning thinking you have an idea what the day will bring, but you don't. Ever.

I stood outside the door listening to the animated stop-and-go burble of Shanna's voice but couldn't make out her words over the sound of the shower. Half a minute later, the burble of words stopped.

"Mortimer? You out there?"

"There's no one out here by that name."

"Oh, for chrissake, *Mort*!"

"Yep."

"I put your phone by the sink. It's still on. Danya wants to talk to you."

"Great. How am I supposed to get it?"

"Come in and *get* it, dope."

Good enough. I got my phone and another eyeful, thinking girls these days weren't nearly as bashful as they were when I was in high school, and a football hero at that. I almost made it to the door when Shanna said, "Hey."

I turned back. "What?"

"Danya and I have been married since April, if that answers a few questions." She looked through the glass, blinking at me, water dripping from her hair into her face.

"It might. I'll give it some thought."

"Do that. Now go."

"Newlyweds. Wow. Hey. Congrats."

"*Go*. Leave. See what Danya wants, then have a smoke or something in the backyard until I get out of here."

"I gave up smoking in the first grade." Delaying tactics are one of a multitude of old codgers' tricks. They usually work, too.

Her lips twitched in what might have been an attempt to keep from smiling. I wouldn't have been able to see that through pebbled glass, so I was happy that the glass was clear. Body language is a big part of communication. "Good for you. Now get out of here," she said, but her voice was softer than before.

I went back to the living room, put the phone to my ear. "So, what's the story, Danya? What's with the *Celebrity News*?"

"That guy didn't see Shanna, did he?"

"Nope. Don't think so, anyway. Not like *I* did."

She hesitated. "What's that mean?"

"Thought I mentioned that she was in the shower. You know, the one with *clear* glass?"

"Well . . . okay. That's good."

Fascinating. "I doubt that he saw her. But he knew her name. Shanna Hayes."

Danya didn't respond to that, didn't give away any stray bits of information. I was still in the dark. She would've made a good CIA agent. When I caught up to her, I thought I might have to waterboard her. I especially wanted to know who her father was—the guy who didn't like me. That still had me going.

"Anyway," I said, "if you're still looking for a gumshoe and think I might do, I probably need to know what's going on."

"A what . . . *gumshoe*, did you say?"

"An investigator." Kids. I looked out a window and saw a red Chevy Cruze slowing as it went by. What were the odds?

"What do you charge?" Danya asked as I tried to keep track of the car.

"Hah? For what?"

"PI work, of course. What're we talkin' about?"

"You still lookin' for a maverick?" At a sharp angle out the window I could see the Cruze idling at the curb, two houses up the street.

"Maybe more than ever, if that tabloid guy is still around. So, how much?"

Ma Clary went for one seventy-five an hour. I didn't think Danya could afford Ma. On the other hand, Maude wasn't here. By now she might be somewhere around Winnemucca, Nevada, headed east.

"Mavericks cost more than your basic run of the mill—"

"Seriously—?"

"How about sixty an hour?" Which is what Ma charged for my time, of which I got twenty-five. "And expenses. But I still don't know what you need or what's going on."

"I'll get back to you on that."

"When do you—" She'd already hung up. Shit fire, she was a hard lady to converse with, but my mind was actually on the creep.

Out the front door, medium-fast jog up the sidewalk, and the Cruze took off, headed uphill—west.

I watched it for a moment, didn't think I could put a bullet through the back window at that distance, then walked back to the house. On the way, I called Danya back. She needed a PI "more than ever," but I still didn't know why. The call went to voice mail again, which was just great.

Okay, there's this tabloid creep nosing around two stunning girls married to each other—interracially, too, which hadn't meant a thing for the past thirty or forty years—and me with no idea what the first girl wanted. Or the second. Which meant, in the absence of the Cruze, that I could sayonara and head down to the Green Room at the Golden Goose and snack on pretzels and beer nuts over a midmorning Moose Drool. Well-deserved, too, I might add, since I'd already seen a highly naked girl and tossed one guy against a garbage can today, and that was my daily quota for both.

The Cruze, however, was still hovering, so beer was out. Too early for beer, anyway, since it wasn't yet noon. Then again, I didn't know if I was being teased or hired. So far, teasing was in the lead—Danya on the phone, Shanna in the shower. If I was being hired, I still didn't know what for, which left things pretty much up in the air, so I still didn't have to call Ma and get her okay. But according to last summer's media circus, I was a world-class gumshoe, and a wet slippery-looking naked girl was loose in the house, and those two facts were somehow related, so I went up the driveway, past the sound of the shower still going full blast behind a window that had been lifted six inches to vent steam, and went back inside.

More hurried snooping, trying to get a handle on things. With the sound of water as a cover, I ducked into the smaller of the two bedrooms and looked around. A computer was on top of an oak desk against a wall beneath a window. An inkjet printer was on top of a bookshelf beside it. I opened the top drawer of the desk.

Stamps, stationary, a ruler, paper clips. Office stuff. Next drawer down held bank statements, phone and power bills. I found a rent receipt for nine hundred forty dollars. Bills were in the name of Danya Fuller. Fuller. I didn't know anyone by that name. The bank statement was from First Interstate on South Virginia. I knew the place, a block or so south of Vassar Street. It wasn't a joint account. She had a thousand and sixty-four dollars in checking. The bottom drawer of the desk held two reams of printer paper and a stapler.

I hurried into the kitchen and opened drawers, found flatware, Ziploc bags, aluminum foil, half a dozen dish towels rolled up into neat tubes, Tupperware. One drawer held the usual detritus that can't be thrown out because it might be useful sometime in the next thirty years—stale rubber bands, nails and screws, picture hangers, pencil stubs, dried-out pens, a modest collection of matchbooks, a bent screwdriver that might have been used as a pry bar, a small rusted claw hammer purchased around the time of the Korean War.

Matchbooks were classic hot-ticket items for clues, so I took particular notice of those—half a dozen big-name Vegas casinos, a few no-name places I'd never heard of on Highway 93, one from the Pahranagai Inn in Caliente, Nevada, site of a hot springs and where a juvenile girls' correctional facility was located.

"Find anything interesting?"

I looked up. She was wrapped in a fuzzy cream-colored towel. Pretty short one, too—one disadvantage of being tall, not that I saw it that way, but I try to see things from the viewpoint of others.

I held up a pen. "You oughta toss this one. It's dried out."

"Danya said you're a private investigator."

"Uh-huh. World-renowned."

"You might investigate the backyard while I get dressed. See if anything looks out of place out there."

"Okey-dokey."

Back outside. A glance down the side of the house toward the street. No Cruze. I went scratching around the yard without a clue as to what might be a clue since I didn't have the slightest idea what Danya or Shanna wanted. The yard didn't look any more promising than it had half an hour ago—dead patchy grass as dry and tough as broom straw, powdery dirt, a few boards stacked in weeds against the back fence, old doghouse, faint funky smell in the vicinity of the garage, which might be a garbage can ready to be hauled out to the curb.

I looked over the west fence into the neighbor's backyard, same to the east and north, didn't see anyone mowing, weeding a garden, hammocking, sunbathing nude—nothing interesting. The day was relentlessly quiet, eighty degrees. Sunshine and blue sky, a few puffy white clouds—

Shanna came out in jeans and a green short-sleeve shirt that did little to hide the curves, hair still damp, brown sandals, hot-pink polish still on her toenails. As she came closer, I refined my estimate of her height to six-one in order to keep my eyes where they wouldn't get me in trouble—though after that business in the shower, I couldn't tell how much it mattered. She was a hell of a sight. And married to Danya. That had taken me by surprise.

"In case you're wondering," she said, "she's Danya Fuller-Hayes and I'm Shanna Hayes-Fuller. Now."

"Bet the IRS hates you two."

"We haven't had to file married yet. Next April we might file 'married filing separately.'"

"Expect an audit." I glanced down the driveway, checking to make sure Vince wasn't still around, then turned back to Shanna.

"You two're really married, huh?" Not that I didn't believe her, but I hoped the question would provoke a bit more elaboration.

She held up a finger with a ring on it I hadn't noticed earlier. Gold, tiny diamond. Not much in the way of elaboration. She looked back at the house. "Um, in there . . . that wasn't . . ."

"No need to explain." Or apologize, I didn't say.

"It's just, you should know—I'm trying really hard not to hate men, all men, since it's like really bad karma."

"Right."

Not hate all men? I got a little whiff of something there. Not sure what it meant though.

Shanna looked around the yard. "So, what'd you find?"

"Look at this place. What's to find?"

She shrugged. I was about to suggest that she phone Danya and get this employment thing settled one way or another. Maybe I didn't want any part of it, terrific-looking girls or not. So far, for all I knew, they'd lost a dog—empty doghouse against the fence—and Ma doesn't take missing-mutt cases, and I wouldn't know where to begin anyway.

Shanna reached into a pocket and pulled out a torn piece of paper. "Here, read this."

It was a note, rough masculine-looking print, barely legible.

> *Get $1000000 redy in smal bills by tusday and I will get him down and take him away no problum. I will fon monday and tok to you.*

The amount was hard to decipher without commas. I had to count zeros. Today was Sunday. I looked at Shanna. "Where'd you get this? And when?"

"It was left in our mailbox four days ago. And, no, we don't know who put it there or why. Get who down from where? And a million dollars? Seriously? It had to be kids. We couldn't figure it out."

It might be why Danya had wanted a PI, though. A *maverick* PI. Maybe she knew what it was about and hadn't told her . . . wife? Okay, I'm a philistine. Her *partner*. Spouse. Significant Other.

"A million bucks," I said, wrinkling my nose as an odor wafted across the yard, like a cat had died somewhere nearby.

"That's what it says. Really, it's ridiculous. We thought it must be kids, some sort of a stupid neighborhood prank."

Maybe. But then why would Danya want a private eye?

"Mind if I keep this?" I asked. "I'll keep it safe."

"Go ahead. Anyway, we couldn't come up with a thousand, much less a million—not that there's any reason to."

Couldn't come up with a grand? At sixty dollars an hour, I was an expense these girls couldn't afford.

I put the note in a pocket. Before I could ask anything more, something clicked in my head. I'd tossed Ignacio against a trash can at the side of the house. A not-unexpected bit of garbage smell there, which is what garbage cans are known for, so what was this miasma drifting across the yard, coming, it seemed like, from the garage? Moldering grass? What grass? The lawn was two inches of brown dry ruff. Run a mower over it and you'd raise a cloud of dust and blow a few ants into the air.

The single-bay garage had one of those ancient one-piece panel doors, held down by a padlock. No other way in.

"Got a key for the lock?" I asked, rapping on the scaly lift-up door, though I might have been able to bust it off its hinges with a modest kick. Near the door, the smell was stronger.

"Danya and I are just renting this place. We're not using the garage. Anything in there belongs to the lady we're renting from. Mrs. Johnson. Thelma."

"Uh-huh. That's not what I asked, kiddo."

"Well, some keys are in the kitchen. Hanging on a hook by the back door. Maybe one of them will open it."

I went back inside, found keys on a ring, came back and found the one for the padlock. As I opened it, screws pulled out of the wood and the hasp fell out. The frame was gouged where a crowbar had popped it out. The marks looked recent. Someone had carefully torn the lock out then shoved it back in place to hide what they'd done. Not good. I grabbed a handle and hauled the door up on twanging springs.

The funky smell got worse. Ten times worse. Twenty.

"Omigod," Shanna said, taking a step back.

The interior of the garage was dark. I went in first. Shanna came in on my heels. My eyes were still adjusting to the dimness when she let out a thin shriek and stood staring up at rapper Jo-X, shirtless, eyes the color of curdled skim milk, blind. He was hanging against the back wall with a rope around the rafters and under his armpits, black tongue lolling, one nasty-looking bullet hole in his forehead, another in his chest.

And . . . funky, putrescent, having achieved in death the apt and essential condition of every gangsta rapper in the country.

And here I was, back in the thick of it.

Ma was gonna fire me. Out of a job, I was gonna end up in a crappy little trailer park in Dubuque.

Shit.

CHAPTER FOUR

"No, no, no," Shanna cried from a few feet behind me. "That . . . that just isn't possible."

Impossible or not, there he was: Jonnie Xenon, Jo-X, in the . . . okay, I was going to say in the flesh, but that would've been gross, given his degree of decomposition in that warm garage, and, of course, the feasting flies. So, there he was . . . in person. Sort of.

According to all the hip, teen magazines—which I didn't read and thought ought to be burned, First Amendment or no, in a last-ditch effort to save what's left of our society—Jonnie Xenon's real name was Aaron Louden Butler. In print he was Jonnie-X, but pronunciation made it Jonnie-Z, which had then become Jo-X in print—still pronounced Jo-Z—because it worked, un-like B-Ob. He had "54" tattooed on both sides of his neck in Gothic print and on a shaved patch on the back of his head—54 being the atomic number for xenon. To his deep-thinking fans, this suggested a cool scientific bent that lent him some cachet. He had spiderwebs tattooed from the corners of his eyes to his ears. A spider in each web was actually a tiny swastika. At last count he had twenty-eight facial piercings in his eyebrows, nose, and lips. And, of course, his tongue, which was pierced by twin spikes . . . which now caught the light and glinted obscenely in the garage.

He had grungy blond hair four inches below his shoulders, wild blue eyes, thin as a whip, and could stick his spiked tongue out a measured—and reported—three and a half inches, which may have accounted for some of his popularity. Onstage, he would tear his shirt off and drive hordes of "Generation Y" girls mad with his thrice-pierced belly button, sunken chest, washboard abs, narrow hips, and unique blend of hip-hop style and toxic lyrics that gave the rest of the gangsta rapper population pause. He was a "bad boy" who gave off palpable criminal vibes, adored by some two million fans, ninety-seven percent of whom were female. By age eighteen, he was a millionaire. Now, at twenty-four, he was worth a reputed thirty-two million dollars—an overt and self-proclaimed user of "recreational" drugs, self-absorbed, self-indulgent, a living, breathing example of why reasonable limits should be put on free speech. You can't shout "fire" in a movie theater, so why are you allowed to "bang yo ho like a drum roll, yo, an' if the ho whole you gotta get down go down go, go, go, y'know?"

Un-freakin'-believable. I didn't know why lightning hadn't struck the diseased son of a bitch years ago.

But now it had, in the form of fast-moving hunks of lead. Two fast-moving hunks, either of which looked fatal. Now Jo-X was dead, and I figured two million fathers would be suspects in his murder. Murder, because I didn't think Jonnie-X's talents extended to shooting himself in the chest *and* the forehead then stringing himself up in rafters.

Trouble was, here I was, in the garage with him, speaking of suspects.

And Shanna.

Or so I thought, but when I turned away from Jo-X she had reached the sidewalk and was disappearing around the front of the house at a dead run, headed east, downhill.

I took off after her, tried to keep up for two blocks, then gave it up because she was pulling away. All I had on were Nikes, not sandals that were actually rocket shoes. I try to run five or six miles several times a week, fast, but I was out of my league here. Maybe that was what Ignacio had meant.

Ignacio.

Sonofabitch.

I trotted back, turned the corner at the front of the house, and Vince was in the garage, snapping pictures of Jo-X. He must've had a spare SD card, or a spare camera in his car.

I didn't call out, but he heard me coming, got off a shot of me bearing down on him, then darted across the backyard. A little hop, and in a surprisingly athletic move, he put one foot on the doghouse and went over the fence like a wharf rat. But—no way was he going to escape. I was fifteen feet behind him. I put one foot on top of the doghouse, and broke through the rotten plywood, barking my left shin and slamming into the fence hard enough to crack a plank. Fuckin' doghouse roof took a hundred forty flyweight pounds but imploded at two hundred eight.

I watched the wharf rat go, through a backyard, over another fence like he'd pole-vaulted it. Speedy little fucker. I couldn't have caught him wearing a jetpack.

The sonofabitch.

*   *   *

Now what?

I walked back across the yard, rubbing my shin. I could phone Ma. If she had coverage on the train, she would probably tell me to get the hell out of there.

Uh-uh. No way. At least not yet.

Which is when my phone rang. It was Ma. Perfect timing. I know God watches my every move, laughing so hard He or She gets side aches.

"Hiya, Ma," I said.

"So how'd it go with that girl—Danya? Is she as good lookin' in the morning as she was last night?"

"How would I know?"

That stopped her. "What's goin' on, boyo?"

"I phoned her at ten. She told me to come over to her place. When I got there, she was gone."

"Well . . . so where are you now?"

"Her place. I chased a tabloid creep out of her house."

"A tabloid creep? What the hell, Mort?"

"That's what I thought." And right then I wondered how the handwriting on the blackmail note Shanna had given me might match that of the creep—although he looked like the kind who would be the teacher's pet and have terrific handwriting by the fourth grade. And quit growing when he was twelve and still pint-sized. Agile little shit.

"What tabloid?"

"*Celebrity News*. Guy looked like a ferret. Or a wharf rat. More like the latter, I'd say, if you want a professional opinion."

"*Celebrity News*? Wharf rat? What are you gettin' mixed up in? I told you not to get mixed up in anything."

Last thing I wanted to tell her about was Jo-X, strung up in the garage like a horse harness in a barn. "I dunno." Which was the absolute truth, just a little light on details. "Where are you, by the way? How's the ride?"

"The ride's fine and thanks for askin' and you sound funny. So I ask once ag . . . what's goin' . . . on't do a . . . thing like . . . las . . . for -od's sa . . ."

"You know anyone by the name of Shanna Hayes, Ma?"

"Sha . . . Ha . . ."

"Ma? You're breaking up."

But she was gone. I would have to thank Verizon later.

Don't do anything, she said. Like what? Don't leave the house here? Don't stay? Good enough. I could do whatever I liked.

So, of course, I stayed.

* * *

Maybe I had a moment. Or not. The garage door was open and it faced the street. The place had no windows. It would be dark if I shut the door, and virulently rank, so I had to leave it open if I was going to do a quick check around Jo-X. With the door open, it was dim inside. He might not be visible from the street, at least I hoped so. As a gumshoe, I was desperate for clues. And I thought I had a pretty good one, too: Jo-X, hangin' against a wall. And another: a note demanding a million bucks. What I didn't have yet was a client.

I hurried over, held my breath because Jo-X dead for several days in June didn't smell as good as Jo-X fresh, or so I thought. I could've been wrong. He was shirtless, his trademark, but he had on a pair of old jeans. I wanted to check his pockets, which would've earned me a big slap on the wrist by my favorite Reno detective, Russ Fairchild. But in all fairness, Danya and Shanna were gone, and Jo-X wasn't, so, as a maverick, which is why Danya hired me, or said she was thinking about it, what choice did I have?

None.

I ran into the house, found a pair of rubber gloves under the kitchen sink, ran back outside. No wharf rat in sight.

I needed information. And I got it. Pulling the wallet out of Xenon's right rear pocket was like fishing around in a snake pit. I found a driver's license issued to Aaron L. Butler. Picture looked like him, allowing for decomposition. Credit cards, a receipt for a motel in Caliente, the Pahranagai Inn—good one, Mort—issued to a Nathan Williams, and, in Jonnie's front left pocket, talk about your basic bingo moment—a flash drive. I turned it over. Written on the back in tidy print was the name "Celine."

Jo-X dead in Danya's garage, flash drive in his pocket with the name *Celine* written on it, wallet intact, motel receipt, tabloid creep snooping around, note demanding $1,000,000. Up to my ears in clues, a dead body about to get national attention, and no idea what was going on. This was great.

My PI training kicked into overdrive. Finally I had a vague idea why Danya might've wanted a maverick PI in her life.

What I didn't have was a paying client.

Sonofabitch. I was working pro bono.

CHAPTER FIVE

OKAY, NOW IT was hell-for-leather scurry-around time. Ignacio was out there somewhere. I pocketed the motel receipt and the flash drive, returned Jo-X's wallet to his pocket, looked around, didn't see anything out of place except me. I couldn't leave. I had to report this mess. Neighbors might've seen things going on over here and taken down my car license, and Vince had my picture, taken right after he got a shot of Jo-X, so leaving the scene of the crime, so to speak, wasn't an option. Vince's photographic journalism notwithstanding, God only knows how many fingerprints I'd left inside the house.

I took out my cell phone and hit 9-1—

Well, hell.

Time to slow down and think.

First thing the cops would do is put me facedown in the dirt and check me for weapons, which they would find if I didn't do something about that. They would find the Caliente motel receipt, the flash drive, and the note demanding money, which made a little more sense now, but still wasn't entirely clear. A million dollars for what, exactly? Body removal? Silence? But I wasn't in the mood to give up any of those things—receipt, flash drive, note, gun—so it was time to scramble around for another few minutes and dig myself deeper into this mess.

I couldn't put any of it in my car, parked a hundred feet up the street. They would probably dismantle the entire thing, take out all the bolts and screws, engine, transmission, spread the whole thing out in a forensic garage. Jo-X was hanging in the girls' garage, not some homeless guy who'd had a little bad luck. Fair or not, that would make a difference. Mort Angel, gumshoe extraordinaire and media darling, was about to get another round of national exposure on prime-time news—talk about your sorry sonofabitchin' moment.

I hoped Ma still had a sense of humor.

* * *

I looked around, tried to think how the police were going to go over the place—the house, the backyard, several yards on the other side of the fence. They would scour the place, look under rocks and boards, take the doghouse apart, strip-search the Mort.

Finally I put the gun, holster, motel receipt, rubber gloves, the thumb drive, Vinnie's SD card, and the note in a big Ziploc bag I found in the kitchen. At the last minute, I remembered the matchbook I'd seen in the kitchen drawer—Pahranagai Inn—same place as the receipt in Jo-X's wallet, what a coincidence, so I grabbed it then scooped up the other matchbooks—clues all—and added them to the Ziploc, stuffed it all up a drainpipe at the side of the house, wedged the wad in place with a couple of kitchen towels, shoved everything as high as I could up the pipe without touching the outside of the drainpipe or disturbing the dust outside it. Then I found a short stick and used it to run the wad another foot up the pipe—all of this being a class-A felony, by the way—dropped the stick in the dust and rolled it around with my shoe, carefully put it right back where I'd found it, and looked around.

I went through the house again. The shower was wet. I didn't think I could dry it and I couldn't wait for it to dry, so I was going to have to explain about the shower, which was going to put Shanna in the thick of this. Danya, too, because why was Mort Angel at this house in the first place? Nothing I could do about that, or wanted to. Jo-X's location alone was going to drag those two neck-deep into this mess. Of course, it was their mess, not mine, or should've been—but here I was, up to my own neck. I had the feeling they'd left out a few things they might have explained in more detail, so my sympathy level was running a tad low.

Five more minutes of snooping around the house didn't turn up anything useful. Ignacio's camera had probably put a time stamp on the photo he'd taken of me, so my time was about up.

Last thing I did was put the knife—without my prints on it—back in a wooden knife block in the kitchen. Shanna had left it on the dresser in the bedroom, and I thought it would muddy the story unnecessarily if they wanted her or me to explain it. And I didn't know if Jo-X had a stab wound or two in his back, which would have been trouble I didn't need. But if he *did*, I was going to double the hourly rate I'd quoted to Danya.

Finally I punched in 911 on my cell phone and gave the public safety dispatcher the gist of the situation, including Jo-X's name and a description of his condition to fire up the police, then I sat on the front porch steps to wait, watching the street, thinking how all this quiet was about to go straight to hell.

* * *

Which it did.

Sirens from two directions—stereo, God love 'em. Three cars. I was flat on my stomach and cuffed by the time the next two cop cars pulled up. I was sitting up on the porch with my back against the front wall of the house when my buddy, Russell Fairchild, arrived in an unmarked car, no siren, and pushed his way through the four cops who had me surrounded.

"You," he said when he saw me.

"I," I said. Our standard greeting under these circumstances, which was getting to be routine.

He was wild-eyed, eyes jittery, hands trembling. Not his usual unflappable self when I came across bodies or body parts of political figures or celebrities.

"You, you, you, what're you, you—"

"Might want to keep the media trolls out of here, if any show up," I said. "And comb your hair 'cause those rotten sons of bitches use telephoto and they won't give you a do-over."

He grabbed me by an arm, got me to my feet, and hauled me around behind the house and across the dusty yard to the back fence. I stumbled along, still in handcuffs.

"What the *hell* are you doin' here, Angel?" he hissed, hitting me with a fine mist of spittle. He'd taken me far from the proliferating mass of cops now flooding the place.

Something of an overreaction, I thought. Then again, he might still be recovering from last summer's media circuses in which I'd played a prominent role and he hadn't.

"Sleuthin'," I said.

"What, why, why, why, why *here*?"

Lots of anxiety, and a powerful emphasis on the *here*. I looked around. "Why not here? Seems like as good a place as any. And these cuffs are pretty tight, Russ. I promise I won't sprint off and leave you in a cloud of dust."

He spun in place. "Je-sus *Christ*, Angel!"

Uh-huh. *Big* overreaction, and he hadn't even seen the body yet. Something was up. "How about we go talk to the other guys, Detective?" I didn't like the look in his eyes, or the gun on his hip.

He hauled me into the farthest corner of the yard. "What the *fuck* is goin' on?" he whisper-shouted. "This is my kid's place."

"Your kid?"

"My daughter, asshole. She lives here."

Oh, shit.

*   *   *

"Shanna's your daughter?"

He slammed me up against the fence. He would've put his face an inch from mine if he'd been seven inches taller, but he got up on his toes and gave it a good try.

"Not Shanna—*Danya*. Where is she, you son of a bitch?"

Danya? She was at least half black. Half, Mort. Might give that another pass through the brain. Well, son of a gun. Twenty minutes ago, this day was looking bad. Now it was worse. Danya had said her father didn't like me, said I was an unprofessional maverick. And dear old dad was my good buddy, Fairchild. Perfect. Last summer, about the time I'd stumbled across my third decapitated head, I thought he was going to hook me up to a transformer and turn out my lights right there in the interrogation room, say, "Oop," and call it good. Now, I thought his stare might accomplish the same thing.

"How about you dial it down a notch, Russ," I said.

Officer Day—last summer's behemoth—lumbered around the corner of the house, gun and a nightstick on his belt, cuffs, baton, radio, sandwich. Five minutes late, but coming on strong.

"Detective Fairchild," one of the responding officers called to us from the garage. "You better take a look at this."

Officer Day—Clifford—lumbered over to Russ and me.

I turned my back to Russ and looked over my shoulder, held my wrists out a few inches. "Cuffs?"

Fairchild's eyes were like marbles. "I oughta keep 'em on you till day after tomorrow." He stared at me for a moment, then said to Day, "Yeah, take 'em off. He ain't goin' nowhere, but Taser him if he blinks." He headed for the garage.

"He was just kidding," I told Day.

"Don't blink, Angel," he said, but I think he smiled, sort of. He popped off my cuffs. He was six-six, three hundred thirty pounds. Every time I saw him, he'd gained another ten. I rubbed my wrists. Now that he had me by a hundred twenty pounds, I didn't think he would need a Taser to put me on the ground—if he could catch me, which wasn't likely.

"You oughta go see what's in the garage," I told him.

"In a while. Right now I'm watchin' you."

"You ever heard of Jo-X?"

"Guy's a shitbug. If it turns out you squashed him, I'll buy you lunch." He looked around. "Where's your partner?"

"Maude? On her way to Memphis."

"Too bad. Unlike you, she brightens up the day."

"Ma? Maude Clary? You gotta be kiddin'."

"She and I go back a ways. You don't."

Maude and Officer Day? Maybe I just got some dirt on her. If so, and I tried to use it to get a raise, she would just laugh at me, so this was going to take some thought.

"You two go back a ways? How far back?"

Day stared at me. "I haven't Tasered anyone this week yet."

"That far back, huh?"

Fairchild exited the garage and walked over to us. He looked shaken. "That is . . . one *ugly* fuckin' sight in there."

"Thought you'd like it," I said. "How's the air in there?"

"Seventh circle of hell."

He'd calmed down a little, but his eyes were still jittery. He jerked a thumb at the garage and said to Day, "Have a look, but take a deep breath before you go in."

Day went. Fairchild glared at me. No one else was within forty feet of us. "I don't believe it," he said. "Gettin' tangled up with you again."

"If you think this is a karmic tie, Russ, you're wrong. This is your fault."

"*My* fault? How'd you come up with that?"

"You told your kid I was an unprofessional maverick. Turns out that's what she thought she wanted, so maybe she listens to you, God only knows why. She came into the Golden Goose last night, the Green Room, and asked for help. Didn't say what for, and I still don't know, but it looks like she and Jo-X have got—"

He shoved me against the fence again, hard, but couldn't figure out precisely why or what to say. He turned and looked at the garage. "Aw jeez, Angel. What the *hell* . . ."

"Anyone know this is your daughter's place?" I asked.

"That'll come out soon enough."

"What I *mean* is, does anyone know *you* are connected to this place? Someone who doesn't like you?"

He stared at me. "What? You think someone's tryin' to get at me through my kid?"

"It's a thought, you being such a nice guy and all."

"Doesn't make sense. That's too . . . complicated." He stared at the garage again. "Je-sus Christ. Jo-X of all the nightmare sons of bitches. Guy's been missing for what now, a week?"

"Six days, I think. Celine, too."

"Celine? Who's that?"

"You don't keep up with the latest in gangster rap?"

"I'd rather pluck out my eyes."

"Celine is Xenon's latest girlfriend, sidekick, squeeze, whatever. She was with him for three weeks before the two of them vanished. It's been in the news. A lot." I watched his face as I said it, but nothing registered.

"Oh, yeah," he said. "Might've heard somethin' about his girl gone missing, too. It's not the kind of thing I pay attention to." He stared into space, then said, "Sonofabitch."

A forensics crew arrived and trooped into the garage. A few of them came out a minute later and began to spread out, through the yard, into the house.

Fairchild handed me to Officer Day. "Put him in your car." Before Day hauled me away, Russell grabbed my arm and said to me in a deathly whisper, "Don't say nothin' to nobody. And I mean *nothin'*."

Several local news crews aimed telephoto lenses at us as Day put me in a squad car, in back where the handles don't work, and I tried to decipher the true meaning of Fairchild's triple negative. Get it wrong and I'd be in trouble. Day leaned against the car, folded his arms across his chest, and watched the hum of activity around the house.

Alone in the quiet, I had time to summarize the situation and determine that, even though I was in the thick of all this and in for a grilling, it wasn't likely that they would hold me beyond an interminable, boring afternoon. Jo-X was partially decomposed, so he'd been dead a few days, no more than six, and he'd been strung up in Danya and Shanna's garage. A garage that came with a rented house, so they would have to check out the owner, Thelma Johnson, see if she'd been nursing a grudge against Jo-X and was using her garage for . . . shall we say, storage.

Continuing my private summary of recent events—Danya was the beautiful daughter of Reno PD's most senior homicide detective. Both Danya and Shanna had run, Danya having more or less hired Mortimer Angel, a gumshoe, for reasons unknown the night before Jo-X had turned up in what the police would take to be her garage as much as Thelma's.

Fairchild would work his way through all that in the next ten minutes if he hadn't already. What he didn't know, and what I had up my sleeve, or up a drainpipe, not that I knew what to do with it, was that Shanna and Danya had found a note in their mailbox a few days ago demanding a big chunk of money and they'd been given a cryptic and ultimately unworkable reason for parting with it. And there was the flash drive, which might or might not have something relevant and useful on it, but the name "Celine" written on it was intriguing.

I didn't have the slightest idea what was going on, but like the previous summer, as a finder of missing persons I had no peer.

None.

Ma was gonna be *so* damn proud of me. I couldn't wait for her to find out.

* * *

The interrogation room at RPD headquarters hadn't changed one iota since my several visits last year, so I had a nice case of déjà vu working as I stared at my reflection in the one-way mirror. Heavy wooden table, chairs bolted to the floor, one sturdy door, and a vent high on one wall giving off an exhausted sigh.

This was going to play hell with today's judo lesson. I was due at Rufus Booth's private dojo at 1:30. My now-deceased fiancée, Jeri, had used judo to toss me around in her home workout room less than twenty minutes after we first met, and her brother, Ron, was one of the top judo masters in the United States in active competition. I thought judo made sense. If Jeri could toss me around like a sack of rice, what might I be able to do with a little training? In the hierarchy of martial arts, Ron was a sixth-dan judo master. He lived over a hundred miles away, not convenient for lessons, but he put me on to Rufus Booth, a ninth-dan master and not the kind of guy you'd ever, *ever* want to attack in a dark alley, not that that's on my bucket list.

But . . . no judo lesson today. I'd been at it for three months, got my yellow belt last week. Jeri would've approved.

Russell Fairchild and Day came in. Russ Mirandized me while a video camera in a corner near the ceiling got it on tape or DVD. Then he reached up and switched the camera off, something they do in Russian prisons all the time.

He turned to Day. "What you are about to hear doesn't leave this room, Cliff."

"You might want to Mirandize him, too," I said.

Fairchild glared at me. "You're a piece of work, Angel. Got a mouth on you that won't quit."

"But I'm a dynamo when it comes to missing persons."

Day's lips lifted a tenth of an inch.

Russell gave me a "come on" gesture with the fingers of his right hand. "Let's hear it."

"Hear what?"

"Guess."

"Starting where?"

"Wherever all of this began, hotshot. Up to you."

I could have had my lawyer present, but Russ and I don't do that since I'm never guilty, just lucky, so I started with quitting my job with the IRS last July and becoming a PI trainee at my nephew's investigative firm.

"Don't start there," he growled.

"After that, huh? You sure? You'll miss out on a couple of great stories. Decapitated heads, severed hands—"

"How about last night? You said my kid came to see you at the Goose. How would she have known where to find you?"

"You'll have to ask her. She didn't say. If she's stalking me, it's probably your fault."

"Pick it up from there, Angel."

That part didn't take long. He seemed to like the part where Danya said her father didn't like Mortimer Angel, thought he was an unprofessional maverick.

"I beg to differ," I groused. "I'm a professional maverick."

Day grunted something that might have been agreement or a laugh. Either way, I liked him better for it.

"Didn't say what she wanted?" Fairchild asked.

"Nope. Just to call her at ten the next morning. She didn't want to talk with anyone else around. Said it was private."

I went through the two calls that went to voice mail, Danya's return call sending me to the house on Elmcrest Drive, which was empty except for one Vincent Ignacio, tabloid creep.

"Hold on a second." Fairchild's face was white. Whiter than usual anyway; guy didn't get nearly enough sun. *Who?*

"Reporter for *Celebrity News*. That's a tabloid rag, in case you didn't know. After I dragged him off the fence and tossed him into—well, *against*—a garbage can, he told me his name was Bill Hogan. But his driver's license was for Vince Ignacio, so he's a liar—not an expert liar like an entrenched politician, but a liar all the same."

"Ah, jeez." Fairchild ran fingers through his hair.

I told him about chasing Vince off, going in the house, having a quick look around, then Shanna at the entrance to the bedroom. I didn't tell him about the knife. Didn't think that needed to enter the narrative. But the shower deal, that seemed unavoidable since the shower was wet—not the kind of thing to try to hide, which would just cause another round of particularly annoying questions. But I managed to avoid details about the eyeful I'd gotten, or the memory that might stick with me the rest of the year.

"She showered, huh?" Fairchild said, squinting at me.

"She'd just come back from the gym and a six-mile run. Girls are picky like that, Russ. Little sweat and they lose it."

"Right. With strange guys in the house, they shuck their clothes and hop in the shower."

"You think I'm strange?"

"I think you're unprecedented."

"Anyway, if you were recording this you could play it back. *I* never said she shucked her clothes. That was you. I'm not even sure what that would look like—shucking, I mean."

He stared at me like I was from Neptune. I get that a lot.

"Fact is, Russ, I think you're stranger than me. We should take a poll. I could be wrong. And when she *shucked* or removed her clothes, I wasn't in the room. About then I got a call from Danya. I told her about the *News* guy and she freaked, wanted me to give the phone to Shanna."

"Which you did, of course. In the bathroom, right?"

"Terrific deduction, since that's where the shower's located and she was in the shower. Whatever they're paying you, it isn't nearly enough."

"And how'd that go?"

"The handoff went okay. I left and they talked for a minute. I couldn't make out any words, then Shanna told me to come back and get the phone. She said Danya wanted to talk to me."

"So, she gave you the phone. When she was in the shower. How'd that go?"

"Pretty good. I'm thinking she might've run track in school because we didn't lose any time on that handoff either. Before I went out the door, she told me she and Danya were married."

"*What!*"

"Married," I repeated, thinking I'd enunciated clearly enough the first time. "Since sometime in April, she said."

"Jesus, *what*? Sonofabitch."

"Uh, let me guess. You didn't give Danya away. She didn't tell dad about the nuptials."

"Ho-*ly* Christ."

"Or, Russ—Shanna could've been lying. Not sure why, but it could've been misdirection, put me on a different track."

That slowed him down. Stopped him, actually. He paced, not easy in a room that size, but his legs were short.

He stopped and looked at me. "I've met Shanna. Lots of times. I thought they were just roommates. Now you tell me they're married. But—lying? You think she might've been?"

"You want an expert opinion?"

He glared at me.

"She showed me a ring. Which doesn't actually mean a thing, but . . . who knows." I hesitated. "You and Danya haven't had any long father-daughter talks in the last year or two, huh?"

"Well, shit. But you still didn't give me that opinion."

"Best guess—yeah, they're hitched."

"Sonofabitch." He left the room.

I looked at Day. "I'm thinking that's his favorite word."

"For you, yeah."

* * *

Five minutes later, Russell was back. "Then what?" he said.

Took me a moment to figure out where we'd left off. "Okay, I went into the living room and Danya wanted to know how much I charge for gumshoeing."

"For what?"

"Gumshoeing. She might've called it investigating."

"Jesus."

"While we were discussing rates, I saw Ignacio roll by in that Chevy Cruze. Ignacio's that tabloid guy, who I'm starting to think knows more about all of this than you or I do."

"Sonofabitch," Russ growled.

I looked over at Day. "Okay, that wasn't me."

"Might've been," Day replied.

Russ stared at me, then at Day. "Hah?"

"Nothing. So then, Danya hung up on me for no reason, which is sort of her MO, and I ran outside, tried to catch up with Ignacio, but he took off. I went back in the house, looked around a little, then Shanna came out in a towel and chased me outside." I didn't have to mention the towel, but spinning Fairchild around a time or two has been a significant part of our relationship, so the towel stayed in.

"Christ. I oughta be a private eye," Russ said, then he caught himself, possibly because he had twenty-five years on Shanna, who might also be his daughter's spouse, which would make her his son-in-law. And, shit—there goes my political-correctness merit badge.

"Okay," Russ said once he'd collected himself. "She comes out in a towel so you go outside."

"Right, and we did it in present tense, just the way you said it. I looked around the yard, didn't see anything, then she came out in jeans and a shirt, no towel."

I decided the note demanding a million dollars didn't need to come into it, especially since it had been stuffed up a drainpipe, so I passed over that part.

"About then I caught a whiff of something rank around the garage, like garbage, but then I remembered that their garbage can was outside by the gate. So I asked Shanna for a key. She told me where they were, I put the key in the lock and the hasp fell out since it'd been jimmied, and, well . . . *that's* why I'm the premier locator of missing persons in all of North America, Russ. All I can tell you is, it's a knack."

"Sonofabitch."

Not only his favorite word, but rhetorical, too. I didn't think it warranted a comment, so I sat there and waited.

"But now Shanna's gone," he said.

"She took off. A good look at Xenon hanging there against the back wall of the garage and she ran. I tried to catch her, but . . ." I shrugged. "She's half my age, built like a freakin' deer. Thing is, she did it in sandals, which I think means Air Nikes and the Swoosh aren't all they're cracked up to be."

"Hell. But, what you say—it sounds as if she didn't have any idea he was in there, strung up in the garage."

"Didn't seem like it. If she knew, I don't think she would've stuck around while I went to get the key. And she didn't know the lock was busted."

Silence.

I said, "You probably ought to know that when I got back after not catching Shanna, that *Celebrity News* guy—Ignacio—was coming out of the garage with a camera."

"Oh, jeez. Oh, Jesus Christ, no."

"He got pictures of Jo-X and a picture of me coming at him, then went over the back fence like a wharf rat."

He stared at me. "A wharf rat?"

I shrugged again. "Fast, nimble. It's an image. I didn't see fur or a tail, but he was wearing clothes."

"Sonofabitch."

"Right. I went after him, but everyone I go after is faster than me these days, although I'm pretty sure I could keep up with Rush Limbaugh. Fact is, I put my foot through the roof of that old doghouse, trying to go over the fence after Ignacio. I saw him run through a yard, pop over another fence, and that was that."

Big sigh from Fairchild. "Then what?"

At this point, what I needed was some slack in the story line, a little time gap for the contraband I'd crammed up the drainpipe, so I improvised. "I went out to the street and looked for Shanna. You can see a quarter mile before the street takes a bend. She was gone. I went down a side street behind the girls' house, tried to spot Ignacio since he went over a fence that way, but he was gone, too. So I went around the block, still didn't see Ignacio or Shanna, came back, phoned it in, and your guys came and cuffed me so I couldn't go crazy and put four or five of them in the hospital."

Another little grin from Day.

Russell was silent for two full minutes, thinking. Then he said, "Okay, we're gonna have to do this again, record it this time. What I did here was, you know . . ." He glanced up at the camera.

"Illegal."

"As a sonofabitch. But Danya's my kid, Angel. I don't know what the fuck's goin' on, but she's my kid. I don't figure she's any part of this, I mean Xenon bein' killed, murdered, strung up in that garage, but . . . fuck."

"I get it, Russ. I've got a daughter, too."

For a moment he was silent, thinking. Then: "Can't think of anything you told me that isn't gonna be on the record one way or another, so let's go through it with the recorder on. Same as we just did."

"PG rating on Shanna in the shower?"

"Tell it the way it was." Then he gave me an extra hard look. "But no surprises, Angel. This'll be on the record. A jury might end up seeing it. If you screw it up, we'll have to do it again."

*   *   *

Two fifteen p.m. My car hadn't been disassembled. In fact, it was in the back lot behind the police station, right where it had been after last year's Q&A sessions when I was finding decapitated heads. It had been vacuumed, which was thoughtful of them. I was ambivalent about the fingerprint dust on the steering wheel, dashboard, door handles, but I didn't say anything about it to Fairchild, who had escorted me out the back door.

"She's not answering her phone," he said. "Danya. I tried to ping her phone's GPS, but she must've pulled the battery."

"You can ping GPS? I mean you, the police?"

"What d'you think?"

Kids these days knew all about GPS, knew how to pull the battery. Things were a lot easier in the Middle Ages. Back then, kids didn't pull the batteries out of their cell phones. Ever. And you could run that comment past a bunch of today's teenagers and get a lot of blank looks.

"Walk with me, Angel." Russ nodded toward the Cyclone fence at the back of the lot.

I gave him a questioning look. He gave me another nod and kept going. The fence bordered the River Walk, a meandering asphalt pedestrian and bike path that rambled along the south side of the Truckee River as it passed behind the police station.

Russ opened a gate in the fence, and we went through, then headed east, away from downtown. It was a nice day. Gentle breeze, blue sky, cottonwoods providing shade. The river flowed around big granite boulders, water eddying and sparkling in the sun. Russ didn't say a word until we were a quarter mile out.

"We still haven't got the guy who killed Senator Reinhart and those others last year," he said. "FBI's got nothing."

"I would've heard if they had, Russ, but the update puts a high note on the afternoon."

He glanced at me. "The guy killed your woman, too."

"Thanks for reminding me. That was and still is the worst day of my life." And it was a she who killed Jeri, not a he, but I couldn't tell him that.

"Sorry about that. Really." He was silent for a minute. "But, Angel, someone phoned it in or we never would've known. A 911 call. A woman. We got her on tape. She sounds older, like over forty, maybe over fifty. Also sounds like she tried to change her voice. She knows it happened and where it happened, so she probably knows who did it."

"Maybe she's the killer."

Russ shrugged. "We thought of that. Cell phone she used was a burner, untraceable, so we've got nothing. I mean, nothing useful. A lawyer named Leland Bye was down in that mineshaft, too, north of Gerlach, and a young hooker, both shot dead, but that's the end of the trail. After that, it's nothing but vapor."

"Well, shit. I sure wish you'd get the guy. I would tap-dance on his grave."

"Me, too. He's still out there. Unless, of course, someone got to him, took care of him. Someone who's kept it real quiet."

"Batman's got the Riddler, I've got you."

We strolled another hundred yards without speaking. I didn't know how Russ had come up with that zinger, but I wasn't going to say another word about it. Might mention it to Ma, though, see what she thought about it, especially since she was the "older woman" who'd made the 911 call.

"No idea what Danya wanted a PI for, huh?" he said at last. "I mean, she didn't say anything about this Jo-X asshole? Man, I hate sayin' Jo-X, like I'm some sort of fuckin' groupie."

"Not a word. I don't think she had any idea Xenon was in that garage."

Another sigh. "This is gonna be a sonofabitch, Angel. No way it's not gonna be a lousy rotten sonofabitch. It's my kid, so they'll take me off the case, which sucks."

"Or it might free you up."

He looked at me. "That's the way you think, huh?"

"It works for me. Anyway, Danya seems like a nice girl."

"She is. She . . . well, her mother and I never got married. I was pretty young, twenty-three. Danya's mother—Denisha—was twenty-one. Denisha Fuller. I've been paying child support for a long time. I would've made a good father. What I mean is, I *am* a good father. I've got a daughter, Josie, seventeen, by my wife. But Denisha . . ." He sighed, kicked a pebble off the path. "She left Reno before she had Danya. She raised Danya in Alabama, south side of Tuscaloosa. Denisha was a real looker when she was younger, but . . . she had that hard edge, even then. Got married twice, divorced twice. She and Danya have had their problems. Danya's been here in Reno since a month after she turned eighteen. She's twenty-two now. Finally wanted her own place, so last year I put my name on the lease for that house she's in. She and Shanna met two years ago. They were roommates for a year, students up at UNR. Danya's a psychology major, taking it kinda slow, eight, ten credits a semester. Not in a big hurry. Shanna's paying a quarter of the rent, Danya's paying a quarter. I'm paying half. Now you tell me they're married."

"It probably just slipped her mind. You know how kids are—they get busy, forget to mention things."

He snorted an unhappy laugh.

"Anyway, that was a lot of background information, Russ."

He stopped and faced me. "Don't laugh or I'll shoot you right here and dump you in the river, but . . . hell . . . I'm thinking I want to hire you."

I stared at him. Finally, I said, "You've got an entire police force at your disposal, Russ."

"Yeah, but there's all those fuckin' rules that get in the way, which is sort of what you mentioned a few minutes ago. I oughta know. This is a goddamn awful situation. I'll be able to keep tabs on the investigation, but Don Kreuger's taking lead. Guy's a square shooter, but a stickler. All I'll be able to do is sit back and watch it roll over her—Danya. And Shanna. So I'm wondering if a maverick isn't what we need, all three of us. And luck. You stumble along, but you're the luckiest son of a bitch I've ever met." He headed east again.

I caught up to him, thinking about luck. Luck came in all sizes and shapes. My kind of luck was different. I hadn't put Ma on a train that morning thinking I'd run into a wet, stacked, naked girl before noon, but there you go—Lady Luck, following me around like a hungry dog. And, of course, there was Jo-X, stinking up a garage, waiting for Nevada's luckiest gumshoe to find him and cause another uproar.

We walked awhile in silence, me thinking about how weird this deal with Fairchild was, or could be, not sure I wanted him involved like this, not sure I didn't, either. In the interrogation room I realized I wasn't going to abandon the investigation, such as it was, since Danya and I had kind of a handshake deal going, but . . .

"Maverick, huh?" I said to get Russ talking again.

"I don't know what's going on," he said. "But two things I'm sure of—you're completely unprofessional, and you've got a way of digging in and finding stuff out. Weird stuff."

I smiled. "It's probably because I don't know what the hell I'm doing. Guess that pisses you off, too. I still remember you giving me the finger in the hospital last summer."

He stopped and jabbed a different finger into my chest. "What I'm thinking is—you can do things I can't. *We* can't."

"You mean the police?"

"Right. I'm thinking you could be something of a parallel, off-the-record investigation—coloring outside the lines so to speak, 'cause that's who you are, the way you do things."

I looked out at the slow-moving river, thinking about it. This might be a mistake, but it might not. It had possibilities.

"I sure as hell wouldn't want anyone to know about this," he went on. "I mean, *anyone*. It could mean my career."

I thought a moment longer, then said, "If I do this, what are you hiring me to do, exactly? Locate Danya since she took off, or find out who killed Xenon?"

"Well . . . both. Either. I mean, whatever, you know, makes her safe, explains how Xenon got in that garage. I want this to go away."

"What if she's guilty, Russ? Or your daughter-in-law." No way I could resist that in-law dig. After all, this was Russ.

He stared at me, finally shook his head. "I know Danya. She didn't do this. She wouldn't know the first thing about that Xenon asshole, lyrics like that. She plays Johnny Mathis CDs at

Christmas, sings along with him. I don't know that much about Shanna, but . . . no way. I think this is just a random piece-of-shit deal, unless someone knows Danya's my kid and is using her to screw with me."

"Whatever I find, assuming I find anything at all, you want me to run it past you first."

"That's right."

"Sounds maverick all right, but not illegal since you're a cop. I would just be giving information to the police, which is the right thing to do."

"You might concentrate on who killed Xenon and stuck him in that garage. Finding Danya isn't likely to be an issue. She's a bit high-strung. She might not think about something like this very clearly, but I think she'll get hold of me pretty soon. If she doesn't, police will probably have her and Shanna rounded up by this evening at the latest."

"Yeah? I didn't think RPD was that good." Another sweet dig, and one I thought might be accurate. Danya and Shanna might not be as easy to find as Russ thought. Not sure why I thought that, but it might've been my gumshoe gene flaring up.

He shrugged, didn't rise to the bait. "Where's she gonna go? Right now we've got fifty cops looking for her and Shanna. So, how 'bout it? I haven't heard you say yes yet."

I gave him a hard look. "On three conditions, Russ."

"Aw, shit. Let's hear 'em."

"Number one, I want access. Right now I don't have that, not like I'll need it. Maude's out of town and I'm not licensed. I can't get a name or address from a phone number or a license plate. I can't track credit card usage or ping a cell phone's GPS. I might have to call you with something like that, and if I do, I'll want it, no hassle, no questions." In fact, I had all that except the pinging. I had Ma's passwords and was getting used to her online investigative tools, but putting Russ in my pocket was the kind of underhanded move Ma had built a career on. If I didn't do this, Ma would show my naked poster all over town. But even without Ma, I wasn't about to let an opportunity this good slip away.

"Two," I went on. "Ma's not going to be involved in this. I'm not going to put her PI license at risk. This is just between you and me. No contract, no legal shit. Just you and me."

"Well, hell, Angel—I was gonna get the guys in the squad room together and make a formal announcement."

Good one, Russ. "What about Day? Clifford. That thing you did, turning off the camera. How's he good with that?"

"Cliff's my brother-in-law. Well, ex. He's a good guy. And if he said word one about any of this, my sister would cut off his nuts since they're still friends."

"That does sound friendly. It also sounds like she knows how to use a chainsaw."

He smiled. "So we're good. I give you access and this deal's just between you and me—don't worry about Cliff. You said three conditions. What's the last one?"

"I want five thousand dollars. Today. In cash."

* * *

"Well . . . horse pucky," he said, smiling. "Now I gotta go hit the bank." Walking back, he had a little skip in his step. Until, that is, he got to thinking about things—like me, his job, Jo-X in his daughter's garage even if the place was a rental—a rat's nest of complications that looked as if it was going to turn into shit stew. Then the skip curdled into his usual flat-footed shuffle, shoulders hunched, face as long as a cold night in January.

"Try phoning her again," I said.

He got out his cell phone and called Danya, got voice mail, left a message for her to call him.

We walked back to the police station, hashing out details. I got his phone numbers, personal and police, same for e-mail addresses. And I got Day's numbers, which I would treasure. I gave Russ both my numbers and e-mail, and told him not to call unless he absolutely had to. Or if he heard from Danya. And I told him if I ever caught him tracking my phone's GPS, he'd never hear from me again. I didn't bother to tell him I was going to go out and get an untraceable Walmart burner, just in case. In case of what, I didn't know, but . . . you never know. If you're going to skate around that razor edge of right and wrong, you take precautions. After last October, I was an expert. And, of course, a murderer.

He stopped outside the gate to the parking lot. "Not actually sure I like you, Angel. Probably won't be having you over for beer and barbeque, but . . . I'm glad you said yes."

He went through, but I stayed behind. He turned and gave me a questioning look.

"I'm not going to tell you how I came up with this, Russ, so I don't want to hear any whining or hassling, none of that, but since you're a client now, you should know that I'm about twenty percent sure that your kid, Danya, is Celine. Maybe even thirty percent." Actually I was only at about ten percent, since Danya was five-eight or -nine and Celine was six-three, almost as tall as Jo-X. I didn't know if they made shoes with six- or seven-inch heels, but there was some sort of a connection there. Danya and Celine were both black, beautiful, and busty, and Jonnie Xenon was hanging around Danya's garage, so I thought . . . maybe.

"Celine?" Russ asked.

"The missing black girl. Girl who's been seen around Jo-X the past couple of weeks."

His jaw dropped. "*That* Celine? You gotta be shitting me."

"Split the difference. Call it twenty-five percent."

"Sonofabitch. How'd you get that? Which can't be true, by the way. I looked into her on the Internet this afternoon—Celine — while you were cooling your heels in your favorite room. No one knows who she is. And she's black as midnight, which Danya isn't. Celine is a looker, but she's taller, like about six foot two. And she doesn't look anything like Danya. Well, not a *lot*."

"There's that whining thing I mentioned."

"Fuck you, Angel. *Celine?*"

"Okay, if it makes you happy, I'll go fifteen percent. It isn't a sure thing. But it makes you wonder, doesn't it—Jonnie Xenon in their garage like that? Why him? Why there?"

He stared. "Sonofabitch." Without another word, he headed for the station in a fast, choppy stride.

"Russ."

He turned sharply, angry. "Yeah?"

"If the police turn up anything about Celine, anything at all, I want to hear about it thirty seconds later."

He chewed on his lower lip. "Yeah, okay."

"And—you know how to find your way to Rapscallion?"

"The restaurant? Sure, why?"

"I'm gonna be there getting a late lunch, since you didn't feed me at the station. Drop by in the next hour or so with five thousand dollars. And bring enough to pick up my tab while you're at it."

He said "fuck" as he went through a back door into the station, just loud enough for me to hear.

CHAPTER SIX

I WAS AT a Walmart still digesting grilled salmon with rice and a pretty good pinot noir when Ma phoned at seven. She'd reached western Utah. She was in the dining car waiting for a New York steak, rare, and a beer. I could tell she hadn't been getting the news since I was all over the place at six o'clock in Reno, four local channels, CNN, no telling how many others. Mortimer Angel does it again. I thought I'd surprise her and let her find out on her own, so I told her everything was copacetic on the home front. I hoped I'd still have a job once she found out just how copacetic things had become.

I wished her a terrific dinner and a safe trip—it was, after all, Amtrak, subject to sudden derailments—hung up, and went back to the Walmart clerk who was ringing up that burner phone —$12.99 and a fifty-dollar phone card with two hundred minutes on it. I got the Drug Dealer Special—though professional dealers probably went with the cheapo thirty-dollar card since the phone would be tossed within a week.

Out the door, the sun was behind the Sierras, nice pink glow on high wispy clouds, day cooling off. I drove to Jeri's place—okay, mine. I was still getting used to it, still saw Jeri in the exercise room tossing me around like a sack of grain. I missed her. We'd been planning an entire lifetime together. What we got was two months, then Julia Reinhart happened.

I got a bottle of Pete's Wicked Ale and sat in the backyard on a lawn chair, watching stars come out one by one, waiting for full dark. Waiting, in fact, for two a.m. to roll around.

Danya-Celine. Celine-Danya.

Weird. Didn't make sense. Danya Fuller was a psych major at UNR. She shouldn't have any connection with a nasty low-life rapper. When Russ had handed over five thousand dollars and paid thirty-six bucks for my lunch, plus tip, he'd given me a photo of Danya taken at his place last Christmas, and a picture of Danya and Shanna at the Grand Canyon last summer.

Celine was . . . unknown. An instant sensation, a media circus all her own, a one-namer like Cher or Beyoncé. Lots of speculation about Jo-X's latest, a girl as black as Jonnie was white. She'd come out of nowhere, replacing some hot, slender bimbo with a nice ass and photogenic boobs revealed by dresses split all the way down to her navel—Krissy Something. Krissy was already old news, off the public's radar, which no doubt pissed her off. It had taken Celine only three days to get on the cover of every tabloid in the country. Krissy might've put bullet holes in Jo-X's forehead and strung him up in Danya's garage knowing, somehow, that Danya was Celine.

But—was Danya Fuller actually Celine? With Jo-X hanging around in her garage, I mentally upped the odds to forty percent. Which left sixty percent that she wasn't, so there was still a lot of room for debate and conjecture there.

And Vince Ignacio, Wharf Rat, was in the picture, snooping around. For some reason, he knew who Danya was and where she lived . . . but, wait. He'd identified Shanna by name, not Danya. But those two were an item, so, if he knew Shanna, he would know Danya. If he thought Danya was Celine and if he thought he had sufficient proof, *Celebrity News* might be gearing up to put out a special edition—Ignacio's hot scoop. Which would put Fairchild in the eye of an epic shit storm.

Fairchild. My brand-new shining contact with RPD. Time to see if that was real or another broken promise.

I got out my phone, rang him up. "Hey, Russ?"

"Yeah? You find somethin' already?"

"No. Xenon's been removed from the garage, hasn't he?"

"Forensics got done about two thirty this afternoon. Guy's at the coroner's office. Why?"

"All I want are answers, Russ, not questions to which you don't want answers. Still got crime scene tape up at the house?"

"Yeah."

"Any police up there, watching the place?"

"A car's out front, in case Danya shows up. Or Shanna. Or your guy, Ignacio. Unmarked car."

"Ignacio's not *my* guy."

"Right. I'm makin' a note of that as we speak."

Smart-ass. "Pull the car at midnight, Russ."

"Huh? Why?"

"Just do it. Figure out a way. Send 'em home. Tell 'em their overtime is only good until midnight, that'll get 'em out of there. If you can't do it, call me back." I hung up, then phoned the Wharf Rat. I had his card, but I'd also memorized his number. Seemed like a good idea.

"Yeah?" he said, in a paranoid whisper. "Who's this?"

"You are not authorized to use that picture of me, Ignacio. Do that and I'll sue you and your scummy rag for a million bucks."

He laughed. "Good luck gettin' a million from me. I got forty bucks in my checking account."

"Forty bucks and no job if you run that picture."

"Jesus, you don't know nothin' about tabloid journalism, do you?" He hung up.

Well, shit.

Five seconds later, my phone rang. Probably the Rat, so I said, "Tabloid journalism is a pimple on society's ass."

"Really? Just a pimple, not a boil or a hemorrhoid?"

I knew that voice. "Hey, Dallas. What's up?" Dallas, my ex, pushing forty-three and still beautiful. She'd been semi-engaged to Reno's missing mayor, Jonnie Sjorgen, until I found his head in the trunk of her Mercedes last July. That pretty much put the kibosh on the engagement, but she got to keep the ring.

"You found another missing Jonnie, Mort. Good work."

"It's a knack."

"I just wanted to call with my congratulations before you got so famous I couldn't get through."

"Thanks. It's always great to hear from you, Dal."

"How's Maude taking it? You and this Jo-X thing?"

"She's somewhere in Utah, on her way to Memphis to visit her kid. She'll be gone two weeks. Amtrak. Her phone cuts in and out, so I think she hasn't seen the news yet."

"No doubt she'll be thrilled."

"I'm counting on it. It's about time I got a raise."

She laughed, hung up, then a minute later my phone chirped and it was Holiday. A phone chirp didn't seem all that manly. I was going to have to come up with a new ringtone.

"Mort, I've been reading. I just turned on the television."

"Yeah? Anything good on?"

"You're totally something else."

"Got that right. Totally."

"Ma's gonna kill you when she gets back. She told you not to find Jo-X, and what do you do?"

"Uh-huh. Can't help it."

"I know. At least this time you found an entire body, not just heads or a severed hand."

"I'm upgrading my act. Doesn't piss off the police as much, waiting around for the rest of it to show up."

"They're saying you found him at a girl's house. Was that the girl in the Green Room last night?"

"This's not for public consumption until it gets out—but that girl was Fairchild's daughter."

Six seconds of silence. Then, "Fairchild? The detective? You gotta be kidding me."

"Nope."

"That girl was black, Mort. *And* pretty. Russell Fairchild is as ugly and white as Buddy Hackett's ghost."

"Good eye, kiddo. The metaphor was a winner, too."

"That was a simile. And . . . *Russell's* kid? I never know when you're serious."

"I am now."

"Interesting. So, how's he taking it?"

"Talk about delighted. The guy is bouncing off the walls."

"I bet. Anyway, I thought I'd let you know Alice phoned a while ago. She misses me, so I'm going to visit her for a few days. I'll drive down tomorrow morning."

Alice, Holiday's aunt, lived in San Francisco. She was fifty-five. She let Holiday bathe with two male cousins until the day Holiday turned eleven. I was so jealous. I never had a cool aunt like that, and I had female cousins the right age, too.

"Good to know. How long you gonna be gone?"

"Four or five days, maybe a week. I'm driving down, and she said something about us going to San Luis Obispo to visit her sister, Irene, so it might be longer."

"Safe trip, huh?"

"Yep. Thanks. I'll let you know when I get back."

The call ended. Everyone was out of town or about to leave. I sat there with Ignacio's snide words drifting around in my head, mostly that crack that I was out of Shanna's league. I hated him until it was full dark and Venus got hung up in the trees over the Sierras. No moon.

Then Venus slid below the mountains.

The night was warm. For a while I contemplated this Danya-Celine thing. Jo-X had been stinking up Danya's—or Shanna's—garage, but what did that mean? According to the covers of half a dozen tabloids, Celine was a "mystery woman"—an expression that sold tens of thousands of additional copies to a relatively low-IQ or easily amused market—so if Danya and Celine were one and the same, in spite of the apparent difference in their heights, then it was likely Danya had an agenda. A hidden agenda, to be precise. Might that agenda include turning out Jo-X's lights for some unknown reason? If so, why the hell would she string him up in her garage?

Made no sense. I couldn't fit Shanna into any of that. And if those two were in fact married, Shanna would know about the Danya-Celine connection—especially if Danya had disappeared for two or three weeks while Celine was making headlines. That would put Shanna in cahoots with Danya, "cahoots" being a word I like to use around Ma. Russell Fairchild must be fizzing like Alka-Seltzer in a glass of Pepsi about now. If—when—the media made that final connection, all hell was going to break loose and Fairchild was going to know how I felt last year, which might make him a better person, more empathetic.

The Wicked Ale was long gone, including its buzz. I wasn't sleepy and I had things to do later that night, so I got up and hiked over to the Green Room, half a mile away.

* * *

As soon as I came through the door, O'Roarke grabbed a bottle of Pete's Wicked Ale and had the top off, the bottle sitting in front of my favorite stool, opposite the TV.

"Nice goin', spitfire. You're four for four now, right?"

"Something like that. I'm beginning to lose count." I pushed the Pete's back at him. "Gimme a Coke."

"Just Coke?"

"Okay, put a twist of lime in it."

O'Roarke frowned at me. "Guy gets famous, suddenly he gets picky. It's a bitch in this place, trying to keep up."

"Yeah, I get that bitch thing a lot."

He set a Coke in front of me, lime on the rim. "Bottoms up. Eleven-o'clock news in ten minutes. You wouldn't want to miss that. You've gone national, baby. Sure you don't want something stronger, like a V and V?"

"V and V?"

"Vodka and Valium."

"You serve that here, do you?"

"We aim to please."

A hooker by the name of Rosa came in and sat next to me. She'd known Holiday last year, knew Holiday and I had a thing going and that Holiday had never really been a hooker. Rosa was a cute little gal, twenty-three, petite, wearing the sort of cleavage-rich dress that attracts business. I didn't complain. Rosa had been in and out of the Green Room a dozen times in the past year, working on a mortgage and car payments.

"I caught your act on the six-o'clock," she said, then turned to O'Roarke. "Caipirinha with cachaca, Patrick."

"Patrick," I said to O'Roarke. "You two are on a first-name basis. That's good. I still call you O'Roarke."

"Unlike you, she's a great customer. That is to say, she pays for her drinks—or someone does. On the other hand, you've still got a bunch of those goddamn free-drink coupons. I gave you too many of 'em last year. How about you don't chase her off before she pays for her drink?"

"I've never chased Rosa away. That was Holiday, and it was last year, long time ago."

To make his day as complete as mine, I thumbed a free-drink coupon out of my shirt pocket and slid it across the bar to him. "Got hers covered, barkeep."

Rosa smiled. "Hey, thanks. These things cost like six bucks, which is a real rip-off."

"De nada."

O'Roarke gave me a cool look, then went off to whip up her drink. I turned to give Rosa the once-over. She looked terrific—the dress was sapphire blue with a plunge that ended an inch below nicely shaped breasts. Her hair was straight, black, all the way to the middle of her back. Holiday told me she got twelve hundred a night or five grand a week and was highly selective.

"How's tricks?" I asked.

"Wow, that's old. Bet you heard it sometime around nineteen eighteen, toward the end of the first world war."

"Ouch. Sorry."

"No problem. I've heard 'em all, every hooker joke ever told and then some."

"Occupational hazard?"

"You got it." O'Roarke set her drink in front of her.

"I could tell you proprietary IRS jokes," I said. "Punch line on a few of them is when someone slits their wrists."

"Dark, Mort. Very dark. But thanks for the drink."

We nursed our drinks for a while—Rosa in a Victoria's Secret dress, keeping an eye out for business opportunities—me in jeans and a polyester shirt from Target. When eleven o'clock rolled around, there was Mortimer Angel in a telephoto shot, being put in the back of Day's cruiser, Day leaning back against the car while Ginger Haley's voice-over explained that the "heads guy" from last year, same guy who got Senator Reinhart's hand in a FedEx package, had been placed in custody after finding the body of bad-boy rapper Jo-X hanging in a garage belonging to the daughter of a Reno police detective by the name of Russell Fairchild.

Uh-oh.

Photos of Danya and Shanna appeared and the voice-over kept up a steady beat. Fairchild would be beside himself. Even at this late hour, the RPD squad room would be a termites' nest of activity. Phones would be ringing.

Speaking of phones, mine lit up and played "Monster Mash" by Bobby "Boris" Pickett, a ringtone I'd put on the phone right before leaving home, hoping for an occasion just like this. I let it play for a while, until Rosa stared at me and said, "You're either seventy years old or twelve."

I swiped the phone. "Yo."

"Jesus Christ, Angel. You still ain't heard from Danya? She hasn't called or nothin'?" Fairchild was bordering on frantic. On TV, a reporter was in front of Jo-X's Las Vegas mansion, a place worth five or six million bucks, one of the larger houses on the Las Lomas Golf Course with a view of the par-five fourteenth green.

"Nope."

"Sonofabitch."

He hung up.

"'Yo' and 'nope,'" Rosa said, looking at me as she stirred her Caipirinha with a tiny red straw.

"It's all about pithy conversation, Sweetheart. Communicate swiftly, waste no effort, get on with life."

She smiled. "Pithy."

"Try it."

"You, me, a room upstairs?"

"Jeez, I thought you were selective."

"I am. So . . . upstairs?"

"Only if it's free and Holiday okays it."

"Well . . . that didn't work. Screw your pithy."

* * *

Two ten a.m., Monday morning. I eased down Elmcrest in the Toyota, checking cars parked on the street—anything with a view of the house. Six possibles, five if cops don't use Zapinos for stakeouts. Russ hadn't called, so maybe he'd come through and cleared them out. The nearest streetlight was two hundred feet away, too dark to see much. Not much I could do except stroll back and hit the interior of the cars with a penlight. If I came across a nest of cops, I would say I was looking for my girlfriend. If that didn't work, Russ would have to bail me out. Pretty good test of our new arrangement, if it came to that.

No cops, so I trotted up the driveway in dark clothing and into the backyard. The garage door was closed, yellow crime scene tape glowing eerily in the night. Same for the back door of the house. But all I wanted was the drainpipe, which wasn't going to be removed in the recommended Home Depot fashion.

Wearing gloves, I grabbed the sonofabitch. It was forty years old, thin sheet metal. I yanked it off the wall, all eight feet of it, stomped it in the middle, folded it, hustled it out to my car, tossed it in the backseat, got in, and took off. No dark sedans swung out behind me with lights and siren, no helicopters, no SWAT team.

Good enough.

Tomorrow there would be an all-points bulletin, a BOLO, for a missing drainpipe.

*   *   *

Back home, I emptied the pipe—everything was still there—then I mashed the pipe flat, folded it into a two-foot wad of scrap covered by scaly bile-green paint, drove it across town to a dark neighborhood, and left it in a weed-enhanced ditch. I stuffed the gloves coated with bits of green paint in a trash can outside an all-night convenience store and went home.

*   *   *

Maude Clary called at eight ten the next morning from somewhere in the mountains of Colorado, west of Denver.

"Jesus, Mort!"

I tried to open my eyes. The left one finally flipped open, but the right one was glued shut. "Yeah? Who's this?"

"Jo-X? *You* found Jo-X?"

"What can I tell you? I don't half try. It's not a teachable skill, so don't ask." Finally, my right eye popped open, and the world was three dimensional again but still blurry.

"The train stops in Denver, boyo. It's the nearest place with a decent airport. I'm comin' home."

"No you're not."

"I'm not?"

"I've got it under control. You've got a kid to visit. Grandkids, too. I'll bet you've even got gifts for the precious little ones."

"They're not so little and not so precious, but of course I've got gifts. I'm their grandma. I'm duty-bound."

"So, stay. Go. Have fun. Relax."

"You've got it under control? *You?* Make me laugh before my first cigarette in the morning an' I'll collapse a lung."

"This was just a hiccup. Anyway, Jo-X is dead. Been dead five or six days, so it's not as if you could resuscitate him. No one's that good at CPR. So, stay. Have fun."

Silence.

I sat up, put my feet over the side of the bed, blinked at the morning glow behind the curtains. "You still there?"

"For hell's sake, Mort . . ."

"Anything else I can do for you, Ma?"

"Yeah. Long as you're on a roll, where's that girl—Danya? They say she's missing, too. And Shanna someone."

"I'm workin' on that."

"Don't."

"Okay, then, I won't."

More disbelieving silence. Then: "They didn't arrest you?"

"Nope. Just like last summer, all I do is find 'em. After that it's up to them to figure things out. They sometimes don't, which you and I both know is a good thing."

"You didn't say anything about all this when I phoned you last night."

"I didn't want to ruin your trip. Now I want you to keep going east and have yourself a mighty fine time."

"Oh, for Christ's sake."

No response needed, so I waited. Sometimes it's better to let it come to you.

"Anyway, are *you* okay, Mort?"

"Never better. Slept like a baby last night." Except when I tore that drainpipe off the wall, which was sort of fun. Reminded me of something I did when I was fourteen. I might tell her about it when she got back home, but now was not the time.

"Well . . . okay, then. Now stay out of it, okay?"

"Fairchild might have a few more questions for me, but I'll do my best." I figured I was safe with the lies of omission now that she was a thousand miles away.

"I'll give some thought about firing you while I'm away. I'll let you know when I get back."

"That's my girl, always on the job."

We hung up. I stood, stretched, didn't feel like hitting the day yet, since I'd been up late, so I went back to bed.

CHAPTER SEVEN

I FINALLY ROLLED out of bed at ten twenty, feeling pretty good after last night's successful clandestine operation. But getting up in the morning is like turning on a computer. Hit the switch and it takes a while to boot up, load memory, move the cobwebs out, get the cursor blinking.

So—coffee first.

Then the morning paper, which I thought would be a hoot.

And there was Reno's very own Mortimer Angel, PI, above the fold on the front page, in full stride, headed for the camera with a lethal gleam in his eye. Ignacio's snapshot. And a nice story—not particularly accurate and missing a lot of critical information— but it had the basics down reasonably well: Mortimer Angel, age forty-two, finding gangsta rapper Jo-X strung up in the garage of the twenty-two-year-old daughter of Reno police detective Russell Fairchild. The *New York Times* would have the picture. And *Le Monde* in France, *Der Spiegel* in Germany, and a paper somewhere in, say, the middle of Colorado for Ma's amusement. Since I may have left out a few details earlier that morning, I expected a call back at any time.

And I figured Ignacio was good for at least a quarter mil after selling those pictures, so my lawsuit was looking quite a bit better now.

Once the coffee took hold, I got a good look at the stuff from the drainpipe. "Celine" was written on the back of the flash drive in a somewhat flowery style. I fired up my computer and stuck the drive in, waited for it to be recognized, then found that it contained two video files. The first was short and shaky, no sound. A time stamp gave the date, which was nine days ago. In a desert field, a helicopter landed not far from a big industrial shed, blowing up clouds of dust. There was a sharp break in the video, then a slender blond girl was walking away from the camera, headed toward the helicopter, dressed in white shorts and a yellow halter. A man in a flight suit walked beside her, several inches taller. The video ended. I started up the second clip. The time stamp showed that it was the following day. In it, Shanna was indoors, at what looked like a restaurant table, wearing the same yellow halter top as in the first clip. A big plate-glass window was beside her with a view of dry gravel in front of the place and a fifty-yard stretch of deserted two-lane highway. She was in profile, staring at something outside. Daylight glare had darkened her features, but I had no doubt that it was Shanna—blond hair with the same pink streak, same lips and eyes, same extraordinary figure. The video bounced around as the camera approached. She looked up with an empty, distant expression as a menu was put in front of her, then the clip ended abruptly.

Shanna.

Alone at a table in what looked like a roadside restaurant or café.

I didn't know what to make of it. Was the name on the flash drive supposed to mean lily-white Shanna was ebony-skinned Celine? Maybe it was body paint. How good was the best body paint these days? Good enough to fool a nation of TV viewers? Maybe. I'd read the book *Black Like Me* years ago in a college sociology class, but the country had moved on and this was an entirely different era. No comparison.

I played both clips again but couldn't make anything more out of them. They had no sound, so that didn't help.

I watched the café video again, looking at the surroundings. The table had the kind of napkin holder you'd see in a small café or roadside diner. The tablecloth was cheap checkered plastic. A ceramic coffee cup was in front of her, still upside down, flatware wrapped in a napkin, salt and pepper shakers off to one side. Across the highway the land looked like flat desert scrub, the day hot and bright, low mountains miles away.

Collectively, the matchbook covers I'd seen at the girls' house had a theme that sang southern Nevada—Las Vegas, Hiko, Caliente, Searchlight, Indian Springs, a few no-name places I'd never heard of. Most of them had addresses on US 93 or 95. One was for a tourist trap on the strangely named Extraterrestrial Highway, State Route 375 between Rachel and Crystal Springs.

But, *Caliente*. I had matchbooks for the Double Down Motel and the Pahranagai Inn, and a Pahranagai room receipt in the name of Nathan Williams.

The SD card I'd pulled from Ignacio's camera held pictures of the girls' house, yard, and inside the house, nothing else.

So—flash drive, a note demanding a million bucks, a motel receipt, matchbook covers. Good stuff, illegally removed from a crime scene that was getting national attention, and I had been at said crime scene, a PI who also got national attention. I thought Police Chief Menteer, Russell's boss, might eventually think to get a warrant to search my place. Russ probably couldn't block something like that. He might not even try, so I put everything in a paper bag and drove over to Velma's place, which took a while due to my fame and the media wolves—three vans had camped out on the street, hoping for a shot of North America's premier finder of missing famous people who turn up dead. I've gotten better at shaking the media, but it still requires effort and finesse. Turns out it's easier to lose them on foot, down one-way streets and alleyways, but today, after twenty minutes of amusing and provocative driving, I was free.

Velma's house backs up to my old place on Ralston Street. I used to go through or over the fence to get there, but this time I parked off the street, on a driveway that runs beside her house, and knocked on her back door.

Velma Knapp is four foot ten, eighty-six years old, a terror for juicy gossip, especially when the conversation gets anywhere near the possibility that I might be getting laid. As a result, she likes Holiday a lot, not that she gets details. She's utterly reliable when I have to duck the media and hide stuff from the police. Last summer she was delighted that I was having an affair—which I wasn't—with a stunningly beautiful woman thirty-four years old, Kayla, ducking her husband—who, thankfully, didn't exist—and the two of us were using the fence between Velma's property and mine as an escape route to avoid trouble—which was true, but not the kind of trouble Velma was rooting for. From time to time, even though I've moved, I mow her lawn and do odd chores and repairs around her place since she's been widowed for fourteen years.

She answered the door in a hair net, a flowery housedress, and a yellow cardigan with toasted tea cake crumbs down the front. Her feet were in huge fuzzy slippers that I'd given her last Christmas.

"Mortimer! Great timing! I have a drain that's plugged."

Yep, great timing.

But the world plays ping-pong with our priorities on a regular basis, so I went in and got right to it after handing her the bag of goodies. I knew right where she kept the drain snake. She looked in the bag as I went to work on the bathroom sink.

"What's all this?" she asked.

"Stuff to keep safe for me."

"From the cops?" she said hopefully.

"From anyone. Including the cops."

"Good. That include Maude?"

"Well, no. You should give it to her if she asks for it."

She sniffed the bag, as if its scent would tell her something she hadn't seen by looking.

"It's about this thing with Jo-X," I told her.

"Who the hell is Jones?"

Her hearing aid isn't always up to par. Batteries are an issue. She hadn't heard a word about Jo-X. She doesn't have television or a computer. No Internet, no iPhone. Just the morning paper, which I'd seen on her front porch as I drove up. Nor would Jo-X have held any interest for her, and I didn't want to explain my latest coup. I especially didn't want to mention his rapper lyrics, which were toxic as a cloud of powdered plutonium. I asked her about her kids to throw her off. Alex and Beth were both older than me by fifteen and seventeen years, respectively, and I had two tea cakes while she caught me up on the latest.

I left Velma with a drain so free of obstructions it could suck down a possum. At eleven twenty-five, I rolled by Danya and Shanna's house, wondering if I'd missed a clue or two in my rush yesterday, but Fairchild and Day were in the backyard, standing at the entrance to the garage. I caught a glimpse of them as I went by. A patrol car was at the curb in front, an unmarked car in the driveway, two vans across the street. The front door of the house was open. I saw three crime scene techs milling around.

I parked up the street and phoned Fairchild.

"Where are you?" First words out of his mouth. No "Hi," or "How's it hangin', Mort." Nothing like that. Caller ID was making it harder all the time to surprise anyone.

"On the street. About a hundred feet west of you. West is the direction in which the sun sets in case you don't—"

"Stay right there. Don't move."

Redundant instructions, but I thought I'd save time by heading toward him anyway. We walked back to the house together. He had a lit Camel jammed in the corner of his mouth, so we trailed smoke. He didn't take the butt out until we hit the driveway.

"Got somethin' to show you," he said.

We went around back, then around to the far side of the house. "What do you think?" he asked.

"About what?"

He pointed with the last third of his Camel. "Someone tore the drainpipe off the wall last night."

I looked around the yard, then over the back fence. "Didn't figure this for a high-crime neighborhood."

"Except for a recent murder, you mean?"

"Okay, that. But, a downspout? Who'd want that?"

"Wouldn't know anything about it, huh?"

I looked up to where the remaining part of the drainpipe had been bent outward, then at Russ. "If I did—hypothetically, you understand—would you want me to tell you about it? And, by the way, I'll let you know when that five thousand dollars is used up."

He connected those two comments, which should have had no relation to one another, then looked down at his feet, took one last suck on the Camel, mashed the butt on the bottom of his shoe, and stuck the remains in a pocket to keep from contaminating the crime scene. What a cop.

"Vandalism," he said with a sigh. "House here has been all over the news. Must've been kids, wanting a souvenir since it was Jo-X. We'll probably never know who did it unless they Facebook it or try to sell it on eBay."

"A drainpipe on eBay. That sounds about right, but I'd look harder at that Facebook thing. Kids can't keep a secret worth a damn. Anything else you want to show me around here?"

* * *

He didn't, so I left. A thought occurred to me, so I drove on down to Virginia Street and left the Toyota on a side street, across from Danya's bank. I sat there for five minutes, then my stomach growled, reminding me of something I'd forgotten to do, so I went into Adelpho's Greek Food on the corner and ordered up a lamb gyro with Tzatziki sauce, then sat at a window seat with a nice view of the front and side entrances to the bank.

Then time crept by like a sloth doing the hundred-yard dash in sub-zero weather.

I had another gyro.

And a Diet Coke.

A lady with a kid in a car seat went into the bank, came out four minutes thirty-seven seconds later. And, yes, I timed her.

Eighteen hundred seconds passed as 12:18 turned into 12:48.

A man in a suit went into the bank, stayed inside for eleven minutes two seconds, came out, got into an Audi, took off south on Virginia Street.

I couldn't pack in another gyro but I was bored. Adelpho—all five feet two inches of him—smiled at me since I was taking up a seat. I smiled back, got another Diet Coke, thought maybe I could order up another gyro to go, eat it later.

A white Pontiac pulled up and an elderly lady, eighty pounds overweight, wearing a Goodwill dress and a wide-brim hat, got out on the passenger side and limped into the bank in clunky black shoes.

I drank the last of my Coke. Slurped it. Stared at the bank.

Goodwill clothing. Big hat. Limp.

Huh.

I got up, ambled across the street, and went into the bank to think about opening a new account.

No old lady in the place, but the bank had restrooms. I could see the Pontiac through a glass door at the side of the lobby.

I sat on a couch in a common area and picked up a magazine on a glass table, sat back, started to read an article about Ibo Island off the coast of Mozambique. Cool place. Might go there on vacation if they weren't beheading Americans.

The old lady emerged slowly from the safe deposit area, came out through a low swinging door, and headed for the side entrance. She was tall, and she had a big purse that looked like it had some heft to it.

I got up.

The lady went outside, and I followed. As she was opening the car door, I said, "I like the hat, Shanna, but that dress has got to go."

Well, I didn't mean it like that, like she should take the dress *off*, right then and there, although I wouldn't have stopped her if she did, but it slowed her down and brought her head up. And, yes, it was Shanna.

She got in the car, moving spritely now. I went around to the driver's side. "Your dad's worried about you," I said to Danya. She had on a dishwater blond wig, dark glasses. Might fool a cop from sixty feet away.

"Tell him I'm okay." She put the car in reverse, started to back up, then stopped. "I didn't kill Jo-X. I mean, *we* didn't."

"Didn't think you did."

"But the whole world does, Mortimer."

"Mort. You should talk to the police, get this cleared up. Both of you, actually, since both of you live in that house."

"Can't do that. Anyway, you're fired. I mean, I never hired you. Gotta go, but it's been nice talking to you." She backed up and cut the wheels.

The windows were rolled down so I gave it one last try as the Pontiac started forward. "You should at least call your dad." I looked at Shanna. "You, too, Celine, if you have family around."

The car lunged as Danya hit the brakes. "What? What did you call her?" Her dark glasses stared at me like insect eyes.

"Celine."

"Fuck."

She hit the gas, stopped as she glanced left on Virginia Street, then went one block north and turned east. Gone.

I had the tag number, description of the car, so I got out my cell phone and called Fairchild.

"Now what, Angel?"

"I just saw your kid, Detective. Me, America's foremost finder of missing per—"

"*Where?*"

"—sons. South Virginia Street. Driving a Pontiac Grand Am, white, couple years old. Last I saw her, she turned off Virginia, east on Vassar. Shanna was with her." I gave him the license plate of the Pontiac, and he hung up on me, probably felt he had things to do, but he didn't give me time to give him a description of the girls, an oversight that was likely to bite him in the ass.

Okay, then. *C'est la vie.*

I went back to my car, headed east on Vassar keeping my eyes open, but the neighborhood was a vast rectangular grid, too many turns and exits, so I came up empty. I did, however, see a sudden increase in the number of police cars patrolling the streets between Virginia Street and Kietzke Lane.

* * *

Now what?

Fairchild and sixty or eighty police officers probably had the streets covered. Danya and Shanna's rental house was a beehive of crime scene activity. I couldn't think of any other place to look. I'd gotten damn lucky, finding them at the bank—luck being the reason Russell had hired me. But luck runs in streaks, and I felt like this streak had about run its course.

So, time to make my own luck.

I drove back to Velma's place, got my bag of clues, checked her drain again, still suckin' it down, then went back home and sat in the kitchen sorting through the things I'd gathered, trying to find a thread I could pull to unravel this sweater. A longneck of Pete's Wicked Ale didn't help, but didn't seem to hurt, either. Fairchild wanted me to skate around the fuzzy edge of the law, avoiding the kind of rules that did nothing but get in the way. Speaking of which, I'd gotten away with a felony or two, which pleased me enough that I rewarded myself with another Pete's.

The stuff I'd found on Jo-X were the felonies. Ripping the downspout off the side of the house was probably no more than a misdemeanor so it barely counted. Maybe I should've kept it as a souvenir. I mean, the downspout of the place where Jo-X was last seen decomposing? You kiddin'? I could have picked up five grand on eBay once things cooled down.

But now, when I thought about it, I had reached the end of this rope, spinning my wheels, hitting a brick wall, mixing metaphors, so I opened a third Wicked Ale and considered other options.

At 5:05 that afternoon, Fairchild called me. I was standing in the kitchen looking out at the backyard, reluctantly coming to the conclusion that things had run their course here in Reno and I was going to have to head south. Vegas was calling; its voice was getting louder. And Caliente. And hot desert temperatures of a hundred five, hundred ten degrees. Things pointed that way, not very tangible or compelling, but in Reno, nothing was pointing anywhere, nothing that wouldn't be neck-deep in police.

"Didn't find her," Fairchild said. He sounded tired. "We got the car. Danya borrowed it yesterday from a boy she knew up at the university, left it on the street in front of his house in Sparks. But they got away somehow."

Maybe because they were in disguise, Russ? Could that have been it?

So they'd made it as far as Sparks, then ditched the car. Sparks is so close to Reno you could set a McDonald's cup on the border between them and the two cities would wage a pitched battle to determine whose union workers would pick it up.

"How close was the car to a bus stop?" I asked.

Silence. "Well, shit on a biscuit. I'll have to check that."

He hung up again.

I fired up a grill and cooked a couple of burgers, ate them with a plate of beans, tried to figure out what the hell I was going to do in Vegas. Finally I decided to wing it, which is what I do.

Six eighteen p.m., Russell was back on the phone. "Checked with the bus driver on the nearest route, two other nearby routes. No one saw Danya or Shanna."

"Sorry about that, Russ."

"You come up with any more ideas?" An indication of just how desperate he was, treating me as an equal. Or more.

"Working on some stuff," I told him. "Nothing definite yet. I'll let you know if I get anywhere."

He wanted to know more about the "stuff" I was working on, but that wasn't our deal. I work best when I skate around the murky edge of the law, which meant working alone. He told me Danya still wasn't answering her cell. They'd pinged her GPS but still hadn't gotten anything. She had a credit card but hadn't used it. Finally, he hung up, unhappy because his kid was doing things he associated with criminal behavior—or using the kind of tricks she'd learned by having a cop for a father.

A hundred ten degrees. The Toyota would hate that, hate Vegas, leave me stranded in the middle of nowhere just for spite. I phoned a car rental place near the airport and ordered up a car for tomorrow morning.

I had five grand. I could run up a hefty credit card bill and pay it in full later, so I made the car a good one.

CHAPTER EIGHT

IT WAS A convertible—a silver Ford Mustang, three hundred ten horsepower, 6-speed manual transmission, great for laying rubber. I thought a convertible would be fun after driving around last summer in Jeri's Porsche with the top down. Paying for it with Fairchild's money was like the cherry on top of a smokin' hot sundae. I figured he owed me fresh air after all the secondhand smoke he'd subjected me to a year ago when we were sorting out decapitations.

First day of July, perfect time to hit Vegas if heatstroke's your thing. I phoned Rufus, told him to put my judo lessons on hold for a while, caught a taxi to the rental place near the airport, picked up the Mustang, then hit I-80 east at 9:40 a.m., top down, happy to be on the road, headed in a direction, any direction. Motion can fool you into thinking you're getting somewhere. It's mental feng shui, good enough that it almost works on Amtrak.

Gumshoe on the loose, road trip, free to turn left, right, or keep going straight ahead. I left Reno with eight thousand dollars in a lockbox in the trunk of the car, a few hundred in my wallet. It was a lot to be carrying around, but cash is still king, and if things got murky in southern Nevada, I didn't want to leave a big credit card trail.

East through Fernley to Fallon, south on US 95 to Schurz, past Walker Lake to Hawthorne, then through serious desert as the temperature climbed into three digits. Left turn at Coaldale, then forty hot, dry miles to Tonopah.

Tonopah, where Holiday and I stayed at the Mizpah Hotel, working the Harry Reinhart caper. The memory was still sharp. And good.

Caper. Another word I need to use more often.

Around a broad swooping bend in the highway, the town appeared to be about eight miles up a long sloping rise. I went eight miles and the town was *still* six miles away. That was the desert for you, full of mirages and vast distances that fool the eye. At an elevation of just over six thousand feet, Tonopah was cool when I finally got there, only ninety-eight degrees.

One thirty-five. Time to gas up. Time for food.

McGinty's Café looked like a fair bet since there was a Texaco station right next door—and a fifties motel, the Stargazer.

McGinty's was doing a modest lunch trade, eight customers in the place, four booths and five tables empty. Two waitresses. The counter was half full, so I sat in a booth with a view of the highway and an occasional car trolling along at twenty-five. I picked up a menu stuck in a metal holder that also corralled salt, pepper, nondairy creamers, sugar packets.

"Hi, I'm Lucy. I'll be your server."

She'd snuck up on me. Eighteen years old, fresh-faced, pretty, auburn hair cut in a short, perky style. Gave me a déjà vu moment, put me back in high school for a few seconds, senior year, thinking about who to ask to the prom.

"Start you off with something to drink first?" she asked.

"Coke or Pepsi, either one."

Lucy stared at me for a moment. Then hustled away, came back a minute later, and set a big plastic cup of Pepsi and a straw in front of me.

"Ready to order?"

"The fried chicken okay?"

"It's dead. How okay is that?"

I stared at her.

"Joke," she said. "It's . . . well, *fried* chicken. I mean, if you were battered and fried, would *you* be okay?"

"Let me guess. Your parents don't own this place."

"Nope. So, how 'bout that chicken?"

"Why not? And fries."

"The Heart Buster Special. Works for me."

She hustled away, slender, trim, curvy, wearing black pants and a short-sleeve white shirt, mouth that wouldn't quit.

I looked out at the street. Watched trucks roll by, spinning up dust devils. Hot blue sky. Weeds. A crow perched atop a power pole, eyeing the asphalt for roadkill. Tonopah is built on a hill, a pile of rocks, actually. Without US 95 going through, the place wouldn't have so much as an outhouse.

One forty turned into one forty-eight, then a huge crash in the vicinity of the kitchen and a man's voice: "Son of a bitch, Lucy! That's it, that's the last goddamn time! Get outta here! Out! You're fired!"

Lucy slowed as she went by. "Your lunch is gonna be late." She kept going, pushed through the door into the hot afternoon, and was gone. The other waitress, fortysomething with big hair and a pen tucked behind one ear, came by. "Chicken'll be another few minutes, hon. Sorry 'bout that. I'm Terry, by the way. Can I get you a refill on that drink?"

"Sure, thanks. Make it a diet. I've reached my sugar limit."

She laughed as waitresses do, got me a refill, hurried away now that her workload had suddenly doubled.

More trucks.

The crow flew away.

A kid on a bicycle glided downhill as the temperature finally hit a hundred.

My fried chicken arrived. Half-size corn on the cob, too. I had a leg and a few fries down when Lucy came in the door with a small suitcase and sat down opposite me in the booth. She had on black nylon running shorts that barely covered her butt, and a lightweight ribbed cotton tank top, pale pink, that hugged half-sized breasts like a second skin, complete with nipple bumps.

"Buy me lunch, Mortimer? I'm starved."

I stared at her for six long seconds. "I've seen pictures of Ethiopia. You don't look starved."

She looked down at herself, then stole a fry off my plate, stuck it in her mouth. "I was about to go on break. That would've been lunch—free, too, but then . . ." She shrugged. "Your plate got loose and Earl reached his limit. Fourth one I've dropped in two weeks, so it's like I'm not supposed to be a waitress."

A beefy guy, fifty years old, wearing a chef's hat, came out of the kitchen as if shot out of a cannon. "Get outta here, Lucy."

"Hey," she said. "I don't work here, Earl. I'm a customer. You treat customers like that in this place?"

"You're not a customer—"

"Yes, she is," I said. I handed her a menu. "What'll it be?"

She put the menu back in its slot. "I pretty much know what they serve here. I'll have a toasted cheese and cole slaw. And fries." She took another one of mine, then looked up at Earl.

"You, you, you . . ." he said. The backs of his hands were hairy. His apron was smeared with cooking grease.

"She's with me," I said. "Toasted cheese, fries, and slaw."

He glared at me for a few seconds, then left. Terry came by, gave Lucy a cool look, me, too, took her order since she was the waitress, not Earl, and departed without a word.

"Thanks," Lucy said. "I was *so* hungry. I've been on since eight without a break—well, a little one, like five minutes, just enough time to go to the bathroom then, wham, in come three truckers and mom and pop with four kids and two other couples and I'm scrambling again and Earl's all grouchy, goin' like hell back there and it's hard to keep it all going—I mean, you'd know what it's like if you ever waited tables, which I never did until like about three weeks ago. Less than three, actually, so it's not like I've had a lot of experience or—"

I made a T with my hands. "Time out, kiddo. Take a breath."

She took a fry instead, dipped it in ketchup, popped it in her mouth. Nice mouth, too. Even white teeth.

"Mortimer?" I said, backing her up to the moment she sat down and asked me to buy her lunch.

"Well, sure. That's your name, right?"

Took me five seconds to say, "Mort."

"Close enough." She aimed a fry at my face. "Nice scars. Kinda sexy. You get them last year from that chick, what's-'er-name, Winter?"

"Yep."

She leaned closer. The tabletop pushed her boobs in a quarter inch, like the kind of solid rubber bumpers you'd find on a boat. "I followed it on TV—when you were finding all those heads. It was like a big soap opera, except it was real, which made it, I dunno, cool and weird and like that—don't know why I got so interested, but there you go. I tracked it every day on the news, even when there wasn't much happening, until you finally caught them— those two crazy women. Which made me glad, you catching them, but sad, too, sort of like getting to the end of an interesting novel. *Then*, you found that senator guy's hand, got it in the mail or something, so there you were again, which was amazing. You should keep eating. It won't take me long to finish up a toasted cheese. Earl will probably whip it up fast to get rid of me."

"How do you do that?"

"Do what?"

"Recite the entire Gettysburg Address in one breath."

"Good lungs?"

I glanced involuntarily at her pink top. Her eyes sparkled in amusement at me. In that waitress outfit she'd looked okay, nice little figure, but in her current getup she was something else, a hot little girl-child with a tight body that was singing an aria. Which, of course, was par since the night before I'd become a gumshoe. But maybe par wasn't right this time; this girl was easily a birdie. Her breasts were a third the size of Shanna's, but perfectly shaped, legs, too, and I consider myself an expert on both.

Her toasted cheese arrived with a solid thump. Terry might have tossed it over from the kitchen. Lucy kicked off a sandal and put a foot up on the seat, heel to her butt, hooked her left arm around her knee, which was almost up to her chin. She picked up a wedge of toasted cheese, took a bite, looked at me, and said, "So, cowboy—which way you headed? North or south?"

I paused with a chicken wing in my hand. "Cowboy?"

She shrugged. "I could call you stud. How's that?"

"How about Mort?"

She shrugged again. "Little old-fashioned, but okay, I can get used to it." She took another bite. "So. Which way?"

"What's it to you?"

"Take me with you?"

"Not a snowball's chance, girl."

"Why not? I've got a good heart. I'm a nice person. You'll see. Anyway, you *have* to take me with you."

"Oh? Why's that?"

"I dropped your fried chicken. If you hadn't ordered it, I would still have a job. So there. And I just checked out of that motel, the Stargazer. Week's rent was due tomorrow anyway, and now I don't have a place to stay, so it's time to move on."

"Not with me."

"Why not? I don't have a car. I saw you on TV all the time. You're harmless."

Not sure I liked that. It bumped up against the noir image I was working on, especially after last year's scars.

"Big problem," I said. "Bigger than just big."

"Yeah? What?"

"Your age, kiddo."

"Really? How old you think I am?" She watched my face like a hawk eyeing a field mouse.

"Eighteen. If I'm lucky."

"You're not. But I am."

"You are what?"

"Lucky. Got a quarter?"

"A quarter?"

"That's money. A nickel would work, too. They're metal, round, pretty much flat on both sides."

Smart-ass little girl. I dug a nickel out of my jeans.

"Flip it," Lucy said. "Don't show it to me."

I didn't want to argue. I flipped the coin. Tails.

"Tails," she said. "Do it again, nine more times." I flipped the nickel, not showing it to her, and she called heads or tails another nine times. "How'd I do?" she asked when I was done.

"Nine out of ten."

"See? Lucky." She looked into my eyes as she poked another fry in her mouth. "So, which way we goin'? North or south?"

I studied her for a moment. Which was nice on the eyes, I have to admit, her in that tight pink top, generous mouth, big blue eyes, bright and dark blue, skin like cream. "South," I said. "Not that it'll make any difference to you."

She smiled. "Yeah? Why's that?"

"Because you're probably only seventeen and that's trouble I don't need."

Her eyes glowed. "Thank you, Daddy."

Jesus Christ.

She picked up another French fry and gnawed it. "Okay, if it bothers you, I'm not seventeen."

"Eighteen wouldn't be much better."

"Seriously? If I were eighteen I could marry you without my parents' consent. That's huge."

I felt my eyes bulge. "Tell me you didn't just say that."

She shrugged. "Just stating a fact. Don't get all hyper. You haven't asked me yet—although, just so you know, I'd probably say yes."

Would a heart attack qualify as hyper? "You're something else, girl."

"So I've been told. Anyway, you get off track pretty easily. So you're going south. Stopping in Vegas?"

"That's the plan."

"Suits me. What're you gonna do there? Investigate this thing with Jo-X?"

Again I stared at her. "Goddamn television."

She laughed. "You are, aren't you? I mean, *you* found him."

"Wouldn't concern you, one way or the other, since you and I are going to part company in—best guess—eight minutes."

She lifted her arms above her head and stretched, which did wonders for everything beneath that tank top. "Really? You won't take me with you?"

"Not a chance."

GUMSHOE ON THE LOOSE

Her arms came back down. "I could help. I'd be a big help. I'm smart. I know things. I can get into places you can't. People trust me. I can act. I could distract people, guys mostly, so you could get past them." She lifted her boobs half an inch. "Think what you could do with a nice little rack like this."

I stared at her—them—her.

She picked up another fry. "What I *mean*," she said, "I've got attributes you could use. I've got good legs, and like I said, I'm real smart."

I was still speechless, but words were tumbling around in my head. I was sorting through them when she said, "Are you listening to any of this? Am I getting through?"

"A little. Mostly I wonder what your high school guidance counselor would think."

"That was Mrs. Lambros. And it's been a while."

"How long is a while? Two weeks?"

She laughed. "So?"

"So what?"

"So I was about to say—not that you were paying attention, because I think you've got a problem in that area—boobs like these are almost like keys. They open doors. Think how much help I could be."

Je-sus. "Okay, it's settled. You can't go with me."

"Why not?"

"You're too withdrawn. We would have long silences during which I would never know what you were thinking."

She tilted her head and smiled. Her eyes sparkled. "So that's a yes, right? I get to go with you?"

"You don't have a car? This is America. Everyone has a car."

"Not me. I've been traveling by bus."

"Which you could still do."

"But not with you, and that's the point here, Mort."

"Got a driver's license? Some ID that gives your age?"

She pursed her lips, then opened her suitcase and dug out a wallet, opened it, handed me a California license.

Lucy K. Landry, five-five, brown hair, blue eyes, a hundred eighteen pounds. And, doing the math, thirty-one years old.

Thirty-one.

I laughed and flipped the license back to her. "Nice try, but I wasn't born yesterday."

"It's real."

"Looking real and being real aren't the same thing."

"So we're good to go, right?"

"I am. You're not."

* * *

Ten miles out of Tonopah, a hundred five miles an hour, Lucy said, "Might want to cool it a little. Truckers say there's a speed trap somewhere around the next whorehouse."

So I cooled it, took it back down to seventy-five.

"What's the rush?" she asked.

"No rush. Just cooling off my brain."

She laughed.

I glanced over at her. "You might be eighteen, but you're not thirty-one. There's no freakin' way."

"I am. Since April. You saw the license."

"It's a terrific fake, even got a hologram. It might keep me from being arrested, giving a minor a ride. A minor girl at that. Where'd you get it?"

"California, of course. And it's not a fake."

"Twenty bucks says it is."

"Great. Now you owe me twenty." She held out a hand.

"Not yet, I don't."

"Hey, no one can ever guess my age. I can pass for sixteen if I need to. You might be able to use that."

"How? To spend twenty years in prison?"

She smiled. "And if I get dolled up just right, I can pass for thirty, maybe thirty-two. I have to really work at that, though."

I glanced at her. "What you're wearing now . . ."

"This'd be like eighteen. You're not so bad with ages. Want to hear my Valley Girl impression? Makes me sound fifteen."

"Please don't. You're not married, are you?"

"Nope. No boyfriend, either, in case you want to know, which is why I'll marry you if you ask." She gave me a look.

I felt a shivery feeling in my belly, like maybe the fried chicken was acting up. "Please don't say that again."

"Maybe later." She sat back and lifted her face to the sun, eyes closed, let the wind buffet her hair around.

We went another three miles in silence.

"How old are you really?" I asked. She couldn't be older than Jeri would've been. Six years older than Holiday? No way. I could probably trip her up if I asked a few more times.

"Thought we covered that already."

"With a fake license, yeah."

"It's not fake."

"Yeah, it is. I didn't just fall off a turnip truck, kiddo."

She looked over at me. "I can tell. You've got little crow's feet in the corner of your eyes."

Shit.

"I've been around," she said. "And around and around. I have a degree in art history from the University of San Francisco. I can tell early Renaissance from late Renaissance, spot a Grant Wood at forty paces, tell you all kinds of weird stuff about Picasso, van Gogh. Know how many homeless people have degrees in art history? It's like, if you don't want to be employed, that's the degree you get. It's sort of like an educational death wish, especially if you don't much care for art."

"Which, of course, you don't."

"No, I like art—now. Not so much when I first started out. The degree's okay with me. I could get a job as a waitress or checkout girl just about anywhere with it. And I did the *Vagina Monologues* last year."

The Mustang swerved two inches. "Say what?"

She looked over at me. "*Vagina Monologues*. You've heard of vaginas, right?" I caught a little smirk in her voice.

I had trouble getting air. "Yep," I said. She still looked like a high school kid to me. No way was she thirty-one. I just needed to come at her in a new direction, and this wasn't it.

She leaned back again, eyes closed. "I played two parts. I did *My Angry Vagina*. That's where a woman rants about all the injustices done to her pussy. But humorously. It's a tirade against tampons, douches, the tools used by OB/GYNs, that sort of thing."

"Uh-huh," I said, stalled on the word *pussy*.

She smiled. "The other part was *Because He Liked to Look At It*. That's where this woman describes how she'd thought her vagina was ugly and she was embarrassed about that. But then she changed her mind 'cause this guy, Bob, liked it so much he would stare at it for hours. Which is just what the title says."

"Uh-huh," I said again. "Hours. Right."

"Okay, now you're totally embarrassed."

"Actually, I'm trying to catch up with the monologues part of this conversation. But, embarrassed by the words you're using? No—if only you weren't seventeen. But we could talk baseball.

Who're you rooting for? Giants, Dodgers?"

"Can you actually say 'vagina'? Let's hear it."

"Vagina."

She grinned. "Okay, good. Anyway, you've never heard of the *Vagina Monologues*?"

"Nope."

"Well, that's a first."

"Talking vaginas? I would think so."

"No, silly. Women talking about their vaginas. Openly. Using words like cunt and pussy—not swearing, just using the words to talk about female anatomy more openly. It's an episodic play by a woman named Eve Ensler. It really is a legitimate play. Thousands of people have seen it. Hundreds of thousands. You oughta go see it, expand your horizons."

"See a vagina? I've done that."

"The play, dope." She smiled at me. "Of course, if it turns out you've got a hankering, I could—"

"*Stop*," I said, setting the volume at ten. "Do you have proof that you're at least eighteen?"

"Proof?"

"Yep."

"You don't think I am?"

"I don't know *what* you are. That fake ID doesn't cut it. I'm not going to talk about . . . about . . ."

"Pussies?"

"Yeah, that—with a seventeen-year-old juvenile delinquent high school kid running away from home. And if you can't prove you're older than seventeen, or God help me only sixteen, you're getting off at the next place that sells gas."

She thought about that for a moment. "Do you have a cell phone?"

"Of course."

"Okay, pull over."

The car swerved again. "Why?"

"Don't worry, I'm not gonna take a selfie or flash you. Not right now, anyway. But driving and talking on a cell phone is dangerous, and I'm all about safety, so pull over."

I got us off the highway and stopped on a wide verge. I didn't expect cell coverage out here, but I was wrong. Guess Verizon was working the US 95 corridor.

Lucy took the phone from me. "What I'm going to do is call my mom, tell her it's me, then hand you the phone, okay?"

"Terrific."

She dialed a number, waited, then: "Hey, Mom, it's me. Yeah, I'm with this really nice guy and . . . yeah, you'd like him . . . no, it's totally cool . . . uh-huh, he wants to know how old I am so tell him, okay?"

She handed me the phone. I took it and said, "Hi."

"Yes, hi."

"Is this Lucy's mother?"

"It is, yes." Nice voice, refined, touch of humor there, too.

"What's your last name, if you don't mind my asking?"

"It's Landry."

Good enough. "And how old is this precocious child of yours, Mrs. Landry?"

She laughed musically. "I'm not sure 'precocious' still applies since Lucy is thirty-one, Mr., um . . ."

"Angel."

"Angel. That's a very interesting name. And I understand your disorientation regarding Lucy's age, but precocious or not, whatever she is, she gets it from me, not from her father."

I didn't know what to say to that, so I thanked her and gave the phone back to Lucy. "I'm back," she said, then listened for a moment. "Las Vegas." She glanced at me. "Yes. He is." Pause, another look at me. "Yeah, he's that, too. Don't worry about me, I'm fine." She ended the call, handed me the phone.

"He is what?" I asked. "And what else, too?"

"Nice," she said. "And way out of his depth."

CHAPTER NINE

SHE WAS A whirlwind. I'd never met anyone like her before. But she wasn't eighteen, nineteen, or even twenty-one. which made me feel somewhat better. A lot better, in fact. I could deal with thirty-one. Thought so, anyway. If only she had a wrinkle somewhere, just one single gray strand . . .

"Out of my depth?" I said, pulling back onto the highway.

"Totally."

"Don't know where you get that, kiddo."

"Just your basic observation. Anyway, Mort, you can relax, I'm not jailbait. It's a family trait, looking young. You should see my mom. She's going on fifty-four, doesn't look thirty-five. My grandmother is seventy-six and passes for midfifties."

She settled herself sideways in the seat and faced me. "Okay, like I said, the *Vagina Monologues* is a legitimate play. It won an Obie Award. Eve Ensler wrote it in 1996. Lots of women have gone to see it. Men, too. It's like a total breakthrough. Like being able to acknowledge and accept and talk about female anatomy without getting embarrassed, use words that used to freak people out, and just . . . get *over* it. I did that for three months in a little theater on Geary Street in San Francisco, sort of an off-Broadway kind of thing. One time there were eighty-five women in the audience and seven men, I counted them, and all the men but two were looking down at their hands and their faces would glow kinda red whenever I or the other actors onstage said 'pussy' or 'cunt,' words like that, especially at first. Just like you did when I said them a few minutes ago. Girl like me says pussy and you're all over the place. So, yeah, you're pretty much out of your depth here."

Felt like it, too.

"But I'm pretty sure we can get you caught up," she said.

"Caught up? We?"

"Expand your vocabulary. Expand your mind. Get you past all the hang-ups."

"I don't have any hang-ups."

"Yeah, right."

"Okay . . . what if I treasure my hang-ups?"

She twisted her lips. "What if you treasure arthritis?"

"Huh?"

"Anyway, we'll work on it. Not all at once, but over time. Vocabulary, concepts. So now we're going to investigate this Jo-X thing, right? That would be cool. He's been all over television lately, especially since you found him, when was it? Day before yesterday? I've never done anything like that. I got this degree in art history that's beyond worthless and I ended up back home, but only for a month 'cause I was going totally schizo there. I mean, what on earth could I learn at home? Back at McGinty's there's Earl, the cook that owns the place?—and he's gruff and hairy and sometimes kinda mean, but I wouldn't get that at home. So, now I've met someone gruff and hairy and mean and that's something, right? It's experience. Which means it's not all bad. Enough of that and maybe I could write plays or novels or something. So if I hang out with you, think of all the amazing things I could see and, you know, experience. I could even end up writing a play about you."

Jesus. I should have stopped her as soon as she said *we* were going to investigate this Jo-X thing, but that would've been like trying to catch a bullet in my teeth.

"And all this"—she waved a hand at the world—"the sun, this terrific heat, all this emptiness. I've never done anything like this before—I mean, not in a car like this. This is a first."

"Well . . . good." It *was* nice. Seventy-five on a highway with few other cars on the road, slipstream of wind blasting over our heads, gorgeous girl beside me, conversation humming along and a trove of fun new words being tossed around.

A few miles went by.

"Thirty-one," I said.

"Yep. Maybe I don't look old because I don't think old. Getting old sucks, if you look around at all the people who are so serious they don't have fun anymore."

"I rode in the WNBR." Okay, that just popped out. I'll have to get a handle on my mouth someday. Or a zipper.

"Well, there's hope then," Lucy said.

I looked over at her and smiled. "You don't have any idea what the WNBR is, do you?"

"Of course I do. World Naked Bike Ride."

Sonofabitch. How out of touch was I? "How did you know that?"

"I've done it four times. Three in San Fran, once up in Portland. Did you do it totally in the buff or wuss out?"

Proudly I said, "All I wore was a little red body paint."

"So you kinda wussed out, but I still take back most of it."

"Most of what?"

"That thing about being totally out of your depth. Maybe you're only eighty percent out."

She dug a bottle of Banana Boat sunscreen out of her suitcase, put a dollop in her hand, and started to rub it over her face. "You're a nice guy, right?"

"Nice?"

"Honest, easygoing, pretty laid back?" Still putting on the sun-block, ears, throat.

"I hope so."

"Sure seems like it. Anyway, you're not mean?"

"Not intentionally, no. I can get gruff at times."

"Still a little hung up, though, the WNBR notwithstanding."

Okay, she was thirty-one. Seventeen-year-old girls do not use the word "notwithstanding." Ever. I felt better.

I glanced at her. "We're back to my hang-ups again?"

"Just sayin'. What you need is a little something to loosen you up, untie a few knots."

I shivered slightly. "Why do I get the feeling you're building up to something?"

"Because I am." She closed the cap and put the sunscreen on the seat beside her.

"Are you gonna make me regret bringing you along?"

"Hope not. Anyway, I've never had a chance like this before and I don't know when or if I ever will again, and I couldn't possibly do it while I'm driving, so now's the time to experience life. There's no way I'm gonna let this opportunity go by, so how 'bout you take it down to like fifty miles an hour."

"Why? You gonna jump out, experience contusions and road burn?"

She laughed. "Fifty, okay?"

I eased off on the gas. The roar of wind tapered off. Sixty-five. Sixty. Fifty-five.

"Okay, now don't flip out," Lucy said.

She pulled her feet under her, then sat up on the back of the seat, up in the wind, and pulled her top off over her head. "Don't forget to steer," she said, then lifted her face, eyes closed, and let the hot, dry wind buffet her body.

I looked up at her, nice flat stomach, great little chest pushed out into a stiff gale, temperature at a hundred three degrees, then looked back at the road, thinking that this PI thing was still right on track, wasn't wearing down a bit. Exactly one year ago, the IRS and I parted ways. After my divorce from Dallas, I'd lived a relatively celibate life as an internal revenue goon for Uncle Sam. Maybe this was catch-up, cosmic style. Maybe I hadn't caught up enough yet and the books were still being balanced. Or—maybe this was part of what it meant to be a gumshoe. Whatever it was, it wasn't worth fighting. Sometimes you go along and enjoy the ride.

Lucy reached down, got the Banana Boat, squeezed some into a hand, and rubbed it over her chest and arms. When she was done, I treated myself to a two-second look.

Her nipples had hardened in the breeze. She caught my look and laughed. "Good. You're not flipping out."

"I'm gritting my teeth, though, trying to make the best of it."

"Uh-huh."

I kept my eyes on the road. That's best if you don't want to slam head-on into a semi. "You probably ought to know—the most impressive chest I've ever seen was on a guy at a beach up at Lake Tahoe a few years back."

"A guy?" Her voice had a frown in it.

"Uh-huh. About thirty years old, long greasy hair. You know the type. He had two human ears tattooed on his chest. The ears were pierced and had rings in their lobes with a chain swinging between them as he walked." I glanced up at her.

Lucy stared at me. "That's brutal."

"Memorable. You got any skin art?"

"Do you see any?"

"Can't see all of you. Most, but not all, and I should point out that you didn't answer the question."

"Well, I don't. No piercings, either, except for my ears. I'm not into that self-destructive stuff. You can change earrings or take them off, but you can't do that with a tattoo."

"Good for you."

The road was two-lane. A big eighteen-wheeler was headed in our direction. Lucy waved as it approached and the trucker blasted his horn merrily as he went by.

"Getting that new experience you were lookin' for?" I asked.

"Uh-huh. This is great. Thanks for letting me do this." Her words were yanked back in the wind.

She gave it another two miles like that, then got back down in her seat. I took it up to seventy-five again. "Got some of those knots undone?" she asked.

"Who said I had knots?"

"It's your aura. Actually, it's sort of sweet. Doesn't match your scars or that little mist of gray in your hair."

"O'Roarke and I talk about my sweet aura all the time. Patrick O'Roarke. He's a bartender in Reno."

"I'm sure. So—want me to put my top back on?"

"Let your conscience be your guide, lady."

"Lady. That's almost an improvement. For the record, I like it when you call me 'kiddo,' too. Makes me feel young again. And, hey, good for you, you aren't totally freaked by this."

"Not visibly. But you'd better be at least eighteen."

She smiled, then closed her eyes.

* * *

Another mile passed in companionable silence while I tried to insert Lucy into my worldview. Holiday would be okay with this since that's how she was. But, man, the guys I worked with at the IRS would be *so* pissed if they could—

Lucy looked up at me. "You're really okay with this? It feels super, this heat and wind, but I don't want to push it."

"Better than okay. Got all my square knots untied."

She smiled and closed her eyes again. "*Square* knots. That's good."

"I haven't seen perky like that in a long time."

"Perky. That's good, too."

Three more miles passed by without conversation. The day was hot as hell, but the heat felt good. It reminded me of my time in Borroloola, Australia, when I put up nearly a mile of fence for a widow named Kate Hardy in the toughest ground God put on this earth. I let my mind go blank and allowed this experience to wash over me without trying to analyze it. Sometimes it's good to shut off the flow of words and just breathe.

* * *

But words eventually sneak back in. Holiday, aka Sarah, was going to graduate with a civil engineering degree and ease out of my life as quietly and with as little fanfare as she'd eased in, back when she was pretending to be a hooker. She was going to give me a peck on the cheek and go off to engineer something somewhere. I wondered about this road trip with Lucy. I didn't know what it was. I had the feeling I was in a wilderness, being marched through fog. Lucy was a free spirit, rather like Kayla, the beautiful girl I'd found in my bed last summer—Mayor Sjorgen's daughter, who had started this surfeit of gorgeous girls, this absolute deluge of women in my life. Kayla and I had driven through the desert in her VW bug, but she wasn't topless. This was a first for me. Lucy's eyes were closed and she sat there like a slender meditating Buddha with a faint smile on her face, head back against the headrest, not a worry in the world, taking life one second at a time. She wasn't posing, wasn't flaunting herself, she was just . . . there. Carefree, relaxed, happy.

I felt loose. Maybe she was untying knots I didn't know I had. Maybe we have more knots than we're aware of, tucked into dimly lit corners of our minds.

Vagina Monologues.

Hot damn.

* * *

Then my phone rang. I slowed to sixty-five and swiped the screen. It was Holiday. I told her to hold on a minute, that I was on a highway and had to find a place to pull off.

"What the hell was *that*?" Lucy said.

"What was what?"

"That ringtone."

"'Monster Mash.' Pretty cool, huh?"

"Wow."

Half a mile ahead I saw a dirt road off to the right. I slowed and pulled off the highway, went three hundred feet up a dusty track to cut down on traffic noise and because one of us wasn't wearing her tight little pink cotton top.

I cut the engine. "What's up?"

"Just wanted to say hi, Mort. Turns out Ravi and his wife are here at Alice's, their kids, too, so it's a busy place."

Ravi was her cousin, two months older than Holiday. He and Dylan had bathed or showered with Holiday from the time she was five years old until she turned eleven. She and Ravi probably had a lot to talk about, interesting memories to share. Not sure about Mrs. Ravi.

"Sounds like good times," I said.

"It is. Right now it's all about ice cream cones. So, you're driving? Where to?"

"Las Vegas. And I've got a topless girl in the car with me. Her name is Lucy." I had to do it. No telling how that would turn out, but I wouldn't lie to Holiday, even by omission. We still had our Tuesday Time together. When I looked over at Lucy, she was staring at me, jaw agape, not looking much like a Buddha.

Two seconds of silence on the other end. Then: "Topless?"

"Very."

"How is very topless different than ordinary topless?"

"Attitude?"

"How old is this girl, Mort? What was her name again?"

"Thirty-one, looks eighteen. Her name is Lucy."

"I should talk to her. Put her on."

Great idea. Oughta be good for a laugh. I handed the phone to Lucy. "Here, kiddo. Converse."

She took it gingerly. "Uh, hi."

I couldn't hear what Holiday was saying. I got out of the car to stretch my legs, wondering which direction my life was about to go. Life is all about choices, forks in the road, some big, some small—tell Holiday about Lucy, or don't. Mention the topless thing, or don't. I'd made my decision. Maybe I'd wanted to know where Holiday and I were going, or if we were going anywhere. It didn't seem likely. Once she got that civil engineering degree, I didn't think she'd stay in Reno, but Reno was home, my place in the world.

I looked back. Thirty feet away, Lucy was slumped in the seat, one bare foot up on the dash, phone to her ear. She waved an index finger at me and smiled.

Good enough. When women talk about me, this is the way it goes. I can't figure it out.

Two minutes went by. Three. I watched a buzzard or vulture floating over a low brown hill half a mile away, hunting.

Lucy got out of the car. She came over in her filmy shorts and sandals. "She hung up. Said a kid dumped an ice cream cone down the front of her shirt. Anyway, that was sort of weird."

"Ice cream down the front is like that."

"Not the ice cream. I mean, she was so nice. You told her I was topless and she didn't mind. Not what I expected. Sarah's that girl you were with when you found Senator Reinhart's hand, right?"

"His right hand, right. And to keep the record straight, it pretty much found me."

"What she did, before she hung up, she told me not to hurt you. Said if I did she'd break my legs, but she said it in a nice way."

"A nice way?"

"Uh-huh. I didn't think anyone could do that. She asked why I was topless and I described it, the sun and the heat, the wind on my skin. I told her it was just an experience—something I might never get a chance to do again, certainly not with someone like you, and she said she understood, especially about you. But the point is, I mean what I *got* is that she cares about you, but it was perfectly okay for you to . . . well, do this. Drive me to Vegas, whatever. Still feels kinda weird, she was so friendly . . . like not only was it okay, but she approved."

"She didn't say anything about gifting, did she?"

"Gifting? What's that?"

"Tell you about it sometime."

"Something to look forward to. I like that. Anyway, here's your phone. Okay with you if I don't put my top on right away?"

"Sure. Enjoy. What's a little nudity among friends?"

She laughed, then looked toward the hills. "She was so, *so* nice about it."

*   *   *

After five more miles, Lucy picked up her tank top, pulled it over her head, snugged it back down.

"Done with the showgirl act?" I asked.

"For now. Don't want to overdo the sun even with sunblock. But it felt good, so thanks. I'll probably do it again later. It's almost like I was born in the wrong century. I could've been Sally Rand or Faith Bacon. Sally, mostly."

"Sally Rand?"

"She did an ostrich-feather dance at the Chicago World's Fair, 1933. Danced entirely naked, partly hidden by feathers. She mostly kept one part of herself concealed, but she showed 'em everything else. Gave the world a topless show that was really something at the time. I'll bet she was pretty much turned on the whole time, too."

I didn't comment on that last, but it sounded a lot like Holiday. I wondered if Lucy had some of that, too.

"Anyway," she said, "you're nice and a little bit goofy but so am I, so I think this relationship is going to work out fine."

"What relationship?"

"You. Me. Us."

"What relationship?"

"It's a work in progress. Guess we'll find out. So, you're investigating this thing with Jo-X? His murder?"

"Maybe."

She frowned. "That doesn't sound very definite."

"It's not."

"Then what're you doing, driving all the way to Vegas if it's just maybe?"

"I'm going to nose around, see if anything pops up. A guy in Reno asked me to look into it. It's sort of a favor."

"A favor, huh? This guy pay you to do this favor?"

I looked over at her.

"Hey, don't look at me like that. It's not like I'm looking for a handout or anything. I've got money. I just want to, you know, hang out with you a while. Especially if you're looking into Jo-X's death, and *especially*-especially since it's okay with Sarah."

"Hang out?"

"Uh-huh. Until you marry me, then it's not called hanging out. In the meantime, I'll learn private eye stuff, help out if I can. I'll tell you why neo-impressionist paintings generally suck, and you can tell me more about those decapitated heads you found, stuff that didn't make it into the news."

"Jesus."

"So even if all you're gonna do is nose around, what's the first step? Do you have a plan? Seems like you ought to. Vegas is a big place. First thing, though, we'll need to get a room."

"Two rooms."

"Nope. One. A suite. I've got an idea about that. Nice big fancy suite and it won't cost us a penny."

"A free suite?"

"Yep. You watch. Like I told you, I'm lucky. Lucky Lucy. Take the 'k' out of Lucky and what's left? Lucy. I was born when four planets were lined up and Mars wasn't one of them."

"That works?"

"Does it ever. You watch."

* * *

We stopped in Beatty, Nevada. Whatever else Lucy wanted to do or see or experience, it was not going to include a big right turn that would take us into Death Valley and temperatures that might exceed a hundred twenty degrees. While I was at the wheel, there was going to be no Furnace Creek, no Dante's View, no Devil's Golf Course, no breakdown in the middle of nowhere, no desiccation of the Mort.

But what she wanted was almost as weird, at least to me. She found a shop that sold nail polish, bought a tiny bottle filled with what looked like fresh blood. I gassed up, and we were back on the road in ten minutes, headed south. She propped a heel on the seat and hunched over a foot, painting her nails. She did the other foot, then her fingernails. When she was finished, she held up her hands and admired her handiwork. Bright blood red.

"Cheap," she said. "Very trailer park."

Women. Go figure.

CHAPTER TEN

WE HIT THE Vegas city limits at 5:20 p.m. First thing visible on the skyline was the Stratosphere. Fifteen minutes later, we were on the Strip, headed south past the Bellagio.

Lucy pointed straight ahead. "The pyramid. Go there."

The Luxor.

Traffic was stop and go past Paris Las Vegas, New York New York, Excalibur. The temperature was a hundred four at almost six in the afternoon. I stopped on a street parallel to the Strip and dug through the lockbox in the trunk. It held weapons and various wigs—long dishwater blond, a snow-white one with shaggy five-inch hair, short black, long brown with a single braid down the back, unkempt light-brown in a bad cut.

Lucy grabbed the white wig. "This one."

"Just what I was thinking."

"I'm sure." She picked up a dark-gray Stetson, held it out. I put on the wig and the hat. Lucy dug through the box and found a salt-and-pepper moustache. "This, too." I put it on, then she gave me a critical look, gave it a little adjustment. Lastly, she found a pair of glasses with just enough purple tint to half-conceal my eyes. She smiled at me, lips twitching slightly. "Perfect."

I was getting used to wearing disguises, even when they itch like a son of a gun. All part and parcel of being world-famous.

I pulled in at the Luxor, valet parking. Lucy and I got out. Lucy got a long admiring up-down-up look from the kid who took the

Mustang's keys. I got my bag from the trunk and Lucy's suitcase from the backseat, money in an envelope out of the lockbox, waved off a uniformed bellhop who had hustled out to grab the luggage from me, and we went inside.

"How much money you got with you?" Lucy asked.

"What's it to you?"

"Jesus, Mort. How much?"

"Eight grand, give or take."

She stared at me for a moment, then said, "Coolarama. Okay, first thing, let's get the hotel desk to hold our stuff so we don't have to lug it around. Then you've got to buy me a dress."

"A dress?"

"Yep. Fairly good one, but not too good. Mostly it's gotta be sexy."

"Sexy."

"Baby-doll sexy."

I didn't ask.

A blond, beautiful desk clerk took our rudimentary luggage without batting an eye, and gave me a claim check. Lucy took me by the arm and hauled me through the pyramid toward a line of interior shops where, without having to interact with the outside world, folks could buy clothing, jewelry, oil paintings, original bronze or pewter sculptures, get a manicure, pedicure, purchase gold coins and unset diamonds, load up on magazines, Snickers bars, key chains, tiny slot machines, Luxor T-shirts, fuzzy dice.

Lucy stopped in front of a shop that sold women's stuff, which was the only way to describe it. "Wait here." She went in, came out ten minutes later carrying a plastic bag with the shop's logo on it. "Got some stuff for later."

Stuff, so I was right.

She handed me the bag. "Don't peek."

"Nice earrings," I said. She'd come out with gold hoops two inches in diameter dangling from her ears.

"You like? Pretty gaudy. Makes me look cheap."

Women. You gotta love their crypto-talk.

We went down two stores to a place that sold dresses, gowns, expensive women's clothing. "Okay, now I'll probably need five hundred dollars," Lucy said. "Or more."

"Nice goddamn dress for five hundred, Sweetheart."

"You kidding? Five hundred'll be low midrange, but I like the sweetheart. Keep it up. It'll play well in this place." She made a "gimme" gesture with her fingers.

I gave her seven hundred. She told me to wait outside, then went in. Mannequins in a window display were draped in silk and leather, sequined dresses, scarves that probably cost two hundred each, purses for a thousand. From the hallway in front of the shop, I watched her amble in wearing a tank top and jogging shorts. I had an image of *Pretty Woman*—hooker going into a ritzy shop on Rodeo Drive. But Lucy didn't look like a hooker, just like a kid who couldn't afford pantyhose in that place, maybe looking for a ladies' room.

She could disappear. Find a back entrance and end up in some sort of a service catacomb that ran behind all the stores, take off with seven hundred bucks. She'd told me to wait outside. But I had five thousand from Russ, so I could afford it if Lucy bolted. She'd been at least seven hundred dollars' worth of company during the drive from Tonopah, so what the hell.

She came out fifteen minutes later in a wow dress. My eyes bulged. Red shimmery fabric, tight around her small waist with a loose cheerleader skirt with a hem twelve inches above the knee that looked as if it'd fly up around her waist in a little updraft; the sweetly rounded tops of her breasts showing, a little red piece of dental floss around her neck to keep the top up, shoulders bare, shapely arms. She was barefoot, a bag in one hand that held the clothes she'd worn into the place, and she had a tiny gold chain around one ankle that hadn't been there before. Now the blood-red nail polish worked, or at least matched the outfit.

"Ho-ly smoke, woman."

She smiled. A pirouette flared the skirt and showed even more thigh. "Like it?"

"Yep. But not if my daughter was wearing it."

"Good. Five hundred sixty-two dollars. Now I need shoes." She handed me that bag, too, turned me into a pack horse, hauled me over to a shoe store, got several more hundred dollar bills, went in and again I waited.

Shoes take longer, but she was a female, so I knew that. I was prepared. I should've wandered off and found a cheeseburger. Forty minutes later, out she came in sparkly silver heels three inches high, which put her at five eight. "How much?" I asked.

"Two-eighty." She handed back a small wad of bills.

"How long have I known you?"

"I don't know. Five hours, maybe six?"

"Call it six. That's a hundred forty bucks an hour."

She stared at me.

I shrugged. "Figures just pop out."

She looked at the front of her dress. "They do, don't they? Nice of you to notice."

"Not that. Well, that, too."

She grabbed me by the arm. "Okay, Daddy, let's go get that suite."

Daddy?

*　*　*

Roulette. Lucy headed for a table with the highest limits—a thousand on a number, twenty thousand on red or black.

"What about my clothes?" I whispered in her ear. I was still holding the bags she'd given me.

"Your clothes don't matter. You'll see. It's all about the idiot baby doll on Daddy's arm."

Baby doll? Daddy? I was beginning to really like this girl, and it wasn't just the way she was filling out that dress.

She sat in a chair at the table, sort of bouncing, and looked up at me. "Sugar needs a thousand, Daddy," she tittered, voice pitched high. She crossed her legs and her dress rode up another three inches. One more inch and we'd be in trouble.

The eyes of the gal running the wheel flickered. Daddy gave "Sugar" ten bills and she hardly looked at the roulette girl as she handed over the cash and received ten chips worth a hundred each. The girl sent the ball spinning around its outer track.

"Uh-uh," Lucy said to her, sounding put out. "One chip, not these little bitty things."

Great.

The ten chips became one chip. Lucy slapped it down on red a few seconds before the girl said, "No more bets." The ball went around the outside a few more times, then clattered around in the wheel and came up black.

Lucy giggled. "Oops." She turned back to me and said, "Sugar needs another hit, Daddy."

I looked at her, and she shot me a look that lasted no more than a millisecond.

I handed twenty crisp Franklins to the girl running the wheel and said, "Two big ones, Honey," in a dumbass voice that matched Sugar's, but was two octaves lower. It matched the wig, the moustache, and the Stetson. Rich old dude keeping his young sexy thing happy. However this played out, I was going to keep enough gas money to limp back to Reno. Without Lucy.

Sugar grabbed the two chips as the ball whirled around the track, wheel spinning in the opposite direction. She closed her eyes and said, "Red, red, red," then plopped a single chip down on red.

Whirr, clatter, bounce.

"Twenty-three red," the girl said. She set a thousand-dollar chip on top of Lucy's.

Lucy let out a little-girl squeal of delight and bounced in her chair. "Lookit, Daddy. I made us some money."

"Real fine, Honey Bunch." I decided not to point out that in fact she hadn't made us a single penny yet.

She closed her eyes and lifted her face toward the ceiling. "I'm gonna let it ride. And this one, too." She giggled, putting down the other chip I'd bought her.

"You do that, Sugar Plum." Three thousand on red. Shee-it.

Christ, what a circus. Half a dozen people were watching. So far we hadn't lost a nickel. Hadn't made one either, but Lucy was betting red and I was thinking black.

The ball whirred around the rim and the wheel spun and Sugar said, "Red, red, red," and the ball clattered and bounced, stopped.

"Nine, red," the girl called out.

Lucy squealed, bounced out of her chair, and planted a big wet kiss on my lips as the girl put three chips on top of Lucy's. A quick breathy whisper in my ear: "Lucky Luce. Look out."

She sat down and picked up her six chips. I was still savoring the kiss. A pit boss eased over, as if drifting on an unseen current. He was bald, wearing a shiny black vest, name tag said Fred. He didn't look directly at Lucy as she toyed with six thousand dollars' worth of chips, three of which had recently belonged to the house.

The wheel spun, Lucy slid all six grand onto red again. "Red, red, red," she chanted, as the pit boss tried not to look as if he were taking a greater interest in the game.

Clatter, bounce. "Thirty-three, black."

"Well, shuckins," said my darling Honey Bunch, pushing her lips out in a pout. She turned to me and said in a giddy voice, "Sugar needs another hit, Daddy." And a sharp flash in her eyes said that, yes indeed, Sugar needed another hit.

So, Daddy shelled out another grand. Down three thousand and counting, not to mention the red dress and shoes.

The ball spun, and Sugar said, "Red, red, red," and the ball landed and the girl called out, "Sixteen, red."

Sugar squealed, which was evidently what she did, and it was a hell of an improvement over, "Well, shuckins."

The pit boss didn't leave. The girl got the ball going again and Lucy moved both chips to black and said, "Black, black, black," and damn if the girl didn't call out, "Two, black."

Sugar squealed, looked up at the ceiling with her eyes closed, moved the four chips to red. The ball spun, the pit boss watched, and Sugar said, loud enough for everyone around to hear, "I gots me that lucky-unlucky feelin', Daddy," and she took a single chip off red and stuck it on double zero.

The ball whirred, clattered around in the wheel, stopped, and the girl said, in a slightly higher register than before, "Double zero."

Lucy squealed and clapped her hands, threw her arms around my neck, and gave me the best-tasting French kiss I'd had in I didn't know how long.

The pit boss's eyes jittered as the girl counted out thirty-five chips and set them on Lucy's double-zero chip, so I guess he had a little strabismus thing going. Suddenly we were up a total of thirty-two thousand dollars.

Lucy pulled her chips in front of her and looked up at me and said, "We oughta get us a suite here, Daddy. I *like* this place."

The pit boss had a two-way radio with a mike on his lapel. He turned away, head lowered, and twenty seconds later a guy was at my side in a two-thousand-dollar suit and a power tie. "Little lady's lucky," he said conversationally.

"Yep. She's a pistol."

He smiled. "We like to treat folks right around here. If y'all don't have a place in town yet, I've got a nice suite that might suit you. Place with a Jacuzzi, full kitchen, sitting room."

I liked the "y'all." He was speaking to the Stetson.

"Don't know," I said. I leaned closer to my baby doll. "Want to settle down here tonight, Sugar Plum? Get us a suite?"

She didn't even look at me. "It's gotta face *east*, Daddy. You know that." She pushed six chips onto red, kept thirty thousand in front of her. "Red, red, red . . ."

"Forgot," I told the guy in the suit. "Room's gotta face east. Got anything like that?"

"Not a problem. East it is."

"And—any upgrades come with that suite? Little lady purely hates all that nickel and dime stuff, drives her nuts."

"We got something that looks like a credit card, but isn't. Good for show tickets, in-room massage, room service or any bar or restaurant in the place, some other stuff, too, no charge."

I pondered that for a moment. The ball clattered, "Eleven, black," the girl called out. "Well, shuckins," Sugar tittered. I looked at the guy at my side. "Sounds good. We'll take 'er."

He slapped me on the shoulder. "Stay right there. I'll send a girl around with keys and a card, get you settled in."

That took six minutes, during which time Lucy won back the six grand she'd lost. I got us checked in under the name Stephen

T. Brewer. T for Thomas. Last October, hunting Julia Fairchild, Maude Clary—Ma—had fake passports, driver's licenses, credit cards, and a bunch of other paper made up for us by a slippery old boy in New Mexico, Ernie "Doc" Saladin. Something of a rush job that ended up costing $12,000 a person. I wasn't inclined to give up the fake ID since the credit cards and all the rest of it was "legit." Now it came in handy. I didn't want Lucy officially tangled up in this and, now that I was once again a household name all across the land of the free, I couldn't run around calling myself Mortimer Angel, the PI who finds bodies and body parts of famous missing people. But the pretty thirty-something gal in a dark green pantsuit who took my information didn't bat an eye at Stephen Brewer, although she raised a discreet eyebrow at the sultry girl at the roulette table who said "shuckins" when her red, red, red came up black, and a small stack of chips was swept away.

"Give it a rest for a while, Sugar Plum?" I asked her when the girl left. "Go have a look at the room?"

"Just one more, Daddy," she said. The ball was spinning. She plopped a chip down on a corner, covering numbers eight, nine, eleven, and twelve. Several more on black.

The ball stopped. "Nine, red," the girl called out, sounding weary. "Corner wins." She put eight more chips on Lucy's one.

"I *like* this place, Daddy," Sugar Plum chirped.

* * *

I did, too. Once the dust finally settled, we were up thirty-six thousand dollars, and I still had my original eight. Seven, after buying Sugar a wardrobe. I stashed our winnings in an account with the casino and got a receipt.

In the suite on the fifteenth floor, alone with Lucy, I looked at her through one eye. "Sugar needs another hit, Daddy?"

"It's all about theater. You're a rich guy being led around by the nose by a dumb sexy little bimbo who has attached herself to his wallet. Bet they've seen *that* around here before."

Okay, *now* I believed she was thirty-one. A girl that age can sound seventeen, but a girl of seventeen can't sound thirty-one.

She flopped down on the bed and hugged herself, smiling. "This is great. I've had more fun today than all last year."

"And I've come closer to having a heart attack today than all last year, Sugar Plum. And it was a pretty bad year, all in all."

She sat up. "Have a little faith, Daddy."

"Had enough 'Daddy' and 'Sugar Plum' yet?"

"For now. Just don't forget who we are." She got up and looked out a window. "Hey, this is nice. Just wait'll the sun goes down and the lights really come on."

We'd given the bellhop a hundred dollars for bringing up our luggage, such as it was, and sent him on his way. Once we were alone in the room, the wig, moustache, and cowboy hat were on a bed where I'd flung them. The place was huge, impressive, and free. Bedroom with two king beds, furniture in glossy golden oak, indirect lighting, windows that sloped inward due to the building's pyramid shape. Big sitting room with a purple couch, overstuffed chairs, floor lamps. A kitchen with a stainless-steel refrigerator, microwave, blender, coffeemaker, juicer, good-sized toaster oven. Sixty-inch televisions in the bedroom and sitting room, forty-inch in the bathroom. I stood at the entrance to the bathroom, checking out a Jacuzzi the size of a small swimming pool. Vegas was in a state of perpetual drought; now I knew why.

Lucy walked over. "I like this dress. It's a hot little number, but real tight on top—which of course it's supposed to be." She turned her back to me, looked over her shoulder. "Unzip me?"

Right away I had a choice—unzip or don't unzip. But in truth I didn't have a choice. I was the only unzipper in the room. And I'd finally accepted the fact that she wasn't seventeen or even twenty-five, so I ran the zipper down, exposing a very nice bare back and a tiny waist; a taut, slender flare of hips.

She turned and stepped out of the dress.

"No bra?" I said, trying unsuccessfully not to stare.

She gave me a look like I was from Mars. "In this dress? You kidding? Anyway, it lifts like a bra. Which, of course, is the whole point. Makes the boobies pop out the top a little."

She rubbed said boobies, then put on her tank top, no shorts. She had on black lace bikini panties. And long legs.

"I'm starving," she said. "Let's eat."

"The room's gotta face east? Where'd that come from?"

She laughed. "Got any idea how much casinos like flakes?"

"I do now."

"So . . . food? Bein' that lucky is hard work."

CHAPTER ELEVEN

LUCY HAD A tabbouleh lettuce wrap—garbanzo beans, roasted tomato, and walnuts with a pomegranate vinaigrette dipping sauce. I had the Australian lobster tail and a small steak. Good stuff. Mine, anyway.

She ate cross-legged on one of the beds in her panties and tank top, flipping through a menu on the TV that advertised the various attractions offered by the Luxor. I sat on a chair, eating off a folding walnut tray worth a hundred bucks.

"We could go see *Fantasy*," Lucy said, pointing with her wrap at the screen where a video clip of the Luxor's "best-on-the-Strip" Showgirl Review was playing. "Topless women, Mort."

"Got that covered already."

She laughed merrily. "It's got guys dancing around in like little jock straps, too. I don't have that."

"Nor will you."

"Maybe not dancing, but—"

"Don't think so, kiddo."

Lucy worked the remote a while longer. "There's Aurora. Nice quiet-lookin' bar downstairs. We could go on down, get ourselves loose, maybe a little bit sozzled."

"Sozzled, huh?"

"Hey, I went to college, picked up a few things. Got that good nineteen-forties vocabulary. Anyway, you might want to unwind after a hard day gambling and riding around with a gabby topless chick seventeen years old."

I gave her a look. "You sure as hell better not be."

"What? Gabby?"

"Seventeen. Gabby is now a given."

"So how 'bout it? Aurora? We're not gettin' anywhere with this Jo-X investigation, and I don't think we're going to find out anything more about him here tonight if we wanted to."

True enough. I wasn't sure we were going to learn anything about Jo-X if we kicked around Vegas for a month.

"You've got that red dress. Got anything else to wear in a place like that?" I asked, nodding at the television.

She smiled. "Turns out, maybe I do."

* * *

She did, sort of. Of course, this was Vegas, so it didn't much matter what she wore as long as it covered the critical parts, or at least pretended to. We rode the elevator down, Lucy in clothes she'd bought in the first shop she'd gone into that afternoon—tight white hip-hugger pants that ended four inches above her ankles, waistline a few inches below her navel, and the absolute *pièce de résistance*, a white crochet cotton halter top with a bit of kite string around her neck, another around her back. The thing was peek-a-boo mesh with eighth-inch holes throughout. It gave no support, but none was needed. It looked airy and cool, and might have weighed a fifth of an ounce. A two-inch fringe on the bottom swayed as she walked. She wore her silver heels and the ankle chain. The outfit left eight inches of flat belly exposed. It might've been legal on the streets in Vegas, but not something I would've wanted to push in Muscogee.

I, of course, was in the white idiot wig and all the rest of it.

We found an empty booth and she ordered a strawberry daiquiri that came in a glass the size of a birdbath. I had a Mojito
made with Pyrat rum, best the place had to offer, even better since
it was on the house. A bottle of that stuff would cost nearly three
hundred dollars.

Lucy looked terrific across the table from me in lighting that
shaded from hot pink to deep blues and purples. She looked good
sipping from a little red straw with pursed lips, too.

Was this a "date"?

I didn't know what it was. I'd started off that morning with no
expectations about anything, including Jo-X's murder, but ever
since Tonopah, the day had been over the top. Not even my recent
year of gumshoe training had prepared me for someone like Lucy.

"Tell me what happened in that basement," she said, looking at
me as she took another sip of daiquiri.

"What basement?"

"Where those two women kept you last year. You were tied up.
What was that like?"

"We could talk about something else."

"We could, but why?"

"It wasn't a good time for me."

She looked at me from the tops of her eyes as she took another
sip. "They said you were naked the entire time."

"That's excellence in journalism for you. Report all the facts.
Don't leave out anything that might sell Jeeps or beer."

"That mean it was true?"

"Yes."

"Well, hell. Now I feel deprived." Her eyes smiled at me.

"We could talk about something else."

"Déjà vu."

"So . . . why art history if you weren't that much into art?"

"I thought mathematics or physics would be a lot of work. Especially since I barely got Ds in algebra in high school. I'm smart, but not like that."

"You could've been an English major."

She shook her head. "I didn't ever want to have to read James Joyce's *Ulysses*, or, God forbid, anything by Montaigne. And I don't like writing essays, which I ended up getting plenty of in art history. Didn't know that would happen. I should've majored in Phys. Ed."

"Did you look for a job? After graduating?"

"I tried. Museums want PhDs, and then there's a waiting list six miles long, or would be if there were six miles of people dumb enough to get doctorates in art history. Bachelor degree in art history and a subway token will get you a ride uptown and then you have to walk back. The first job I got was arranging and decorating mannequins in a store window, if you can believe that. Like in that place in the casino here where I bought the dress. That was at Macy's in Frisco. Lasted all of a week. Then I was a receptionist for a dentist for a year and a half in Reno. Then I was in Seattle for two years, working for a florist, arranging flowers. Best job I ever had. Finally I got tired of rain so I went down to Phoenix, got a job answering the phone and taking orders for a fat guy who rented out party equipment, amplifiers and speakers, fold-up stages, laser lights. He would do this DJ thing, too, play music on a monster computer console that stored like twenty thousand songs. Then he started hitting on me, tryin' to anyway. Third time that happened, I was at my desk the next morning and I happened to look up. There was a scorpion on the ceiling. A *scorpion*. On the ceiling. Just *standing* there, if that's what you call it when things are upside down. Who knew they could do that? It could've dropped on my head. So I got the hell out. As it turns out, I'm not into poisonous bugs on ceilings or chubby guys hitting on me."

"Just old guys," I said.

She pummeled me with a look. "Hey! You're not that old. You might have a few years on me—not that many, actually—but you look good. And you haven't hit on me, but it would be okay if you did. And—bein' here with you—for me there's a bonus."

"What's that?"

"Two things, actually. First—you're a private investigator. It's not like I have anything like a career going. So maybe I could stay with you, learn how to investigate stuff."

"Stay with me?"

"Well, stick with you, then. Run around with you. Help out, which I totally know I could do if you give me a chance. And . . . whatever. Learn things."

"That would be a decision you might live to regret."

"Doubt it. And, you're kinda sexy—well, more than kinda—so running around with you would be that kind of nice, which is the other bonus."

I stifled a laugh. Me, more than kinda sexy? Ri-i-i-ght.

She smiled. She had a fresh, innocent face. The alcohol had put a little color in her cheeks. "You don't think so?" she said.

"Nope."

"Maybe it's those facial scars. Gives you a nice piratey look. Better even than Depp since his are fake."

"Piratey. I don't think that's a word."

"It is if I shay it is."

"Shay?"

She stared at her drink for five seconds. "I think a shay is like a carriage or a surrey. Not sure why I said it though." She looked up at me. "Truth is, I'm not a big drinker. This thing's got a pretty good kick to it. Sneaks up on you."

"We could go take in that show—*Fantasy*. Drink plain Cokes. You could watch guys leap around in jock straps."

"And you could check out a bunch of topless women." Her eyes locked on mine. "But—"

"But?"

She tilted her head. "Too much of a good thing . . . ?"

"Right. I might've reached my limit for the day. Or week."

"It sure better not be for a week."

"Sounds like you've got ideas cookin' in that head of yours."

She toyed with her drink. Took another small sip. Gazed down at the slush. When she looked up, her voice had changed. "This . . . this thing we're doing. I don't want you to think we have to keep doing it."

Uh-oh. Serious talk. Didn't see that coming. I thought I had a handle on this girl, but maybe not.

"This wasn't your idea," she said. "At all. I get that. I pretty much bulled my way into your life, Mort. Back in Tonopah."

"It's been a trip and a half, Luce."

She gazed into her drink again. "You should know—I'm not going to sleep with you tonight."

I blinked. "I didn't think you would."

"That right? No expectations at all after everything we've done today? After what I did in the car on the way here?"

I thought about that. "I will acknowledge that the possibility crossed my mind, but it never rose to the level of an expectation. And I wondered what I would do if things looked like they were headed that way. I still think you're too young. At least you *look* too young."

She smiled. "I'm not too young. At all. But you're a really nice guy, like you've got no hard edges. And I will acknowledge that the thought crossed my mind, too. About a dozen times today, actually, especially in the car. But I don't want to do that, and I don't want to lead you on. This is our first day of . . . of whatever this is. I mean, maybe it's nothing, even though I'd marry you right now if you ask. But it could end up as a kind of partnership or an employer-employee-trainee sort of thing. Anyway, this is just the first day of whatever it is and no way am I ready to sleep with you—if, as you say, it starts to head in that direction."

"I'm glad. Relieved, actually."

"Although." She smiled, reached over, and took my hand. "I can be kind of a tease. It's not like I'm oblivious. I know guys like to look at undressed women and it can get them wound up."

"Hey, it's still a trip and a half."

"Well, good. But the thing is, it sort of heats me up, too, if you want to know. Guess that's one reason why I do it. I was going a little bit in the car today, even if you didn't know it."

"Going."

"Yep. Little bit. Anyway, I needed to say all this, and I think this drink has made it easier—but I'm not really a huge, evil tease, like I would just tease you until the end of time. I'm not a virgin, Mort. Not even close."

I was about to say something, not sure what, though I think it was going to be something to do with Holiday and being impervious to being teased, which might or might not be true, but she held up a hand and stopped me, which was probably a good thing. "Gotta say one more thing here, Mort."

"Okay, shoot. I'll shove a word in edgewise later."

She smiled at that. "If . . . if you want to get rid of me, I'll go. No big scene. Not even a little scene. But if you do, it would be nice if I got, I don't know, maybe a third of what we won? That wouldn't be too awful of me, would it? Like maybe ten or twelve thousand for being lucky. You keep the rest since you put up the money."

"If that's what you want, sure."

Her eyes flashed. "*No!*" Her voice got softer. "That's not what I said. I just don't want to be . . . in the way, like baggage you don't want. That's the last thing I'd ever want to be."

"You're anything but baggage, Lucy."

She smiled hopefully. "Does that mean you're gonna keep me around a while? Like I might be useful and I'm sort of fun to be with?"

"More than sort of. It's been a terrific day. All of it—the topless show, the conversation, the gambling, the outfit you're wearing right now."

Her smile blazed in the dim room. "Good." She pushed her drink away. "Enough of this. What I'm *really* in the mood for is that Jacuzzi upstairs. With company, if you can stand it."

"If I can stand it, huh?"

"Well . . . yeah. Knowing it won't lead to anything later. Not tonight anyway. That hasn't changed just 'cause we had this talk."

"Hey, I'm tough. I can take it."

*　*　*

Tough. That's me.

And then . . .

"Hey, look," Lucy called to me from the bathroom. "Bubble bath. Really good stuff, too."

I came into the room. She had a towel around her waist as hot water filled the tub. I had the towel's twin around my waist. Lucy took a look at me and straightened up. "Whoa."

"Whoa?"

"You . . . uh, you're kinda, wow, Mort."

"Went off your Prozac again, huh? That's what happens."

"I'm serious. I mean, you're not like Schwarzenegger, which is actually a good thing, but you . . . you're buffed. Totally."

"It's the Borroloola workout."

"Borroloola? What's that? Is it anything like Pilates?"

"Probably not. Tell you later."

"Got a lot of stuff to tell me later. Gifting, Borroloola workout. You might tell me about that girl who told me not to hurt you, too. Sarah, Holiday, whatever her name is."

"All in good time."

She looked great, standing there topless in that towel as hot water poured into the Jacuzzi and the room filled with steam. She'd put on soft music, easy listening stuff sans lyrics.

She crumbled a bar of Rose Jam Bubbleroon under the faucet as the tub filled, and the air took on a humid rose scent.

"Tough guys don't take bubble baths, Sugar Plum."

"Too late, tough guy." Bubbles multiplied like hell, piling up in the tub. Bubbles, for Christ's sake. I had a sudden vision of my ex, Dallas, in a similar tub last year. I had a second vision—that of my hard-won tough-guy image flying off into yesteryear never to return. Rambo never took a bubble bath. Too busy killing bad guys and stopping his own bleeding.

"Hop in," Lucy said. "Don't worry, I won't peek."

I dropped the towel and got in. Lucy unwound her towel and tested the water with a foot. Man, she was something. Slender and tight, with a short, neat triangle trim, not a Brazilian. And, like she said, not a tattoo anywhere.

"You didn't jump right in, Sally Rand," I said.

Her grin took on a Cheshire look. She struck a little pose.

"You look . . . strong," I said.

"That'd be gymnastics. Five days a week from age five until I was sixteen. I was pretty good on the balance beam. I keep up with some of it. Want to see me stand on my hands, arch my back, and touch the soles of both feet to the top of my head? I can still do that."

"Sure. Since no one can do that."

"Wanna bet?"

"Right now? That'd be a hell of a sight."

She laughed. "Maybe later. Like in a day or two or three."

She got in, sank down into a froth of iridescent bubbles with a sigh, leaned back, closed her eyes. "Omigod, Mort."

Yep.

Neither of us said a word for the next five minutes. We faced each other in water up to our chins, legs touching, not moving. Lucy slid a foot along my calf. That was all, no words.

Then I said, "We could turn on the jets on this thing."

"Uh-huh. If we want bubbles all the way out in the hallway, get management thinkin' they made a big mistake with us."

Another five, wet, warm, silent minutes went by.

"Mort?"

"Yeah?"

"If I ever get so grown-up and serious that I don't want to do anything like this anymore, will you please shoot me?"

"Sure thing, Sugar Plum."

A smile in her voice. "Thank you, Daddy."

"You're welcome. By the way, very little of what's happened in the past twelve hours feels real to me."

"Uh-huh." Her voice was soft, dreamy.

"Sure you're thirty-one years old?"

"Shut up, Mort."

* * *

We floated weightless in bubbles and music with our legs en-
twined, hers silky, mine not so much. Hammer never had it this
good. Or Spade, Moto, any of those guys. Didn't know about
Hercule Poirot. With a name like that, bubble bath might've been
the norm, but I was fairly certain Spade and Hammer had never
bubble-bathed with the dames. This, then, was a whole new chap-
ter in the pantheon of the world's greatest PIs.

PIs—that would be private investigators.

Wake up, Mort. What about Jo-X?

Lucy's comment about us not getting any closer to looking into
his murder began to drift around in my head like a shark circling
meat. My newly discovered PI gene was acting up. We had work
to do, and this wasn't it. She wanted to help, wanted to "stay with
me." A few hours with America's preeminent locator of missing
persons, and she wanted to learn the innermost secrets of the
gumshoe's tradecraft.

Well, so did I.

Too bad Ma was in Tennessee, a lady who actually knew a few
innermost gumshoeing secrets.

Warm. Drifting. Jo-X fading back into oblivion . . .

"Mort?"

"Yep?"

"Water's cooling off."

"Um-hmm."

"We probably ought to shower off these bubbles."

"Right."

"Hey, wake up."

"Yup. Wide awake."

"Are not. We could shower together or separately."

"Yup."

Her foot nudged my knee. "So? Which one? Together, I could scrub your back and you could scrub mine. But I can see where that might lead to a series of escalating complications."

Seventeen-year-old girls do not use phrases like "escalating complications." Good deal.

"You go ahead, kiddo. I'm good."

I kept my eyes closed, my erection under water where I thought it belonged. I heard her get out, pad over to the shower, heard the shower come on, heard her humming to herself over the music.

Hammer *never* had it so fuckin' good.

* * *

News at Eleven, and there was Mortimer Angel again, a five-second shot of me getting stuffed into a police car, looking guilty. And photos of Danya and Shanna who were renting the house. Nice long mention of "Celine," dark and luscious in a two-week-old clip of her and Jonnie-X as they got into a limo somewhere. No mention of Vince Ignacio. No floods, riots, no nukes in the Middle East, so the story was still the top item of the evening. It seemed as if it had happened a week ago, but I totaled it up and it had only been sixty hours since I'd found Jonnie-Boy. A lot had happened since then, warping time.

I turned off the television. Probably twenty million adults were cheering Jo-X's passing while a million little souls were crying their little hearts out because, one by lonely one, there was no longer any hope that they might ever feel his manly arms pressing their trembling little bodies to his bony sunken chest. Tragedy, American style.

Waists wrapped in towels, Lucy and I spent a few minutes at a window, looking down at the lights of the Strip, a thousand people below, neon up the wazoo in the psychedelic night, traffic as thick and slow as molasses as midnight approached.

Finally she went up on tiptoe, kissed me, dropped her towel on a chair, and slid between satin sheets in the bed nearest the window. "'Night, Mort."

"'Night, kiddo."

"Lucy."

"Lucy."

I gave it another two minutes, then crawled into the other bed, closest to the door. I lay on my back looking up at the ceiling, dimly illuminated by a muddy wash from all the multi-colored lights below.

Felt Lucy over there, eight feet away.

She still looked eighteen, except in that red dress, which put her at about twenty-four. Tangling with her was like being caught in a tornado, tossed around like a rag doll, but the truth is I'd made a *choice* back in Tonopah. I could have left her there. She would've been fine. I'd been under no obligation to haul her down here to Vegas, and had no obligation to keep her with me now. She could have all the money she'd won, and I could get on with this Jo-X investigation, such as it was. But all of that would have been like throwing the gift back in the face of fate. I was a gumshoe. I had cast off the IRS lamprey mantle. Girls flocking to me like pigeons to a statue was my reward for discovering I had a soul.

I heard her turn over. She sighed softly.

But forget the girl for a moment, big guy. Now what? Jo-X was dead, murdered, and I'd stumbled across his body, which is what I do, no skill involved, no idea how to follow up. Danya and Shanna were still missing. I was in Las Vegas with not much more to go on than the thinnest of evaporating vapor trails.

Lucy turned over again, thumped her pillow with a fist.

I had an inkling of the truth about the mysterious and elusive Celine, something the world at large hadn't picked up on yet—except possibly for the Wharf Rat, Ignacio. And I had a connection between Shanna and what appeared to be an unknown little diner somewhere in a hundred thousand square miles of desert. And maybe there was a clue or something in Caliente, but I didn't know what, other than it was a good place to go if you wanted a mud bath or needed to stock up on matches.

"Mort?"

A-a-a-and, here we go. "Yeah?"

"This doesn't feel right. Would it be okay if I—?"

"Sure, kiddo."

"Not to like *do* anything. But it would help me get to sleep if I could just sort of snuggle up for a while—if, you know, that's all that I did . . . that *we* did, 'cause this isn't working."

"C'mon."

She slid into bed with me and wriggled closer. "Thanks."

"De nada."

"Sure you're okay with this?"

"I'm sure it'll be a hardship, but I've endured worse."

"Worse than this, huh?" She kissed my shoulder.

"Like you wouldn't believe. Don't give it a second thought."

"Well, okay then. 'Night."

"'Night."

And that was that. In a dark corner of the room, Hammer and Spade were cat-calling and firing off rude names at me. Finally they left, disgusted.

I lay there with a dynamite girl tucked against my side, the rest of me humming happily, no bumping or thumping necessary. A real gumshoe might've had her flipped onto her back by now. A real gumshoe might've paid for her lunch and left her in Tonopah with a twenty-dollar bill. If I weren't a trainee, I might have checked out leads the minute I'd hit town—alone. I might be out rustling clues right this minute, if I knew how to do that. A real gumshoe would at least have some idea of where to start, conjectures to explore, but the only real investigator I knew was in Memphis, Tennessee. I thought all that was true, but I had the feeling that Lucy would've been a game changer even for Mike Hammer.

Were we partners, or just two people sharing body heat, about to part company in the next day or two? Should I tell her about the "Celine" video? Could I trust her?

Trust her? Seriously? My eyes flew open at the thought. Trust her after we'd been together barely twelve hours? That sounded like the definition of an idiot on wheels.

And Holiday? Other than telling Lucy not to hurt me, she was so far out on the ragged edge of this Jo-X thing that she was invisible. Holiday wasn't a PI, didn't pretend to be. But she thought I could be hurt? Tough, invincible me? What did she know that I didn't? Hurt Mort and I'll break your legs. Which meant what? Make him happy?

I *was* happy. Very. And Lucy was already asleep, pressed up tight against me. The palm of my left hand was at the small of her back, fingertips riding the sturdy swell of her rear.

Every single thing that had happened in the last two days felt so unreal right then that I thought I might levitate off the bed and find myself stuck to the ceiling come the dawn.

CHAPTER TWELVE

WHEN I SAT up in bed the next morning, Lucy was in pale green bikini panties, standing in the middle of the room, bent forward at the waist with her forehead touching one knee, the other leg up over her body, toes pointed at the ceiling. Both legs were as straight as rulers.

She turned her head and looked at me. "Morning." She held her position.

"Christ, you can do that before coffee?" I asked.

"You've been totally conked. How do you know I haven't had coffee already?"

"Well, okay. How about bringing me a cup?"

"Haven't made any. I don't drink coffee."

I stared at her. It was too early to process all that.

She said, "If you need caffeine on board before you do this, there's a Mr. Coffee or something in the kitchen."

"I would, but I prefer not to show off. What *is* that exactly? What you're doing? It sure looks like fun."

"Stretchies. I've got this routine I do every morning. Most evenings, too. Have to, if I don't want to lose it. I want to be able to do this when I'm fifty." She switched legs and went into her stance again.

"If I end up in hell, that looks like one of the exercises they'll make me do."

She laughed. Held the stance for thirty seconds, then stood up, squared her shoulders, and bent over backward, arms straight, farther and farther, until her hands touched the floor behind her feet, breasts stretched tight as drums, pointed first at the ceiling then behind her, which looked impossible. Her spine was doubled into a U shape. Then one leg came up, then the other, and she was in a handstand. Held that for a few seconds, then one leg continued on over and touched the floor, then the other, and she stood up, all of it done slowly and in perfect control. She did that nine more times, traveling backward half a foot at a time.

I said, "Deer can reach back and lick the middle of their own backs."

"It helps that they have three-foot necks." She sank to the floor, down into fore-and-aft splits. Lifted her back calf, arched her back, and put the sole of her foot on top of her head.

"You don't have a backbone, do you? You're a jellyfish, or an eel."

"Eels have backbones. I might be a shark, though."

"Whatever. The point is, God didn't give you a bunch of rock-hard inflexible concrete cast-iron splintery vertebrae like the rest of us, did He?"

"Rhetorical question. And He's a She."

"Do you own a bra?"

"Another rhetorical question."

"Not that one."

"Jog bra, yeah. Don't wear one if I'm not jogging, so, no, I sorta don't own what you'd call a real bra. Never really needed one, either." She twisted on the floor and the fore-and-aft splits became side splits. I winced.

"How 'bout I buy you one?"

"Naked breasts disturb you all of a sudden?"

"Not at all. It's just that . . . aw, the hell with it."

"Not getting a little worked up, are you?"

"Who? Me?"

"Sounds like a yes. Do you think my wearing a bra would help with that?"

"I don't know. It might."

"I could go do this in the other room."

"Not sure I want that, either."

She stood up and faced me, hands on her hips. "Well, what *do* you want?"

I put my feet on the floor. "Right now, breakfast." Buck naked, I headed for the bathroom.

Behind me, Lucy whistled, then said, "Hey, wait a minute, you. That was definitely a yes."

"Fair's fair, Sugar Plum. Cool your jets."

* * *

We ate at the Pyramid Café, then went "outside," into the rest of the building. If it were raining in Vegas, we would never know it. Measured by the amount of empty space it contains, the Luxor is in a class of its own. Its scale is lost from outside, but inside you see how vast the place really is. Its interior was a huge hollow pyramid, big enough to launch a dozen hot-air balloons.

The bigger Vegas casinos are like little cities. Management doesn't want you to leave, at least not with your wallet—unless your wallet has been gutted like a fish—so they do their best to provide everything under one roof: shopping, gambling, dinner, breakfast, bar, hotel, ATMs, banking, floor shows, video arcade, childcare, the works. The only two things you can't get are river rafting and open-heart surgery.

Okay, I'm not sure about the surgery.

Lucy and I had been inside for sixteen continuous hours. I was starting to miss the only things missing: real sky, clouds, wind. But there was something I had to do first, no choice.

At the main cashier cage I got twenty chips out of my Luxor account and handed them to Lucy.

She drilled me with her eyes. "What's this for?"

"Fun. Gambling. Whatever. I've got to go out, Lucy. Alone."

"Where to?"

"Just . . . out. There's a certain kind of confidentiality private investigators are supposed to honor. I've got something I need to do." I brushed her cheek with a finger. "I'll be back in, say, three hours. If you want, you could get some more sun. Morning sun's good. Meet me at the pool in back?"

She looked unhappy. "I don't have a bathing suit."

"Cash in a chip, buy yourself one." I left her there, walked away a few steps, turned back. "Three hours," I said, then I left.

*　*　*

Twenty thousand dollars. I didn't care about the money. As far as I was concerned it was hers, but I had to know what she'd do. I felt crummy about that, but didn't feel I had a choice. I couldn't tell her about Celine possibly being Shanna, not without getting the okay from Fairchild. For all I knew, Danya was Celine, though that was looking less likely now. My certainty level, having watched the video on the flash drive and finding Jo-X in that garage, was edging toward eighty percent that it was at least one of them, but that left twenty percent unaccounted for.

Outside, I had the valet bring around the Mustang. I gave the kid twenty bucks—big spender—got in, hit the Strip, headed east at the next intersection. I went far enough that Lucy couldn't see me from a window in our suite if she went back up. I pulled to a curb and phoned Russ.

"Yeah, what's up?" he answered, guarded.

"Can you talk?"

"Give me a minute."

I waited, top down on the car. Ten fifteen a.m. The day had already hit a hundred degrees. I wondered what Lucy was doing. If she wanted to split, now was the time to do it.

"Angel?" my favorite RPD detective said.

"Yep."

"What's up? You find Danya?"

"Not yet. Obviously you haven't either. But I'm just getting started down here."

"Down where?"

"Vegas."

"Vegas! What the hell's down there? I mean, other than Jo-X's got a big place down there, but they've already been through it, the police. Didn't find much of anything, except . . ."

"Except what?"

"Rohypnol. Guy had some in a drawer in his bar. Son of a bitch has his own in-house bar, thirty million bucks, and he needs a date rape drug? I'm glad that lowlife fucker is dead. Especially if Danya is Celine. You still think it's possible?"

"Anything's possible. Right now I'm at about fifty percent." I wasn't, but I was at least at fifty percent for Shanna.

"Last time it was twenty-five."

"This is Vegas. Odds change every few minutes down here."

"Well, shit. Got anything else goin' on?"

"I don't know. Might be something. But the police have things pretty well covered up there. I'd just get in the way."

"So what's down there? What've you got?"

"Not sure. I'll let you know if or when I find anything."

"If you find that goddamn secret hideaway of Jo-X's, let me know. That is, if there is such a place."

Which is what everyone else on the planet wanted to know. The fabled Jo-X "retreat," his private getaway place when he'd finally had his fill of screaming fans and wanted to be alone. The place was a castle in the sky, a fantasy, media conjecture. It might not exist. Opinions varied. But Jo-X disappeared from time to time. When he did, there was no sign of him. Nothing at all. Then he would reappear, and when asked where he'd been, his response was invariably to stick his tongue out that also-fabled three and a half inches, except that wasn't a fable but a tape-measured fact. Gross one, too.

"Haven't come across it yet," I told Russ. "What I'm doing, I'm following up on something of a lead down here."

"What kind of a lead?"

"A vapor trail. Maybe a little less than that."

"A vapor trail . . ."

But that Rohypnol thing might've thickened the mist. I would have to think about that. "What I need, Russ, is your okay to get someone else involved in this."

"Someone else? Like who?"

"An assistant that I . . . that I came across."

He was all over that half-second hesitation. "An assistant? You 'came across' an assistant?"

"Yep."

"How's that work? How do you do that?"

"It's a knack."

Well, he'd heard *that* before. "Jesus Christ, Angel. It's a girl, isn't it? Who is she? What's the story?"

"Her name is Lucy. I'm checking her out as we speak, but it's up to you, how much I tell her. Thing is, it'd be damn hard to work with an assistant who doesn't know what's going on."

"How old is she?"

"What's it to you?"

"How old?"

I gave him a weary sigh. "She says she's thirty-one." No need to tell him how old she looked.

"She says? I don't like the sound of that."

"It's been more or less verified."

"How do you 'more or less' do that?"

"I got a second opinion."

Silence. Then: "You're a hell of a hard guy to talk to."

"So I've been told."

He wanted to know more about my assistant so I gave him the bare-bones gist of how we met and how we decided to travel together, leaving out all mention of the various outfits Lucy had or hadn't worn, or that she said she'd marry me, which might've been a joke and didn't seem relevant in any case.

"Twelve thousand? She won twelve thousand bucks?"

"Rounded off a little, yeah." Rounded down from thirty-six thousand, but he didn't need to know that.

"How the hell'd she do that?"

"Roulette. She's a pistol."

"Sonofabitch, twelve grand is almost three months—"

"Is that a yes on the assistant, Russ? Tell her about Danya possibly being Celine?"

"Christ. You figure you can trust this girl, huh? Lucy?"

"We're in test mode right now. If she passes, then, yeah. I have the feeling she'll pass, and I have the feeling I could use the help. She seems like a nice-enough kid."

"Kid?"

"It's an expression we old farts use. And she's sort of like having a set of keys, so there's that."

"Keys?"

"She's the type that might open a few doors."

"Sonofabitch. She that good-lookin'?"

"Pretty much."

"Je-sus, I'm in the wrong—"

"Yeah, yeah. But I still haven't heard that okay, Russell."

"Yeah, fine. Do what you gotta. Just don't let the media get hold of that Celine thing."

"One other thing."

"What?"

"Get me Jo-X's address down here. I don't know where it is."

"And here I thought you were a PI, Angel."

"I am. Good one, too. I've got a police detective in my pocket. That's one way I get the information I need. Quick, too."

"Shit. How old you say that girl was again?"

"They found Rohypnol? That's really something. Call me back with that address. Shouldn't take you five minutes."

* * *

I could've had Russell try to check out Lucy, but I didn't want to do that—not after that call to Lucy's mother. Lucy hadn't told the woman her name or age, and both had checked out. There was no way Lucy could have been waiting for me to show up in Tonopah, no way to set up that kind of a coincidence. That was just paranoia talking. Now it was up to the money I'd given her. In effect, I was betting twenty Gs that she would still be there, that everything she'd said was true. And if I was wrong . . . it was only money. I had a lot more than I needed and, hell, it really was hers. I would have bet it all on black, lost my ass.

* * *

Back at the Luxor, she wasn't at the pool.

I'd driven around, then walked around the UNLV campus for an hour, chewed up some time, tried to think about Danya, Shanna, Celine, Jo-X, didn't get anywhere with that. At some point, Fairchild phoned with Jo-X's Vegas address. Finally, I went back to the hotel.

The pool at 1:05 was bustling with tiny bikinis and speedos on hairy guys with beer bellies; lotion, kids, two hundred baking bodies, a dozen kinds of music. No Lucy.

So there you have it, Mort. Easy come, easy go. Once again, I was a gumshoe on the loose. Already I missed her, but I had a job to do, an address to check out.

I went up to the room, opened the door, and she hit me in the chest with a fistful of thousand-dollar chips.

"Don't *ever* do that again," she said with a feline snarl.

"Do what?"

"Test me like that. And don't tell me it wasn't a test or I'll rip your heart out."

Ouch.

"Sugar Plum, I—"

"Don't. Just don't."

I saw tears. She turned away, went to a window, and looked out. Her body was rigid, shaking.

I stood there like a great ape, wondering what to do next to screw things up. What I came up with was, "I didn't have a choice, Lucy."

She whirled. "I thought we were partners."

She was hurt, but, in fact, it was time for a reality check, even though that could cost me a gorgeous assistant. I took her by the shoulders. "Look at me."

She tried to turn away, but I held her, kept her facing me. "You want to be my partner? Well, this is part of it. I was paid to do this. I have a client. What I tell you is up to him, not to me. So if you're hurt, *tough*."

At the word "tough," she looked shocked.

"It's been like a game so far," I went on. "We've had fun. But I told you I didn't have a choice, and that's the real world. Yes, it was a test. If we're going to work together, you'll have to know a few things that are highly confidential, so I had to know you could be trusted. And after knowing you less than twenty-four hours, how was I supposed to do that? So—do you want to 'stick around' with me in the real world too, even if it isn't always 'fun'?"

A single tear rolled down her cheek. "Yes."

I kissed her. I had to. Last thing I wanted was to knock her out of herself, make her stop being who she was. But the kiss missed her lips, landed on her forehead instead. My bad.

For a moment she was like a block of wood, then suddenly she was in my arms, crying. I let that run its course, didn't try to fix it, say anything. I'd learned that much in life anyway. When women cry, just hold them. Anything you say will be wrong.

Finally, she backed away a few inches. "Just, please, don't do anything like that again, okay?"

No fancy words, no "Sugar Plum," no typical dumbass Mort comment. "Okay."

* * *

And I *still* didn't know what the hell I was doing with this girl. Which was par for the course. I had eleven years on her, not what I'd thought when we left Tonopah in spite of that glimpse at her driver's license. Eleven years. Not even close to what I'd thought at first sight at McGinty's Café. She was smart. Maybe she could be my assistant. As if a lone-wolf PI-in-training could even *have* an assistant.

One thing I noticed, finally, was that Lucy was wearing a real shirt, sleeveless. It wasn't mesh, wasn't see-through. She had on tight white pants, barefoot, no ankle chain, no hoop earrings, no belly showing. The shirt had a collar. It was robin's-egg blue, seersucker with a kind of checkered design, something a real estate agent might wear in hundred-degree heat, showing houses.

She looked more grown-up, looked more like . . . twenty-two.

I crouched down and started to pick up chips. As I went along, I began to notice that there seemed to be too many of them. In fact, there were thirty-six.

"I kept four of them, put all the rest on red," she said, standing over me.

I stared up at her. "Red, red, red? Sixteen chips?"

"Yep. Pit boss guy looked like he was gonna faint. One spin of the wheel. I was mad. But even mad, I'm still lucky."

Jesus.

"They looked pretty upset when I won, but now that we're up another sixteen thousand, they might put more upgrades on the suite," Lucy said with a hesitant smile, already starting to turn back into herself.

I stood up. "Not sure what else they could give us, kiddo." But we were up fifty-two thousand now, so maybe they would give us the penthouse if we asked. And a limo and a driver.

Her smile widened. She gave me a peck on the cheek. "They could send up a few guys in jock straps to dance around."

"Yeah. That'd really brighten my day."

* * *

As we went past the main cashier's cage on our way out, I had Lucy put twenty-six chips in an account in her name alone. Now we each had twenty-six thousand at the casino, which seemed fair to me. It gave her the option of leaving any time she wanted. I still had four thousand in a money belt, a few hundred in my wallet. Money was not going to be an issue.

Back in the Mustang, one forty p.m., Jo-X's address plugged into the car's navigation system. The temperature was a hundred six and still inching upward. I had on dark gray khaki shorts and a lightweight green shirt with several buttons undone, a black wig, dark moustache, dark glasses, and the Stetson. Before we left the room, I showed her the two videos of Shanna, brought her up to speed on that front, which might have still been a risk, but she'd had thirty-six thousand dollars and hadn't taken off. I told her to put on her running shorts and partly see-through crochet halter top. The clothing was cooler and more likely to turn heads if we needed heads to turn. No telling what we would run into.

"That moustache looks pretty funky," she said.

I touched it. Last year I'd worn one the size of a shoe brush, running around with Jeri while we dodged media jackals. This one was more sedate, two-thirds Pancho Villa.

"You no like, senorita?" The top was down on the Mustang, sun beating down. Hot. Lucy wore a floppy, wide-brim hat.

"Makes you look, I don't know, with those shades and from a distance—Mexican, maybe Cuban."

"So you got yourself a hot Latino. Be happy."

She laughed. "Or not. But you look kinda Texan with the hat."

I kicked the Stetson back on my head. "You no like the hat, too, Barbie? You're a hell of a hard dame to please."

"No, I like the hat. It's just that funky 'stache. The thought of kissing you gives me the willies."

"*USA Today* has me listed as more recognizable than the vice president, not that that's a ringing endorsement—I'm not sure I could pick the VP out of a lineup—but still not good since we're going to be in or around Jo-X's place. So the 'stache, as you call it, shall remain in place."

We were half a mile past the Mandalay Bay Casino, headed south. Lucy held her hat on with one hand. We were doing fifty in a forty-five zone. "Glad we got that cleared up, and since you brought it up, what're we gonna do at Jo-X's place anyhow?"

I shrugged. "Dunno."

"Perfect. I'm learning stuff already."

"If you must know, we're gonna scout the place, see what we see."

"Scout it, right. You should have a Dan'l Boone hat."

In addition to the other disguise elements, I had four hats in the lockbox in the Mustang's trunk. The box also held binoculars, a hefty .357 Magnum revolver and a little .32, a tool kit, other odds and ends. You never know what you're going to run into. Lucy was proof of that.

But no Dan'l Boone hat.

Might have to pick one up to round out the collection.

CHAPTER THIRTEEN

JO-X'S ESTATE WAS something shy of a full-on mansion, not like the kind of places you'd find in Florida—Naples, Little Bokeelia Island, Longboat Key. It only had two stories. How could you call it a mansion if it didn't have at least three stories? But it was a nice stucco Mediterranean in shades of desert sand and basalt with a few desert palms in front, and, as advertised, it overlooked the fourteenth green of the Las Lomas Golf Club—a daily parade of color-blind guys in funny hats swatting balls and cussing. What more could anyone ask?

"Now what?" Lucy asked.

Now I still didn't know what. A single patrol car was in front of the mini-mansion, a forensics van, and two unmarked cars that might have disgorged detectives, chiefs, and others of that ilk. No way in, nothing to do but gawk with the others, and there were a great many others—about twelve carloads, mostly young, mostly girls, which gave us plenty of cover as we cruised slowly by, also gawking. I slouched behind the wheel while Lucy sat up and gave the place a good long look.

The mansion was eighty-two hundred square feet plus the pool and grounds, so the forensics guys and gals had a lot of territory to cover. Jo-X had been found in Reno, but he could have been killed anywhere—and by anyone, including twenty million civic-minded adults. The size of the suspect list might've given

Russell a modicum of comfort—*if* I hadn't found Jo-X in his daughter's garage.

But Lucy and I weren't getting anywhere, which was par for me. I wasn't sure about her. What had I expected, coming out here? A drive-by look at the house? What would that tell me? The thought that cops would be going through the place had occurred to me, but I'd wanted to check it out to be sure. Skulking Jo-X's mansion in the wee hours might be out of the question, but not necessarily. However, I did something like that last summer and almost got myself killed.

"Now what?" Lucy the Trainee asked.

"Now—oh, shit, duck."

"Duck?"

"Well, me. You don't have to." I slumped way down. "What I should've said was, don't stare at that blue car at the curb." Which was like saying, "Don't think about elephants."

"Which one?" Lucy asked, sitting up straighter, staring, head swiveling. "There's two of 'em."

"The one with the redhead in it."

"How will I know which one not to stare at if I don't look at both of them?"

Aw jeez. "Okay, then don't look at either one of 'em."

"If there's a problem, how's that supposed to help us?"

"Eyes front, girl."

We kept going. I drifted to the curb when we were a hundred yards beyond the car with the redhead behind the wheel.

"What's goin' on?" Lucy asked.

"Remember Shanna?"

She thought for a moment. "Tall, busty, naked blond girl in the shower you described twice in profuse exuberant detail but who's keeping track? Sure. So what?"

While briefing Lucy earlier, I might have given her an excess of information, but during investigations you never know what will be important. Cases often turn on trivia.

"That was her."

"In one of those blue cars?"

"Yep. The Ford Focus, not the SUV."

"You sure?"

"Nope."

"Perfect."

I handed her a digital camera. "Get a close-up of her. Make it look like you're taking pictures of Jo-X's place."

She said, "I feel like Nancy Drew," then popped out of the car and trotted back to where Shanna—maybe Shanna—was observing the activity at Jo-X's house. I watched in the rearview mirror. Lucy looked seventeen or eighteen, not much older than the quintessential groupie. Perfect cover. I pulled a quick U-turn and got the Mustang aimed in the same direction as the Focus, crept another twenty yards closer, then watched as Lucy walked up to the car in question and snapped a few pictures. Two minutes later, she was back.

I flipped through five pictures on the little screen. Good shots. Lucy had come through.

"That her?" she asked.

"Yep. Wearing a wig and sunglasses, but it's her."

"It's *she*, you mean."

"So you're colloquially challenged, Miss Prissy. I'll have to keep that in mind."

She smiled. "Okay, now what?"

"Now we try to follow her." Which meant I couldn't ditch the moustache, wig, or Stetson for a while.

"How about I drive? You could slump down, keep out of sight better that way."

"Got your license with you? Think you can keep up, not lose her?"

"Does a bear poop?"

I stared at her. "Something's missing from that time-honored aphorism, doll."

"Listen very, very carefully, Mort. Does a bear poop?"

"Well, yeah. They don't hold it until they die. If they did, they wouldn't last long."

"Okay then. The bear thing is like a total yes, I can keep up with her. What's the problem? Change places with me."

I did, head whirling slightly. I still couldn't keep up with her. Quixotic damn broad.

We sat there for another ten minutes. The Focus stayed at the curb. Finally it pulled away, slowly, as if Shanna were reluctant to leave but had no choice.

Lucy waited a moment then eased out behind her. She kept Shanna's car within view but hung back nicely.

"You've done this before," I said.

"Nope. But believe it or not I've watched all the seasons of *Justified* and I think I picked up a few pointers. And, by the way, Timothy Olyphant is a hunk and a half."

"I wouldn't know."

"Trust me. Don't feel bad about it, though. He's not real. You are. And you're totally Borroloola'ed, whatever *that* is."

* * *

Olyphant wasn't real. Good to know.

North on Decatur to I-215, a jog over to I-15, then through the heart of Las Vegas, parallel to the Strip. Lucy waved bye-bye to the Luxor as we went by.

Through Vegas, North Vegas, past Nellis AFB, signs telling us we were headed for St. George, Utah, Salt Lake City. Shanna held it at seventy and on we went, staying nearly a mile behind.

Road trip, motion, heat, freedom, cute girl in a crochet top, and Shanna in a Focus. Shanna, last seen leaving a bank parking lot in Reno wearing a Goodwill dress and bad shoes. Finally I was getting somewhere.

"Hope it doesn't get cold wherever we're going," Lucy said. "What I'm wearing is all I've got. Everything else is back at the Luxor."

I pointed to the temperature readout on the dash. "Right now it's a hundred seven degrees. Unless you slam us into the back of a refrigerated tractor-trailer, cold isn't an option."

"Might be later, though. You might have to hold me. Where do you think she's going?"

"Caliente."

"You think? Just 'cause of some matchbook covers?"

"And a motel receipt. Let us not forget that."

"That sounds really thin," said my trainee. "Fifty bucks says you're wrong."

"You're on. You should stick to roulette."

"Hah."

Twenty-two miles out of Vegas, Shanna turned left onto US 93 and headed north. We were half a mile back.

"Caliente," I said.

"We'll see."

We took the turn. The world got even more dry and empty, hot enough that you could safely eat roadkill. The billboards thinned out. We passed a rusty sign that read: Caliente 101 miles.

"Caliente," I said.

"Well, poop. Anyway, we're not there yet."

More emptiness, almost no traffic. Lucy let the Focus get nearly two miles ahead. We lost sight of it on the bends, picked it up again on the straightaways, and the road was mostly straight.

"So," Lucy said. "Gifting."

I stared at her. "Huh?"

"*Gifting*. What is it? You said you'd tell me later. It's later now and this road is really boring."

"Forgot I'd mentioned it. Any explanation I give you pretty much depends on how open your mind is, kiddo."

She laughed. "Like I've got a problem with that."

So I told her. I didn't know who came up with the word gifting, but I'd first heard it from Ma as we were driving to Bend, Oregon. The concept, however, was Holiday's. She'd come up with it as we were leaving Tonopah last year. It wasn't a difficult concept, but its ramifications ran dark and deep in the subterranean caverns of my mind. Still did, truth be told. In a nutshell, my fiancé, Jeri DiFrazzia, had "gifted" me to Holiday, loaned me out on Tuesdays.

"To do what?" Lucy asked.

"To watch and observe Holiday in various states of undress."

"Why?"

"To get her going. Revved up."

"Sounds like fun, like something out of the *Monologues*. What else? I mean, after she got revved up?"

"Last year when this was going on . . . nothing else."

She stared at me. "Nothing?"

"I believe a boob rub was discussed in the early stages but not acted upon."

"That's too bad. Boob rubs are fun."

"About the time I thought Jeri would seriously approve of things getting even that far, she was murdered."

Silence for several seconds. "I'm sorry," she said quietly. "You mentioned that earlier, but I'm still sorry."

"Me, too." Turns out, some scars never heal.

"They ever catch who did it?"

"No." Which probably meant Julia Reinhart would've gotten away with it, like Ma and I had thought back then. "And that," I said, "brings us to Borroloola."

"The workout routine that got you totally buffed."

"Totally, huh?"

"Well, I did see something like two ounces of fat around your middle yesterday. It must be a pretty great routine."

"It is. What you do, you lift a sixteen-pound iron bar up two and a half or three feet, and slam it down into the earth about three hundred thousand times."

She stared at me. "Tell me you didn't really do that."

"Borroloola is a town in Australia, Northwest Territories. It's a tiny little nothing place. I was digging holes for fence posts, every eight feet for nearly a mile. The holes were the hard part, hence the iron bar, but there was also setting the poles in slurry and putting in side rails. I did forty feet a day, twelve hours a day in the sun, in temperatures of about a hundred degrees. That's the Borroloola Routine. Highly effective and recommended."

"I'm thinking that's not going to catch on."

"Yeah? I was hoping to go national by October. Tours down under, weight loss guaranteed."

"If I were you, I'd rethink it." Lucy glanced in the rearview mirror. "There might be someone following us."

I turned and looked. A mile or so back, swimming in and out of the heat mirages, was a vague dark dot.

"How long's it been back there?"

"Ever since the interstate."

"We're doing seventy. There's nowhere to turn off. If that's fast enough for them, they'd stay behind us."

"Just sayin'," she said. "I'll keep an eye on it."

"You do that, Honey Bunch."

She slapped my thigh, then rubbed it. She looked over at me. "Hey, I gotta do something to keep myself awake."

"Do what you gotta. I'm gonna catch a nap."

She looked ahead at Shanna's car, a mile and a half away. "Borroloola, huh? At least the name's catchy."

* * *

Twenty miles later, Lucy said, "Uh-oh."

I'd been dozing off, drugged by the heat.

"Uh-oh?" I sat up straighter.

She pointed. "Got a few buildings coming up ahead. She's turning off."

"How's our gas situation?"

"Little over half a tank."

"Probably good enough. Let's see what this place is."

Lucy took it down to fifty-five. The buildings began to take shape. The smaller one was Arlene's Diner, a dried-up place of peeling clapboards. I didn't get a good look at it because I had to sink down below the level of the windows as we got near, but the roof looked like it could use work. Lucy pulled off the highway. I kept out of sight so Shanna would think the girl in the car was alone. Trouble is, I didn't think that all the way through.

"There's a motel here, too," Lucy informed me. "Midnight Rider Motel."

"Spiffy name."

"Suits the place. You oughta see it. It's only got four rooms. It probably has dead bodies decaying in the floorboards. And there's a little house trailer behind the diner that looks like total scurvy crap."

"Where's Shanna's car?" I was curled up beneath the dash, squashed between the shifter and the passenger door. They ought to design Mustangs with more leg room for times like this.

"Parked in front of the door to the diner. She's not in the car, so she's inside, eating or using the restroom, speaking of which."

"Pull off. Park away from her car, far as you can. Did she see you taking her picture back in Vegas at Jo-X's?"

"I don't think so. I was just some no-name girl, and she was staring at his house like it was on fire. She never looked at me."

"Okay, go in, see what's what."

"If I can get some food, you want anything?"

"Yeah, beer and a restroom would be great."

She laughed, eased the car to a stop. No shade anywhere around, which figured. The sun was blazing straight down on my head. I should've had her put the top up, but I need stuff to hit me between the eyes before it makes an impact.

"Don't wander off," my smart-ass assistant said as she got out and headed for the diner.

* * *

Hundred nine degrees, me hugging the floor wondering if I was going to die there, end up rendered into a blob of tallow.

Three minutes.

Five. Five is a long time at a hundred nine fuckin' degrees.

Then footsteps on gravel. They stopped. I looked up. A huge guy in grimy coveralls was looking down at me.

"Whatcha doin' down there, dude?" he asked. He had a black beard as dense as a bramble thicket, inch and a half long, eyes that looked like two narrow-set bullet holes.

My impression was that this was not the brightest flame in the candelabra, but I'm often wrong about that. "Got a cramp in my calf," I said.

"Yeah, those suck. You oughta get out, walk around. And drink more water."

He left. A minute later a diesel engine snorted to life. I raised my head far enough to see a big rig pass by thirty feet away with a huge backhoe on a flatbed trailer, headed for the highway. I caught a glimpse of *Buddie's Excavating* printed on the driver's-side door.

Another three minutes and Lucy was back. She stood outside the car and handed me a bottle of cold water and a plastic bag.

"Damn," I said. "They were out of beer?" I was still on the floor, sun blasting down.

"Alcohol's bad for you in heat like this. I was afraid you were gonna die out here. Drink up."

I did. Opened the bag and found two more bottles of water, two Snickers bars, Oh Henry, Mars bar, Twix. "No beer, but these're good for you?"

"It's all the waitress girl in there had at the register."

"Girl, huh?"

"Probably midtwenties. I didn't know what you'd like so I got a selection. And that girl, Shanna—she's like, wow—tall and beautiful and . . . you know . . ."

"A little bit busty."

"*Totally*. About to fly out of that halter she's wearing. And her hair was long and red, so if you say she's blond, then she was wearing a pretty good wig. Anyway, she was getting a sandwich to go, so I couldn't order anything and have us keep up with her, so I got what I could."

"You forgot the restroom."

"No, I went." She grinned, then said, "Okay, that's not fair. I could drive you around back. There's a shed back there you could maybe pee behind."

Well, hell. Things were approaching critical. "Do it," I said.

She got in the car, jumped back out. "Ow, ow, *ow*! Son of a *bitch*, that seat is hot!"

"I coulda told you that, Sweetheart."

"Well, why *didn't* you?"

"Heatstroke?"

She poured cold water on the seat, then got in, ignoring the wet, and drove around behind the diner. As I ducked behind a wooden shed that offered all the privacy I was going to get, Lucy said, "She just got in her car. She's leaving. Better hurry."

Some things don't hurry as well as others. But US 93 was a flat, empty strip. I didn't think hurrying was strictly necessary. We were in a hot Mustang, Shanna was in a Ford Focus—so, no contest.

A Chevy Impala with scabrous paint was parked behind the diner. No one in sight. I faced away from the diner/motel combo, peed away from the shed. To my left and around the corner of the shed was that house trailer Lucy had mentioned. Old, no sign of life. In weeds behind the shed were lengths of rusting iron pipe, a tree saw with teeth three-quarters of an inch long, tangled coils of baling wire, old paint cans, an aluminum ladder. A quarter mile away in the desert, an industrial building of some sort gleamed in the sun, big enough to house four or five motor homes. Glare off the roof was like looking into the face of the sun.

When I got back, Lucy had the car facing out, ready to go.

"She kept going north," she said.

"As expected. I doubt that many people come this way for a sandwich at the diner here, then hustle on back to Vegas."

"Smart-ass."

"Gumshoe 101. She's headed to Caliente."

"We'll see. By the way, that car I thought might have been following us went by. Small red sedan. I don't know cars all that well so I don't know what kind it was. I mean, who gives a darn about cars?"

"Or about the kind of planes that were flying overhead in or around the Philippines in, say, nineteen forty-three."

She gave me the same look Jeri used to give me. Dallas still does on occasion, when we're together.

"Sometimes, Mort, you're unintelligible."

"Yup."

She smiled. "And inarticulate."

"Yah."

As we left Arlene's, I sat up and looked back. The building was the color of dust, a scorched place in the middle of nowhere. A lone gas pump sat beside the building. The Midnight Rider Motel was thirty yards from the diner, just four units and as sand-blasted and dehydrated-looking as the roadside diner.

Then we were on the highway and the Focus was four miles away. Lucy took it up to a hundred for a while then settled down to a sedate seventy, keeping two miles back.

"Back there," I said, "that's the diner in the video."

Lucy looked at me. "I know. I even saw the table where she was sitting. By that window."

"That shed a quarter mile out in the desert? I'll bet that's where he kept the helicopter."

"Maybe we need to get nosy around that place."

"Uh-huh. Later. Right now we've got to stay on Shanna."

"Which—observe—I'm doing."

"And a great job of it, too."

Ten miles out we passed the big rig with its backhoe on the trailer. No sign of life, trees, anything, in the mountains rising up around us, just a few buzzards looking for something tasty that had finally given up. I ate the Oh Henry bar and a Snickers, then drank another bottle of water.

"Next time I buy the lunch, kiddo."

"Fine. If we end up following Timothy Olyphant, I'll stay in the car and you can go inside and check him out. He's got a great butt. Otherwise, quit complaining."

"You'd stay in the car? Really?"

"No way."

CHAPTER FOURTEEN

PAST ALAMO AND Ash Springs to the junction of US 93 and Highway 375. We turned right onto the Great Basin Highway.

"Caliente," I said.

"Well . . . poop."

Up ahead, the red car passed Shanna's. Lucy stayed a mile behind the Focus.

Forty-three miles later, after winding through a canyon, we pulled onto Front Street and into the town—population just under twelve hundred, previously known as Culverwell. Flat and hot and dry, but it had a casino, Sinclair and Exxon gas stations, a bank, a few motels, all contained within low, scorched hills. We stayed two hundred yards behind Shanna as she cruised through the business section and out the other side. She pulled into a tree-shaded parking lot for the Pahranagai Inn at the north end of town. Lucy sped up as Shanna turned off, trying not to lose her.

"Motel receipt in a kitchen drawer will do it every time, Sweetheart," I told Lucy. "Pay attention. And notice that we're in Caliente, so you owe me fifty bucks."

"Well, crapola. I don't have that much with me so you'll have to accept fifty dollars' worth of something else later."

"What'll fifty bucks get me?"

"Wait and see."

We pulled into the lot just in time to see Shanna disappear into room nine. Lucy parked forty feet from the Focus. The place was nicer than anything else we'd seen in Caliente—cedar siding stained a dark brown, probably one of those indeterminate names on the paint can like Sunrise Sienna or Overland Umber, which meant you had to look at color swatches.

"Now what?" Lucy asked.

"Now we go see what's what."

"You said they were married."

"Yeah? So?"

"So, you might want to give them a little privacy for like, I don't know—half an hour or something."

Christ, the things that never cross my mind. "Nope, let's get in there before anything like that gets fired up."

"Your call, boss."

Boss? I gave her a sidelong look as we walked to the room. Curtains were pulled across the windows.

"Tell 'em you're from the office," I whispered.

"Okay. Then what?"

"Wing it, partner. Show me your stuff."

"Showed you pretty much all of my stuff yesterday."

"Not that. Let's see how well you improvise."

She shot me a sudden panicked look as I knocked on the door and stepped to one side, pressed myself against a wall. At the last moment I pushed her in front of the security peephole and told her to smile.

"What is it?" Shanna's voice called out.

"Office, ma'am."

I gave my assistant two thumbs up and did a little side step to avoid a kick in the shin. Testy.

Shanna's voice through the door: "What d'you need?"

"There's a blank spot on the registration form you didn't fill out."

The door opened. It hit the security chain and stopped. Like all security chains, it was a joke. Good enough. I set my foot against the bottom of the door to hold it, then gave it a good bump with my shoulder, tore a few screws out of the door jamb, and went inside.

"Well Christ on a moped," Danya said, sitting cross-legged on the bed. "Look who. Thought I fired you, Mortimer."

* * *

"Mort," I said.

I pulled Lucy into the room, then shut the door. Shanna had her wig off. She was back to short frizzy blond hair with the pink streak in it. She had backed away, trying to catch up to this unexpected development. And, like Lucy said or implied, she was wearing a halter that wouldn't hold another ounce without coming apart. But it was hot as hades outside, so I didn't think badly of her for it.

"I can see why my dad doesn't like you," Danya said. "You really *are* a maverick. *And* unprofessional. Who's gonna pay for that busted chain and stuff?"

"Not a problem," I said. "You are."

Danya looked past me at Lucy. "Who's the teenybopper in the 'fuck-me-like-crazy' outfit?"

"Who're you callin' a teenybopper, Chicklet?"

"Whoa, whoa," I said. "Let's back up and take another run at this. Turns out we're all on the same team here."

"Who says?" Danya uncurled her legs and stood up. She was in lime green panties and a scoop-neck T-shirt held out in front by a couple of Texas Ruby grapefruits, or something like that.

"Me," I said loudly, hoping to cut through the estrogen and this round-robin jealousy thing that had erupted. "Danya, this is Lucy, and she's a lot older than either you or Shanna, so have a little respect for her age."

"No way," Danya said. "She's older than me?"

"Than *I*," Lucy said, no sugar-coating on the tone.

I rolled my eyes. "Okay, grammar will not be an issue right now. Right now, it's all about truth and a dead Jo-X, and I'd like to keep it that way, so if it looks like there's gonna be a catfight, I'm gonna pull my gun."

"Since you obviously don't have a gun on you," Danya said, "I assume that means you're gonna pull out your dick."

Aw, jeez.

Lucy laughed. "You should," she said to me. "Loosen things up in here. This room has got some seriously ugly knots."

Danya looked at me and smiled. "Got yourself a live little wire there, don'cha, Mortimer?"

"Mort, and yes I do."

"She good in bed, too?"

"I don't know, but she's great in a Jacuzzi and her name is Lucy and now that we've got the introductions and the personal stuff out of the way, let's see if we can't stay focused on what's import- ant here. Which is to try to save a couple of girls' asses now that Jo-X turned up in an awkward location."

"Fine," Danya said. She sank back down on the bed and went cross-legged again, which gave me a panty frontal, not that I no- ticed, her being a married woman and all. Shanna sat next to her and put an arm around her waist, the other hand on a thigh, not her own.

Danya looked at Shanna. "Did you get into his place?"

"Couldn't. Cops were totally all over it."

"Well, hell. It was worth a try, but the guest book's probably gone by now anyway. That's gonna totally suck."

"What guest book?" I asked.

Danya stared at me for a moment. "Why're you here? I fired you."

"Couple hours later, your dad hired me."

She laughed. "You oughta do stand-up."

"Turns out he wanted a maverick, too. You'd disappeared and Jo-X was in your garage. Your dad said something about the police having to operate with too many rules. He wanted an off-the-books parallel investigation going on. Which is my forte."

"Sounds like him. When he wasn't totally pissed at you, I think he kind of admired you."

Next time I saw him I would have to tell him that, see if he'd kiss me on both cheeks or pull a gun.

"And," I said, "I don't think your dad wants our arrangement to become public knowledge, so keep it to yourself."

"Well, hell. I've got CBS and NBC on speed dial." She gave me a hard stare. "As if I want the public all over this."

"What guest book?" I asked again.

"At Jo-X's house in Vegas. He had a party four or five weeks ago. My dumbass sister was there and she said she signed the stupid thing. Her name is Josie, J-O-S-I-E. So now there's her name, Josie Fairchild, right there in that book, and Jo-X dead, found in my garage—Danya *Fairchild's* garage, if the police stumble across that possibility even though my actual name is Fuller. Has been all my life. How long do you think it'll take the cops to put two and two together, drag my sister into this? And then me, and probably my dad."

"Two and two? That's a tough one. Could take up to a year and a half."

Danya smiled. "Don't let my dad hear you say that."

"Given where Xenon was found, you're already in this up to your neck whether you're Fuller or Fairchild."

"Which still doesn't make sense, him being there. But then if my sister also gets dragged into this because she signed that book at his party, that would be an unbelievable mess."

"Josie," I said. "Pronounced the same as Xenon's Jo-X. Terrific."

"Yeah. She thought that was so cool, their names sounding the same. Maybe that's why she started listening to him."

"How old is she?"

"Seventeen."

"And she went to a party at Jo-X's place? In Vegas."

"Uh-huh. Smart, huh? She went to a concert in Reno at the convention center and got way up front. Some girl came around halfway through the concert and gave her a pass to go backstage. Jo-X was flying out right after the concert, but he told her there was gonna be this party at his Vegas mansion in a few days and she was invited. She told Dad she wanted to go to Vegas, gave him some song and dance about staying with a girlfriend who moved down there, and, of course, he said no way. I think he may have actually said no *f-ing* way, not that it matters. But Josie's always been a rebel. She told him she was going to stay the weekend with me, then took off with an equally retarded girlfriend, and they drove down in the girl's car." She looked at Lucy, sitting beside me on the other bed. "If you're older than nineteen, I'll shit a brick."

"What a lovely expression," Lucy said. "I'll treasure it and the image, but adobe or concrete, either one, that's gonna hurt."

"She's thirty-one," I said quickly, before things got out of hand again.

Danya stared at Lucy. "Not possible."

"It's been verified," I said. "But if you want, we could cut off an arm or a leg and count rings."

Lucy chucked me in the ribs with an elbow. It didn't hurt the way it used to when Jeri did it. But that they both felt compelled to do so on occasion must mean something. Then she sat closer to me and put an arm through mine, hugged it close.

"So your kid sister went to a Jo-X party and your dad didn't know," I said to Danya. "That's about right for a kid these days. Punishment for that is taking away their cell phone for half an hour, give it back right before they go suicidal. How did Xenon notice her? She pretty, too?"

"Pretty? She's a lot more than just pretty. She's five-ten and looks like a showgirl. And you should see what she wore to that concert. So, yeah, that evil bastard picked her out of the crowd."

"Okay. How'd that get you involved? And what's with this Pahranagai Inn? I found a receipt in Xenon's wallet. The name on the receipt was Nathan Williams."

"Never heard of him, but it's probably Jo-X." Danya glanced at Lucy, then stared at me. "Can she be trusted? This isn't . . . this is getting into some really private stuff, Mortimer."

"Mort. She can," I said.

"I can," Lucy echoed. "And his name is Mort in case you hadn't picked up on that yet."

Danya gave her a hard look, then turned to me. "Josie woke up here. In this room. She was at the party in Vegas. There were like sixty people there, she remembers that. And she had a few drinks, then . . . nothing after that, until she woke up here, naked, a hundred fifty miles away, and she knew she'd been raped."

"Rohypnol," I said. "He roofied her."

"That's what I thought, too. Nothing else made sense."

"What I mean is—they found Rohypnol at Jo-X's place. The police did when they searched it. Your father told me."

"Well, shit. That rotten *asshole*. Jo-X, not my dad."

"Jo-X—who, let us not forget, ended up in your garage."

"Which is *still* one unbelievably weird goddamn mystery I don't know shit about," Danya said harshly.

"Or me," Shanna said, and I felt Lucy's arm tighten on mine at the lapse in grammar. I bumped her shoulder, indicating that she could keep it to herself, vent later.

"Josie phoned my cell," Danya said. "I was in Reno. She was crying. She told me where she was and asked me to come get her and bring her some clothes 'cause hers were gone. Jo-X took 'em, the bastard. Don't know why. All she had were towels and bedsheets from in here so she couldn't leave the room. And she wanted me to bring her a 'Plan-B' pill."

"Plan-B?"

"A 'morning after' pill. Just in case. But if you're thinking we should've gone to the police, Josie said she'd been douched. She didn't do it, but she could tell. Douched her when she was unconscious? How evil is that? And she's older than sixteen and he's famous, which meant everyone would think she was just a dumb groupie, which maybe she was, so the police might figure it was consensual and she was looking for a payoff—and on and on. You know how it goes. Famous rich guys almost never get prosecuted for rape. For them it just goes away and the girl is stuck with everyone knowing or thinking she'd been raped, or that she's a gold-digging liar. So we handled it."

Handled it. That sounded familiar. "How'd you do that?"

"Hey, if you're thinking we killed the fucker, think again. This all happened about a month ago. And stringing him up in our garage would've been a super way to cover it up. What we *handled*, was Josie. Getting her back home, talking to her, not letting Dad find out what had happened 'cause he would've gone totally ballistic and done something really stupid."

"And the retarded girlfriend who drove her down to Vegas didn't notice the car was empty on the return trip?"

"My dumb sister told her Jo-X said he'd buy her a plane ticket back if she wanted to stay until that next afternoon or the day after. And, of course, she did, and, of course, the girlfriend had to get back or her parents would find out, so she left the party kinda early and went back to their motel."

Sounded like a couple of typical dumb kids, all right.

The room went quiet for a while.

Okay, who killed Xenon? Danya?

Motive, I thought—check. Opportunity was iffy since Jo-X was usually surrounded by fans and various sycophants. Means? A bullet in the chest, another in the head? She could manage that if she could get him alone, which was that opportunity thing again. But string him up in their garage like some sort of a trophy afterward?—no way in hell. In fact, Jo-X in their garage was like being given a get-out-of-jail-free card. They should have stayed in Reno. Running and hiding out like this was stupid.

I looked at Danya. "You said this is the room Josie woke up in?" Quickly I turned to Lucy and said, "I ended that sentence with a preposition. Is that okay?"

She bit my shoulder. "Poophead."

"Ow," I said, mostly for show since she didn't draw blood. I looked at Danya.

"Yes," she said.

"And here you are."

"We didn't stick around very long when we got Josie. We looked around a little, but mostly Shanna and I got her dressed and hustled her out, fast. We had to get back to Reno. I'd told Dad Josie was staying with me. Then, later, things got too hot in Reno after Jo-X turned up—which is the kind of weirdness that makes you believe in ghosts—so we came back here to keep out of sight. And, yes, this is the same room. I was hoping we could learn something by staying here, but it's been cleaned, obviously, so now it's just a place where hopefully no one will find us. But Jo-X ended up in our garage, and since we didn't put him there, something's goin' on, maybe in Vegas or maybe around here— something we don't know anything about—Shanna and me—but we'd like to find out, which, if you're wondering, is why we're here and not in some little no-name motel in Idaho or hiding out in Pahrump or Beowawe."

Nevada postage-stamp towns. Her explanation for being here sounded about half reasonable. What else? Only two other known facts I could think of offhand that didn't fit their narrative.

I shuttled a look between the two of them. "What about that note demanding a million dollars?"

Danya glanced at Shanna, then back at me. "I found it in the mailbox. That's all I know about it."

"Except by then Jo-X was in your garage."

"I didn't know that. I mean *we* didn't know anything about Jo-X being there, or even being dead. Everyone thought he was just missing, which, of course, he was. The note didn't make any sense, so we thought it must be kids fooling around."

"You should go back to Reno, talk to your father. It's likely that note would get you off the hook for anything having to do with Jo-X."

Danya's eyes narrowed. "Think so, huh? Bastard turns up in Danya Fuller's garage, except her father's name is *Fairchild*, and this happens a month after Josie *Fairchild* signs his guest book? And Danya and Josie are half sisters? Who's gonna think that's a coincidence? That note wouldn't mean I'm innocent. The police might even think I wrote it or had someone write it for me."

"Why would you do that?"

She stared at me like my hair was on fire. "I *didn't*. So how would I know why anyone would think I wrote it, other than cops are suspicious and they want to solve murders."

That note was nothing but trouble. It meant someone else was in the game. Danya or Shanna could have written it, but that would mean they knew about Jo-X in the garage. But why put him there in the first place? Why not get rid of him? And if Jo-X's murderer wrote the note, why would he think the girls would pay $1,000,000 instead of calling the police and reporting the body? The note-writer must've thought they would pay, or might, but why? No answers to any of that, which brought me to the second thing that didn't fit the narrative.

"Josie is one thing. She might even be a motive for murder." I looked at Shanna. "Now tell me why you became Celine."

CHAPTER FIFTEEN

THERE ARE MOMENTS of dead silence in the world, when you can hear your heartbeat, worms tunneling underground, clouds floating by, a leaky faucet in a neighbor's house. This was one of those.

Finally Danya said, "You called her Celine at that bank in Reno. Why would you do that? Where did you come up with a mega-bizarro thing like that?"

Mega-bizarro. I filed that away for future use. You never know when you might want to sound twelve years old.

"You look at Celine on TV then at Shanna and their figures and heights are the same." I wanted to see how that absurdity would play before hitting them with something more concrete.

"Their figures?"

"Boobs, if you want to get technical."

Danya gave me an incredulous look. "You're a tit expert?"

"Sort of. Yeah."

"That's beyond ridiculous. Kind of nasty, too. And Celine is black, Shanna is white."

"No argument with any of that, including my being nasty."

"Shanna isn't Celine. That's totally ludicrous."

"Would be, if it weren't true. But luckily there's more." I pulled out my cell phone. I'd uploaded the two videos from the flash drive. I got a video going and held it out to the girls.

The video was silent. Danya and Shanna stared at it in shock as someone approached Shanna in a roadside diner and handed her a menu. Shanna was wearing shorts and a yellow halter top.

The video lasted less than ten seconds. When it ended, I said, "Want to see it again?"

"It was that bitch waitress," Shanna said. Danya put an arm around Shanna's shoulders.

I let that tender moment run for a moment, let them consider the implications of what they'd just seen. Then I said, "Okay, there's no sound so how about you narrate this one for me." I played the first video, the one with Shanna in that same yellow halter walking toward the helicopter with a guy in a flight suit.

"Well, shit," Shanna said when the clip ended. She dropped her head and her shoulders sagged. Then she sort of shook herself and said, "Wait. How does any of that mean *I'm* Celine?"

"'Celine' was written on the flash drive."

"Yeah? So?"

Yeah, Mort. So?

"What if the flash drive belonged to Celine?" Danya said. "She might've written her name on it."

I looked at Shanna. "That doesn't explain why you're in the video, or the droopy, defeated look you had when you saw it just now."

"I'm tired. I get all droopy when I'm tired."

"That's unfortunate. Now guess where I found that video."

"In a box of Wheaties."

"Close, but wrong. It was in Jo-X's pocket when I found him in your garage."

They both stared at me.

"Consider the myriad implications," I said to Shanna. "Dead, disgusting rapper in your garage, video of you in his pocket, the name Celine on the flash drive, helicopter pilot who can probably be identified as Jo-X by experts. Guy had to get a pilot's license somewhere. You are in this up to your eyeballs. Or would be if the police got hold of this. And you can thank me later for having removed it."

"It's not my garage—I mean, *our* garage. It belongs to that lady we rent the place from, Mrs. Johnson."

"You could explain that to the police. I'm sure they would understand. This is all a great big misunderstanding."

Silence. Shifty eyes.

Okay, enough. "I guess Lucy and I will have to go back to that diner and have a talk with the waitress, maybe show her the video, see what she has to say about it."

"Don't," Danya said quickly.

"Why not?"

"Just . . . don't."

"That mean you've got something more to add to the saga of Shanna and Celine and Jo-X?" I asked.

Danya slid off the bed and took Shanna's hand. "Excuse us for a moment." She led Shanna into the bathroom, shut the door.

"Might be a back window," Lucy said, first thing she'd said since calling me a poophead, a term of endearment I would treasure in memory as much as my first Lionel train set.

"I'll tell you a funny back-window bathroom story later. Right now, how about you hustle around back and have a look? Fast."

"That's redundant. Hustle means fast. And you think they'd go out the window in panties?"

"You never know. They've also got towels in there. Go."

She went soundlessly out the door. I got up and stood close to the bathroom door. I could hear voices in there, so maybe they weren't headed for Canada in attire that might draw stares. Or they were having trouble getting the window open.

They came out two minutes later. A few seconds later, Lucy came back inside. We all settled into our customary places.

"Got your story straight?" I asked the two girls.

"There's nothing to get 'straight,'" Danya said. "It is what it is, but we had to decide how much of it to tell you."

"Why not tell us all of it?"

She ignored that. "All of this is sort of my fault. After we got Josie home, I drove back to Vegas and spoke to Jo-X. Well, I screamed at him, if you want to know. I wasn't thinking clearly. I didn't know what I thought he'd do, but he raped my little sister. I went to his house and his bodyguards or servants or whatever they are, one of them called him on a little radio thing."

"So they can identify you," I said. "Great."

"Maybe not. I wore a blond wig and sunglasses and some other stuff. Anyway, they let me in, probably because Jo-X likes girls, good-looking young women, and when I saw him I just screamed at him, which I know was dumb but I couldn't help it. He laughed at me. Just laughed. Told me I was crazy and had two guys drag me off the property, back out to the street. And that was that. I figured I couldn't get close to him again after that."

"Then," Shanna said, "I did. He's always got a girl on his arm. If you check the archives you'll see that the girls change every few months. It's what he does, like part of his act. They're mostly white, but sometimes black. He'd had two white girls in a row so I figured he'd be ready for a black girl. So—you've seen Celine on TV—I was really dark, which was a good disguise, always wearing a wild red wig, dark glasses, a little bit of stuff in my cheeks to round out my face, bright red lipstick, and—well—wearing outrageous dresses to show off my ... my ..."

"Got it," I said.

"I didn't want her to do it," Danya said. "Except ..."

"Except that you did."

"I wanted *him*. I wanted him in prison. I wanted him to get *raped* in prison, hoped that would happen anyway."

"How about where he is now?"

"In hell? That's perfect, too. Maybe he'll get raped there."

Nice.

"So," Shanna broke in, "I got close to him. I was dressed in a typical Celine outfit. It was at a concert in Phoenix. I had on body paint, turned myself into a very dark black girl. I bribed a security guy two hundred dollars to let me go backstage. Soon as I saw Jo-X, I hooked an arm around his neck and pulled his face two inches from mine, and said something like, 'Know what you need to take your act to the next level? Me. White as you are, black as I am. We make a statement, not like you with that Snow White Krissy bitch.' And he totally snapped it up, the boldness of it, what I was wearing. And, yes, breasts were a big part of it, if you want to know. Perfect for his raunchy act."

"And you did all that in order to . . . ?"

"Get close to him, of course. Like I said. Go to parties. Keep a close eye on him. Wait for him to roofie someone. Catch him in the act, if at all possible. What I *really* wanted was to get a video of him raping some unconscious girl, shut his life *down*."

"And sex?"

She laughed. "Sex was not an option. I was arm candy. I made that clear up front. I was career enhancement—I was for show only. I told him he could have any girl he wanted, no problem, all I wanted was *money*, which gave me credibility. I told him he'd make a lot more with me than with Krissy. His fan base was mostly young teen girls. I could pull in the boys. I told him I'd wear any outfit he asked me to, no matter how revealing. I figured that would hook him. I was onstage with him, visible in restaurants, limos, hotels, everywhere he went. I was mysterious and unknown, instantly famous. I made him a lot of money. I was Celine for a few weeks, and now I'm not."

Then she gave me a cold-steel look. "So *what?*"

So what? Suddenly I didn't know. I found that I hadn't put a lot of thought into the question of what it might mean if Shanna or Danya really was Celine, where that might end up. But at least I was a hundred percent sure now, something I could report to my favorite RPD detective. Maybe. I would have to give that some thought. Josie was a significant problem. Did I want to tell Russ about her being raped? How much could he take?

Lucy said, "So what? *Here's* what—he didn't roofie anyone so you couldn't catch him. So you killed him instead."

"And hung him in our garage to stink up the neighborhood and get the police involved," Danya said. "That's brilliant."

"You killed him and someone else put him in your garage."

Danya stared at her, then at me. "When you pick up women— well, high school girls—you should have them checked for rabies before taking them out in public. She's delusional."

Rabies. Interesting. That had never occurred to me. "Okay, now tell me about the helicopter," I said to Shanna.

She looked down at her hands. "The video was at that place where I first saw this girl this afternoon"—she nodded at Lucy. "Arlene's Café, Diner, whatever. A lot of people think Jo-X has a secret place, some sort of a hideaway somewhere, no one knows where. Turns out it's true. I don't know who all knows about it, or exactly where it is, or how he managed to keep it so secret, but I was there. Before that, I was with him for almost three weeks, then one afternoon he gave me an address and told me to be there the next day at one p.m., not to be followed, and not to arrive as Celine, but as me, since by then he knew I was white, but not my real name, who I was, or even that I was from Reno, so he called me Celine like everyone else.

"So I did. I put the address into the system and left his house in Vegas as Celine in a car with dark tinted windows. I had to get rid of some media lice, which took a while, but all they knew was they were following a car from Jo-X's place, didn't know it had 'Celine' in it, so they probably didn't try as hard as they would have. I pulled off the highway and changed back into myself, which took some scrubbing to get off the black, but it's just body paint, expensive stuff meant to do just what it did. When I finally got to that diner, I went into the bathroom and made sure all the body paint was off, then I waited. I was there for over an hour, then a helicopter flew over the diner and came down behind the place. A few minutes later, there's Jo-X, but you wouldn't know it since he was wearing mirrored sunglasses, a hat, and a flight suit like the kind a real pilot would wear with a bunch of pockets and zippers. I guess that was in case anyone else was at the diner, but if you think about it, the owner, maybe that waitress since she was kinda old and didn't really act like a waitress, has to know that the guy was Jo-X. If so, she probably phoned him and told him I was there, waiting."

"Two hours ago the waitress there was young," Lucy said.

"I saw her. That wasn't the same one. The one who took the video was in her fifties or sixties. Jo-X came inside and got me. We walked out to the helicopter and he flew it. I didn't know he could fly one of those. Turns out he really was a pilot. I don't think anyone in the media knows. If they did, you would've heard about it on TV—more Jonnie Xenon hype to thrill the girls. He took off, kept low, circled around a bunch of canyons and hills and made a lot of turns, then finally landed at this place in a sort of valley way up in the mountains. What we flew over was all dry desert, like a maze. I couldn't find the place now if I had to.

"He was more relaxed, not so wild or hyper, not like the Jo-X everyone sees onstage and television, but he tried like hell to get me into bed. Maybe that was why he took me there. Probably was.

Thing is, I'm a lot stronger than I look. Meaner, too. And I knew he'd roofied Josie so I didn't drink anything but bottled water from bottles where the cap was still sealed at wherever they bottle those things. I figured he could even roofie an ice cube. And I slept in a different bed, different room, with the door locked and the back of a chair stuck under the knob. He tried, but didn't even get to first base."

"First base. That's tits, right?" Lucy said.

Shanna glared at her. "You oughta know, girl." Then a glance at Lucy's chest—"Okay, maybe not." She looked at me. "Anyway, he flew me out the next morning, back to that diner, and that was the end of Celine since Celine didn't put out and she maybe called him a few pretty bad names. He told me to get my stuff out of his Vegas house by noon since I was staying there, which didn't give me much time. He told me Celine was done, gone, adios, he never wanted to see her again."

She shrugged. "And that's it. I didn't get him. I was at five parties and sort of young girls were all over the place, but I didn't catch him roofying anyone. Maybe I should've fucked the fucker at his hideout to stay with him, I don't know."

"No, you shouldn't," Danya said, kissing Shanna's shoulder. Shanna's eyes were on me as Danya did it, a defiant stare with a fair amount of carborundum in it.

"Then you ate at Arlene's," I said, working on the timeline.

"I was hungry," Shanna said. "*Starving*. That asshole flew me out of there early that morning, before I could get anything to eat. The diner was right there. The drive to Vegas would've taken over an hour. So then that waitress came over and called herself Celine."

"Celine?" I said.

"Yeah. There wasn't any sound in that video, but the bitch freaked me out, saying that, told me she'd be my waitress and her name was Celine. She was like fifty or sixty, cigarette smoke in the air around her, in her clothes and hair. But then . . . that was all. She took my order and the cook in back made me an omelet, not a very good one, either. But I guess that old bitch made a video with a hidden camera, like in her hair or clipped to her shirt or something."

"Wonder why she would do that?" Lucy said.

It seemed like a reasonable question, and Lucy hadn't asked it in an aggressive way. A sign of progress?

Shanna shrugged. "Who knows? Maybe because she knew the pilot was Jo-X? Really, I don't see how she couldn't. There's a big metal building in back of the restaurant where he keeps the helicopter. How could he keep himself a secret for however long, like a year or two or three? She's got to know. So then she comes up and calls herself Celine, maybe to see what I'd do? Or"—she looked at me—"maybe my figure sort of gave me away like you suggested, but I doubt it. I think she knows more about Jo-X than about anyone else on the planet."

* * *

Lucy and I left. I gave Danya my cell number, just in case. In case of what, I didn't know, but this investigation had become a Hydra, with tentacles all over the place. No telling what might happen. Too bad I said all that out loud.

"A Hydra has a bunch of heads," Lucy said. "Not tentacles."

"My bad."

"You should keep me around. Learn cool stuff."

CHAPTER SIXTEEN

ROAD RUMBLE AND wind. White noise. Unlike gangsta rap, white noise doesn't interfere with thinking. Gangsta rap inhibits not only all semblance of thought but all emotional growth and maturity. You can see it when cars thump by, emitting rap like a person pounding an empty ten-thousand-gallon water tank with a sledge hammer, the person behind the wheel looking like the reincarnation of Attila the Hun. People who listen to gangsta rap should not be allowed to vote.

Beside me in the passenger seat, Lucy was quiet. The temperature was still in the nineties. The sun had gone behind the hills and high thin clouds were illuminated in orange and rose.

So, white noise and thinking...

Waitress goes outside and makes a video of a girl—Shanna—walking toward a helicopter with a guy dressed like a pilot. Odds are she knows the guy is Jonnie Xenon, has known it for a while. Next day she makes another video of the girl sitting at a table in the diner. The videos end up on a flash drive in Jo-X's pocket in Shanna and Danya's garage, and a note demanding a million dollars ends up in their mailbox. Add it up, big guy. Put two and two together.

Yeah, right. Like this was a two-plus-two deal.

How about this? The waitress kills Jo-X, puts his body in the girls' garage, and demands money? Does that work? Uh-uh. That had so many holes in it I didn't know where to start counting.

Someone put Jo-X in that garage. But who? Couldn't be the newlyweds. That didn't make a lick of sense.

Okay, try this: the waitress is Jo-X's mother, stepmother, aunt. One way or another, they're close. That explains why she's willing to keep a secret that she could sell for tens of thousands. Then why wouldn't Jo-X take Josie to the Midnight Rider Motel right next to Arlene's? Why take her to the Pahranagai Inn?

To keep her away from mom, of course. To keep the police from snooping around mom's place if things went bad with the girl. I doubted he would think that way, but she might—if she knew he was roofying girls, and I had no proof or hint of that.

But, wait. Mom has a son worth thirty million dollars and she lives in a decomposing shack attached to the back of that craphole diner? She's not in a big luxury house somewhere with maids flitting around all day dusting stuff, a cook whipping up culinary delights?

I couldn't see it.

I couldn't see anything. But when you can't figure out where to start, you grab a string and start pulling, so I pulled on the video string. The waitress made two videos. Why make videos of Shanna—or at least of an unknown girl about to meet Jo-X? She might've called herself Celine to see what kind of a reaction it got. That made sense. Maybe Shanna's "figure" had entered into it. Then—how and why had the videos ended up in the dead rapper's pocket?

I was tired. I still didn't have enough information. So much for white noise enhancing thinking. Maybe this one was going to require gangsta rap to figure out.

I missed Ma. She would probably know where to go from here.

Something I'd heard earlier was lodged in my head, but it was staying there. My brain was a clotted mass of disconnected facts.

"Lot of boobs back there," Lucy said, breaking the silence.

"An interesting and salient observation for sure."

"Just sayin'."

"Which is why it's so interesting."

She was quiet for half a mile. Then: "I'm starting to think maybe I got shortchanged."

"Hey, kiddo. I've seen big and I've seen small. You're about as perfect as it gets."

She hit me with a two-hundred-watt smile. "Think so?"

"Yep. You got lucky, hit that happy medium."

She settled back. "Well, okay then. If you think so, then tonight you should rub massage oil on 'em. That'd be nice."

"Be still, my heart."

"You wait. It'll be good for you. Get another knot untied. Good for me, too. Really, there's nothing like a good boob rub."

"I wouldn't know."

"Trust me."

* * *

The sky darkened to cobalt blue. The temperature slipped below ninety. Desert cools off quickly when the sun goes down.

Lucy looked over at me. "You believe any of what those two broads said back there?"

"The best lie is ninety-seven percent true. So, yeah, I believe most of it."

"Ninety-seven percent of it?"

"Yep."

"How'd you come up with ninety-seven percent?"

"Ninety-six percent is an obvious lie, ninety-eight percent gives too much away."

"Oh, jeez."

"Stick with me, kid. Improve your mind."

"Yeah, I feel that happening. So if ninety-seven percent of what they said is true, then three percent is a lie."

"Or missing. When they ducked into the bathroom, they decided how much to tell us."

"So there's more."

"More than just a little. I think that missing three percent is more like twenty-five."

"Your math totally sucks, in case you didn't know."

"Math is like that."

"True."

Stars were starting to appear when the lights of the motel and diner appeared in the gloom, two miles ahead.

"We oughta stay there tonight," Lucy said. "Check this place out. Maybe we'll see that old waitress."

"I was thinking the same thing—if they've got a room. The place only had four units."

"Midnight Rider Motel. Name gives me the willies. We'll have to stay in the same bed so I don't get scared. If this place has scorpions on the ceiling, though, I'm outta there. So, same bed? We did okay last night."

"Dressed like that, you still look seventeen. Was that really your mother yesterday? She wasn't lying? You don't have a sister and the two of you didn't cook up a story?"

She laughed, which wasn't an answer. Scary.

I might have to give Fairchild a call, have him check out Lucy Landry, see how old she really was.

* * *

The sign in front of the motel had the vacancy sign lit, a nice little blood-red glow in the night. A Lexus LX SUV, dusty but new, was in front of unit four, farthest from the diner. Thing was worth nearly ninety thousand dollars, but I figured we could take it in a drag race in the Mustang, easy. It might have power, but it would still accelerate like a tuna boat.

No office at the motel. A sign lit by a tiny light directed us to the diner. Inside, at a glass-front counter, a tall, thin woman who reeked of cigarette smoke took fifty-two dollars and gave us a key to room one. She had a smoker's voice, red hair, gnarled fingers, thin lips, eyes that evaluated the two of us, lingering on Lucy's crochet top. From what Shanna said, that would be the waitress who took the video.

She told us the diner would be open for another half hour. The kitchen shut down at ten. Tonight's special was meat loaf—no doubt warmed over and over for the past three days. Special indeed. Good thing we'd eaten before leaving Caliente.

Back outside, Lucy said softly, "Spooky lady. That's gotta be her. The video waitress."

"Yep. And that's 'gotta be she,' not 'gotta be her.'"

"I'm working on my colloquial English."

"Okay, then. Just don't let it get out of hand."

Room one was a swayback queen-size bed in a twelve-by-twelve room—not much space for morning stretchies. A fifteen-inch color television with a picture tube was anchored to a wall with a chain—an antique, probably worth more now than when it was new. No remote. I didn't know if I still remembered how to run one of those things, turn it on and off, change channels. The bathroom was a rust-stained toilet, old sink, a shower stall with a leaky shower head, a grimy back window that faced west with a view of empty desert and the last dregs of light above low black hills. An overhead bulb put out twenty-five watts, barely enough to keep us from bumping into things. A swamp cooler blew cool humid air into the room with a weary hollow rumble. The whole place looked and felt early nineteen sixties, about the time my mother was running around in diapers. I would have to text her and let her know I was thinking about her. She'd be thrilled.

Lucy bounced on the bed, which I decided is something women do. Maybe they test for squeaks to see if it could be a problem later. "Which side do you want?"

"We could be back at the Luxor in an hour and a half," I said. "An hour and fifteen minutes if I push it."

"And here I thought you were a PI."

"I'm used to nineteenth-century conveniences."

"Which would be the eighteen hundreds, Mort. Outhouses or chamber pots. Not much in the way of TV back then either."

"No television would be a big improvement."

"Of course. Back then, people still knew how to read." She got up and peeked out the window at the highway. "That video of Tits Galore was taken over there in the diner. Which I thought was why we're here, sleuthing like crazy. Which means we have to stay here tonight, so—no Luxor."

"Tits Galore. Nice."

"I forgot her name."

"And sleuthing like crazy. I'll have to remember that."

She looked around. "There's only one bed. No choice about the sleeping arrangement."

"Uh-huh."

"And there appears to be a shower in the bathroom. Water might even come out of it. Don't know how hot, though."

"Rugged little pioneer chick, aren't you?"

She unhitched her top, took it off, and dropped it on the bed. "I thought you were okay with little."

"I'm fine with it. And look at you, Miss Speedy."

She stepped out of her running shorts. "It's been a hot day. You up for a shower?"

"Go ahead. I'm going to have a look-see around this place before it gets completely dark."

She stood there in bare feet and panties. The look on her face might have been disappointment. "I could get dressed again," she said. "Go with you."

I was still wearing dark khaki shorts and the green shirt. "I was thinking of keeping a low profile. In that white top you'd stand out like a beacon. I'll be back in a while."

I went out the door, left her standing there, then looked around at the night. Empty highway, sliver of moon hanging over the western hills, fluorescent lights in the diner, small floodlights illuminating an old sign on the roof that read *Arlene's Diner*, temperature still dropping, faint breeze drifting in from the west. Country and western music was playing so far away it was like an aural hallucination.

Dim light leaked between curtains from unit four. The Lexus parked in front of the room reflected tiny pinpoints of light.

I went around behind the motel and let my eyes adjust to the night, which took a while. The moon looked like a tooth, stuck in the black top of a hill. A minute later it was gone.

My cell phone rang. I'd forgotten I had it with me. Not a good idea to have phones ringing in the night when you're trying to skulk around.

"What's up, Ma?" I said quietly after checking the screen.

"Just makin' sure you're not gettin' into any more trouble, boyo."

"Who, me?"

Silence. "Okay, that don't sound good. Where are you?"

"At a motel between Caliente and Vegas."

"There ain't nothin' between Caliente and Vegas except Gila monsters and vultures."

"And a motel. And a diner. Not sure about Gila monsters, Ma. I'm thinking that's New Mexico."

"What the *hell* are you doin' down there? Do I want to know what you're up to?"

"Probably not."

"Okay, then. You're fired." She hung up.

She was so cool, I could hardly stand it.

I was about to turn the phone off when "Monster Mash" started up again. "Sonofabitch," I hissed. "Yeah? What?"

"You find anything yet?" Russell asked.

My favorite pudgy cop, talk about luck. I looked around, didn't see anyone headed my way to check out my new ringtone. "Workin' on it, Detective."

"That's not what I asked, Angel."

"If I find anything that you oughta know, I'll let you know."

"*Anything* you find out, I oughta know about it."

"Well, okay, if you insist, pi is approximately three point one four two. Got that last year from Holiday. There'll be a quiz on that in the morning, so study up."

He disconnected. Maybe he knew Ma.

I called him right back.

"*Yeah?*"

"I need you to check on someone. Name's Lucy Landry."

"Lucy? That assistant you 'came across'? I thought you said you trust her."

"I do. A lot. Just get her birthday for me."

"Birthday?"

"Date of birth, Russ. Month, day, year."

"I know that," he growled. "What I want to know is *why*."

"If I miss it and don't get her a gift, I'll never hear the end of it. You know women."

"Oh, for Christ's sake."

"Do it, Russ. Get back to me within ten minutes. She's got a California driver's license, if that helps. Middle initial K."

I ended the call.

The night pressed in dark and quiet around me. I set the phone on vibrate, then walked slowly around the back of the diner. The ground was black on black. Maybe I would get lucky and not fall into an open pit.

CHAPTER SEVENTEEN

MEANWHILE, BUDDIE WAS rubbing Arlene's feet, as he did every night about this time. Her feet hurt, even if she wasn't on her feet all that much. She didn't do much waitressing. She had Melanie for that. The cook and his wife lived in the trailer behind the diner. Melanie was the dimmest of a wide selection of low-wattage bulbs, but the cook, Kirby, didn't glow much brighter. Both were in their twenties, neither of them a high school graduate. Melanie also did the rooms at the motel in the morning, at which time Arlene had to do the waitress thing. Mostly she ran the cash register for the diner and the motel, ordered supplies, kept the diner and motel stocked up—food and sheets, little bars of soap. Buddie did basic maintenance around the place and ran the backhoe as far away as Hiko to the north, Moapa to the south, which brought in nearly twice as much money as the diner and motel combined.

Except, maybe . . .

Room four.

Room four was the cash cow. Four was the retirement fund, or so Arlene had thought in the beginning when she first came up with the idea. But it hadn't worked out quite as well as she'd hoped it would, back when she told Buddie to install two video cameras with lenses so small they looked like fly specks up in the corners of the ceiling. He'd also installed the microphones and put the wireless in the wall. He could use a drill, do basic tasks if they weren't too complicated. Arlene had had to hook up the system to the monitor in their private living space in the diner's back rooms where Melanie and Kirby weren't allowed.

Arlene's eyes were closed. A cigarette burned in a corner of her mouth. This was the best time of the day, Buddie rubbing the pain out of her feet—maybe there was something to that foot reflexology crap after all, she thought. What was it about feet that connected them to other parts of the body? Rub a certain spot and it helped settle the liver? Did she really believe that? Oh, but it felt so good. And her son, Buddie Junior—Big Bud dead of an altercation with a lawn mower twenty-three years ago, the dumb ass—had worked on her feet from the time he was eight years old, twenty-six years ago, when he was just a little thing. Now he was six-seven, a three-hundred-fifty-pound monster, but pretty good with a Case 695ST backhoe digging septics and trenches, and great with his big hands on her feet, kneading out the pain. Twenty-six years of it, he knew what she liked.

"Got that nice Lexus outside four," Buddie said, breaking the silence.

"Uh-huh. Don't stop."

"Think the guy's worth it? It's been a long time. Ten months since we got us one."

"Maybe." Arlene's eyes were still closed. "Let's hope." She sent a stream of smoke toward the ceiling. Ten months. About average. The longest had been sixteen months between catches. Longer than she'd thought when they'd started, thinking they'd catch one every month or two. But maybe it was for the best. So far the law had never come around, at least not in any official capacity, although her heart about skipped a beat whenever a cruiser pulled in, Nevada Highway Patrol guys coming in to eat. Which didn't happen often. Arlene's Diner was a last resort.

"What'd you see?" Buddie asked.

"Money belt. He put it under the mattress."

"Yeah? That's good. Sure wish we could sell the car, though. That'd be worth a lot. Lot more than the belt, most likely."

"We've talked about that, Buddie."

"I know. Still wish we could."

He was an idiot. She found it hard to be patient. "Not easy to do something like that and not have cops all over us."

"Big sonofabitch, that Lexus."

She laid back, sighing as Buddie's thumb worked a groove up the sole of her right foot.

"When will he be completely out?" Buddie asked. He looked at the monitor. Looked like the guy was out now, crashed on the bed. But he'd had trouble in the past when he'd gone in too soon. Trouble made noise. He liked it quiet and easy.

"Better plan on midnight, maybe one o'clock."

"After the *Tonight Show*," Buddie said. "Good deal. Hate it when I miss that." He stood up and stretched his back. "It's gettin' late. I better get the backhoe out there, ready to go."

"You do that, Sweetheart."

"We got someone in one," Buddie said. "I seen a car."

"Some guy about forty and a young girl looks like she's a high-end hooker, outfit she was wearing. Don't see any money there. I put them as far away from Four as I could."

"Okay, good."

Just then the buzzer for the motel rang, doorbell push-button on the jamb to the restaurant, someone wanting a room.

"Hell," Arlene muttered, putting her feet into flip-flops. "It's like frickin' Grand Central Station around here tonight."

Not good, but she really wanted that money belt.

CHAPTER EIGHTEEN

I HEARD A car engine moments before headlights swept over the ground between the diner and the motel, illuminating gravel, weeds, dirt, aluminum cans. Then the engine went silent.

Footsteps on gravel, a moment of quiet, then they headed for the diner. I stood in shadow at the back corner of the motel as Vince Ignacio appeared in a pale wash of light spilling from the diner's windows.

The Wharf Rat. Terrific.

I went around the front and saw a red Chevrolet Cruze nosed in between the Mustang and the Lexus.

I wanted to keep my night vision intact, so I waited in the lee of the building. Six or eight minutes later, Ignacio came out and headed back toward the motel.

"Hsssst."

He stopped, night blind. "Who's there?"

"Over here, Vince."

He hesitated, peering into the gloom. I came closer, grabbed him by the front of his shirt, and hauled him squawking into the darkness behind the motel. I told him to shut up, rammed the suggestion home with a knuckle to his chest as I pinned him to the back wall.

"What're you doin' here, Ignacio?" I asked. I almost called him Wharf.

Took him a moment to recover, then he said, "Hey, it's still a free country, Mr. Angel. I'm just ridin' the highways."

"Sure you are."

"You could turn loose of my shirt."

"I could, but I won't. I told you you couldn't use that picture of me. So now I've got this big sonofabitching lawsuit in the works. Once the dust settles, I'm gonna be rich. I figure you made a bundle with those Jo-X pictures."

That slowed him down for a few seconds.

"Didn't hear nothin' about any lawsuit," he said.

"You'll get the subpoena when they finally track you down. If I were you, I'd be thinking Brazil, maybe Uruguay."

He chuckled. Which meant he was over the shock of being dragged off into the night. "Subpoena. I'll believe it when I see it. Anyway, you finally got that 'Celine' thing nailed down, right? Things come together for you today in Caliente? Like maybe you're not engaged to her like you said?" He snickered. "I still don't think you're her type . . . Stud."

Man, I hate it when intimidation fades off into burlesque and low comedy. The sky was nothing but stars, Milky Way glowing bright. White as he was, Vince's face was a pale blob against the black side of the motel. Good thing I couldn't see his grin.

I heard distant scuffling noises, then the big backhoe's diesel engine fired up, thirty yards behind the diner, beyond the shed I'd been forced to use as an outhouse earlier. Headlights came on. The rig backed off its trailer, warning beeper chirping away.

I shoved Ignacio toward the front of the motel. "Keep away from me," I said. "Keep following and I'll put you in a dumpster somewhere and lock the sonofabitchin' lid down."

He went. I watched him scuttle ratlike around the back of his Cruze. I went behind the motel again to see what this backhoe business was all about. Who fires up a backhoe this late at night?

I stood in the dark, watching. The backhoe swiveled and bounced, headlights briefly illuminating the helicopter shed, then it surged away, churned west into empty desert, lights dipping and swaying over the uneven ground. It went out a little beyond the helicopter shed, then stopped. Moments later the engine died, lights went out, and the night was quiet again.

My phone vibrated.

"Yeah?" I said softly.

Fairchild gave me Lucy's birthday. She was born on April Fool's day. Interesting. And the planet for Aries was Mars—the planet that *wasn't* lined up with four others when she was born. Also interesting.

Russ said, "She's thirty-one. Isn't that a little young for you?"

"In what way, Russ? She's my assistant. How old does an assistant have to be?"

"Yeah, right. I pulled up her picture. She's an assistant like I'm Brad Pitt."

"Not sure that analogy works, but if it makes you happy, use it." I hung up.

Thirty-one. Yes, indeed, I was hopeless with ages, but I had a hell of a girl on my hands.

I waited in the dark. Three minutes. Four. Then a dark figure emerged in the night and went into the back of the diner, where the owner lived. Looked tall. Huge, actually. Had to be that big guy with the beard I'd seen earlier that day.

Again, the land went deathly quiet. Then that ethereal sound of western music got me moving quietly around the back of the diner, alert for further signs of activity.

As I passed the shed, the music got louder, coming from the vicinity of the house trailer.

I walked closer, not knowing what to expect. If anyone asked, it was a nice night and I was out for a stroll. Weak, yellow light came from the trailer's windows. I was circling around the far side of the diner when a woman's low voice said, "Whatcha doin'?"

"Walking," I said. I couldn't see her. I headed toward the sound of her voice.

"Pretty dark out for walkin'." Sounded young, a lot younger than the fiftysomething lady in the diner who'd taken our money for the room and very likely made the Shanna videos.

"Uh-huh. Stars are bright though."

"Always are, out here. Most nights, anyways."

Finally I saw her, a dark shape in what might've been a lawn chair beside the trailer. The end of a cigarette flared as she took a drag, then it was just a dim red-orange glow again, like a firefly about out of gas.

"You live here?" I asked.

"Uh-huh." Silence. Then, "You in the motel?"

"Room One," I said.

"Shower head in there drippin' all the time."

"That's the one."

Five seconds of quiet, then, "Anyways, hi. I'm Melanie. Not many folks come out back here, 'specially in the dark like this."

"Mort," I said.

"What's a mort?"

"That's my name."

"Funny name. Sounds like, I dunno, some kind of a bug."

"Blame my mother."

She laughed. "I do the rooms. Cleanin'. In the morning if the people're gone. Then I waitress all day till six or seven. Later if we got enough business. That don't happen often, though."

"You work a lot."

"Not so much. Four rooms is all. Half the time nobody rents one, even in summer. Diner is empty a lot, too."

She wanted to talk. Good. "I've heard there's a helicopter that comes and goes out there in the desert." I was at the edge of a yellow glow emanating from a window. I pointed out behind the diner.

"Yeah, it does."

"Know whose it is?"

"Nope. Just some tall skinny guy's."

"I think a girl flew out with him a while back. Not long ago. Maybe a week or two."

"Yeah, I remember that. Girl was in the diner for about an hour, had an ice tea, then off she goes with that guy."

"Were you her waitress?"

"Nope. Arlene tole me to take a break, said she'd handle it."

"So, the guy left with the girl, then he flew her back the next morning."

Melanie was quiet for a moment, then: "I don't think so."

"No?"

"Uh-uh. I mean, she come back all right, but in a car. One of those SV whatchamacallits."

"SUV?"

"Yeah, that. It was a big one. Black."

"She didn't fly back?"

"Nope. Some guy at the motel left early. I was doin' the room when that girl come back in what you called it, that SVW? Big one—almost like new."

"Tall girl? Blond?"

"Yep. Great big titties, too, like holy Jesus big."

Nothing identified Shanna like her breasts.

"Pink streak in her hair?" I said.

"Uh-huh. You know 'er?"

"I've seen her around. She been in here before?"

"Don't think so. I'm here 'bout always. My man's the cook. Kirby. He's twenty-seven. I'll be twenty-four in August."

"Hey, if I don't see you in August, happy birthday."

"Yeah, right. Twenty-four. I'll be freakin' old."

Which made me what? Prehistoric?

"Anyway," Melanie said, "that helicopter guy come back later that afternoon. He flew in, walked over from that building out there, kinda hunched over like he was hurting, and took off in that black car, the one the girl left. She was already gone, drove off in a car she left overnight outside the diner."

"You remember all that?"

She shrugged. "Ain't much goin' on here. I pay attention to stuff. Like in that shed back of the diner there's a safe Arlene bought like a week ago on Craigslist, except she didn't get the combination so she can't open it. Not like her to be dumb like that, not get the combination to open it for chrissake. So then this guy had to come out all the way from Henderson to look at it, try to bust it open or something. It still ain't open yet. He's gonna try again in a couple days. Kirby tole me about it since he works in the kitchen an' the storeroom in back with the shelves and the freezers. Heard 'em talking in a back room, Arlene an' her kid, Buddie."

"Buddie. Guy with a beard? Big guy?"

"Like holy Jesus big, yeah."

A safe. I would have to think about that.

"Helicopter guy looked like he was hurting, huh?" I said.

"Pretty much. Looked like he got kicked in the balls. Hard, too. Like you see in the movies, guy gets kicked. Except in real life they don't get up so fast an' keep on fightin'."

"Which way'd he go when he drove away?"

She pointed. "That way. Toward Vegas. Came back like four hours later, late afternoon. Looked like he was feeling better. He flew off in that chopper." She took another drag and blew out a stream of smoke that hung almost motionless in the air. "Christ, I hope I don't get knocked up an' have a kid to keep track of, too. That'd be a bitch and a half, everything else I gotta do."

* * *

So, Jo-X had flown back in, hunched over. Maybe kicked in the nuts. Sounded like his luck with Shanna was quite a bit worse than she'd told us. That morning she'd returned in an SUV, not in his helicopter like she said. Another lie.

And the woman who ran the place bought a safe without the combination. If I bought a safe, Craigslist or new, I'd be sure I could open it before I took delivery. I looped around the front of the diner and went back to the motel. In the room, Lucy was in a towel too small to wrap and tuck. She held it pinched at her waist as she glared at me. She needed another towel, but I didn't point that out since her feathers appeared to be ruffled.

"Find out anything?" she asked. "You've been gone half an hour."

"As a matter of fact, I did."

Her voice softened. "What? A car pulled up out front while you were gone. It was Timothy Olyphant, wasn't it?"

"Close," I said. "It was the Wharf Rat."

Took her a few seconds to process that. "Wharf rat. That's that scrawny guy in Reno you said took a picture of you?"

"The very same."

"Well, hell. That's interesting."

"Ain't it?"

"Ain't ain't a word."

I squinted at her. "That was irony, wasn't it? I have trouble with irony."

"Uh-huh. So, where's the rat now?"

"Probably six feet away, right through that wall." I pointed. "He might have his ear stuck to a glass against the wall."

Lucy hit the wall with the pad of her fist. "Take that, Rat."

"So, how about we keep it down in here?" I said. "Unless you want to end up on the front page of a tabloid."

"What else did you find out?" Lucy whispered.

"A big backhoe went out into the desert, then stopped."

"A backhoe? Wow, News at Eleven. Hope you got video."

"And the gal who cleans the rooms here said Shanna didn't fly back that morning like she said she did. She drove herself. In a black SUV."

Lucy thought about that for a moment. "The girl who cleans the rooms told you that? She could be wrong."

"I don't think so. She lives here. Don't think she has a PhD in anything, but she was pretty specific. What she said and the way she said it rang true."

"So, Shanna lied."

"Apparently."

"I wonder why. Might have to give that some thought."

"Or track her down and ask."

"That'd work. But now, how about that shower?" She let the towel unwind and held it in one hand.

"You didn't get wet and clean while I was gone?"

"Uh-uh. I waited for you. The shower looks spooky. In fact this whole place is like that, including the name. I got scared, figured I needed someone in the shower with me to keep me safe and maybe help scrub these."

Aw, jeez.

* * *

I never served in the military. Worse, I was an Internal Revenue thug for sixteen long years, so I'd done more damage to the country than good. Eventually I discovered I had a soul. But a guy by the name of Warley Sullivan was still at the IRS, and he was born without a soul and never managed to acquire one along the way. He was fifty-four, six foot two, had a beak nose and vulture's eyes, and had never married since no one would have him, for good reason. His greatest joy was finding that mom and pop hadn't paid enough in taxes four years ago and the penalties and interest had added up enough to make Christmas a mean season for their three kids. I figured I could finally contribute to the welfare of the country by giving him details about that shower with Lucy, at which point Warley would be forced to kill himself. It would be like having served in the Marines.

* * *

News at Eleven: Backhoe in the desert.

Lucy was snugged up against me like before, fast asleep. She wasn't ready for things to go beyond that point. Couldn't say I was either. Lucy wanted closeness, warmth, contact. We hadn't known each other forty-eight hours yet. This was only our second night together, though it seemed like a long week. It might have come as a surprise to her that abstinence suited me—if I'd told her—but some things are better left unsaid. Naked and wet, she looked nineteen. Or eighteen. A nymph. My daughter, Nicole, is twenty-one. Lucy had ten years on her, verified so many times I finally had to accept it. It was still a stretch to see her that old. Impossible, really, but in fact she was two years older than Jeri would have been, so this thing, whatever it was, wasn't the worst thing that had happened to me recently.

The shower took place quietly, though, because Wharf Rat was in the room next door. That put a little damper on things, for which I would have to thank him later without telling him why.

Midnight came and went. I was still awake at 12:55. Lucy was warm, breathing so softly I could barely hear her. We were covered by a sheet and a thin blanket. Every fifteen or twenty minutes a vehicle of some kind blew by on the highway creating a brief flare of light on the walls and ceiling.

Lucy had one of those bodies you don't get tired of seeing. If she had an ounce out of place, I didn't know where it was. If she needed an ounce more, I wouldn't have known where to put it. And, how about focusing on the case, Mort?

Okay . . . Shanna hadn't come back in Jo-X's helicopter. She'd driven herself back in a big black SUV, which apparently belonged to the dipshit himself.

She'd lied.

I wondered why.

Later that same day, Jo-X had flown in, evidently in pain, and taken that SUV south, toward Vegas. Came back four hours later and flew away in the helicopter. No black SUV anywhere around now, so it had been driven away. By whom?

The rear window of the bathroom was open a few inches to let in fresh air. It also let in the distant sound of a diesel engine snorting to life. Being a world-class gumshoe, I lifted Lucy's arm off my chest and rolled out from under, got to my feet to check on the continuing late-night action out back.

I put on jeans sans underwear, shoes sans socks, then went out into the night sans shirt. The Lexus was no longer in front of the motel. The red Cruze was there, so Vinny was in his room. The temperature had finally dropped into the high sixties.

I went around to the back of the motel. The backhoe was lumbering away, moving farther out into the desert.

"Where do you think it's going?" the Wharf Rat said in the dark, not six feet away.

I nearly jumped out of my skin, which is an expression I hate but understand better now. I was surprised my hide wasn't lying in folds on the ground.

But the shock wore off quickly and there we were, together in the night, sharing the weirdness of the backhoe headed away from us, taillights looking like the eyes of a vampire bat. For a moment I had the eerie sensation that Ignacio and I were pals, sharing this unlikely apparition.

"Dunno," I said after a few deep breaths to get my voice right. "What time is it?"

Vince checked his watch. "One fifteen."

"That Lexus is gone. Guy who was in the end room."

"I heard it start up. Half an hour ago. Didn't see which way it went."

I shrugged, a gesture Vince didn't catch in the dark. The Lexus wasn't my concern. We stood there another five minutes, watching, not talking. The backhoe was out about a half mile, well beyond Jo-X's helicopter shed, no longer moving away. Its lights were small in the distance. The diesel engine revved up and down. No doubt it was digging, but why?

"Kinda strange," I said.

"Probably putting in an outhouse."

"That'd be my guess. Long walk to go potty, but it would keep the smell down, so, yeah—outhouse for sure."

"Whatever it is, I'll bet it's nice to get the work done when it isn't a hundred twenty degrees out."

"That's a thought."

More silence. Finally, he said, "I'm not really a bad guy, Mr. Angel. I just, you know, work for a tabloid. I know they suck if you have half a brain, and my job is pure trash to most normal people, but I'm good at it and it pays really well. Like twenty times better than waiting tables, which I've done."

"How'd you figure out Celine? And when?"

"Two weeks after she first showed up on Xenon's arm. She got lonely or something and drove up to Tonopah to visit that other girl, Danya, who'd driven down from Reno to be with her. I followed Celine up there. She left Xenon's place as a black girl and ended up in Tonopah pure white. They stayed the night at a motel, then Celine went back to Vegas. She was black again. I didn't know anything about that other girl, so I followed her. She went back to Reno. I found out where they live and did some checking, found out Celine's real name is Shanna Hayes and that she married Danya Fuller in April. Then I went back to Vegas to stay on Celine, see what else I could find out."

"You kept all of that to yourself the past two weeks?"

"Had to. Break a story too soon and you lose the best part of it forever. Things shut down. Other people move in on it. I had that happen a few years ago, lost the best half of a big story. The only way I would break this one before I've got it nailed down is if someone else was about to. I keep a close watch on things, but no one's been on Shanna's tail except you, and all you do is find dead people, so I figure I'm the only one near it so far."

A finder of dead people. Catchy. Something to have carved on my headstone. I would have to get that in my will.

"You think there's more to Celine's story than what you've got now?" I asked.

"Sure. She's married to that girl, Danya. So why was she with Jo-X? What was that all about? My guess is that's the real story. I don't want to let out what I've got before I get all of it."

"How are you following these people?"

"Just . . . practice. It's what I do—following people. Well, one of the things. I've been doing it for years."

Good at it, too. The sonofabitch oughta work for me. Or Ma.

I said, "Then Xenon disappeared, and the girls live in Reno. How'd you end up here? This motel, of all places. And Caliente."

"Long story, sorta."

"I've got nothing but time. Let's hear it."

"Celine was the key to the story, so I stayed on her. I mean, Xenon's been around for years, but Celine was new, big, hot. I followed her from Xenon's Vegas mansion a second time. She stopped off the highway for a while, finally ended up here, white, not black, and flew off in a helicopter. I didn't know what that was all about. I watched from the highway with binoculars. I didn't know who the pilot was or where he and Shanna were going. I waited all that day for her to come back, then finally got a room at the motel here when it started to get dark. I was tired. Nothing was happening. I figured when the helicopter returned, it would wake me up and I'd get back on Celine's tail.

"But it never did. I woke up about ten that next morning. Celine's car was gone and a black SUV was parked where her car used to be. So I missed her. I would've woke up for sure if that helicopter came back, so I didn't know what had happened. I went back to Vegas. Two days later, Xenon missed a big concert in Seattle. Celine was missing, too, media starting to go crazy, no one knew what was going on, so I went back to Reno.

"Then that girl, Danya, spotted me at their house so she took off, but I followed her to a motel on Fourth Street. She got a room. Knew where she was, so I went back to their house to try to pick up that other girl, Shanna. The back door was unlocked so I called out names, got no answer, so I went in. Then you showed up and chased me off after roughing me up."

"Sorry about that."

"Uh-huh. You owe me an SD card—thirty-two gigs. Then Shanna came back. After a while you found Jo-X in that garage and Shanna scooted. Fast, too. I got pictures, then you came after me. I went back to the motel where Danya had checked in. Her car was still there. I waited half a block up the street, all day and all night. Pizza guy showed up at the motel. The girls never came out. They didn't come out until that next afternoon, then they got into a different car that some college-looking guy left before he took off in their car, which was weird. They went to that bank—I saw you there in the parking lot—then they took off, went out to Sparks and ditched that car, got into Danya's car again, which had been parked a block away. They took off, and I followed them all the way from there to Caliente. Easy. Duck soup."

"On little or no sleep?"

He put a shrug in his voice. "It's what I do. Red Bull's a lifesaver. One time I stayed up for seventy-five hours. Had to. Just have to ignore the more lurid hallucinations. After one of those, I crashed for twenty-two hours, which is a little disorienting when you finally wake up. So, who's the girl with you?"

"About her—keep your distance or I'll put you in the hospital. I can almost believe you and I might end up friends, but mess with her and you'll spend a month in traction."

"Okay, then. Forget I asked."

"Where'd the expression 'duck soup' come from?"

"I Googled it a few years ago. Turns out, no one knows."

"You Googled it?"

"Sure. You can find out anything on the Internet."

"Except where 'duck soup' came from."

"Yeah. Except that. If I ever find out, I'll let you know."

CHAPTER NINETEEN

SUNRISE WAS AT 4:58 a.m. It started as a bright orange spark of
light in a notch in the eastern hills. The Lexus was still gone—as
I'd expected. The backhoe-loader was back on its trailer behind
the diner. All was quiet. Ignacio's Cruze was still in front of the
motel. No sign of the Rat.

By five fifteen, Lucy and I were back on the road, headed
north. It was eighty miles to Caliente, and I wanted to catch the
girls by surprise. The temperature was still in the sixties. I had the
top up on the Mustang and the heater on low since Lucy was in
jogging shorts and that crochet top, which was about as warm as
wearing nothing at all.

We got to the Pahranagai Inn at six thirty. I knocked on the
door to room nine. A minute later the peephole went dark, then
the door was opened by a sleepy-eyed Danya.

"This better be awful goddamn good," she said with a growl
in her voice, possibly because she was in panties and no top, but
maybe that was just who she was in the wee hours.

"It is." I bulled my way past her. She followed me and Lucy followed her. Shanna was in bed with the covers up to her chin.

"What I'm wondering," I said to her while Danya worked a
T-shirt on over her head, "is why you lied about Jo-X flying you
back to that motel and diner the next morning."

"Who says I lied?"

"I have sources. And you lied."

"What sources?"

"They shall remain nameless, but you *lied*, Shanna." In fact, she might not have lied. The girl last night, Melanie, could've been mistaken, but I didn't think so, so I was putting on the pressure.

And, as expected, Shanna caved.

"Okay. So Jo-X didn't fly me back. So what?"

"So I'm wondering *why* you lied."

A moment of hesitation, then: "Because I roofied the rotten son of a bitch, that's why. Which is none of your business and I didn't want to advertise it, especially since he turned up dead."

I stared at her. "You roofied him?"

"Uh-huh. Probably the last thing that asshole ever expected, it happening to him. I asked around and got it from some loser guy at one of Jo-X's parties, just in case, hoping I would get a chance to use it, which didn't seem likely. But then Jo-X invited me to his hideout, so that was perfect."

"No one else around? Just you two?"

"Just us. He doesn't have anyone up there on a regular basis, like maids or cooks or anything. I think he gets fuel delivered, and maintenance guys probably come up to do stuff on occasion, but he's got the place looking like it's sort of a drug rehab facility so delivery people and workers don't ask questions."

"Drug rehab. Perfect."

"Thing is," Shanna said, "if it ever got out that I roofied him up there, people might think I killed him when he was out cold, so if you want to know why I lied, that's why."

"So you didn't kill him?" I knew she hadn't, since Jo-X had flown back later that day, according to Melanie, but it's never a good idea to give out too much information.

"No, I did not. What I did, if you must know, I super-glued his cock to his belly."

I gaped at her. "You did *what*?"

"Put a big glob of superglue on his dick and stuck it to his belly, aimed up. The fucker. Glue takes like two seconds to bond flesh to flesh. Then I left him a note explaining why, told him to think twice before he raped girls. It was sort of like *he* got raped, but not nearly as bad as what he did to Josie. Until he got his dick unstuck, he'd be pissing himself. He's lucky I didn't glue his dick *shut*, 'cause I thought about it. Then I found the keys to his SUV and drove out. Only one road into the place, so that was easy. Anyway, he was fine when I left him, except for the glue. But obviously someone killed him. A guy like that's got to have a ton of enemies, so it looks like someone finally got to him."

"And strung him up in your garage."

"Which is so bizarre I don't know what to think about it."

Bizarre, yes. She'd been standing behind me when I tried to open the padlock on the garage and the hasp had fallen out, no key needed. She didn't see it happen. She didn't know the lock was jimmied. Anyone could have put Jo-X in their garage. It also meant whoever did it didn't have access to a key.

"Why would anyone think you could pay a million dollars?" I asked.

"She was Celine," said Lucy the Trainee, nodding at Shanna. "Whoever put him in the garage probably knew that."

"Well, hell," Danya muttered.

"Yeah, what'd that pay?" I asked. I gave Lucy's waist a little squeeze. Good job.

"Not enough," Shanna said.

"You told him you would do it for the money. It must have been enough to convince him. How much?"

She shrugged. "I got twenty a concert."

"Twenty?"

She stared at me like I was the guy texting who walked off a cliff. "Twenty *thousand*. What'd you think? Twenty bucks?"

Great. Love it when a gorgeous girl puts a sneer in her voice.

"And," she added, "a thousand a day, just to go around with him, be seen, wear revealing clothes."

"How many concerts?" I asked.

"I went to four."

Eighty thousand. "Did you get the money up front?"

"What d'you think?"

"She did," Lucy said. "For sure." Shanna shot her a baleful look, then nodded.

"How many days were you with him?" I asked.

"Nineteen or twenty. About that. I didn't get my thousand a day for those."

Kids hadn't written that note. It was someone who thought the girls had money. Might not have known how much, though.

"Anyway," I said, "there's a road into Jo-X's place and *you* know where it is."

"It's not like it's invisible from the highway. But it's just a dirt track with 'No Trespassing' signs and a wire gate. The gate isn't locked or anything. It's one of those wire loop things. Then, if you get up into the hills, still like about three miles from the house, there's a sign saying the place is a private hospital or something, like a detox place, and Keep Out signs are all over. And there's one of those tire-shredding things, and a call box and a camera so they can see who's there if someone shows up and wants in."

"He's got a tire shredder?"

"Uh-huh. Like those ugly steel teeth you see in parking lots where they warn you not to back up. I figure there's got to be a switch or something in the house that someone can throw to lower the teeth. If you tried to drive over it going up to Jo-X's place, you'd blow all your tires. And they put big rocks beside the shredder and dug trenches. All that is right at the mouth of a canyon. It'd be hard to get up there in a car or truck if someone didn't want you there."

* * *

After Shanna had driven Jo-X's SUV out of his hideaway, he'd flown out in his helicopter. Then, according to Melanie, he'd walked hunched over to his SUV. Now I knew he might've had something tugging on his pecker. Like his belly. Talk about your basic all-purpose revenge move. But it still wasn't as bad as Lorena Bobbitt's solution to life's little ups and downs. Lorena and her Ginsu knives had spawned a song: "Lorena's in the car takin' Willie for a ride." She was born in Quito, Ecuador. Maybe they did things differently down there. Like cut off the offending member and chuck it out a window on the way to Walmart.

Hurts just to think about it. Superglue was bad, but not that bad. I wondered where Lorena was now, if she had found another boyfriend or if guys were keeping their distance.

Back on the road, top down on the Mustang. Lucy and I had eaten breakfast at the casino on Front Street in Caliente and were on the road by eight twenty, temperature already approaching ninety.

I looked for the turnoff to Jo-X's hideaway, thought I spotted what might be it, but wasn't sure. Shanna told us it was on the west side of the highway, eight or ten miles north of Arlene's Diner and the Midnight Rider Motel.

Speaking of which, as we passed Arlene's, Lucy was sitting up on the back of the seat with her top off, eyes closed, and we were doing fifty-five miles an hour. And Ignacio was in front of his motel room with what looked like a cup of coffee in his hand, eyes bugging out as we blew on by.

*   *   *

We reached the Vegas city limits at ten fifteen. Lucy put her top on two miles before we reached I-15, but she had a forty-mile top-less run in good morning sun, hair blowing around in the blast of wind. I was inordinately proud of the fact that I'd looked up at her only eight or ten times and whistled at her only once when I caught her with her back arched and her eyes closed.

In my white wig and moustache, I valet-parked the Mustang at the Luxor and we went inside. I kept the key that opened the lockbox in the trunk. It might raise eyebrows if some curious kid were to open it and find guns and disguise paraphernalia.

In our suite we found two maids working on the room. There wasn't much to do since we hadn't been there in twenty-four hours, hadn't used the towels or the bed. I gave them each fifty dollars and chased them out.

"Jacuzzi," Lucy said, shedding clothes as if they were on fire. "The shower in that motel sucked."

"I thought you had fun."

"I did. A lot. But the water was only tepid and the pressure was low. Now get naked, Mort."

"Naked? *Moi*?"

"People often bathe naked. It's like a custom." She came over, pulled my head down, and gave me a kiss. "But I'm not a tease and this is still just getting clean, nothing else, I mean nothing that you'd call exercise or aerobic—so you don't actually *have* to participate if it would leave you unfulfilled and unhappy. But you did earlier, participate, I mean, so I'm kind of making an assumption. Sometime later, not sure when yet, it's likely I will 'put out' as the old saying goes—if you want, that is, and I hope you do when the time comes, and if you think Holiday wouldn't freak out—which from everything you've told me she probably wouldn't—but right now we need to scrub off about three hundred miles of desert dust."

"Impressive. I believe you said all that in one breath."

"Good lungs."

"It's called logorrhea."

"You probably think I don't know what that means."

I gave her a long up-and-down look. "Are you *sure* you're thirty-one, kiddo? You don't look twenty-one."

"You should get naked."

* * *

Which I did, and the next thirty or forty minutes were a lot of fun. And I've been trained in the art of enjoying the sights without having to take a role more active than helping to get chests really clean, a skill at which I believe I have become more skilled than the average Joe since practice makes perfect.

After the Jacuzzi and shower and toweling off, Lucy piled into a bed and suggested that it would be nice if I piled in after her and held her for a while. Being a good sport about such things, I piled in and let the world of wharf rats and dead gangsta rappers and spooky motels drift off into mental vapor.

We stayed like that for about half an hour, during which time I contemplated, drowsily but happily, what it had meant to dump the IRS and become a world-famous gumshoe. Tried to, anyway.

Then Lucy fell asleep and so did I.

*   *   *

"We should lose ten thousand dollars," Lucy said. She was on the floor, doing splits that would've torn every tendon and muscle in my body from crotch to toes, so I didn't join in.

"Right. Exactly what I was thinking."

She laughed. "Not. You were looking at my boobs."

"Okay, Lucifer, why should we drop ten Gs?"

"Lucifer, cool. To keep the suite, of course."

I thought about that. Did we need the suite? I liked it, but the investigation appeared to be relocating itself to Arlene's Diner or Caliente or points in between—like Jo-X's hideaway if we could find it. But the suite was fantastic, free, and only an hour and a half drive from the Midnight Rider. Besides, losing ten thousand dollars? I couldn't imagine that much fun.

We got eleven chips, thousand bucks each, cashed one, and she bought another baby-doll outfit—white jogging shorts and a white tank top with spaghetti straps. She was into white clothing. The top was short at both ends—that is to say, both high and low. The plunge neckline exposed enough breast to turn heads, and three inches of exceptionally tight belly showed. She wore white sandals. White looked terrific on her. She was an extremely hot little baby-doll bimbo, having fun with Daddy's life savings. I told her so and got a big smile with a hint of promise in it.

She tucked an arm through mine and we drew stares—well, she did—as we went through the casino to the same roulette table, which caused a hefty-looking pit boss to ease over. The ball was already whirring around its track when Lucy plunked down a thousand-dollar chip on red, said, "Red, red, red," and the ball came up black, and someone said, "Well, shuckins."

Not the same pit boss, but he'd evidently been schooled in the ways of Daddy's Girl. He looked worried. Lucy put down another thousand on black, said, "Black, black, black," and the ball bounced into a red slot and stayed there.

"Well, *shuckins*, Daddy," she said, pouting up at me.

Then she put all the rest of the chips down, four on red, four on black. Wow. I felt my eyes bug out.

"Uh, Honey Bunch . . ." I said.

She reached up and put a finger on my lips, said, "Shhh, I'm gonna win *somethin'*, Daddy," and I saw the pit boss smile.

The ball whirred and the wheel spun and Lucy said, "C'mon, c'mon, c'mon," and the girl running the wheel gave me a look like I was with the world's all-time dumbest bimbo and therefore I was the world's all-time dumbest Wallet, then the ball clattered and bounced around, came to rest on green zero.

"Well . . . shuckins," Honey Bunch said, staring at the table in disbelief as the girl raked in all eight chips.

Honey looked up at me. "Our room still faces east, don't it, Daddy?"

"Yep. Still does, Sugar Plum."

She stared at the table again. "*Double* shuckins."

* * *

We ate lunch before leaving. Well, I did. Lucy had a spinach salad enhanced with beets, cucumbers, and more kinds of inedible vegetation than you'd find on a Mississippi riverbank. By three thirty we were on the road, headed for Arlene's Diner and the Spooky Motel. We'd put her suitcase and my travel bag in the Mustang's trunk, in case we needed a change of clothes.

Lucy drove, because I was still drowsy from the Jacuzzi, the nap, and the lunch, and she wasn't. For an old broad, over thirty, she was pretty tough. Before we left Vegas, I hit a Walmart and had her buy black pants, a dark shirt, dark blue tennis shoes, clothes for night skulking that she didn't have. And I stocked up on food and water, bought a small ice chest, a bag of ice.

Still in her white shorts and tank top, Lucy got us headed out on I-15. Without either of us saying a word about where we were going, she turned left onto US 93. No need for words. There wasn't any real choice of destination. All the activity with Jo-X and Shanna was in the neighborhood of Arlene's Diner and the Midnight Rider Motel. Somewhere around there, up in the hills, was Jo-X's private retreat, which I wanted to see, if possible, even if we had to walk in once we reached the tire shredder.

"Four thousand on red, four on black," I said.

"I couldn't win one lousy penny. All I could do is lose. I'll bet they've never seen anything that dumb in forever."

"Priceless. You made the pit boss very happy."

"I'm glad. I bet they'll let us keep the suite for a month after that show since we've still got forty thousand of their money."

Ten miles north of I-15, in the middle of nowhere, we'd been riding along in silence for five minutes, Lucy in her sun hat, when she let out an abrupt laugh that faded into a round of girlish giggles.

"What?" I asked.

She grinned at me. "Superglue."

"Ouch," I said.

"Yeah. But what I wouldn't have given to be a fly on the wall when he woke up and had to pee." She looked over at me. "Well, maybe not. That'd be gross. But for the record, I've heard his lyrics, so he deserved what he got. And if he raped that girl, then he deserved the bullets, too."

* * *

We'd learned things. I didn't know if any of it was useful, but anything new added to our store of knowledge, which gave me an
idea. I hadn't spoken with Russell since last night, so I gave him a
jingle. Maybe he'd found something useful up there in Reno and
hadn't gotten back to me yet.

"You find her yet?" Russ asked without preamble.

"In fact, I did." He'd forked over five thousand smackeroos so I
figured I owed him that much. Smackeroos was a word I'd picked
up in Gerlach last year at Waldo's Texaco. It filled a niche.

"You *did*? Where?"

"Caliente."

"Caliente? What's she doin' down there? How'd you find her,
anyway?"

"Do you have any idea who you're talkin' to?"

Dead air for a few seconds. "Well, yeah."

"Doesn't sound like it. You are talking to the most successful
locator of missing persons in all of North—"

"Oh, for chrissake, yeah, yeah, yeah—"

"—America, and you oughta stay away for a while. She's with
Shanna. They're fine, keeping their heads down. Until we get a
handle on what's going on and who might've killed Jo-X, I'm of
the opinion that they're in as good a place as any. Pick them up
and you've got a circus on your hands."

And you'd also have a bubbling fountain of information on
your hands, I didn't tell him—*if* he could get it out of the girls.
Last thing I wanted him to know was that Shanna had roofied
Xenon and super-glued part of his anatomy to another part of his
anatomy. Which, if I thought about it, wasn't a topic I wanted to
pursue in any depth now or in the future with Russ or anyone else.

Odds were Jo-X's autopsy had already given Russ that tidbit. No need to bring it up, which I couldn't anyway without revealing more than I wanted to at the moment.

"Where at in Caliente are they?" Russell asked.

"I'm gonna protect you from yourself and your inclination to do exactly the wrong thing and not tell you—or tell Lucy what you said because she'd correct your English."

"Jesus Christ, Angel—"

"Seriously, Russ. Don't go there. Leave 'em alone." Which was up to him now. If he went to Caliente, it would take him about ten minutes to find them; the place was that small.

"Where're you staying? Caliente?"

"Nope. Suite at the Luxor."

"A *suite*? Je-sus, Angel. But, look, I paid you to find—"

"Hello," I said. "Russ? You there? You're breaking u—"

"I hear you just fine and—"

"Russ, you there? Damn it, call must've dropped out—"

"I'm here, Angel. I'm right here. *Hey*—"

"Guess he's gone," I said to Lucy, and into the phone. "Cell coverage out here must not be that g—" and I ended the call.

Ten seconds later, my phone rang. "Monster Mash" played for a while, then the call went to voice mail.

I looked over at Lucy. "You takin' notes?"

"Yeah. You need a new ringtone."

"Not that. What I said to Russ."

"How to screw your client and run a maverick operation? Uh-huh, I think I'm gonna be good at this."

CHAPTER TWENTY

The shimmering motel-diner oasis rose out of the afternoon heat mirage like a ghastly ghostly rotting galleon emerging from the murky depths. I told all that to Lucy.

"Don't count on a Pulitzer. Are we stopping?" she asked half a mile before we got there.

"Let's see if we can find that road to Jo-X's. Shanna said it was west of the highway, eight miles past the diner."

"Eight to ten."

"Good. You're keepin' notes."

At the Walmart where Lucy had bought her dark clothing, I'd also bought a small backpack to carry food and water. Shanna had estimated that the tire shredder was three miles from Jo-X's house. Not far, but in hundred-degree heat and no shade it would make for a hot hike. The longest day of the year was only a week or so ago. The sun would be up for four more blazing-hot hours.

As we went by the motel—no sign of the red Chevy Cruze—I reached over and reset the trip odometer.

At seventy-five miles an hour, the miles piled up quickly. Lucy slowed when we'd gone eight of them. I looked ahead for any sign of a road. After another mile, I saw something.

"Slower," I told her.

At nine point two, a dirt road appeared to the left. Lucy made the turn onto a rutted washboard trail. Fifty yards off the highway we came to a gate of sorts—a section of barbed wire fence held across the canted trail by a loop of wire around a wooden post, a common arrangement in western rangeland. Lucy stopped the car and I got out, lifted the loop of wire from the post and dragged the gate—four strands of limp wire nailed to a vertical board in the middle of the road—out of the way.

As Shanna had said, NO TRESPASSING signs were nailed to each of the posts flanking the trail. And a PRIVATE PROPERTY sign, and one that read: KEEP OUT. TRESPASSERS WILL BE PROSECUTED.

Given the condition of the road, the number of signs seemed like overkill. Ignoring the signs, the unlikely prosecution, and an even less-likely protracted trial by a jury of my peers, I waved Lucy through and hauled the wire crap back across the road and secured it in place.

I went around to the driver's side. "Move over."

She scooted nimbly across the center console. I got behind the wheel. "Know how to use a gun?" I asked.

"Big one like a rifle, or a little one?"

"How about a revolver? That's a little one. A handgun."

She didn't answer for a few seconds. Then: "My dad and one of my uncles took me to a firing range when I was thirteen or fourteen, something like that. I shot a .22 rifle and—I think—an automatic. It might've been like a .33 or something. Didn't have a big huge kick to it."

"They don't make a .33. It might've been a .32 or a .35."

She shrugged.

A few miles from the highway, on a slope into the foothills, nothing but rocks and weeds all around, I stopped the car and we got out. I opened the trunk and the lockbox, got out two revolvers—a sturdy SP101 Ruger .357 Magnum with a 2.9-inch barrel, and a little S&W .32.

I handed her the .32.

"We gonna kill things?" she asked, holding the gun between thumb and index finger as if it were a dead fish.

"The way you're holding that gun, target practice might be a good thing. Just in case."

"In case of what. Jihadists?"

"In case of anything. Trouble. Jo-X is dead, in case you forgot. We don't know what might be going on around here."

She looked at the gun, dangling from her fingers like a piece of week-old road kill. "Is this thing loaded?"

"Not yet."

I took the gun from her, opened a box of .32 ammo, swung the cylinder out and put in five rounds, snapped the cylinder back in place. "Now it is," I said.

"Oh, great."

I handed it to her. "Keep it pointed away from yourself or me. Or the car. You need to think about what would happen if the gun were to fire, even accidentally, where the bullet would go."

"Great," she said again.

I loaded the Ruger. On the drive from Vegas, we'd each had a 20-oz plastic bottle of water. I got a viciously sharp CRKT knife out of the lockbox and cut the tops off the empties. I scooped up enough dust to weigh them down, set them a couple feet apart about twenty-five feet away, then came back.

"Okay, here's the way it goes. You don't just blast away. You get a reasonable sight picture before you pull the trigger. If that takes you an extra half second, it's worth it."

"A sight picture?"

I drew her a diagram in the dust. "Like this." I pointed out the front and rear sights of her .32, had her line them up on a bottle. She closed one eye and wrinkled her nose as she squinted along the barrel. "Got it?" I asked.

"I guess."

"If you have to use the gun, odds are your target will be less than thirty feet away, usually less than fifteen. In a gunfight, six or eight feet wouldn't be uncommon."

"A gunfight. Smokin'."

"Beyond thirty feet you can pretty much forget about hitting anything—unless you're an expert."

"Right. Gunfights at thirty feet."

"Here's a little factoid: If your aim is off by just two degrees at thirty feet, you'll miss by more than a foot. Which means it's unlikely you'd hit anything useful. Like a man."

"Learning stuff like crazy."

I gave her a look. "Are you taking any of this seriously?"

"Sure. Thirty feet. Aim. Don't blast away."

I sighed. "Okay, watch. I'll take the bottle on the left." I gave her some foam earplugs, packed two in my ears, then lined up the sights, squeezed the trigger, and missed. Well, the bottle was only two inches wide, and I'd forgotten that the Ruger, with its fixed sights, fired a skosh left. I fired four more rounds, hit the bottle three times in eight seconds.

"Okay," I said. "Your turn. The gun will kick a little, but not a lot. It won't hurt you. Take your time."

At which point she dropped into a stance, two-fisted combat grip, and hit the right-hand bottle four times in five seconds.

"Well, shit," I said, staring at the perforated bottle. "You blasted away. I told you not to do that."

"Was that okay?" she said with enough sugar in her voice to put a diabetic into a coma.

"I've been fuckin' had."

"Not yet, you haven't. But you will. If not tonight then, I don't know. Sometime soon."

"I meant right here, now."

"I know what you meant. Kinda fun, though, listening to all that NRA stuff. It never hurts to review the basics."

"Shit. So, what's the story, Sugar Plum?"

"The story is that I've had a concealed carry permit since I was twenty-one. My dad insisted since I've been sort of traveling around by myself. I've got a .38 in my suitcase loaded with plus-P ammo, and I find a firing range five or six times a year and fire at least four boxes, sometimes as much as eight, fifty rounds a box. Dad insisted, and I like doing it."

"Well, shit."

"But this little .32 was fun. Hardly any recoil." She popped the cylinder out, ejected the brass, handed the gun back to me, barrel down. "It's pretty wimpy, though. If you don't mind, I'll use my own. It's got a lot more stopping power."

"You never said a word about having a gun."

"You didn't ask. And there's lots of things I haven't told you. You don't even know where I went to high school or if I went to the prom."

"Well, shit."

"Your vocabulary could use upgrading, though."

"Well, fuck. And—no prom. Entire junior and senior class was probably terrified of you."

"That's better. And, wrong, I wore a dark blue gown."

* * *

We packed up our stuff. Before we left, Lucy got her .38 out of her suitcase and buckled it around her waist in a black nylon holster. Not knowing what we might run into, I did the same with my .357. We took off, headed uphill. I drove. Two miles later, I said, "Art history major, shit."

Lucy just smiled.

The miles were rough. Another six miles from the highway we reached the tire shredder. Except it was . . . shredded, more or less. The entire thing had been pulled out of the ground, dragged to one side. The hole it left was filled in with dirt, which made it just another minor bump in the road.

"Must've been an earthquake," I said. "Bad one. Not long ago, either."

In fact, given two or three uninterrupted hours, I think I could have jacked the mechanism out of the ground with chains, short sturdy I-beams, and a couple of 20-ton hydraulic jacks.

A sign on a post by the defunct shredder read:

PRIVATE
Edward L. Jacobson Addiction Treatment Center
By appointment only
KEEP OUT
Trespassers will be prosecuted

"Addiction treatment, sure," Lucy said. "People roofying each other. Easy to get addicted to that kind of kiddin' around."

"Anyway, we won't have to walk in."

"And I was so looking forward to the exercise in this heat."

"Hop out. I'll meet you up at the house."

She slugged my arm. "Drive, Daddy."

The road, such as it was, entered a narrow dry arroyo of weathered basalt that wound up into the mountains. We gained a thousand feet of elevation in two and a half miles before the road began to level out. Small rocks pinged up into the wheel wells. A plume of fine brown dust followed us up the hillside. Around an outcropping of rock, we stopped at another fence with a gate across the road.

The gate had been left open. Two gates and a tire shredder so far. A sign on this gate read:

VISITORS MUST CHECK IN AT THE RECEPTION AREA.
Patients may be walking around the facility. If you have
no business here, you may be liable for damages of up to
$250,000 for loss of treatment to patients.

"They take their Rohypnol seriously here," Lucy said.

"Wouldn't you?"

I drove on, ignoring the quarter-million-dollar scare tactic. A faint odor riding a gentle breeze gave me a sense of déjà vu, but I couldn't place it.

Half a mile farther, Jo-X's hideout came into view. By now the odor was much stronger, the chemical smell of ash. The house was a low rambling structure, sandstone colored, with big picture windows and a four-foot decorative adobe fence around the perimeter of the building that encompassed little courtyards.

I spotted a broken window with soot on the outside wall above it. More windows, more soot. I was in the fifth grade the first time I encountered a house that had burned down. It was half a mile from my house. A friend of mine and I went through it a week later. The odor of fried insulation, plastic, wood, metal, electronics, and wallboard is distinctive. And rank.

"Fire," Lucy said.

"Days old." No smoke was coming from the house, just the smell.

"Probably has something to do with that tire shredder thing someone tore out of the ground."

"You're gonna be a first-rate gumshoe in no time, kiddo."

She stuck her tongue out at me. It made her look sixteen, which was scary.

The driveway curved around to the right and ended at a six-car unattached garage. In front of the garage was a blue Focus and a red Chevy Cruze.

Looked like a party was in progress. Perfect.

* * *

I drifted the Mustang beside the Cruze and cut the engine. Shanna and Ignacio were by the front door, or what remained of what I assumed had once been the front door, now ash on hinges.

"Hola," I called out cheerfully, wondering what the hell was going on. "Barbeque get out of hand?"

"You're late," Vince said. "The canapés are all gone and all we got left is a warm six-pack of O'Douls."

I was liking the Wharf Rat more every time I ran into him.

"You know this character?" I said to Shanna.

"Yeah, sure. His name is Bill."

"Bill Hogan, right?"

She frowned at me. "That's right. So?"

"So you're aware that he's the guy who scared Danya away from your house the day Jo-X turned up in your garage."

She stared at Ignacio. "You didn't say anything about that."

Vince shrugged.

"He has CIA-like following skills," I informed her.

"Following skills?"

"He followed you all the way from Vegas to Tonopah, and Danya from Tonopah to Reno. Later he followed you and Danya from Reno to Caliente. And," I added to give the party a boost, "his name isn't Bill. It's Vincent Ignacio, *Celebrity News*." I smiled at him. "Just gettin' it all out in the open so we can get things figured out."

"Yeah, thanks a bunch." He didn't look happy.

"No problem, Vinny."

"Jesus H. Christ, the tabloid guy." Shanna backed away from him.

"Just the tabloid guy," I said. "Christ was someone else."

Lucy snickered.

I nodded at the house. "How's it look inside? Ready for a party now that everyone's here except Danya?"

Shanna was in her summer usual: jogging shorts and a halter top with prominent nipple bumps. Vince's chin came about to her cleavage, which meant this might be the best day of his life—until Lucy and I showed up, that is.

"Merry Maids would be a plus," Vince said, recovering. "And new furniture, electricity, and water. And a ceiling."

Shanna still wasn't through with him. "How do you live with yourself, creep, working for a toilet-paper rag?"

Creep. She and Danya had been talking.

Vince's face turned a shade of pink. I didn't think tabloid rats had any internal mechanism that allowed them to feel shame. Or maybe it wasn't shame. It might have been a natural reaction to the lights coming on, like roaches scurrying into dark corners. But that may have been uncharitable of me, especially since Vince and I appeared to be approaching buddyhood, almost on a first-name basis.

"Good stuff," I said. "Bigfoot loose in Manhattan's subways. 7-Eleven spotted on the far side of the moon. You and Danya are serious front-page material."

"Well, fuck," Shanna growled. "The fuckin' *News*."

"Language," Lucy said.

Then, of course, Vince stepped in it, which is what tabloid

rodents do. His eyes shifted to Lucy, taking on a kind of glow. "You're Lucy Landry, right?" Couldn't resist showing off. Don't know where he got that, but the lad was good. I would have to keep him away from Ma so she wouldn't hire him, fire me.

Lucy was six feet from him. She took two quick strides and jabbed a finger into his scrawny chest, which happened to be covered by a T-shirt with Mickey Mouse on it. The rat had been to Disneyworld sometime in his youth, and the joy of the place had made a lasting impression.

"*Miss* Landry to you, bucko," Lucy said. "Don't make me pull this gun."

His eyes shifted again, this time to the .38 at her hip, which might not have registered before with two great halter tops to check out. "Yes, ma'am," he said.

But not to be outdone, he went around his Cruze, opened the passenger door, and reached beneath the front seat, pulled out a black automatic—a .45 Glock 21 in a Blackhawk tactical holster. He came toward us, strapping it on.

"Whoa," Lucy said. "Nice piece, Rat."

Vince stared at her. "Rat?"

"Cool it, Luce," I said. I looked around. "Everyone feel safer now that we can hold off a small invading army?"

"I do," said the Rat. He looked an inch taller with that gun on his hip.

"I don't," said Shanna.

"Me either," Lucy said, giving Vince the eye. "You ever fire that thing?"

"Couple of times, yeah. You ever fire that little popgun?"

"Okay, great," I said. I looked at the house. "What's inside? Shall we go have a look?"

It was a standard burn-out—the cloying ash and chemical odor you get when household goods and the surrounding house goes up. There wasn't much left of this one. It had burned itself out without anyone so much as pissing on the flames. The roof beams were gone and afternoon sunlight slanted through, illuminating black ashy lumps. Stringers of blackened electrical wire hung in loops in what little wall remained. A fire marshal might've been able to locate the source of ignition, but I had the feeling it would turn out to be lawn mower propellant—gasoline. And a single match, or a flick of a Zippo. Who might've done it and why were questions without answers.

So, what could be learned in this mess? Damned little, was my guess. DNA and fingerprints would probably be gone. If the place had been robbed, an inventory of the ash might reveal that, but that would require a list of what had been in the house. I wondered if Jo-X had such a list or where it might be, especially given that this place was a national secret and didn't exist.

We were only a step or two inside. "I wonder who built this place," I said. "And who the contractor thought he was building it for."

Lucy wrinkled her nose. "We're not really gonna go through it, are we?"

"Have to."

She looked down at her feet. "Well, I can't walk around in here in sandals." She held out a hand. "Key."

I gave her the key to the Mustang. She went out and popped the trunk, got out her new tennis shoes and put them on.

Back in the house, she looked around. "What're we looking for, anyway?"

"Missing stuff, charred bodies, the usual."

"Bodies, that's wonderful. But missing stuff? How would we know if anything's missing?"

I turned to Shanna. "You were here, what? A week or two ago? Do you remember any of it, like furniture?"

"Furniture thieves," Vince said. "That's good. They do this a lot. Grab a couch, then burn the place down."

Shanna laughed, which probably made his day.

I said to her, "Anything at all?"

"This is just the entryway. Was. Over there, that's the living room." She stepped gingerly through the ashy crud. "The main one, anyway. Guest room I was in had a big sitting room."

We followed her through the devastation to what had been an open room with huge windows, even more open now with the latest in designer skylights and stumpy walls.

"What was in here?" I asked.

"It all looks so different, burned up like this. I'm not sure what was where."

"Close your eyes. Try to visualize how it was." I didn't know what good that would do, but it couldn't hurt to try. It felt very Zen, like I was a freakin' hypnotist-investigator.

Shanna closed her eyes and stood still for nearly a minute. Then she turned in a circle. "There was a sofa about here," she said. "I guess this is it." She nudged a pile of soot with a foot. "And another one over there. And a couple of like La-Z-Boys. An entertainment center was against that wall, and a huge TV. I remember that."

All piles of charred lumps. Hopeless. A forensics team might be able to make something of this, I thought. At least figure out what had been what, if it mattered.

"There was a room down a sort of short hallway that he kept locked," Shanna said. "When I roofied him, I still couldn't open it. I couldn't find the keys."

"You roofied him?" Vince said.

"Put that in your rag and I'll track you down and blow off both your kneecaps with your own gun," I told him.

"I'll keep that in mind," he said, looking thoughtful.

Shanna led us down what used to be a hallway, now a channel between charcoal nubs where wall studs had burned almost to the floor. Finally she stopped. "It was in there, I think."

Except for an outside wall, the room hadn't been destroyed as completely as the rest of the house. A wall had been torn out and was lying in pieces on the ground outside. Interior walls were still standing, and I saw why. They were clad in sheet metal, maybe an eighth of an inch thick. The metal was buckled but still upright. The door was open, possibly sprung by the intense heat. Everything inside the room had either burned or melted. Not much remained except the room itself, but the metal sheeting was a clue as to its purpose. If I had to guess, I would say it had held valuables, things he kept under lock and key. He was away from this place for days or weeks at a time, maybe with no one to watch over it, or a caretaker once a week he didn't entirely trust. The signs along the road would keep most people out, but there was always that tenth of a percent willing to take risks for easy profit. This room, I thought, might have held a safe, which made me think about Melanie's words in the dark outside her trailer—the diner's owner, Arlene, buying a safe on Craigslist. A safe that had been delivered without the combination or keys needed to open it. Steal a safe, you might have trouble opening it.

The room wasn't big, ten by ten feet, big enough to hold a good-sized safe. A pile of ash littered with blackened hardware might have once been a cabinet with drawers. I rubbed the ash with a foot, didn't see anything that might've been jewelry.

"I didn't see any power lines coming in," I said to get Vince out before he saw too much. "Maybe he was on a generator."

We trooped outside and around the house. On a pad west of the house I saw Xenon's helicopter, a hundred fifty feet away, far enough that the fire hadn't damaged it. Two steel sheds were fifty feet from the main house, still intact and unlocked, paint slightly scorched. The first held shovels, rakes, shears, and other tools I couldn't imagine Jo-X using. The second had housed a generator big enough to power the house. The generator itself was gone. Stubby bolts that might have held it in place were embedded in a concrete slab floor. A wire as thick as my wrist dangled from a three-hundred-amp power panel. The cable ended in a socket that would connect to the generator. Big air-conditioning condensers were outside the house, so I thought the generator was at least 50kW, maybe more. The floor was scored, as if the generator had been dragged outside, and I saw what looked like blood spots on the concrete slab. The blood, if that's what it was, was beneath the scrape marks the generator had made. So, blood first, then the generator was removed. If it was blood. Sure looked like it.

I thought about that. If I wanted to put a bullet in him out here, I would monkey with the generator, turn it off or cut off the fuel. Power goes out. When he came out to see what the problem was, putting a bullet in his skinny chest wouldn't be hard to do, one more in his head to make certain.

Behind the shed was a thousand-gallon tank of diesel that hadn't gone up with the house. A gauge on the tank indicated that it was less than a quarter full.

I turned away from the shed and looked back at the house.

"Now what?" Lucy said, putting an arm through mine.

"Now I don't know what."

"I like it that you're always so modest." She stared at the black smelly ruins of the house with me. "Anyway, this was fun. You sure know how to show a girl a good time."

* * *

Back at the cars, Vince sidled over and said, "Bigfoot loose in Manhattan subways? That's pretty good. Okay if I use it?"

"Be my guest. If you write it up, send me a copy. I want to know how it turns out. Do they finally catch him and give him a job with the IRS, or is he running loose with occasional above-ground sightings, like shinnying up the Empire State Building?"

"Those're good, too, IRS especially." He got in his car, hung a U-turn in the driveway, then stopped opposite me. "I think he'd still be loose, living on rats and small dogs, terrorizing people. It'd read better that way and I could do follow-up stories. But I like that IRS bit, too. If you ever want a job at the *News*, I'd say you've got the chops for it. Let me know and I'll put in a word for you." He gave me a grin and drove away.

Shanna stood with Lucy and me, shading her eyes with a hand as she looked back at the house. Finally she turned away. "I wonder who did this? And why."

"Same person who killed the Zee, probably," I said.

She widened her eyes. "Wow, you're good. Probably make private eye of the month on the street where you live."

Man, I hate irony. Especially when it comes in short shorts and a straining halter.

Shanna opened her car door, started to get in.

"Back to Caliente?" I asked.

"Where else? This place is . . . gone."

"Danya didn't want to check it out with you?"

"Obviously not, but as a private eye you're on top of things like unreal. Awesome, really."

"Go, before I'm forced to hurt you."

"Pussycat. I worry more about the junior high chick you're hooked up with." She got in, banged the door shut.

"If you're smart, you'll ditch the shoes," I said to her.

"Yeah? Why's that?"

"You'll never get them clean. Investigators could tell you've been up here. If that's a concern, that is."

She looked at me for a moment, said, "Thanks," and took off down the mountain after Vince.

"So, what have we learned here?" I asked Lucy.

"Don't play with matches, don't smoke in bed, don't slosh gasoline around your house, remember to ditch your shoes, and Shanna's a bitch?"

"All good observations for sure, but besides those."

"Whoever burned the place down might've stolen a big-ass generator."

"An even more cogent and useful observation. What else?"

"High-capacity halter tops are made of Kevlar, and Shanna's a bitch and a *half*?"

I gave her a one-eyed squint. "Kevlar might be useful as a reinforcing agent, but I was referring to other things."

"Actually, I think it's totally interesting that Shanna was even here. And the darling little tabloid guy."

"Totally, huh? You're so Valley. And given darling Vinny's propensity and skills, it's likely he followed her here. But you're right about Shanna. Last thing I expected was to see her up here."

"She's a bitch."

"You could let that go."

"Don't see why. One thing she did right, though, she roofied Jo-X, gave him a superglue special, and left here by car."

"Probably couldn't find the keys to the whirly."

"So, she knew where the place *was*, Mr. PI. Then she comes back but didn't know the place had been set on fire. I'll bet she was looking for something. She might have left something that would point to her being here and she wanted to get it back."

"She might still be looking for that guest book Josie signed."

"Possible, but people don't usually haul those around." She stared at the house. "No one reported the fire. Look at it. It went up, burned right to the ground. No fire trucks, nothing."

"Another tremendous observation."

"So, what did *you* get from this place, Smarty Pants?"

"Ash in my throat."

She laughed. "That and an eyeful."

"An eyeful?"

"Her halter top. Jeez Louise, it was like she was shoplifting honeydews. I bet she could've asked Jo-X for thirty thousand a concert. *I* would've. Well . . . *if.*"

CHAPTER TWENTY-ONE

I RESET THE odometer, then drove us out past the first gate, the tire shredder, then the gate near the highway. I dragged the gate back across the road to keep the riffraff out. The distance from Jo-X's hideaway to the highway was fourteen point seven miles.

"Where to?" Lucy asked as I stopped the Mustang a few feet from the highway.

Left was Caliente, right was Vegas. I checked the time—5:50. Temperature readout on the dash was dead on a hundred.

"How about your favorite resort?" I said.

"Back to our Jacuzzi. Perfect. Get the smell of ash off us."

"I meant the Midnight Rider and its shower."

She didn't respond for a few seconds. Then she shrugged. "The water was tepid but the shower was still a blast. I could get you all lathered up. Which I haven't really done yet."

I sighed deeply.

She smiled. "What?"

"You never quit, do you?"

"Hey, I'm only *thirty*-one, not a hundred one, and it's been a while since I've . . . since . . . anyway, we haven't checked out the food at the diner. The place might be a sleeper. It might have a nice crab salad or a world-class lobster thermidor."

"Right. And the ceiling farther back might be plated with gold or painted with a Michelangelo fresco."

"Yeah. That, too. We should go see."

* * *

"Back again?" said the lady behind the counter, head tilted slightly to the left, eyes dark behind reading glasses with violet frames on a beaded chain. Smoke filled the air around her like the ash in Jo-X's former hideout.

"We're traveling between Ely and Vegas," I said. "My oldest sister died. We got a bunch of family stuff to sort out."

"That's never fun. I'll put you in room four. That's—"

"Actually," I interrupted, "we were in One the other day. I'd rather stay there if it's all the same."

"Four's a better room. Same price."

"Even so, how 'bout we take number one again? It's closer to the diner here if we get hungry."

She hesitated, lips twitching. "If you insist, One it is. That'll be fifty-two dollars, cash. Fifty-five if you use a credit card."

I gave her three twenties and got change. "I don't suppose you have lobster thermidor tonight in the dining room?"

I don't know if it was the "thermidor" or the "dining room" that made her laugh, but she did. Maybe. Her smoker's voice transmogrified it into a fragmented cackle. Spooky.

* * *

Our waitress was Melanie. Hard to believe she was eight years younger than Lucy. Before we were seated, she told us the closest they had to lobster in Arlene's Diner was a tuna salad sandwich made fresh yesterday or a bowl of clam chowder out of a can, take your pick.

Lucy stared at me. "We could be at the Luxor in an hour and a half. Less if I drive."

"We've already got a room for the night here."

"Jacuzzi over there. Clean sheets. Free food in the casino. They might even have lobster thermidor."

"Good 'nuf."

I said so long to Melanie and we left, which felt weird, but I had a plan of sorts rolling around in my head.

We arrived at the Luxor at seven forty-five. The sun wouldn't set for over an hour. Temperature a hundred and one degrees. Vegas runs hot. Up and down the Strip, half the women were in clothing that showed quite a bit more than the usual amount of skin you see in Iowa, which was both good and bad. As a result, Lucy fit right in as we rolled into the valet area and she got out in running shorts and her peek-a-boo crochet halter. Even with the competition, she drew stares. There is skin and then there is skin. Lucy's was the latter variety.

"Got any thousand-dollar chips on you?" she asked.

"One." I adjusted the wig and moustache.

"Gimme it. I feel lucky."

"Last time you said that you lost ten thousand bucks."

"They'll be overjoyed to see me. They want their money back, Daddy. They figger it's just a matter of time."

"Go get 'em, Sugar Plum."

Which she did. Red, three times, letting it ride, then she put down a "shuckins" to keep them guessing, and we headed to the suite with seven chips, up another six thousand dollars.

"Why the hell do you want to be a PI?" I asked her when we got in the elevator. "A few days here and you could retire."

"Everything we've done since I got rescued from Tonopah, of course. Luck can change. But you should try waiting tables, sometime. Or renting party stuff, talking on the phone, telling people what they can rent. Same thing over and over and over. Prices, terms, and conditions. Scorpions on the ceiling. Now I'm running around with a hot PI who carries a .357 Magnum."

"Hot, right. They have anti-psychotic drugs now, you know. Keeps people like you from being institutionalized."

"You don't think?" She took my hand. "Smile. You're about to get happy with a girl who knows how to use a .38 loaded with plus-P ammo and who's a little bit worked up at the moment."

"Worked up?"

"Well . . . yeah. Little bit more than a little bit."

"That can't be good. When'd that happen?"

"I dunno. It just did. I'm thinking of maybe doing something about it, too."

"Like what?"

"Wouldn't you like to know?"

"Kinda would, yeah."

"Okay, I'll give you a hint."

We were in the midst of a tremendous kiss when the elevator doors opened. We walked down to the room a little faster than usual, sort of a lope. I opened the door and there was my all-time favorite detective, sitting on a bed, watching television.

Our television.

Shit.

*   *   *

"Ho-ly smoke," Fairchild said as he got to his feet. "I mean, uh, this is the assistant you were talkin' about? Lucy?"

I took off the hairpiece and the moustache, tossed them on a chair. "What the hell are *you* doin' here, Russ?"

"Hey, it's nice to see you, too, Mortimer."

"Mort."

Russ held out a hand to Lucy. "Russell Fairchild, Reno PD. And you are . . ."

"Out of your jurisdiction, obviously."

Russ lowered his hand and shot me a look. Then Lucy said, "Lucy. Mort's assistant. And I've like been to Reno a few times, but I'm really sort of from like all over, totally."

She said all that in the voice of a fifteen-year-old Valley Girl, and the "likes" were just great. Her "totally" at the end was like the cherry on top of a sundae. Russell knew how old she was, but still. Here she was in color and 3-D, 3-D being the main thing, especially in that halter top with seven inches of tummy showing. When he looked at me, I saw new respect in his eyes, which were jittering slightly.

"Think I'll go put on something different," Lucy said. She went into the bathroom and shut the door.

"Holy Christ, Angel," Russ said in an awed whisper.

"Yeah. And whatever your mouth thinks it wants to say next, don't let it."

"That is . . . is she . . ."

"What?"

"Is she any good? I mean, as an assistant?"

"She's fantastic."

He didn't know how to take that. He shook his head and said, "I am in the wrong . . . Je-sus. Okay, before she comes back, I got something to tell you about that Jo-X dipshit. Boyce found it during the autopsy, figures it must've happened a week or two ago. Xenon . . . well, he, he . . ."

"Had a little superglue accident with his pecker, would be my guess."

His eyes widened. "Where the *hell* did you get that?"

"I have these vivid dreams."

"Sonofabitch."

"I'm a gumshoe, Russ. Good one, too."

"Sonofabitch. Boyce was backed up. He did the autopsy two days ago. We kept that superglue business hushed up. There isn't six people who know about it, so I'd really like to know—"

Lucy came out barefoot, wearing a white Luxor terrycloth bathrobe that ended at mid-thigh, left a lot of nice leg showing. As Hammer would say, she looked like a million bucks.

"Okay, Mr. Reno Detective," she said. "What're you doin' here? How'd you get in this room?"

He gawked at her for several seconds, then said, "You just called me 'detective.' That's how I got in."

"Detectives can float through locked doors? I didn't know that. I'll watch while you float back out."

"If you *must* know, I knew you two were staying here at the Luxor. I've got a friend works security here. I asked him if a girl won big at roulette in the last day or two, and he said some ditzy broad was driving them nuts at the table, playing like a complete idiot but winning big." He gave me an accusing look. "Upwards of forty thousand dollars big, not twelve."

I shrugged. "I rounded it off. And we won a little more after I talked to you. Then lost ten grand."

He stared at me, then said, "My friend owed me. He knew which room the 'ditzy broad' was in. He got me in here where I could wait in comfort, be sure to see you if you came in. Which, as you can see, worked." He offered Lucy a tentative smile.

"Give you ten minutes, then I'll kick you out myself," said my young, volatile, gorgeous, somewhat-underdressed assistant.

Fairchild's smile faded.

"Nine minutes fifty-five seconds and counting," she said. "You're interrupting things."

Smooth.

"Interrupting what?" His eyes swiveled to me.

"Dinner," I said. "We haven't eaten yet."

"Hey, great, I'll buy. We could go on down and—"

"I need a bath," Lucy said. "Dinner can wait. Nine minutes forty seconds. Say what you gotta say, then take it somewhere else and have a nice day."

Russell's eyes ping-ponged between us for a moment, then he said, "Where in Caliente is Danya? And Shanna?"

"And here I thought you were a detective."

"I could find 'em, no problem. I thought I'd see you first, find out what they're doing there, get some information before I bust in on 'em."

"You should stay away."

"That's my *kid*, Angel. How'm I supposed to do that?"

Good question, actually. What would I do if it were Nicole? My daughter. Answer: I would move heaven and earth to protect her. Fortunately, she was two thousand miles away from all this.

"Pahranagai Inn," Lucy said. "Room nine. Now how about you get out and leave us alone."

I stared at her. She gave me a bland look in return.

"Well," she said, "he's got to know where they are. But"—she faced Russ—"if you're smart you'll play it cool. Right now she's safe. Make a big deal out of it and you could screw it up."

"I just need to see her. Make sure she's okay."

"She's fine. She's with Shanna," I said.

"Yeah, well, I figured that."

"And they're married—unless they're lying about it, which doesn't seem likely, so you'd better factor that into whatever you think you're gonna do or say to her."

"How about, 'congratulations'?" Lucy said. "Since it looks like you kinda missed that part."

Fairchild's head whipped between us as if he were watching a jai alai match. Finally he said, "Parana-what?"

"Pahranagai Inn," Lucy said. "Room nine. It's at the north end of town. *Caliente*. Hundred and fifty miles from here so you oughta get a move on."

"Yeah, well, thanks," Russ said.

I got a pad of Luxor stationary out of a desk. "Before you go, I want you to find out everything you can about a woman named Arlene." I wrote on the pad with a Luxor pen. Damn fine pen, too. No skipping, no ink blot. Thought maybe I'd keep it since they buy them by the truckload.

"Arlene," Russ said slowly.

"I don't know her last name. But it's likely she's the owner of Arlene's Diner. You'll pass the place on the way to Caliente. It's in the middle of nowhere on US 93. Can't miss it. She's in her fifties or sixties, if that helps."

"So, what do you want to know about this person?"

"Whatever you can find out. Does she own the place? How much did it make the last few years? Does she have relatives nearby? And there's a motel there, too, the Midnight Rider Motel. Does she own it? If so, for how long? If not, who does? Does she own other property anywhere? Rent anything? How long has she been in the state? Where was she born? Is she educated?"

"Jesus," Russ said. "Who is this woman?"

"That's what I want you to find out."

"Four minutes, twenty seconds," said my assistant. "But I'm thinking of trimming that ten minutes down to like eight."

Russ stared at her, then back at me. "What's with this Arlene lady?"

"I don't know. Place is a little odd," I said. I didn't want to mention that Arlene almost certainly knew that Jo-X flew in and out of the place, and that she knew Shanna was Celine—which I wasn't ready to reveal to Russ yet.

"Odd how?"

"Minute and a half," said my assistant, giving me the kind of look that could mean only one thing.

"Odd as in strange," I said to Russ.

"Strange how?"

"Strange as in a little bit off."

"Shee-it. Talk about runnin' me around in circles."

"Just find out everything you can, Russ. I don't know what's important, but I'll sift through it."

"Fifty-five seconds."

Russ gave me a look. "What's with the countdown timer, Angel?"

"She needs a bath."

"So? Who's keeping her? Bathroom's right over there. It has a door. She was just in there."

Lucy's eyes narrowed. Her lips parted and her teeth showed. "In thirty-eight seconds I'm gonna throw you out a window."

"Jesus, Angel. Okay, I get this information, how'm I gonna get it to you?"

"You've got my number. Cell phone coverage is sketchy out in the desert. Keep trying. You might confide in your overgrown behemoth sidekick, give him the information. Or have him get it for you, if he can do that. I'll phone you. If I don't get through, I'll phone him. One way or another, I'll get it."

"Okay, great. We all done here?" Lucy said.

Russell stared at me. "Your assistant's kinda—"

"Out," Lucy said. She hauled him toward the door by a sleeve and propelled him out into the hallway.

I blocked the door with a foot so she couldn't slam it in his face and further damage what had evolved into a useful working relationship.

"She's new," I said. "We're still workin' things out—"

Lucy's bathrobe landed on my head. When I got it off, Russ was staring somewhere behind me with eyes the size of tennis balls before I got the door closed.

I turned around. Lucy was wearing nothing but a grin she'd borrowed from an Alice in Wonderland movie.

"*She's new*," she chirped, jumping up on me, arms around my neck, legs wrapped around my waist.

"Hey, wait—" My hands automatically grabbed her rear to keep her from falling and hurting herself, which turned out not to be necessary—but it was the kind of warm, firm, rounded butt I would be able to feel in my hands for the next twenty years.

"And pretty worked up," she whispered. "So you've got a lot of work to do—you know, like you told him—workin' things out."

CHAPTER TWENTY-TWO

DINNER WAS LOBSTER thermidor and a very fine Vouvrey from France's Loire Valley, courtesy of the Luxor who had lost another three grand to Lucky Luce minutes before we sat down and got menus. I was almost starting to feel sorry for them, especially the pit boss who watched a month's salary walk away after just six minutes of play. It wouldn't be long before Lucy was banned from roulette in this place. They did that in casinos. Casinos were notoriously sore losers. *Notorious.* Card counters were regularly escorted to the sidewalk by the seat of their pants, but this thing with roulette would have them scratching their heads. She didn't have a system and she used the word "shuckins." She'd bet on both red and black at the same time, which qualified her as a genuine idiot. They might check her birthday, discover that four planets had been lined up like duckpins, none of them Mars, then run us out to the sidewalk and put us in their infamous Black Book, which they claim doesn't exist—except that it does.

On the way down to the restaurant, my legs had felt rubbery. I hadn't been used like that in a while. In fact, it had been about nine months. First there was the Jacuzzi, then a shower, then a brushing of teeth, then a bottle about the size of my thumb that produced dabs of liquid on her chest and inner thighs that smelled faintly of musk and orange blossoms, then she led me over to a bed and, if memory serves, there was quite a lot of pre-fooling-around and girlish giggling—not mine; I try to suppress it since it plays havoc with my PI gravitas—before things got serious. Words from the *Vagina Monologues* were used. At one point, one of us said, "Giddyup, Mort," in a breathy whisper and I'm ninety-nine percent certain it wasn't me.

"Wow," she said, flat on her back and naked. "I haven't been roughed up like that in . . . like forever."

I was on my back, too, unable to produce lifelike sounds.

Lucy sat up nimbly and straddled me on hands and knees. She bent down and brushed my lips with a nipple, then gazed into my eyes. "Speak. I want to hear signs of life."

"Can't," I croaked.

"How about a little CPR kick start?"

"I'll let you know."

"We should go get dinner then do this again. Okay?"

"I'll let you know."

She giggled, then stretched out full-length on top of me and tucked her head beneath my chin. "You do that."

* * *

Luck is a guileful thing. Good luck is sometimes disguised as bad. You miss your flight, stomp around angry, and the plane ends up scattered all over a mountainside somewhere. Good luck isn't always apparent at first glance, but give it time. What looks like bad luck can save your life.

Lucy and I were in the Mustang headed north on the Strip. We were the first car at a red light, The light turned green, I hit the gas, and we were T-boned by a sixteen-year-old kid running the red. He was joyriding in his daddy's Mercedes SUV, green, same kind of car that Jeri, Ma, and I were tracking last October, driven by Julia Reinhart. It seemed like a cosmic sign to me, but I misinterpreted it, which I tend to do.

It wasn't a full-on T-bone, didn't hit the passenger door. The SUV got the front quarter of the Mustang, gave us a one-eighty spin, glanced off and got a full T-bone on a zippy little Chevy Volt in the lane to our left, pushed it across the intersection where the Volt was hit head-on by a limousine. After our one-eighty we got front-ended by a Forester that had been behind us. When we came to rest, we were facing due south, watching the traffic that used to be behind us pile up, horns honking, as if that would help clear a five-car accident. Lucy's side airbag had deployed, then deflated, leaving her with a thick dusting of talcum powder and cornstarch.

"You okay?" I asked her.

She didn't answer for a few seconds, then she spit out some talcum and said, "Well, poop. I liked this car."

"Is that a yes?"

"Uh-huh. My first ever car accident."

"Good thing it was a rental. Not so much paperwork."

Lucy and I had been headed back to Arlene's since that seemed to be the epicenter of this Jo-X-Danya-Shanna case. That trip had just experienced what's called an unexpected delay.

It was 10:08, full dark, or would've been if we hadn't been on the Strip with a billion watts of neon illuminating the scene. Once I got my head back in the game, I thought about the lockbox in the trunk with its guns and disguises. It was probably a nonissue since the accident wasn't our fault, but we were about to get inundated with cops and tow trucks, so I needed to keep that lockbox in mind.

I got out, checked the damage. The right front tire was tilted inward, crushed up against the engine. It looked like the entire front axle assembly was a total loss, steering, too, the hood was crumpled, radiator leaking, windshield had a big crack in it, lots of extraneous damage. Fifty-fifty odds, they would total the car.

Lucy and I endured the snail-paced paperwork nightmare that results from a major non-injury accident. Police statements, license, rental agreement. I'd taken the insurance policy with the rental, so they could hash it out with the insurance company of the kid's father, who, as luck would have it, was an assistant DA. Later I found out there were three of them in the car, and the kid had a point one six blood alcohol level and they had been passing around an open bottle of Smirnoff's vodka. The usual dumb.

An hour later, Lucy and I were in a taxi, headed back to the Luxor. I had the lockbox on my lap. Thing was constructed of sixteenth-inch steel plate. With weapons, ammo, knife, wigs, and so on, it weighed thirty-five pounds.

"Anyway," Lucy said, "that rounded out the evening."

"Yup."

"We need a new car. Gonna get one in the morning?"

"Yup."

She stared at me. "Your needle's stuck."

"Yup."

She poked me in the ribs, then kissed me. "So, no Midnight Rider Motel. We'll have to tough it out in the suite. And if you say 'yup' one more time, I'll sleep in the other bed. Alone."

"The other bed has fleas. And the suite's got room service and a Jacuzzi, kiddo. This was meant to be."

"Fleas, huh? Okay, then. Same bed."

The taxi driver was a woman in her forties. She gave me a wink in the rearview mirror. Nice.

* * *

One of the perks we got with the suite was hassle-free car rental service. An assistant concierge contacted Avis who were thrilled that the Mustang might be a total loss, and we ended up with a Cadillac XTS. The convertible had been nice, but I'd been concerned about the lockbox. Go through the ragtop with a utility knife, drop the rear seats, and there was the box. Someone could take off with it in thirty seconds. So now we had a hardtop, which was that aforementioned bad-luck, good-luck thing. Up in the suite I signed the new rental agreement, and the Caddy was delivered to valet parking. The claim check was left for us at the front desk. Done.

I had to get out of the Jacuzzi when my phone lit up with "Monster Mash." I caught it on "a graveyard smash." Lucy was in bubbles up to her chin. She gave me a whistle and said, "Wow. Now *there's* a sight."

"Down, girl."

She laughed. I told her to shush, then swiped the phone.

"Yeah?"

"You told my dad where we were, you cretin."

"Cretin. That's not a big word, two syllables, but it's not in common usage. I'm impressed."

"Shithead."

"A term of endearment I've been called before."

"For good reason, I'm sure," Danya said. "Why the *hell* did you tell him? My dad?"

"Because he's your dad. And he loves you. And he was more than a little worried."

"You're still a shithead."

"Okay, then, keep in touch."

I ended the call. It hadn't lasted long enough for me to lose the erection, so I got a leer and a smile as I stepped back into the

Jacuzzi. I kept the phone where I could reach it because I have these premonitions.

"Danya?" Lucy said.

"Uh-huh."

"She called you a cretin?"

"Sure did. And a shithead. Twice."

"She's beautiful, but she's got rough edges."

The phone sounded off again. I swiped the screen. "Hola, kiddo. Guess we were cut off."

"Yeah, right," Danya said. "Don't do it again."

"That all depends. What's up?"

"That's what *I* want to know. That tabloid guy was up at Jo-X's hideout place. How'd he find out about us? Or you?"

"You first."

"I don't *know*. That's why—"

"What I *meant* was, he knew about you two first. Shanna, actually. He tracked Celine all the way to Tonopah, except by the time she got there she was Shanna again. Then he tracked *you* to Reno. He found out later who she was, after she got back to your place when Xenon dumped her. I wasn't involved in this mess until you hired me and got me involved."

"Well, shit. Is there any way to keep him from writing the story?"

"You could kill him. That always works."

"Get real."

"Not that I know of. Something about freedom of the press, First Amendment rights, that sort of thing."

"What about libel?"

"If he tells the truth, good luck with that."

"If anyone in the media found out Shanna had been Celine, we would never hear the end of it."

"Sure you would. You're giving the national attention span too much credit."

"That's still not a nightmare I want us to ride out."

"Gotta go, Danya. Good luck. If you need more advice, I'm here for you." I ended the call.

"She's gonna kill the Wharf Rat?" Lucy asked.

"Probably not. But next time I see him, I might give him a heads-up. Anyway, I'm hungry. You ready to get out of here, go track down something to eat?"

* * *

My phone rang at six forty-five the next morning.

"Please get that soon, like *now*," said my brusque assistant. She had an arm across my chest, warm resilient breasts tucked tight against my ribs, one leg flopped over one of mine.

"'Monster Mash,' Sugar Plum. Really good stuff."

"Before I throw it against a wall, okay?"

"That's right, threaten the phone." I swiped the screen and said, "Yo?"

"Yo?" Ma replied.

"Do you know what time it is?" I asked.

"Eight forty-five."

"Not here, it ain't."

"You don't come on the news until after the first commercial break, Mort. The story's starting to fade."

"Good to know, and it's six forty-five here."

"So what's goin' on? Where are you? Still at that motel?"

Took me a moment to catch up to that.

"Not that one. We're in Vegas. At the Luxor where, guess what, it's now six forty-*six* in the morning."

"We?"

Oops. That one got loose.

"Got me an assistant, Ma."

"No, you don't."

"I don't?"

"Who the hell said you could have an assistant? I'm not paying for anything like that. And it's a she, isn't it?"

"Wait, I'll check."

"Don't bother. How old is she?"

"Thirty-one."

Silence for a moment. "That don't sound so bad, not that you can have an assistant."

"Thanks, Ma."

"She good? I mean, as an assistant? And don't think my asking means you can keep her. Jesus, I don't mean keep her like a hamster. What I mean is, get rid of her. Unless of course she's useful. And free."

"She's useful. Like a set of skeleton keys."

More silence.

"What's that mean?" she asked. "That don't sound good."

"You'll like her, Ma."

"At least tell me she's not there in the room with you."

"She's not here in the room with me."

"Liar."

"You told me to tell you that. Now, if you want to know where she is, she's right here in the room with me."

"Early in the morning, too. So . . . what's she weigh?"

"That's a hell of a question."

"Again, I ask: What's she weigh?"

"Depends. When she's in a supermarket, she weighs apples, nectarines, grapes, stuff like that."

"Je-sus Christ. You evasive son of a bitch. She's beautiful, ain't she?"

"Beauty is in the eye of the beholder, Ma."

She hung up.

"That your ma?" Lucy asked, head propped up on an elbow.

"Nope. That was Ma."

She stared at me. "Let me know when you wake up."

* * *

Twelve thirty-five p.m. Temperature 105 degrees and creeping upward.

The Caddy was a hardtop, a good solid ride with tinted windows, leather seats, navigation system, intermittent wipers. The lockbox was in the trunk. I had on the white wig, matching moustache, golfer's hat, sunglasses. Lucy wore sunglasses so big they made her look like an insect.

"And look," I said. "It even has air-conditioning."

"Wowie. Imagine that. I liked the Mustang."

"Me, too."

"Won't be much point in me taking off my top in this thing. It doesn't even have a sunroof." She was wearing her form-fitting pink tank top from Tonopah, complete with bumps. Latex-thin stretchy cotton was a hell of a good invention.

"Really?" I said. "That's too bad."

She gave me a smug look. "Thank you."

We cruised by Jo-X's Vegas mansion. The circus had been downgraded to a carnival. One cop car, one forensics van, and four carloads of anguished girls barely old enough to drive, Jo-X rap issuing from three of the cars, polluting the neighborhood. Crime scene tape was still strung up. It had only been five days since I'd found Jo-X and sent a million teenage souls into a death spiral of mourning, sort of like Kennedy's assassination, which, to keep the record straight, was fourteen years before I was born.

Five days? It felt like two very long weeks.

I pulled over a quarter mile away, swapped the white wig for an unkempt brown one so I could dump the itchy moustache.

"Now what?" Lucy said.

"You drive. I'm gonna get Fairchild on the horn."

She gawked at me. "On the *horn*? Seriously?"

"Before your day, kiddo."

"You, on the other hand, used a 'horn' before they had rotary dial and Bakelite phones."

"You're fired, smart-ass."

She smiled. "You didn't know they used to make phones out of Bakelite, did you?"

"Tell me why it matters."

"It matters because I know a ton of cool stuff so you can't fire me. That and I'm really good in a Jacuzzi."

"Excellent points both. Now are you gonna drive this thing or do I have to fire you?"

We switched places.

"Where to?" she asked, fastening her seat belt.

"Just drive. Jo-X rap is coming through the windows. Lyrics like that will rot your brain stem."

I downloaded a new ringtone while we headed back north, then speed-dialed Fairchild. He picked up on the second ring.

"Yeah?"

"Bit terse on the howdy there, Russ," I said.

"What?"

"Where are you?"

"Cali-fuckin'-ente."

"You're breaking up, Russ. When we're back in Reno, I'll tell you what it sounded like you just said. It'll crack you up."

"What the hell do you want, Angel?"

"That lady, Arlene, Arlene's Diner, what'd you find out?"

"I put Day on it. That would be your buddy Officer Day. Ask him. You still got his number?"

"I keep it in a special place in my wallet."

Lucy looked over at me, then back at the road, lips lifting in a little smile.

"Call Day. I'm busy." Russ ended our horn session the same way Ma did that morning.

"What's in a special place in your wallet?" Lucy asked.

"Officer Day's phone number. Well, numbers."

"I sure hope Officer Day is a woman."

"I haven't told you about Day yet?"

"Nope."

"Well, then, you're in for a real treat."

"Why? She pretty?"

"You'll have to tell me when you two meet. Now shush." I got Day on the first ring, which was great. Now I had two RPD cops in my back pocket. "Officer Day. How's your day?"

"Got any idea how many times I've heard that dumbass line, Angel?"

"Nope. I'll puzzle it out later, get back to you on that. So, tell me about Arlene of Arlene's Diner."

Five seconds of dead air. Then, "I can't talk here. I'll call you back." My phone went dead.

"Call back," I told Lucy.

"Caught her at a bad time?"

"With Day, there's never a good time."

"That makes her sound like something of a bitch, Mort."

"Right. Keep your eyes on the road, woman."

My phone's new ringtone fired up. I let it play for twenty glorious seconds.

Ten seconds in, Lucy stared at me. "What on earth is *that*?"

"'Purple People Eater,' by Sheb Wooley."

"Wow. When did *that* come out?"

"Nineteen fifty-eight."

"People must've been totally schizo back then."

"Here's a thought. When was your father born?"

"Well, poop and a half. Nineteen fifty-seven."

"Right. Eisenhower was president. Ike founded the CIA. I know cool stuff, too. Now shush." I answered the phone. "Sorry about the delay, Officer. Had a little ringtone issue. So what's the poop on Arlene?"

Lucy looked at me and mouthed, "Poop?"

"Arlene Faye Hicks," Day said. "Fifty-nine. Got a son thirty-four years old, Buddie Hicks. Buddie with an 'ie,' not 'y,' no middle name. She owns the diner, motel, too—been there going on fifteen years. Place made just over seventeen thousand last year, diner and motel combined. She didn't pay a nickel in federal taxes, income that low. Sounds like a high-end goddamn place out there, Angel."

"You should go there on vacation, check out the fishing and boating. What about her son? He runs a backhoe."

"Buddie's Excavating. Guy made thirty-one thou last year, paid his taxes. No kind of a police record. Her either. They've got the same address so the kid's still living with his mama."

"They own any other property?"

"Didn't find any. She's driving a 2005 Impala worth about a buck thirty-nine. She's got a storage unit in North Vegas. T&T Storage. Unit seventy-two. Sixty-five bucks a month."

"TNT, like the explosive? Classy."

"You could drop by, tell 'em you don't like the name."

"Oh, but I do like it."

"I'm glad. Makes this a damn good week. What else you want to know, Angel? Checking out this lady and her kid was as boring as watching bat shit pellets harden in the sun."

"Not an image I would've come up with."

"So you're unimaginative. You should read more. If that's all, I gotta get back in the station, keep Reno's streets safe."

"A sense of humor. Who woulda thunk—" The line went dead. People hang up on me a lot. Don't know why.

"*Totally* weird conversation," Lucy said.

"You should've heard the part about bat shit pellets drying in the sun."

"Bat shit pellets? Seriously?"

"That's Officer Day. We have an interesting relationship."

"Still do? I wouldn't want to get in the middle of anything. If, you know, you've got something goin' on with her."

"Trust me, you don't have to worry about that."

"She find out anything good?"

"T&T Storage, North Vegas. Arlene's renting a unit there, number seventy-two, sixty-five bucks a month. Which is where we're headed, kiddo. And her full name is Arlene Faye Hicks."

"That's all your Officer Day got? Arlene's not wanted by the police or anything?"

"Nope. But that Impala she's got parked behind the diner is a 2005 model. How about that?"

"Talk about a sucky car . . . *and* your new ringtone."

"Give it time. It'll grow on you."

She rolled her eyes.

I got into Google Maps, typed in T&T Storage, got a map and an address, got Lucy aimed in the right direction on I-15.

"'Purple People Eater,'" she said.

"I wasn't born yet, but Mom says those were America's best years. After Korea, before Vietnam. *American Graffiti* years, if you saw the movie. Of course, the Soviets had hydrogen bombs, so there's that. She described hiding under her desk at school. They taught you how to duck and cover, kiss your ass good-bye."

"A one-eyed, one-horned . . . what?"

"Flying purple people eater."

"People eater. That's a little bit gross, actually."

"In fact, it's funny and tame. You want gross, listen to Jo-X's lyrics. That's like scuba diving in a backed-up sewer."

She made a face. "I get your point, and that's an image I'll spend the next month trying to forget. So, here we are, headed off to check out a storage unit. That's exciting."

"Arlene made all of seventeen thousand dollars last year. She pays nearly eight hundred for storage. That's a pretty good percentage of net. I wonder what she's got worth storing for eight hundred a year."

"Maybe it's where she keeps her gold bars."

"Yeah, that'd be my guess."

* * *

T&T Storage was a low-rent place behind a rusting chain-link fence topped with a languid coil of rusting razor wire. A push-button entry pad would roll a gate open for vehicles. The office comprised part of the perimeter fence. A door gave access to the office, and a door inside the office gave access to the yard. The office windows looked like LA smog had been concentrated, compressed, and baked into translucent plates.

We went in. I kept sunglasses on, but Lucy settled hers on top of her head.

A guy in his forties was behind a gouged countertop with a hoagie in one hand, a Danielle Steel paperback novel, *Magic*, in the other. Half a dozen tottering stacks of romance novels sat on a table beside him, ninety or a hundred novels. A rackety air conditioner had taken the temperature down to the mid-eighties. The hoagie was leaking vinegar and oil onto his T-shirt. All in all a fine tableau. The guy had four or more chins. Easy to lose count. His gut flowed and sagged around him, much of it in his lap, but five hundred pounds will do that.

Five hundred.

Easy.

"Hi, there," Lucy said to him. "What's your name?"

Prettiest girl who'd spoken to him in twenty years. He stared at her with a bit of lettuce hanging out of his mouth, made him look like a cow that had paused while grazing.

"Stan."

"Well, Stan. My dad here wants me to get one of those storage shed thingies, so whatcha got?"

Dad? Shit. We'd talked it over, how to do this. If it was a guy, she would do the talking. If a woman, I'd take over. That was as far as we'd taken it. She hadn't said anything about me being billed as her father. But, of course, it worked since she was in shorts, that skintight tank top, looked about nineteen, and I had "good-old-dad" written all over me.

Pinned down by gravity, Stan struggled to his feet. It took him half a minute to get in position behind the counter. "What size unit you lookin' for?" His eyes lingered on her chest for five seconds before finally getting up to her face.

A partly open door to a back room showed an unmade bed, clothes on the floor, a kitchen counter buried beneath fast-food containers. A popcorn and dirty-clothes smell hung in the air.

"I don't know," Lucy said. "How 'bout you show us around? I need to see how big they are to decide."

In spite of the little she was wearing, movement—showing us around—evidently didn't appeal to Stan. Maybe his forklift was parked too far away. Or the hundred-seven-degree outside temperature was daunting. He glanced at a wall-sized diagram of T&T's facility, covered by a yellowing sheet of Plexiglas. Units were marked up with grease-pencil.

He said, "You kin go have a look around. Available units are open, so check 'em out. Bay six is small, thirty-five a month. Fifty-one is a medium, fifty bucks. Seventy is large, sixty-five a month. If you want to store an RV, it depends on size."

"Yeah? How much for an eighty-foot yacht?"

He gaped at her.

"Kidding, Stan." She tittered like a girl I sat next to in first-year algebra, freshman year. Stan grinned, eating it up.

He gave us a sheet with a map of T&T's yard on it, put Xs on the units he'd mentioned, and pointed at the door to the yard. "Out thataway. Have yourselves a ball."

We went outside. Stan had a golf cart parked outside the door. It had a substantial frame, beefed-up suspension. Lucy gave it a little pat as we went by. "Hi, ho, Silver," she said quietly.

Without sunglasses, two minutes in the yard would have liquefied my retinas. The place was doubling as a blast furnace, all one and a half acres. No shade, dark asphalt, glare off steel-sheet doors.

"Holy cow," Lucy said. "Must be a hundred fifty out here. You oughta at least take off your shirt."

"You, too. At least."

"Yeah, right. In case you hadn't noticed, Stan has cameras all over and a monitor in his office to keep an eye on the place."

"You could probably get yourself a nice discount."

"That would be *so* worth it, Daddy."

"Which reminds me. *Dad?*"

"Worked, didn't it? So where is this unit of Arlene's?"

I checked Stan's map. "Down this way. Number seventy-two. Look for security cameras. I'll mark them on the map."

"Security cameras?"

"They could be a problem. Later."

"Groovy."

Unit seventy-two was twelve feet from seventy. Seventy was marked on the map as a large unit, available. I tested the handle before grabbing it. Good thing. Best guess, it was running about two hundred ninety degrees.

"Shirt," Lucy said.

"Come again?"

"Take off your shirt, use that."

"You just want me out of my shirt."

"You're being difficult because you want me out of mine."

So I took off my shirt, folded it, used it to lift the articulating door to unit seventy since Stan was probably watching. We went in for show, looked around.

"I totally *love* it," Lucy said. "I could like *live* in here."

Ten by twenty-four feet, dust on the floor, ten-foot ceiling, interior running a hundred forty degrees. Lots of things wouldn't survive a summer in there.

Back outside.

"Now what?" Lucy said.

"Have you noticed that the padlocks on the sheds are all the same?"

"Uh-huh. So?"

"So, I'll bet you fifty bucks he won't allow any other kind of lock on a door and that he sells 'em in his office."

"Why? You want one?"

"Two of 'em, yeah. Now that I've seen 'em."

"Don't know why. But that fifty-dollar bet reminds me I still owe you fifty for when that girl ended up in Caliente."

"You can pay me later. But getting back to the locks, which are the issue here—they look pretty goddamn husky."

"Means you're thinking of getting into Arlene's unit, right?"

"Right."

"But probably not with Stanley watching, so tell me we're coming back tonight."

"We're coming back tonight."

"Groovy."

*　*　*

We went through T&T's yard, noting the placement of cameras, checked the small and medium units for show, looked at the chain-link fence and the desert scrub beyond it, then I put on my shirt as we walked back to the office.

"See anything ya like?" Stan asked.

"Still thinking about it," Lucy said. "But probably."

"You sell locks here?" I asked.

"Sure do." He set one on the counter. "Only padlock I allow in the place. This one's one secure son of a gun, lemme tell you. I haven't never had anyone break into a unit."

"That's a double negative," Lucy said, elbows leaning on the counter. "So you've had break-ins in the past, right?"

"Huh? No. I just said—"

"Don't mind her," I told him. "She's an English Nazi, thinks she's gonna be a lawyer. Prosecutor. I'll buy two locks."

"Two?"

"Got a backyard fence that could use one."

"Hell of a lock for a backyard. So, which unit you want?"

"We're leaning toward a medium. Have to get back to you on that, though. For now, I'll just take the two locks."

He shrugged. I paid fifteen dollars each for the locks, then Lucy and I went back to the Caddy.

She gave me a quick kiss on the cheek. "English Nazi. I like it." She got behind the wheel again. "Where to now?"

"Home Depot. I saw one a few miles back, where we passed a Target, Walmart, Best Buy."

"Home Depot. That's like my all-time favorite store."

"Ever been in one?"

"Nope."

"Well, you're in for a treat. Table saws, plumbing supplies, tile flooring, pressure-treated lumber, cordless drills."

"Perfect. My idea of heaven."

We went in and I took her to the tool department. I went straight to the biggest bolt cutters they had, ones with three-foot handles. I picked up a Klein, hundred forty bucks, and tried to cut one of the locks I'd bought at Stan's. They made a fair dent in the locking bar, then stalled. Lucy followed me to the pipe department. I found two three-foot lengths of iron pipe, slid them over the handles of the cutter to give me four-foot handles, gave it a try, grunted like a guy trying to lift the front end of a '47 Chevy to impress his girl, turned my face red, and that fuckin' lock finally gave up.

"Wow," Lucy said. "I could use a lock like that on my chastity belt."

I gave her a look. "Little late for that, Sugar Plum."

She hooked an arm through mine. "Now what?"

"Now we run around town, buy more stuff."

I bought the bolt cutters and the iron pipe, paid cash to keep it off my credit card since the cutters could be misconstrued to be a burglary tool.

Behind the wheel of the Caddy, Lucy said, "Okay, more stuff to buy. Where to?"

I pointed across a busy four-lane street. "Walmart, then back to air-conditioning, a shower, Jacuzzi, maybe catch a little nap."

"Now you're talking."

"And . . . I might pick up a Danielle Steel novel in Walmart before we hit a checkout lane."

"And I'll pick up a Bic lighter to set it on fire."

CHAPTER TWENTY-THREE

NINE FORTY-EIGHT P.M. Ninety-five degrees. The last bit of sunset was a deep burgundy glow above the mountains to the west. We parked the Cadillac in the side yard of a raucous country bar called Little Joe's—raucous because it was Friday evening—as far from the entrance as possible, then hiked a quarter mile through sand and sage with the glow of untold millions of watts of distant neon faintly illuminating the ground. Lucy was dressed all in black. I had on black jeans and a dark green shirt. We wore ball caps with good-sized bills pulled down low. Before heading out, we put dark blue body paint on our faces. I carried the bolt cutters and pipes, a thirty-pound load, so the trek to T&T's yard was a high point of the evening. Lucy took along two small flashlights, a pair of gloves, and the lock I hadn't destroyed at Home Depot.

We arrived at T&T's east perimeter fence, nearest approach to unit seventy-two. The Klein cutter went through the chain-link like a Samurai sword through a chicken neck. I cut vertically up four feet, over three, peeled the section back, and in we went.

This was not the sort of thing to savor slowly, like dinner at Tavern On The Green. We went straight to number seventy-two, and I hit the lock with the bolt cutters. Well, hit the lock makes it sound easy. What I did was, I grunted and gasped, damn near did a barrel roll hanging onto those pipes, and finally with Lucy helping and the pipe pulled out another six inches for increased leverage, the lock gave up with a snap and a clang.

"Whew," said my assistant. "We should cut off a few more while we're here."

"Go ahead while I check out the shed here." I put the pieces of Arlene's lock in a pocket then rolled the door up using a glove to keep from leaving prints. Going in was a squeeze because the generator was a big one, and parked next to it was an ATV with fat tires and dried mud on the frame.

"Jo-X's generator, you think?" Lucy asked.

"That'd be my guess." It was a Triton 80kW, painted yellow, with a slightly dinged outer shell. Six feet tall, three-and-a-half wide, nearly fourteen feet long, about three tons worth. I figured it wasn't going to be here long. Even dinged and used it'd go for ten thousand dollars. Not sure how Buddie got it all the way over here and in the shed, but that wasn't my problem.

"Arlene and Buddie killed Jonnie-X," Lucy said flatly.

"Could have."

"You don't sound so sure."

"I think things are still weird. This generator probably came from Jo-X's place. A serial number would tell the police that, if they can get a warrant to have a look at it. I'm pretty sure those two are thieves. They took this generator and probably the safe that girl, Melanie, told me about. Most likely more stuff out of Xenon's place, like this ATV. But they might be more than just thieves. That video Arlene took of Shanna? How's that fit? Why'd she take it? And Jo-X strung up in the garage with a video of Shanna in his pocket? It has to be connected to that note asking for a million dollars. Jo-X gets himself superglued, later that day he arrives at the diner in his helicopter, drives off in the SUV Shanna arrived in, probably sees a doctor, comes back later that afternoon and flies back to this hideout, ends up sporting a few bullet holes. It's a mess. We're not going to figure all that out right now, so let's give this place a quick once-over and get the hell out."

The generator was right up front. Stuff had been shoved to the back to make room for it—furniture so crappy it was unlikely that Goodwill would take it, a five-foot floor lamp, other junk, two sixty-inch televisions, couple of TiVo minis, and a metal box the size of a toaster oven with a cheap combination lock on it.

The bolt cutters laughed as I cut the lock. Five pounds on the handles did the trick. Lucy lifted the top and shined a flashlight in.

"I was right," she said.

"Yeah, what?"

"Gold bars."

* * *

Yeah, right.

I nudged her aside, and . . . gold bars. Not many, but size beats quantity every time.

There were three—not the one-ounce kiddie-size bars but big, fat ten-ounce Perth Mint bars, 99.99 percent pure, worth around twelve thousand dollars each at today's spot prices. Tossed in like an afterthought were three or four little one-ounce Asahi bars, *9999* stamped on their golden faces.

"It's amazing," Lucy said, "how much you can accumulate when you save milk money starting in like the fourth grade."

"Ain't that the truth." I found a little paper envelope, opened it, and a safe-deposit key slid out onto my palm. I put it back. Nothing else of interest in the box. I put the pieces of the lock in a pocket. A missing lock would say less than a lock that had been cut.

"Now what?" Lucy said.

"Now we get out of here."

There was no thought of taking the gold. We weren't there for that. We weren't thieves. No telling where or how Arlene had gotten that gold, although I wasn't thinking milk money.

I rolled the door back down and secured it with the second of the two locks I'd bought from Stan.

Speaking of which, something like a golf cart rolled around the corner of a line of sheds and Stan himself yelled, "Hey! Hey, you!" A heavy-duty flashlight lit us up.

We ran.

A golf cart carrying five hundred pounds doesn't accelerate like a Formula One racecar. Doesn't corner well either. It wasn't a real contest. Lucy took the two pipes, and I had the bolt cutters. We made it to the fence well ahead of Stan, popped through, and high-stepped through the sage aided by the beam of Stan's big flashlight, tracking us until we were over a hundred yards out.

Three minutes later, we were outside the Cadillac at Little Joe's, scrubbing blue paint off our faces with washcloths we'd prepared in advance. Iron pipe and bolt cutters in the trunk. I got behind the wheel, nosed the car into the road, and a cop car went by with lights, no siren. Not going fast, either, so it was hunting.

"Probably looking for us," Lucy said.

"Uh-huh." I took off in the same direction as the cruiser, turned off south at the first opportunity. Back at T&T, Stan would look around but find nothing wrong with the units unless he happened to notice that one of them had a new lock on it. Arlene would have a fit next time she tried to get into the place.

I took a right at the next big intersection and went west until I saw Interstate 15 ahead, circled around to find an on-ramp, then took us north and east.

"Back to Arlene's?" Lucy asked.

"Yep. Gotta hustle if we're gonna get a room."

"Good. I love that place."

I took us up to eighty-five, held it there until we reached the turnoff to US 93, then went north at seventy.

Lucy rubbed my neck. "You were gonna tell me something. Said you'd tell me later. It's later now, and this road is boring, especially at night, so now's a good time."

"I don't remember. How about a hint?"

"It was something about a bathroom window, which sounds kinda iffy."

"Iffy? It's a true story *and* my finest hour."

"Sounds like I'm in for it, but go ahead."

So I told her about the chickadee in Bend, Oregon, last year and how I'd gone through a window in the men's room to escape. The chickadee was Sophie, a voluptuous Mexican girl, and she'd called me a shithead in the back alley behind the bar after I'd landed on the ground. I still didn't know how she'd thought to go out back in time to watch me slither headfirst out that window.

As it turned out, the road was so boring I ended up giving Lucy more of the story than it required. She was quiet for half a minute, then said, "All these women have huge tits, Mort."

"Not my fault. I don't plan these things."

"Still."

I glanced over at her. She was a shadow in the dash lights. "I told you about my fiancée, Jeri. She was about your size."

"On top, you mean?"

"Yes. She was perfect, too. Like you."

She didn't say anything for another mile. Then, "I would still marry you. Tonight, if you ask. We could go back to Vegas, be all hitched up two hours from now. You said not to say that again, but it's been three days, and nothing's changed."

Sometimes words just get you in trouble. I reached over, took her hand, and kissed her palm. Didn't say a thing.

She made a happy sound. "That mean we're engaged?"

* * *

After ten miles of silence, Lucy said, "Picasso."

"Gesundheit."

She ignored that. "What do you think of his paintings, since it's still boring out here?"

"Picasso's?"

"Uh-huh."

"Is that what his stuff is called? Paintings?"

She sighed.

"Well," I said, "most mornings before I get out of bed I give his work a moment of penetrating thought—"

"Seriously, Mort."

Seriously—I had a flashback to a discussion I'd had with my ex-wife, Dallas, about orchestras, classical music, and my being a philistine. My position was that the conductor was nothing but a glory-hog who could be replaced by one of those wacky wind-puppet things that whip and twist in the wind, promoting fast food and tire sales. All those anorexic gals intently sawing their violins and cellos never look up at him. They're focused on the music. They've played it before. They know how it goes. Once the conductor says, "go," he could duck out and have a brewski or two and get back in time to take his unearned bows. All that arm waving, hair whipping around, and sweat flying off his brow was nothing but theatrics.

"Picasso," my assistant said, not giving up.

"That's the guy who doesn't know where noses and eyes go on people's faces, right?"

Lucy laughed.

"I did that sort of thing in the second grade," I said. "Dogs looked like cows or chickens. No one gave me a million bucks for my work, though, so how's that fair?"

"It's called Cubism."

"What is?"

"Picasso's style."

"Right. No one ever called my art Cubism, either. Bunch of Mickey Mouse no-nothing tourists. I oughta sue."

*　*　*

Half a mile from Arlene's Diner I pulled off the highway onto a wide patch on the verge. I killed the lights, and we sat there with the engine ticking in the quiet as it cooled.

"Slight change of plans," I said.

"That backhoe, right? We're gonna go see what it was doing in the middle of nowhere."

"It was out there at one in the morning, so, yeah. We're right here. Might's well have a look."

She leaned over and kissed my cheek. "This's why I want to be a PI. Sneakin' around, having fun."

"Anyone ever tell you you're a spooky kid?"

"My dad. Lots of times. Makes me wonder why he bought me a BB gun when I was ten."

We got out and walked up the highway toward the diner in ball caps, dark clothing, guns on our hips. And flashlights, but we kept them turned off.

Headlights appeared, north of Arlene's, a few miles away. We had plenty of time to ease off into the desert and hunker down as a pickup truck went by. Then back out to the highway. Two hundred yards south of the diner we headed west into the desert, skirting the diner, motel, Melanie's trailer.

Only one light was on, the one illuminating the sign on the diner's roof. I guided off it, trying to estimate where the backhoe had gone. We kept going west, into starlit emptiness behind the buildings, wending our way through tough, gnarled sage.

A car glided by almost silently on the highway, a quarter mile away. Minutes later the diesel growl of an eighteen-wheeler went by in the other direction. Then all was quiet except for a lone coyote yipping in the distance, farther in the hills.

We went past the helicopter shed, kept going. After a while, I stopped and looked around. "Somewhere around here, I think."

"Sure is dark out here."

"Beautiful *and* observant."

Something backhanded my ribs in the night. Didn't see what it was. Stars were bright. The Milky Way was a glowing ribbon, but the dirt and scrub around us was all but invisible.

I risked turning on a flashlight, aimed away from the diner and motel. I swung it around, didn't see anything.

I clicked it off and we walked another thirty yards west before I tried again. Still nothing.

We did that a few more times, then Lucy said, "What was that over there?" She aimed her light at a place where the dirt didn't look natural. We headed that way.

It was a rough rectangle of loose, scuffed dirt, ten by twenty feet, several inches high, different color than the rest of the desert floor. Twisted bits of broken sage poked out of the torn-up dirt, scenting the air. Huge tire tracks were pressed into the earth.

"What do you think it is?" Lucy asked.

"Dirt."

"Huh. Do you need a PI license to get that, or should I have figured it out without all that training?"

"It was the license. Don't beat yourself up about it."

"I won't, since you don't actually *have* a license. And on a somewhat more serious note, what do you think this is? What was he doing out here?"

"Vince and I thought he was putting in an outhouse, but now that we're out here, that's probably not right."

Lucy flicked her light to the right. "There's another one."

We headed that way, found another patch of dirt twelve by twenty-five feet, sagebrush torn up, older than the one we'd just seen. I swung the light farther to the west. The beam dissipated into darkness after about sixty yards, but in that distance I saw three more almost-invisible mounds.

Like graves.

"Kinda spooky out here," Lucy said, half whispering.

A huge spotlight came on, over by the diner. Several million candlepower blasted the desert floor forty yards to our left, then swept toward us. We hit the deck, flat out in the dirt as the light passed over us. It kept moving, sweeping to the north.

"Well, poop," said my vocabulary-challenged assistant.

"Run."

I lunged to my feet. Lucy was already up. We ran south. I tried to keep up with her, but it was like trying to keep up with Shanna or Vince.

Man, being forty-two sucked.

The light raked the desert to the north, then came back, panning like the searchlight of a prison. We ran another twenty yards then hit the dirt before the light rolled over us. I'd seen *The Great Escape,* Steve McQueen as the Cooler King. I didn't have much faith in the ability of a searchlight to pick out people in the dark but I wasn't about to stand up as it went by, either.

We got up, ran. It headed back, scything across the desert. I hit the dirt. Lucy landed beside me.

"Still want to be a PI?" I said.

"Of course. This's so cool. Want me to try to shoot out that light?"

"Half a mile away with a .38 revolver? Why not? No telling who or what you'd end up hitting."

The light hunted us for three or four minutes, then went out. Twenty minutes later, Lucy and I arrived back at the Cadillac. I was breathing hard. She wasn't. She took the driver's seat.

"We're probably not gonna get that room at the Midnight Rider, huh?" she said.

"Not tonight. Arlene and Buddie will be at DefCon One, then we show up in dark clothing covered in dirt."

"DefCon One? What the heck is that?"

"Tell you later. So, do we head back to Vegas or keep going to Caliente? It's seventy miles back, eighty miles if we continue north. You choose."

"Caliente has hot springs," she said.

"Uh-huh. Beds'll do that when you really get 'em goin.'"

She stared at me. "No way you just said that."

Well, hell. Things pop out. My ex, Dallas, still gives me The Look on occasion, a kind of long-suffering incredulous stare. My mouth might be why she divorced me. That or she was terrified of the IRS, knowing agents will audit their own wives if it would get them a promotion. I'll have to ask. She would level with me now that I have a soul.

I said, "Soaking in a hot spring might be just the ticket."

"Just the ticket?"

"An expression of approval. And hot springs? What could be better, since it didn't even reach a hundred ten today."

She sighed. "Ever been in a mud bath? And don't answer with something so wacky I'd have to shoot you."

"Mud bath. Sounds like your basic oxymoron, but to answer the question without getting shot—no."

"If they've got hot springs, they might have mud baths. Very therapeutic. We should find out."

"You're driving, Sugar Plum."

* * *

As we sailed past the motel, I saw Ignacio's Cruze parked outside. So the Rat was still nosing around.

First stop in Caliente was the Pahranagai Inn. I rang a buzzer on a countertop in the office, and a lady thirty years old came yawning out of a back room. She checked us into room six, told us the hot springs north of town wouldn't be open that time of night, which by then was early in the morning.

"Well, poop," someone said.

So . . . shower and sleep. It had been a long day, starting with Ma's wake-up call before seven that morning. The shower was quick and workmanlike, goal-oriented, without the kind of undercurrent that might have delayed things. Lucy fell asleep on her side two minutes before I did, so I tucked her butt against my belly, got hold of a nice warm breast, and spooned her.

* * *

Outside the room the next morning, nine twenty-five a.m., temperature eighty-four degrees and rising rapidly, there was RPD Detective Fairchild, my buddy, pacing, puffing on a Camel. And, of course, Lucy came out the door right after me, wearing shorts and a tank top molded to her like a second skin, revealing rounded contours.

"Morning, Detective," I said.

Russell stared at me. "Nice wig. I could use one like that at our next Halloween party at RPD." He leaked smoke as Lucy came up beside me. "Miss Lucy," he said, giving her a nod and a brief appraising look. "By the way, what's your last name?"

I'd asked him to check on her birthday, so his question was a bit of misdirection for which I would have to thank him later.

Her eyes narrowed. "What's it to you?"

"Just wondering."

"You're kinda nosy."

"Sorry about that. I do it for a living." He turned to me. "Funny, you two showin' up here. What's the story?"

"No-o-osy," Lucy said.

I put a hand on her shoulder. "Take it easy, kiddo. Detective Fairchild here more or less qualifies as a friend."

"More or less?" Russ said.

"A friend?" Lucy said. "Seriously?"

I was thinking about distributing Valium to get things under control when Danya and Shanna came out of unit nine in wigs, hats, sunglasses, and hot-weather clothing that revealed enough skin to put a father into cardiac arrest. Perfect. Southern Nevada didn't have that much Valium so I took a step back to let nature take its course.

Danya shook her head in disbelief when she saw the three of us standing there. She and Shanna drifted over.

"How about some breakfast and a powwow, everyone?" I said before Danya could start in on us.

"Powwow?" she said. "You gotta be kidding." She turned to her father. "I thought you were gonna get a different motel, leave us alone."

"I am leaving you alone."

"Yeah, right. There's a motel the other end of town."

"So I'll go. Today." He turned to me. "Breakfast where?"

"Wherever the locals feed. That's always best."

We cruised the main drag and ended up at Dottie's Kitchen. We went in three cars, Cadillac, Focus, Russ in a dark blue Ford Explorer three years old.

The breakfast crowd at Dottie's was thinning out. We found a booth away from the remaining customers, Danya and Shanna in one side, Lucy and I facing them, Russell in a chair at the end.

Our waitress was in her forties with big hair, a plastic stick-on smile, five menus. She took drink orders and left.

"My treat," I said. "Order up."

After a while, Big-Hair took our orders, left again.

"So, Dad," Danya said, "you said he's unprofessional and a maverick and you don't like him, so what the *hell* is he doing here?"

"Nice," Lucy said.

Russ shrugged. "He's got other qualities I'm finding useful, in addition to the two you just mentioned."

"Perfect." Danya looked at me with her usual hint of venom. "So go ahead and powwow, Mr. Useful."

I pulled out my cell phone. "Got something to show you," I said to Russ.

"Oh, no. *No!*" Danya yelped.

"Got a problem with this?" I asked her. "If so, why?"

"What is it?" Russell said.

Danya looked down at her hands. "It's . . . just . . . *shit.*" She shot me a lethal *j'accuse* look, then slumped back in the booth. "Go ahead. Whatever. I give up."

I showed Russ the two Shanna videos. Twice each.

He looked over at his daughter and his . . . daughter-in-law. "What's that all about? Where was that taken? Who took it?"

"Someone at this table is the fabled Celine," I said.

Russ stared at Danya. "How could you?"

"I couldn't. Did you actually *look* at that video, Dad?"

Shanna said, "*I'm* Celine. I mean, I was." She looked at me. "And thanks so much for bringing this up, Mortimer."

"*Da nada*. And it's Mort. We've got a hell of a problem, ladies. You two in particular. It isn't going to go away until it's dealt with, so let's deal with it."

Russ stared at Shanna. "*You're* Celine? The one with Xenon? The missing girl everyone's talking about?"

"I was. For almost three weeks."

"Why? I mean how? I mean . . ." He stared at me. "You thought it was Danya."

"I goofed. It was her bride."

Lucy laughed softly.

Danya shot her a look. "We're married. So what? Maybe you could act like you're at least fourteen." She used the same look on me. "And 'bride'? You could clean up your act, too."

"Sorry. Groom didn't seem to fit. But if you want to take a stab at it, be my guest."

"Je-sus, you're . . . you're . . ."

"Let's back up," Russ said quickly. "Who took those videos you just showed me?"

So, with Shanna butting in from time to time, the two of us told him about Arlene, Arlene's Diner, Shanna's night at Xenon's hideaway, and the super-gluing of the rapper appendage.

He stared at Shanna in wonder. "You super-glued his . . . his . . . but *why*?"

I knew why. I leaned closer, wanting to hear this. She wasn't going to put Josie into this, so what was the lie this time?

"Because," Shanna said, "he never said anything about sex before he got me up there. Then that's what it turned into, and it was hard to get him to back off, take no for an answer."

"But he did," Russ said. "Back off, I mean."

"Eventually. He was drinking and I helped that along. I got him really drunk, but before that, it was like attempted rape. It's a good thing I'm strong. After a while he finally passed out, but I was still super pissed off."

"Man, I guess so." He shook his head. "So you're the one who did that. Jesus. This's getting complicated. Who else knows you did it?"

"Far as I know, everyone at this table, no one else. I figure he got separated from himself at some doctor's place, but I doubt he'd tell his doctor who glued the dork to the dork."

Lucy laughed. "Perfect."

Separated from himself. I would have to remember that if the situation ever came up again.

"You went up there with him," Russ said. "Why would you even risk doing that?"

Shanna shrugged. "Everyone thought he had a place, a secret hideout. If he did, I wanted to see it, that's all. He never said anything about sex. I told him up front that wasn't gonna happen, then he comes onto me like a freaking maniac."

"So, now you're caught up, Russ," I said. "The issue now is, what're we gonna *do* about all this?" I looked at the two girls. "Jonnie-X was in your garage. It's become public knowledge that you two are married, although the world at large doesn't know you were Celine, Shanna. You're both wanted for questioning. Your father and father-in-law is a cop." I couldn't resist that. No way. I think I caught Lucy's chuckle with an elbow right before it leaked out.

The father-in-law thing went by without comment. What I'd laid out was serious, and it was evident that no one had a ready solution to put out there. In fact, it wasn't easy, in thirty words or less, to say exactly what the problem was.

"Your thoughts, Russ," I said.

He let out a breath, as if he'd been holding it for the past twenty minutes, then he gave Shanna a piercing look, as cops do. "Why? *Why* were you Celine?"

Right to the crux of the matter. It wasn't my place to bring Josie into it, tell Russ that one of the world's greatest lowlifes had raped his youngest daughter. That was up to Danya. Or Josie. I gave her a silent questioning look. One word and Russ would turn into Vesuvius, but how could Danya explain Shanna's being Celine without bringing Josie's rape into it?

I was about to find out.

"For the money," Danya said. She gave me a rock-hard look that warned me to keep my mouth shut or die.

"What money?" Russ said.

Shanna took up the lie. "Money for school and like a decent car since mine is old and always breaking down. Jonnie gave me twenty thousand dollars a concert, and a thousand a day. Just to go places and be seen with him and be up there onstage to . . . to wear what I wore and show myself off."

"Twenty thousand . . ." Russ stared at her. But he shook it off quickly and said, "Then the guy ends up in your garage with bullet holes in him. How'd that happen?"

"That's the totally insane part," Danya said. "We don't know a thing about it, who put him there or why."

That "why" couldn't go unchallenged. It left too much up in the air. Time to bring more into it, now that the Josie factor had been sidelined. "There was a sort of weird blackmail note, Russ."

"A note? Blackmail?" His head whipped between Danya and me. "What for?"

For an instant, she gave me a cold stare, then she shrugged and slumped in the booth. The note was their out. The note made her and Shanna innocent. "It was left in our mailbox," she said. "Some idiot demanded a million dollars."

I got a Xerox copy of the note out of my wallet, handed it to Russ. He read it twice and I read it again: *Get $1000000 redy in smal bills by tusday and I will get him down and take him away no problum. I will fon monday and tok to you.*

Russ set the note on the table. "Mind if I keep this?" he asked me.

"All yours. The original is in Reno if you need it." I got out my cell phone and took a picture of the note. My copy.

"At first we thought it was a joke," Danya said. "The kind of stupid thing kids do. But then I thought it might not be a joke since Shanna was Celine, or had been. By then she'd left Jo-X, but it would be a big huge deal if it got out. The note didn't make *sense*. We didn't know Jo-X was in our garage, but Shanna had super-glued him. Maybe he told someone. But 'get him down, take him away'? And a million dollars? That was just crazy. So I kind of hired Mortimer—*Mort*—to look into it since"—she gave her father an accusing look—"*you* said he's a maverick."

"So my involvement is your fault, Russ," I said.

Danya glared at me. "But I never *really* hired you. I just told you to phone me so we could talk."

"Then *you* hired me," I said to Russ, "since that maverick thing appealed to you."

"Big mistake, Dad," Danya said.

"Or *not*," Lucy spoke up. "Mort's the only one who's been putting things together. All you two have been doing is hiding out and playing house in that motel room."

"*And*," I said, loud enough to yank everyone's attention away from Lucy's comment, "we have a reporter for *Celebrity News* running around with about eighty percent of the story ready to go, so the shit's gonna hit the fan sometime soon. When it hits, the splatter is gonna be something else, kids."

Danya made a face. Probably didn't like the image.

"*How* soon, you think?" Russ asked.

"Don't know. Right now he's sitting on it, but if he gets a whiff of anyone else on it, it'll probably be in the next issue or a special edition." I looked at Shanna. "He knows you're Celine. He found that out the first two weeks. He knows Jo-X was found in *Celine's* garage, and he's got pictures. There's not much more to this story, so I doubt he'll put it off much longer. All in all, the longer you girls stay hidden, the more guilty it makes you look."

"Keeping out of the public's eye doesn't make us guilty, it's just common-freakin'-sense," Danya said.

"Right. Tell that to John Deere out in Iowa."

"I don't give a rat's ass what anyone thinks in Iowa."

"Well put, but"—I turned to Russ—"you're the father, but also the cop, and I think a professional opinion is warranted. Should they turn themselves in?"

He didn't jump to answer that one. He thought about it for a while, then sighed, letting out enough hot air to lift a dirigible. "Probably not, at least not right now. We need to chew on this a while longer. I know where they are. If it comes to that, I'll take the heat. I can say I told 'em to keep out of sight—not as a cop, but as a father who is a cop."

"Which could end your career," I said.

He shrugged. "Maybe I'll be a private eye, like you."

Good one, Russ. I heard Spade and Hammer yucking it up in the next booth. "Something I'd like to see," I said.

"You got any idea how many cops end up as PIs?"

"I'll have to get back to you on that. And if your advice for Danya, Shanna, and 'Celine' is to stay out of sight, fine, I'm on board. But to drag all this back to the issue we're still tap-dancing around, guess what, folks?—somebody killed Jo-X."

That shut down the conversation for several minutes.

Finally our food arrived and we tucked into it. That delayed the conversation another ten minutes, but I could feel the cams and wheels working in everyone's head. Except mine. I was tired of it. Time to let someone else jump out there with suggestions and solutions.

And still Josie wasn't in it, at least as far as Russ knew. I didn't know if he had bought Shanna's explanation for why she'd been Celine, but twenty grand a concert was a pretty convincing reason, if you needed money and didn't mind being associated with lyrics that had already rotted fifty thousand brain stems.

"He had a ton of enemies," Russ said, breaking the silence.

"Yes, he did," I said. "That'll help. But he ended up in Shanna's garage and Shanna is Celine, or was. That's not general knowledge. Let's hope it stays that way. Not even Xenon knew who she was. But it would be nice if we could figure out who did the world a favor and killed that troll and why he ended up in 'Celine's' garage and not yours, Russ, or mine, or in the empty desert somewhere, which would've been the best option."

Russ tapped the table with a finger. "Someone asked for a million bucks. Whoever it was knew Shanna was Celine. Had to. Then they killed Jo-X and strung him up in that garage."

"Yet we're still spinning our wheels," I said. "Something is missing. Why kill him? Why put him in *that* garage?"

"Money," Danya said. "*Someone* knew about Shanna. They killed him and tried to blackmail us. What's so hard about that?"

"A million bucks, that's what," Russ said. "Who would think you could come up with that kind of money?"

"We should get the Wharf Rat in on this," Lucy said. "He knew Shanna was Celine. Not that I think he killed Jo-X, runty little guy like that. Of course, he did have a gun."

Russ stared at her. "Huh? Wharf rat? A gun?"

Lucy bumped my shoulder. "Tell him."

"That reporter for the *News*," I said. "I told you he went over the back fence at the girls' house like a freakin' wharf rat—hence the name. He made the connection between Shanna and Celine." I looked at Russ. "What caliber bullets was Xenon shot with?"

"Thirty-eights. So what?"

"So he didn't do it. At least not with the gun we saw up at Xenon's hideout. He had a .45, looked like it would knock him over if he fired it. I doubt that he knows how Jo-X ended up in the garage, but it's possible he knows something about all this, something obscure, and hasn't put it together yet."

"He should be here with us now," Russ said.

"Like I said," Lucy muttered.

"I might be able to round him up," I said. I didn't tell Russ I'd seen his car at the Midnight Rider Motel on the way past the place last night. I didn't want a parade headed down that way. Turns out a parade would have been a good thing. Hindsight, as they say, is 20-20, but when you're on the front line, vision runs about 20-800.

"See if you can do that," Russ said. "We'll be here." He looked at Danya. "Somewhere in Caliente."

"Sundowner Motel," Danya said. "Or the Double Down. I saw 'em on the way over here." She put a hand on his arm. "It's not like we don't want you staying at our motel, Dad, but . . ."

"But you two don't need me right next door."

"Something like that. But actually, now that you're here, I'm glad you are. I mean, we don't know what's going on. You've got my cell number and you'll be less than a mile away since this is a really small town."

After a moment of silence, Russ looked at Shanna. "I never got a chance to welcome you to the family, but . . . welcome. I'm still not sure about that Celine business. Looks like it attracted attention none of us needed, but we'll deal with it. Somehow."

"Not sure how this fits, if at all," I said, "but I think those two at that diner, Arlene and her kid, Buddie, stole some stuff from Jo-X's hideaway up in the hills before or after the place burned down. Most likely before. In fact, they might've burned it down to cover their tracks. I can't tell when that happened, but it might've been right after they heard Xenon was dead. Soon as they heard that, they'd be at his place within hours, loading up."

"What stuff? What'd they take?"

"A good-sized generator. Eighty kilowatts. And maybe a safe they can't open. Probably a bunch of other stuff, as much as they could cart away. The woman who took those videos, Arlene, probably knew the helicopter pilot was Xenon. I think it would have been almost impossible for him to have kept that a secret. If I had to guess, I'd say he was paying her to keep quiet."

Russ stared at me. "Christ, Angel, she probably killed him. Her and what's his name again—Buddie? What're we doing, tap-dancing around here?"

"It's certain they're opportunists and thieves, not necessarily murderers though."

"Break one law, it's easier to break another. Kid breaks into a house, next thing he's pulling armed robberies in a parking lot and someone ends up dead."

"If Xenon was paying her to keep quiet, killing him would have cut off the money spigot. Don't see that happening."

"Maybe." He didn't look convinced. "So where'd you learn about that generator thing? How'd you get that?"

"Officer Day dug up information on Arlene. She's got a shed in a storage facility. I went in and had a look—"

"*We* had a look," Lucy said.

"You weren't there if I say you weren't there," I told her. "And you weren't there." I turned to Russ. "There's an eighty-thousand-watt diesel generator in there. A generator is missing from Jo-X's place in the hills. Two and two, Russ."

"How the hell did you 'have a look' in her shed? Place like that is usually fenced-in, keypad access."

"It was something of a maverick operation. Which is why you hired me. You would never have gotten a warrant—'you' meaning Vegas cops. You want details?"

He shook his head. "Not now. Maybe never. I could put the Lincoln County or state police on Arlene and her kid, though."

"Not yet. There's no telling how that'd screw things up. We still don't know who killed Jo-X."

"Yeah, well, horse pucky," he said. "But I'm still thinking I'd like to keep a real close eye on that Arlene woman and her kid. Real effing close."

"'Effing,'" Lucy said. "Cool."

CHAPTER TWENTY-FOUR

"Hot springs," she said when we got back in the Caddy.

"First we clean our guns."

"Of course. I was just thinking that." She waited a moment. "Why?"

"All that dust diving we did last night."

"Oh, yeah. That."

We hadn't given up our room at the Inn yet. Checkout time was in forty-five minutes. From the lockbox in the trunk I got out basic gun-cleaning supplies. We sat at a table in the room and wiped the guns down, ran patches with a splash of Hoppe's No. 9 on them through cylinders and barrels, ran a few more patches through, put a single drop of oil in the mechanism, wiped off the excess, reloaded.

"We didn't use that bed there," Lucy said, eyeing the king.

"You didn't sleep? That's too bad. I did."

"Very funny."

"They're gonna kick us out of here in fifteen minutes."

She thought about that. "Okay, hot spring."

Ryder's Hot Spring was a six-minute drive north. Private room for an hour ran forty bucks. We got naked, took a quick rinse-off shower in a kind of alcove above the pool. The pool was down half a dozen steps, a ten-by-ten-foot concrete square just under four feet deep. The bottom was a layer of smooth pebbled gravel that gave a great foot massage. Water temperature was a hundred three degrees.

Lucy went down the steps first, then crouched down slightly. The water hit her at mid-nipple. She closed her eyes and leaned against a stone wall, letting the water support most of her weight. "Heaven."

She opened her eyes and smiled as I came down the stairs. "Now *there's* a promising sight," she said.

"Says the nineteen-year-old vixen with the fake ID."

"Get in here. I want to cop a feel."

"If you must."

She trudged through the water, producing a little swirling wake, put her arms around my waist, and pulled me close. "A week ago I was waiting tables at McGinty's. Now look."

"Yup."

"So articulate." She kissed my neck then put her left leg between mine, curled it around my right calf like a python. Off in a corner I thought I saw Sam Spade in a mask and snorkel blowing laugh bubbles.

"Yup."

"A man of few words."

"A man who knows when to keep his mouth shut."

"Yeah? When did that happen?" Her lips brushed mine, then she backed away a few inches and said, "That sort of tickles. Not that I mind."

"What?"

"*This*, Cowboy. What did you *think*?"

And so on.

* * *

I pulled the Caddy up in front of room one at the Midnight Rider Motel. The time was four twenty p.m. We'd run an hour over at the hot spring and paid another forty dollars. Then there was lunch at Dottie's Kitchen and a leisurely walk around Caliente to see what the place had to offer. The town was pretty basic. Not many people in Manhattan or San Francisco were going to be in a rush to sell their high-rises and move out there. At a dim saloon called Jerry's, I found a Pete's Wicked Ale and Lucy had iced tea.

Ignacio's Chevy Cruze wasn't anywhere around the motel or Arlene's Diner when we got there, so it looked as if we weren't going to pick his brain anytime soon.

"Well, poop. Where'd that dodo-head go?" Lucy wondered.

"He'll turn up when you least expect it. Or want it. Next time we see him we'll tell him about that dodo-head thing."

"Are we gonna stay here tonight?"

"Might's well. Weird things happen around here. But I think we'll keep our guns ready just in case."

Arlene had the register's cash drawer open when we went in. When she saw us, her fingers stopped in the midst of counting a thin wad of bills. Her eyes were bright on us, searching.

"How about a room?" I said.

She gave me an appraising look. "What's the attraction here? You could be in Vegas in little over an hour."

"That's a pretty high-pressure sales pitch," I said. "I'm not sure I can resist."

"It can't be the food."

"It's the unbeatable views and the curb appeal. You oughta be on a list of Best Western motels."

If a virus could smile, that's how it would look. Her eyes had all the warmth of an alligator's. "I'll put you in number four."

"How about that first room? We're used to it."

"Shower head was leaking. I've got my kid working on it. He has to get a part at Lowe's, down in Vegas. I'll put you in Four. It's a better room anyway, same price." She pushed a check-in form toward me, and a pen, then said, "Was that you two, out back in the desert last night?"

I stared at her. "Out where?"

She aimed a crooked finger. "Behind the place here, half a mile or so west."

"Nope." A lie works best without elaboration.

I filled in the form, gave her three twenties, got change, and we headed for the door.

Just then a two-way radio on the counter beside the register squawked. A man's voice said, "Got tracks in the dirt out here, Ma. People been walkin' around, but I don't see nothin' much."

Arlene didn't answer, didn't pick up the radio. Eyes like the muzzles of machine guns tracked us to the door.

I opened it, then stopped and offered Lucy the open door with a little sweep of my hand. "After you."

She took the hint. "You opened it. You should go first."

"Really, kiddo, I insist."

"I think the saying is 'age before beauty.'"

"That was during the nineteen hundreds. Now it's more like 'if you don't go first, I'll kick your butt.'"

"You and who else?"

"Ma?" said the radio. "You there?"

Good. I was hoping we'd hear more about tracks in the dirt out in the desert.

Arlene put the radio to her lips. "Hold your damn horses." Her voice was a sharp smoker's rasp. She stared at us.

And that was that.

I went outside and Lucy followed.

She glanced through a window as we headed toward the motel. "She's on that radio now, watching us. Spooky old bitch."

"Language, Sugar Plum."

"Spooky old cunt, then." She hugged my arm. "And just so you know, that word is in the *Vagina Monologues*."

"I bet they don't use it that way."

"Well, no. But it suits her."

* * *

As we walked to the motel, I saw a pickup truck out in the desert, a guy walking around. Buddie. I opened the trunk of the Cadillac. Lucy got out her suitcase and I retrieved my travel bag.

I looked over at the diner. "Want to shake a tree, see what falls out?"

She turned a full circle. "You see a tree around here?"

"It's an expression, kiddo. But to be clear, how about we take a stroll behind the motel here in broad daylight, meander up to where that backhoe was digging the other night—"

"A meandering stroll, huh?"

"—and see if our walk gets another mention."

"Or if that kid of hers tries to run us over with that backhoe. Which, in case you hadn't noticed, is parked behind the diner. Or maybe comes after us with a shotgun since they're concerned about something out there."

"A shotgun would be a big something falling out of a tree. Shaking trees is an old PI's trick. And I've got Russ's number."

"He's an hour away."

"Which is why we will go armed."

"Probably a good idea. But we better at least wait 'til Buddie gets back, since he's still out there. You really want to yank this tiger's tail?"

"We need information. I want to shake things up, if there's anything to shake up."

"There is. Pretty obviously, Mort. Not sure what, though."

"You got that lucky-unlucky feeling?"

"Sure do. C'mon." She headed for the room.

Outside, attached to a wall in the shade between rooms three and four, a thermometer registered a hundred two degrees. Inside, the temperature was about ninety. The room was marginally nicer than number one—king-size bed instead of queen, the shower head wasn't leaking, the carpet was somewhat newer. I turned on the air conditioner, set the thermostat at seventy-two degrees. It started up with a shimmy that shook the wall, then settled down.

"Now what?" Lucy said.

"Whatever you like. I'm gonna read." I flopped down on the bed with Berney's *Whiplash River* that I'd been carrying around since I'd left Reno.

Lucy watched me for a moment, then removed her top and started doing inhuman "stretchies" in a small open space between the bed and a wall.

I didn't watch. Much. During the next half hour, I managed to read three whole pages.

* * *

Arlene squinted at the monitor.

"They still there?" Buddie asked on the two-way. "What's goin' on? What're they doin'?"

"He's just reading. And, good heavens, that ridiculous little girl is in a handstand, doubled over, not wearing a shirt."

"There's nothing out here. "I'm comin' in."

"Those two are very strange. I need to think about this." She turned off the radio, watched the monitor a while longer, then went back into the diner.

* * *

We gave it an hour, then saddled up. Damn wig was too hot so I went without and the hell with it. I wore jeans and kept my short-sleeve shirt untucked to keep my gun out of sight. Given what Lucy was wearing, she didn't have any way to hide her gun, so she left it in the lockbox in the Caddy's trunk. She'd slathered herself with sunblock. She wore her sun hat, sunglasses. I wore my Stetson, which made me look like John Wayne—except for the sunglasses. Wayne was always riding around on a horse in bright sunlight, which is the reason he had a world-class squint.

We headed west. No sign of life, so I veered toward the diner as we went by to have a look at the back of the place in daylight. Not much to see, old Impala parked outside the back door, junk piled up behind the building—a refrigerator on its side with the door missing, four-by-eight-foot plywood sheets leaning against a scaly clapboard wall, a toilet still in a wooden crate, used tires. Buddie's backhoe was on its flatbed trailer, parked near a power pole. Power lines looped black against the bright blue sky into a gooseneck head and a conduit that led down to a service panel. The old shed back there still had a slight, tired lean.

We were fifty feet past the diner when a panel truck pulled up behind the Impala in the dusty area between the diner and the shed, Henderson Lock & Safe printed on the side.

"Interesting," Lucy said.

"We could go over and watch."

"That bitch or Buddie would shotgun us for sure."

Arlene came out a back door, followed by Buddie. Buddie was the guy I'd seen while crammed into the foot well of the Mustang a few days ago. He looked a full head taller than Arlene, which would put him at six foot six or more. Big guy, looked like Sasquatch. He gave Lucy and me a long look, said something to

Arlene, then the guy in the panel truck was out with a clipboard in his hands, and they had to deal with him.

Good time to wander around where they didn't want us to go. I was happy to have a .357 Magnum on my hip.

The sun bore down and did its best to broil us. The walk out was so pleasurable that I thought we ought to go up into the hills, a mile or more away, see what was on the other side. Lucy said go ahead, report back, so that discussion ended early.

We went out half a mile. Daylight made finding the place— whatever it was—a lot easier. We followed the backhoe trail and finally found tire tracks all over as the backhoe had made dozens of three-point turns. Low mounds of disturbed dirt were more evident, ten or twelve of them lined up on the playa where the land sloped up toward the hills.

"This one looks sort of new," Lucy said, rubbing dirt with a shoe.

It was at the end of the row. The smell of torn sage was strong, the dirt was slightly darker, but there was still nothing to indicate what Buddie had been doing out there—although I was starting to get a fairly unpleasant idea.

We looked around awhile. Tire tracks, vague places where the earth seemed raised. Others that seemed slightly lower.

Then a pickup truck came bounding across the desert toward us from the direction of the diner.

"Company coming," Lucy said. "Kinda fast, too."

I unsnapped my holster, left the gun hidden.

The guy in the beard rolled up, cut the engine, got out. He was more than six-six, weighed well over three hundred pounds, arms with muscle like you see on anacondas. "Whatcha doin'?" he asked.

"Rock hounding. Lots of interesting minerals out here."

"Yeah? Like what?" He came closer.

Now what? Let him get within reach? Pull the gun? This was a lousy situation. I motioned for Lucy to move away, let me handle it, which I did by drifting sideways, away from Lucy, keeping the guy at least ten feet away. I circled around a big sagebrush, didn't think he could leap over it at me. I picked up a rock that looked about as likely to be valuable as a wad of used Kleenex. I gave it a scientific look. "Looks like you got some good kinorthosite out here."

"What's that?"

Kinorthosite was nothing at all, but it had a minerally sound and enough syllables to keep this guy off balance. "You find it where you find deposits of decomposed agarnalite."

"What's that?"

If I kept this up, he was gonna wear me out. "It's used as a base in road construction."

"Sounds like it's worth about twenty cents a ton then. You're staying at the motel, right?"

"So far."

"So far. What's that mean?"

"Might move on. Haven't decided yet." I pointed to a nearby place where the earth had been disturbed. "What're you doing out here?"

"Burying septic tanks."

"Probably have to flush twice to get shit this far out."

His laugh was a baritone rumble. "Old used tanks, dude. I put in a new septic, people pay me five hundred bucks to haul the old one out. Suckers stink to high heaven, so I bury 'em out here, far enough out so you can't smell 'em. You want, I'll dig one up and you can have it, no charge."

"That's tempting. I'll think about it." Lucy was forty yards away, looking at me. "Well, nice talking with you. Gotta see what we can find up in the hills. Interesting geology around here."

I started walking, headed away from the diner.

"Not much gold up there," Buddie said, "but I've seen a lot of sidewinders. They're hard to spot in the sand. Good luck in those shoes."

I stopped for a moment.

"They taste like chicken, sorta," he said. "But you gotta cook 'em real slow or they're tough as boot leather."

"Good to know." I headed out again.

He stood there and watched me go. I caught up to Lucy and we kept walking west, away from the diner.

"What'd he say?" she asked.

"Our shoes suck, and watch out for sidewinders."

"That's what? Like rattlesnakes?"

"Yep."

"Well, poop. How 'bout a piggyback ride?"

*   *   *

So we walked that mile up into the hills, after all. Below, Buddie watched us for ten minutes then gave up and drove back to the diner. The panel truck was gone. The guy might've opened the safe like it was a cheap tin breadbox. Or failed quickly. Either way, he was gone and Lucy and I were alone with Arlene and Buddie. And Melanie and the cook, Kirby. Every ten or fifteen minutes, a car or truck would roll by on the highway. We didn't see any sidewinders and, like Buddie had said, there wasn't any gold in the hills, at least not decent-sized nuggets.

We arrived back at the motel-diner, dusty, hot, and thirsty. Arlene wasn't in the diner, but Melanie was wandering around, fussing with the tables, menus, salt and pepper shakers.

"How about some water," I said to her. "Four bottles."

She got the bottles out of a tall cooler with glass doors and a Pepsi logo. "Eight bucks."

I gave her a ten.

She handed me two dollars change. "You were that guy I talked to out back a coupla nights ago, right?"

"That's right."

"You sort of like this place, huh?"

"It's a lot like Venice, only hotter."

"Really? Venice is like . . . like in France or Spain, right?"

"Close. You nailed the right continent."

"Cool."

"Did they finally get that safe open?"

Her face shut down. She turned and looked toward the back of the diner. "What safe?" she said, almost a whisper.

I kept my voice low. "The one you said was in that shed out back."

"See, the thing is, I'm kinda gettin' behind here, mister. I gotta fill the ketchup bottles on the tables, so if that water was all you wanted . . ."

"Right. Nice talkin' with you."

Lucy and I left. We headed for the far room of the motel. "When did they move Venice?" Lucy said. "I didn't catch that."

"Place was sinking into the sea. They moved it a month or two ago, Sugar Plum. It's in Corsica now."

"Corsica. That's in England or Holland, right?"

"Yeah. One of those."

"Guess I can be kinda bitchy, huh? Hope it's not enough to scare you off."

"I'll let you know."

* * *

We showered. I read. Lucy stretched awhile, but there's only so much of that a person can do before their bones are so flexible they can no longer take Earth's gravity, so she went out to the car, found a battered James Lee Burke novel in the trunk, *Cadillac Jukebox,* and settled down beside me on the bed. I wondered when or if we would hear something more about our walking tour out in the desert.

Hunger eventually drove us back to the diner. A car had pulled up and a couple with two boys about six and eight years old were in the dining room—the boys running amok, playing grab ass, toppling a few chairs while the parents took a break from parenting.

Arlene came out of the back, went back, came out again, went back, didn't pay us any attention. Melanie took our orders. They were out of lobster thermidor again so we settled for greasy fried chicken, baked potato, cole slaw in a side dish.

"Yum," Lucy said, picking the skin off a chicken breast.

"Calories, dear."

"That's about all it is."

The sun went below the hills. Long shadows crept eastward across the shallow bowl of the valley.

"Got apple or berry pie for dessert," Melanie said. "And ice cream, vanilla or chocolate."

"Berry pie with vanilla ice cream for me," I said.

Lucy looked up at her. "Nothing for me, thanks. I'm saving myself for my wedding night."

Melanie stared at her, then shook her head and left.

"Not sure you should do that to her," I said.

"Maybe I'll have a little of your ice cream when it arrives."

"Don't. You won't be able to wear white at your wedding. People will talk."

"I'll wear white. You'll see, since you'll be there."

Dessert arrived. Lucy nipped a single spoonful of ice cream. I paid, we went outside. To settle the food, we walked half a mile up the highway and back. The land grew dark and infinite around us. The Milky Way filled with secrets.

"Nice out here," Lucy said as we stood outside the motel. The world was dead quiet. "Except for . . ." She nodded toward the diner. "Those two weirdos, Lizzie Borden and Bigfoot. Still got your gun on you, right?"

I slapped my hip. The revolver was on my belt under my shirt and it would stay there, maybe even when I was in bed. Which I told Lucy.

"In bed? That's so *cool*. I could put that in my diary. I slept with Wyatt Freakin' Earp. You *are* gonna wear the hat, too, aren't you?"

"Of course. And spurs."

"Oh, great. I hate it when those dig in."

CHAPTER TWENTY-FIVE

THE SMOKE ALARM above the bed went off seconds after I woke to the smell of smoke. First Alert gave off that ear-piercing shriek that catapults you out of bed and yanks your brain inside out. Lucy was out of bed on the other side, a ghost in the dark. She grabbed the blanket as I tried to find my clothes on a chair beside the bed. Too late. The smoke drove me away. I headed for the door naked, eyes stinging, watering.

Lucy ran outside with the blanket in her arms. I followed on her heels and ran into a brick wall outside the door that slammed me back into the room on my back, dazed. Then something grabbed my foot, dragged me out into the night, and a weight like a Jeep Cherokee landed on my chest. Then something grabbed my head and banged it onto the concrete walkway, hard, and all the lights went out.

* * *

I woke to a murmur of sound that slowly got louder. In time, I recognized Arlene's pre-cancerous smoker's rasp, interspersed at intervals with Lucy's voice. When I finally cracked my eyes open, Arlene was in a chair ten feet away, a cigarette drooping at the corner of her mouth, smoke curling up past her face. She held a snub-nose revolver loosely in one hand and was looking a little way off to my right.

"You didn't have to kill him," Lucy said.

Kill who? Me? I wasn't dead. Yet. I wanted to tell Lucy I was still alive, then Arlene said, "That little shit was in our shed, the one out back. He saw the safe." Her cigarette bobbled as she spoke, sending ash down the front of her sweater. She took the cigarette out, held it between index and middle fingers as she brushed her sweater. "I could've handled that, but he also found a solid silver sculpture of a mountain lion bringing down a nine-point buck. The artist was famous. One of those western guys, like Remington. The thing was on display in one of the bigger Vegas casinos for half a year. They'd presented it to that Jonnie-X guy with all kinds of whoop-ti-do, so thousands of people had seen it, knew it belonged to him. It weighs forty-four pounds. At today's silver prices, it's worth about fourteen thousand dollars so Buddie just had to have it. He doesn't know when to leave something that could ruin us. We'll have to melt it down, of course, and soon. It's worth over fifty thousand as a work of art, but it's too well known so there's no way to sell it like that."

"So you killed him," Lucy said.

I still didn't know who'd been killed.

Arlene shrugged. "What was I supposed to do with him?"

My eyes felt droopy and I was having trouble making sense of the conversation. Maybe I had another fuckin' concussion. Goddamn things were gonna be the death of me yet.

"Wrrr-mi-cloz," I said. I heard my own voice and the words hadn't come out the way I'd hoped. Not even close. I was in a chair in jockey shorts, nothing else, wrists held together in front of me by a plastic strap. A loop of rope was around my waist to keep me in the chair. The knot was somewhere behind me, out of reach. I'd asked where my clothes were, tried to anyway, but my voice wasn't working right. The gravel sound of it, however, drew Arlene's grackle eyes in my direction.

"Ah, it's awake."

"Mort!" Lucy said. "Are you all right?"

"Shuuu," I said. "Yeauuu." Didn't sound right to me, so I tried clearing my throat, which about took the top of my head off, then I said, "Sor'v. Yep."

"He needs a doctor," Lucy said.

"As if," Arlene responded.

So, no doc.

I felt chilled. We were in a room with a washer and dryer, a deep sink, cupboards, rolls of toilet paper on shelves, cleaning supplies, old refrigerator, cardboard boxes, a water heater. A door behind Arlene was closed. An overhead light fixture full of bugs cast a yellowish glow into the room. The floor was bare concrete with a few spidery cracks in it. Off to my left, a window was black, so I figured it was still night.

"Whz time zit?" I asked.

Arlene glanced at the wall behind me. "Two forty, not that it matters."

"Wer's Bud-d-dee?"

"Digging. Got a little backhoe work to do."

"Got ano'er steptic t'brry?"

She tilted her head at me.

I gathered up my tongue, blinked to try to get her to quit being double since one of her was more than enough, and tried again. "He bury'n anoth' sebtic tank?"

She laughed. "He told you that old story, huh? No, Mr. Angel, we don't bury septic tanks out there."

I didn't want to know what they did bury, but even in my sorry state I had a pretty good idea. My telling her wasn't likely to give them any new ideas, so I said, "Cars."

She tilted her head again. "Bravo. Give that man a giant stuffed panda." Her voice held not a trace of humor.

Still, she'd tried to be funny. I thought killing her would be even more amusing.

Lucy said, "They killed the Wharf Rat, Mort."

Arlene stared at her. "Wharf Rat?"

"Vincent Ignacio," I said, the words coming out quite a bit better that time as my mouth and brain finally connected. I felt sick, though, knowing he was gone. Knowing we were next.

"Who?" She still looked perplexed.

"You might know him as Bill Hogan. He drove a red Chevy Cruze."

"Oh, yes. Mr. Hogan. He was snooping around the shed out back, got inside, and ended up rather dead."

"Is 'rather dead' more dead or less dead than just plain dead?"

She smiled, lips pressed together as if they'd been sutured. "You're quite famous, Mr. Angel. Too bad your legion of fans will never know what became of you." She looked at Lucy. "Or you, but you're nobody special."

"Says *you*," Lucy said.

I looked over at her. She had a raw patch on her left cheek and a cut on her forehead that had bled a little. Her hands were also bound with a plastic strap, feet, too. I tried to move my legs, but they were strapped together at the ankles. Second time in less than a year I'd been tied up. That part of this PI thing was starting to get on my nerves.

"How long've I been out?" I asked.

"Two hours," Arlene said. "Give or take. Enjoy your life while you can, Mr. Angel. Soon the lights will go out forever. You and this little woman-child can race off to eternity together."

Lucy was in shorts and her pink tank top. Her feet were bare. She gave me a sad smile and said, "I'm sorry, Mort."

"What for?"

"I don't know. Just . . . everything. This . . ."

"Not your fault, kiddo." To Arlene I said, "Lot of smoke, but there wasn't any fire, was there?"

"Of course not. Not in the room. That isn't cost effective. We got a smoky fire going at the intake to your air conditioner. Fills the room quickly. People tend to panic, come running outside with their eyes watering, not looking around."

"What hit me? Buddie?"

"Well, it wasn't me, Mr. Angel. Of *course* it was Buddie, and I imagine it was like running full tilt into a redwood tree. And I'd like to know where you heard his name."

"So would I."

Her eyes looked like bullet holes in sheet metal. She lifted the revolver, aimed it at me. Short barrel, not worth a shit at long range. A Rossi .38 special, wouldn't take plus-P ammunition, but I still didn't like it pointed in my direction. I also thought I was looking at the gun that had killed Jo-X. "A bullet in the knee would hurt," she said. "Quite a bit, I should think."

I did, too. "How about *Buddie's* Excavating, printed right on the side of that flatbed truck of his. Which might be nothing but a wild-ass guess on my part, but I thought it was—"

"Okay, enough. Shut up."

So I shut up.

She sat there and stared at me, then at Lucy. Her cigarette burned down and she used the butt to light another.

"Cost effective," I said. "Chain smoking saves on matches."

She said nothing, but a corner of her mouth lifted a sixteenth of an inch.

"Gets the lung cancer going faster, too," I said. "Which, in your case, is good for the entire country. Patriotic, even."

Arlene huffed out a cloud of smoke. "I could put a bullet in her knee instead. Maybe *that* would shut you up."

So I shut up again.

We sat in silence. I could hear a clock ticking somewhere behind me, a very faint click, click, click. And, in the distance, the barely audible on-and-off diesel growl of Buddie's backhoe.

Finally Arlene said, "How did you get onto us, here?"

"Onto you how?"

She lifted the muzzle of the gun half an inch. "Here you are. You're nosing around. This place isn't for shit. And don't bother giving me a surprised look. No one sniffs around here. People only stop when they have to. Crappy little oasis in the empty desert, and there you two were, snooping around two nights ago. What put you onto us? I know you, Mr. Angel, were the one who found Xenon. You were in the news for days. But that was up in Reno. How on earth did any of that get you pointed down here?"

The only hope we had was to make her think the police were about to land on her and Buddie with both feet. And soon.

"The videos," I said. "You shouldn't have taken them. I still don't know what that was all about."

"What videos?"

"The ones you took of Celine. Who, by the way, isn't black, but you know that. You made a video of her walking with Xenon over to his helicopter. Then another one, the next morning, when she was in the diner. You walked up and gave her a menu."

Her eyes took on a murderous shine. "That isn't possible. Those videos are on my computer and nowhere else."

"Except, of course, on my cell phone. I showed them to a cop yesterday. He'll be along anytime now."

She levitated out of the chair, not a bad sign. "Show me," she said in a choked voice.

"No problem. I'll get right on it. Just get these straps off my wrists and ankles."

She sank slowly back onto her chair. "You described those videos, so I'm forced to believe you. Now *how* did they get on your cell phone, Mr. Angel?" She said it with deadly calm, gun aimed at Lucy.

If I clowned around right then, Lucy was dead. I could see it in Arlene's eyes. "They were on a flash drive in a pocket of Jo-X's jeans when I found him in that garage. I kept the flash drive, copied the videos to a computer, then e-mailed them to my cell phone. This is the digital age."

"A flash drive," she said slowly. Then a light dawned. "That stupid, stupid son of a bitch. It was Buddie. Had to be."

"He's your kid, so son of a *bitch* sounds right," Lucy said.

Don't, I thought.

Arlene's gaze swiveled to Lucy. "I'm going to let that go since we've got something more interesting than a bullet for you and bullets are messy, but you should watch your mouth, girl. You could end up without teeth for the last few hours of your life. You might find that unpleasant."

To distract her, I said, "You knew Buddie put Xenon in their garage?"

"But of course. That was my idea. Buddie would never have come up with it. When that girl, Celine, left here that morning, Buddie followed her all the way up to Reno. She stopped only once for gas, in Tonopah. He phoned from there, told me where they were. He wanted to know if I wanted him to keep after her and of *course* I did. He found out where she lived. I had him take pictures of the house and yard, so when he came back, I told him to take that piece of shit rapper up there, dump him in their laps. I saw that garage in the pictures he took. It looked old. He could get it open, one way or another. I thought it was a marvelous idea to have Xenon turn up four hundred miles from here, right where 'Celine' lived. Once he was found, the police would go crazy, as would this entire silly country, as it so often does. Celine would be exposed. It would be a typical American circus, Celine in the center ring, media over it like maggots, the entire country agog at what she'd done."

"So why would you tell Buddie to leave that flash drive in Jo-X's pocket?"

"I *wouldn't*. I videoed that phony Celine girl inside the diner and put the video on my computer. And on a flash drive that I left in my desk. That goddamn thing pointed a finger right back at us. Buddie did it because he's an imbecile and a moron."

Family. The ones who know you best. Not much love there. I thought it likely that she would kill him at some point, haul him into the desert, let the coyotes and buzzards have him. He would make a hearty meal.

"Why make the video in the first place?" I asked.

"Insurance. No specific reason. At the time, I realized it was the one and only chance I would ever get to do it. I didn't think I would need it, but if I did, I would have it."

"Then it was Buddie who wrote the note," I said. "Figures. It looked like it was written by an eight-year-old." If her love for him was as wobbly as I thought, the note might put her over the edge. Worth a try.

Her dark eyes locked on mine. "What note?"

"A note was left in their mailbox. In Celine's mailbox, at the house where she lived."

"What on earth did it say?"

"It asked for a million dollars."

"A million . . . oh, good Lord, what a *stupid* . . ." Her gaze turned inward for a moment. "I will skin him alive. That stupid damn kid of mine. Always so greedy."

"Like his mother."

"*Not* like me. I control it. I am patient. It hasn't always been easy, but I've kept him under control."

"Until you turned him loose to follow Celine. Four hundred miles from mom, he got ideas."

She shook her head. "What else did that damn note say?"

"I left it with a cop yesterday, but I took a picture with my cell phone. The spelling and grammar will make you proud."

"That's Buddie. He almost made it to the eighth grade."

Almost. I liked that. Seventh-grade education in a country that promotes kids based on age, not accomplishment. See Spot run would probably tax his little brain.

"Did you kill Jo-X down here or up in Reno?" I asked.

"Neither. We found him dead in that hideaway place of his, up in the hills."

"Sure you did."

Arlene gave me a funny look. "We did. That girl flying off in his helicopter was a bad sign. I figured Xenon was about to go off the rails, taking that girl up there. He'd never done anything like it before. Maybe it was the size of her bust. Men are like that. Buddie found the place over a year ago. We figured Xenon had to have all kinds of stuff up there, worth a lot of money. But he was giving us three grand a month to keep quiet about who he was. Thirty-six thousand a year, just to keep his secret, let him know if anyone came snooping around, let him know if the diner was empty and it was safe for him to fly in. Buddie doesn't even make that much with his backhoe.

"But all of that would end if people knew where he was hiding out, then that damn girl goes up there. The next morning she came back in Jo-X's SUV, alone. He flew in later, looked like he was hurting, then he flew back up to his place that afternoon. I didn't like any of that, so when Buddie got back the next day after tailing that Celine girl to Reno, I sent him up there the next day and he watched the place for a while, told me he didn't see anyone moving around, so he came out of the hills where he'd been watching. Doors weren't locked, so he went in. He looked all over, finally found Xenon dead, shot twice."

I believed her. She said it with matter-of-fact simplicity, no sign of duplicity. "So you raided the place," I said.

She shrugged. "What would *you* have done? Of course we did. Well, Buddie did. He used the backhoe to rip out something across the road that blows out tires, then went up and got a big safe out of a locked room. Backhoe took out a wall in nothing flat. Buddie said he tipped the safe into the scoop with a big iron bar and loaded it onto the flatbed, brought it back here."

"He got the generator, too. It was in the shed where he found Xenon's body."

She cocked her head and gave me a long look. "How do you know where he found him?"

"I know lots of things. But if you're wondering how I knew *exactly* where he found Xenon, I went up there and had a look around. There was blood in the generator shed and no generator."

"And you're sure Buddie stole it, not someone else?"

"I would only be ninety-nine percent sure except that I found it in that storage unit of yours, the one at T&T Storage in North Vegas. So, yeah, I'm a hundred percent sure."

A kind of shudder went through her. "How on earth did you find out about that place?"

"Police got it for me. If you listen very carefully, you might hear sirens."

She listened for a moment, then shook it off.

"You might've gotten ten grand for the generator, except this game of yours is just about over, Arlene. Really, I'm surprised the police aren't all over this place right now."

Buddie came in through a back door behind me. I heard him but didn't see him until he came around and got a bottle of water out of the refrigerator behind Arlene.

"He says he got into our shed at T&T," Arlene said to him.

"That right?" Buddie gave me a reptilian stare, then opened the bottle and took a long drink.

"He found the generator you put in there."

"And the gold bars," Lucy said.

Another tremor passed through Arlene. "You took them."

"Nope," I said. "Unlike you, we're not thieves."

She thought about that for a moment, then looked at Buddie. "Tell me you didn't leave a note in a mailbox in Reno asking for a million dollars. Please tell me you aren't that stupid."

His mouth dropped open, and he stared at her, lips wet. Made him look like a baleen whale, scooping plankton.

"You *are*," she said, shoulders slumping in defeat. "You are utterly, dismally, terminally hopeless."

"That Celine girl would've paid," Buddie said with a whine in his voice. "She'd gotta have made millions bein' with Jonnie-X, Ma. A million bucks we coulda had."

"You think she got a million dollars in less than a month?" Arlene shook her head in disbelief. "*And* you left a flash drive on his body with those videos I made."

"No, I didn't . . . I mean, so what? That chick would've found it. Then she would've *had* to pay up."

Arlene gave me a tormented look, as if I cared. "'So what,' he says. 'The chick would have found it.' See what I have to put up with? He can run a backhoe, but his brain is full of mush."

"Sorry," I said. "Though it's probably genetic."

She must not have heard that. She stared at Buddie. "Police could be on their way here as we speak. You've got to get rid of them. Immediately. Do it fast."

"Hole's ready," he said. "I'm good to go."

"Then go. Get it done and get back here. I'll start cleaning up. Maybe we'll get out of this mess you've made."

Buddie untied the rope around Lucy's waist and lifted her as if she were a doll stuffed with feathers. She struggled, but this was Bambi vs. Godzilla. He carried her out the back door.

Arlene gave me a dead look. "Good riddance to both of you. You have been the worst thing possible."

"Too bad. Expect the police—soon."

"They won't find anything."

"Cars buried out in the desert. They'll find 'em."

"I had Buddie put down one septic. If anyone wants to know what he buried out there, he'll dig it up. The smell will knock them down. That'll keep them away."

"How many cars?" I asked.

"Thirteen so far. No, fourteen. We put that Hogan guy down yesterday night. You'll be number fifteen."

"You bury people in their cars?"

"Of course. Buddie puts them behind the wheel, in the trunk, whatever he feels like. It hardly matters. You'll see."

"Why are you doing this? Killing people?"

"That's a silly damn question. For *retirement*, of course. This place is perfect for that, but it's a horrible place to live. I'm not going to stay here forever."

"How did you pick your victims?"

"As if that'll matter to you in another hour or two."

"Or to you, so tell me."

She shrugged. "Room four is wired for sound and there's two tiny little cameras way up high in the corners hooked up to a monitor in our back room. Some guy comes in alone, got a fat wallet or we see a money belt, find out he's got a lot of cash, no one knows he's here, I roofie him, Buddie packs the guy in his car and runs him out back, puts him in the ground."

"Alive."

Arlene shrugged again. "No one's complained yet. You're the first."

"You're insane. Both of you."

"Least of my worries."

Buddie came back inside, untied the rope around my waist, got me under the knees and the back of the neck like a forklift, folded me almost double, picked me up like a sack of grain, not even a grunt, and hauled me out the door into the night. It was an uncanny feeling, like being four years old again.

The Caddy was parked at the end of the building. The trunk was open. He dropped me in, banged the lid down, and the world went dark as hades.

I was half on top of Lucy, half on the lockbox. It dug into my ribs. Lucy was crying softly. The engine turned over, caught, and the car bumped over the uneven ground, bouncing us around as it headed out into the desert.

We were crammed in awkwardly. I worked the lockbox off to one side. The trunk was so cramped I could barely roll over. The effort made my head throb. "Did they open the lockbox?" I asked Lucy, keeping my voice down. "Did they get your gun?"

"I don't know. He practically tossed me in here."

She moved around, grunting. Then she said, "It's open. Got hats and wigs and other stuff in here. And that knife."

"Where is it? The knife?"

"Right here."

"Open it. See if you can cut these straps on my wrists."

I heard the click as the knife opened. "Careful," I said.

She groped around, got hold of my forearms. She fumbled around, clumsy with her wrists held together, and I felt the knife slice into the pad of my left thumb. "That's me you're cutting," I said.

"Sorry."

She felt for the strap, kept sawing away, then the strap came loose. I took the knife from her and cut the strap from around her wrists, then pulled my legs up, cut the strap binding my ankles. I gave her the knife. "Get your ankles loose, then fold the knife up and give it to me."

The jouncing continued, getting rougher.

"No gun in the lockbox?" I asked.

"I couldn't feel one."

"Try again. They're going to bury this car with us in it, and everything we had. Keeping our guns would be stupid."

"Like they're geniuses."

"He wouldn't think of it, but she would. Feel around."

We came up with a jack handle, clothing, shoes, no gun, no flashlights, then the bouncing stopped. A door opened, the Caddy gave a lurch as Bigfoot got out, then the door slammed shut.

"Let's see if we can fold the rear seat down," I said. "Maybe there's a catch or lever here in the trunk."

I felt around on the left side, Lucy worked on the right. Then the backhoe's diesel fired up. Seconds later a grinding rasp of metal on metal came from the back bumper as the Cadillac was shoved from behind. The front end tilted down, rocks ground harshly along the undercarriage, metal scraped against rock, then the Caddy leveled out again. Finally it quit moving, tilted up a few degrees in front.

"We've got to find a latch, something."

"He's gonna *bury* us, Mort."

"Don't give up. Find a latch."

I scrabbled all around that left side, didn't feel anything. How did the engineers who designed these things expect people stuck in the trunk to get the fuck out?

"There's nothing," Lucy said.

Then the entire car bounced as an unearthly roar of rock and sand landed on the roof. Lucy whimpered.

"Move over," I told her. "Give me room."

I worked myself around and got on my side, folded up, and wedged my shoulders against the back of the trunk. I hammered the back of the rear seat with a foot, about where I figured a catch would have to be. Nothing gave. More dirt landed on the roof with a sickening thud.

I slammed the seat again. And again, again, again. In bare feet, it hurt like a sonofabitch. Another huge load of dirt landed on the car, then suddenly the latch broke and the backseat on the driver's side flopped down.

"Go through," I told her. "Turn on the overhead light. There should be a switch on the fixture. Fold the other backseat down, then see if they put our guns in the car. Check under the seats."

She crawled forward, catching me in the face with a foot, which hurt. The darkness was complete. More dirt landed on the roof. I could feel the weight of it, deadening the car's suspension. I sensed it pressing like death against the Caddy's windows.

Then the dome light came on, bathing the interior of the car in weak yellow light. Dirt covered the outside of the windows. This is what it would look like from inside a transparent coffin. A shiver of raw fear crawled up my spine. Earth pressed against the windows like a malevolent force, eager to get in, snuff us out, fold us into its black arms forever.

I crawled out of the trunk. Felt more than heard a muffled thump as more dirt landed on top of what was already there.

"I got all three guns," Lucy said breathlessly. "They were in back, on the floor."

"Loaded?"

She snapped the cylinders out. "Well, shoot. No bullets in any of 'em. But it's not like we're gonna get a good sight picture in here, Mort."

Gallows humor, God love her.

Outside, I didn't hear anything. "Quiet," I said. "Listen."

We went still. All I could hear was a hiss of dirt sifting over the windows and along the skin of the car. I closed my eyes. No, there was the faint sound of a diesel engine, and as I strained my ears, it grew fainter, fainter still, then it was gone.

We'd been buried alive.

CHAPTER TWENTY-SIX

"NOT MUCH AIR, not much time," I said.

"I know that."

"Stay back. Find our clothes. Make sure you get our shoes. Try to conserve air."

She didn't ask why. I'd taken the jack handle with me as I'd crawled out of the trunk. I lowered the backs of both front seats as far as they would go, then slammed the jack handle into the windshield, passenger side, felt the glass crack.

"What're you doin'?"

"Only thing I can think of, kiddo." I swung the handle again and again, finally broke through the glass. It was tough, hanging in webs of flexible plastic—a lot safer if we'd been in a traffic accident, but I wanted the glass *out*.

It took more effort than I'd anticipated. Dirt and dust sifted in. I felt the air in the car start to go stale. Not a lot, but it was going to get worse, and soon.

I kept pounding the glass, hammering around the edges of the hole I'd started until it was finally big enough for me to get my shoulders through. A few hundred pounds of earth had come into the car—gravel, dirt, sand. Most of it ended up on the floor. I reached into the hole and dug furiously with my hands, shredding my fingernails.

"Can I help?" Lucy said.

"Not enough room in here for two, Honey."

"Honey. I like that." Her words sounded forced, airless.

I pulled dirt into the car, shoved it down to the floorboards. It was the only way. I couldn't push the dirt out so I had to pull it in. I hoped there was enough volume in the car to take enough dirt, and that we wouldn't run out of empty space or air before I burrowed a hole to the surface.

A rock wedged in the hole. I had to knock out more glass to pull it inside. It weighed at least two hundred pounds. I hoped there weren't any more up there. I shoved it onto the driver's seat then rolled it down into the foot well on that side.

With both hands up through the hole, I pulled more dirt into the car. It poured in like sand through an hourglass, jamming frequently. The passenger foot well was almost full. My mouth was full of grit. The air was getting bad.

About the time I couldn't reach up any farther, an avalanche of dirt cascaded down through the windshield. I gagged, spitting out a mouthful of dirt.

"Let me," Lucy said. "Trade places."

She'd been shoving dirt back into the trunk. I clambered into the back and she took over at the windshield.

My breath came in tight gasps. Not much oxygen left. Lucy pulled dirt inside, and I pulled it back over the console between the front seats. She crouched on the dash with her shoulders and chest through the hole, windshield even with her waist. She dug furiously. Dirt came down around her, then suddenly she stopped.

"Lucy?"

No answer. Her feet kicked. I grabbed her and pulled her back inside the car along with another hundred pounds of dirt.

She lay on her stomach, spitting, gasping.

Not much time left. I was going to have to be a gopher and maybe die trapped in a vertical shaft of earth or the two of us were going to die in that car.

I pulled more dirt inside, worked my shoulders into the gap, then shoved myself upward, hands first, grabbing dirt, elbowing it down past my body, trying to shove it down and away with my feet. I felt the blackness start to get hold of me—when the brain feels those first cobwebs of floating thought and you know there isn't much left, then there's a kind of strange unearthly plateau when it doesn't seem to matter very much . . . but I kept digging, digging, and then I saw a tiny, tiny light, a single star, and a ghostly breath of air and oxygen hit me in the face and I began to cry.

*   *   *

I gulped in air. We weren't out of the woods yet. This could all go to hell in a heartbeat. The dirt around the hole was unstable and the hole was very small, but there was hope.

I scraped gently at the dirt. It filtered down around me, and I moved around, tried to get it to go down past my body. It wedged between me and the surrounding earth. Then the hole closed in on me, wouldn't go past my chest, and all I could do was work my way back down.

I slid back into the car, felt dirt thud into the hole I'd created above, sealing off the air.

"Mort . . . I can't . . ."

"Go up, Honey. There's air. But be very, very careful. Don't dislodge much dirt. Go straight up, hands first. Don't make a big hole. Keep it small."

She crawled into the hole and stood. I couldn't tell what she was doing. Dirt sifted down around her, then she stopped and a few seconds of dead quiet went by. Finally, I heard her breathing, great gulps of air. But now there wasn't much left in the car. I felt myself starting to slip away again.

I tapped her leg. She came back down. More dirt piled in after her. This was delicate, dangerous work. One misstep and we'd be down there forever.

"Your turn," she said. "It sort of collapsed again."

I reached up and pulled dirt out of the vertical shaft, shoved it to one side, then worked my shoulders through the windshield again. Pulled more dirt down, got some air, gently widened the hole, saw two stars now, then lowered myself back down.

Back and forth we traded places, getting air, slowly making the hole larger. On the surface it widened like a funnel as the sides kept collapsing, dirt tumbling in through the windshield. The trunk was almost full of dirt. It wouldn't take much more. If we ran out of room, that would be the ball game.

Finally, after my fifth or sixth turn, I lowered myself into the car and said, "Try to get out. I'll lift your feet, boost you up."

"And leave you here?"

"One of us has to get out first. That someone is going to be you, no argument. And don't worry, I fully intend to get out of here, too."

"Okay. Be careful."

She gave me the world's grittiest kiss then crawled into the hole and stood up. I crouched on the dirt as close to the hole as I could get. I cupped my hands around one of her feet, then put all my Borroloola strength training into lifting her as she scrabbled to the surface.

Then she was out.

I felt my eyes well up with tears. She was precious. I was not. I was just a former IRS goon and a scruffy old half-assed PI, but she was pure diamond. This rattletrap, sometimes-obnoxious universe could get along fine without me. Without her, it would be a far less valuable place.

"Your turn," she said. Her voice came down muffled.

"Here, take this," I said, passing clothing and other things up to her. She reached down, got hold of it, took it up the rest of the way.

Half-assed and scruffy or not, I still wanted out. What I needed was leverage, a place to put my foot. I reached up and back, scraped dirt off the roof to create a step for my foot. More dirt rattled down into the car. At least I had air.

It took a while, but finally I stood up through the windshield, feet on the dash. My eyes were level with the ground outside. I lifted one leg high enough to get my toes on the car's roof, and with Lucy pulling on one hand, hauled myself out of the grave.

She slammed into me, hugging hard, crying.

"Oh God, God, God, thank you," she wailed.

I felt like wailing myself, but I am a rock, I am a . . .

Okay, I cried, too, came about *this* fuckin' close to wailing, but managed to hold it off. If we'd been in that ragtop Mustang, we'd be dead already. Saved by a drunk kid in daddy's car.

"For a while I didn't . . . didn't think we were gonna make it," she said. Her voice sounded blubbery.

"It was close. Good thing you were born when the planets were lined up just right."

She hugged me tighter.

Finally I looked around. Never had stars looked so beautiful. Never had ordinary air smelled so sweet. Never had I wanted to kill two people so much. Well, one person—Julia Reinhart. To stay alive, I'd had to know she was no longer on this earth. I had *needed* to kill her, and I had.

Now, there was Buddie and Arlene.

* * *

Except . . . maybe not.

Could I do that again? Hunt someone down and kill them? I wasn't a judge or jury. I had been grievously wronged, as had Lucy. Buddie and Arlene had tried to murder us and had come within a hair's breadth of succeeding. But they hadn't, so now it was up to the law to deal with them. Those two weren't going to escape society's wrath and vengeance for having tried to kill us, for murdering Vince Ignacio and killing a dozen others over the years. The evidence was buried. It could and would be retrieved. No doubt most of it would be horrible beyond imagining. Buddie and Arlene were headed for lethal injections.

Another problem with our hunting down those two—Buddie was a monster. Six foot seven, three hundred fifty pounds, well fed, psychotic, and—I was guessing here but I think I was on the right track—he would make every effort to kill us and stuff us back in the ground if we showed up. Also, Arlene had a gun and she had bullets, so going after those two didn't strike me as the swiftest move we might make that night.

Lucy shivered. "Now what?" Her voice was a whisper, as if the night had ears. Which, around here, maybe it did.

I looked toward the diner. Lights were on over there. Those two were probably scrambling around, removing any last-minute traces of evidence in case the police showed up. Buddie would be certain we were finished, but you never know what a Yeti is thinking. The last thing we needed was for that spotlight to come on again in a final paranoid sweep and get lucky.

"Not sure," I said. "But get dressed. Dark clothing."

I was still in jockeys. They were so full of dirt they sagged on me. I took them off, shook out a pound of Nevada, put them back on. My mom wouldn't have approved. What would people think if I got in an accident? The thought passed through, but I can't say it had much weight.

Beneath the starry sky we dressed, put on shoes, gathered up what seemed most likely to be useful—the knife, jack handle, one gun each. They didn't have bullets, but a revolver aimed at a person's heart tends to intimidate. It could alter behavior, cause hesitations. I took my .357 Magnum, Lucy kept her .38.

So now . . . choices.

Best option was to give the diner a very wide berth and walk out to the highway, flag down the next vehicle to come along. Get the hell out of there. Call the police.

I couldn't bring myself to do that. What I wanted was to fire up that backhoe and drive it through the diner and level the place, hopefully run over Bigfoot and his bitch mother in the process.

That, of course, was just the worst kind of wishful thinking.

But we were dark, invisible out there. We could get close to the diner and motel, see what was going on. A thought clattered through my head, something about curiosity, a cat, and a bad outcome.

Man, I hated those two.

Really, though. We could get a little closer, listen, maybe get an idea of what was going on.

Or, with luck, we could find a phone, call the police, be right there when those two were packed into a police car in handcuffs.

Stupid thoughts.

We walked quietly toward the diner's lights. Not many lights were on. I saw two yellowish glows. We were still over a quarter mile away.

"What're we doin', Mort?" she whispered.

"You're not hurt, are you? You can run if you have to?"

"Yeah, but . . . what're we *doing*?"

"Seeing how much we can see."

"Are we gonna kill them? I hope."

Okay, we were on the same psychological page here. But it wasn't a good page.

"Nope."

"Why not? They tried to kill us." Her voice was low, savage. It wouldn't carry far into the night, but it would carry pretty deep into her psyche. Well, she'd never had anyone try to snuff her out before, and I had. I was experienced. I could handle it.

Sure I could.

"The law will take care of them," I said. But I felt no sense of satisfaction at the words, no sense of justice. The words were dust in my mouth. They were logical, dead, and empty, so I had a fine little skirmish going on in my head.

"That what you want?" Lucy asked. "Put the law on them?"

"No. I want to roast their hearts over an open fire. But having them arrested is the right thing to do. And a lot safer."

Arrested.

An anemic, tepid, civilized word. It had no bearing on what Buddie had done to us. It had no quality of justice. Marching the two of them away in cuffs sounded marginally better, but it had none of the hot-blooded appeal of that open-fire thing.

We went another hundred yards in silence. Finally she said, "If that's what you want, okay." I could barely hear her words.

"If you hear anything, like someone coming after you, run."

"Whatever."

Curious response.

A light went out inside the diner. Moments later, the last one went out. All that was left was a kind of halo where a floodlight lit the *Diner* sign on the roof where it faced the highway. Lucy and I were still a quarter mile out, at the helicopter hangar.

"Beddie-by," Lucy whispered.

"Maybe. Don't count on it."

We went past Buddie's backhoe on its trailer. We made it to the shed behind the diner that held the safe they'd taken out of Jo-X's place. We stood behind it. I looked around a corner at the diner, still holding the jack handle. This close to the place, I saw a faint glow in a window from somewhere inside—a night-light, or maybe they weren't asleep or in bed yet.

Lucy pawed through junk behind the shed. "Ouch." Then, "Look what I found," she whispered. "Careful. It's sharp."

It was the old tree saw I'd seen several days ago. A two-foot gently curved blade, long jagged teeth. I remembered seeing it—a rusty, nasty-looking, possibly useful weapon in exactly the right circumstances, which wasn't the case here. Here it was un-wieldy and hopelessly inadequate.

"If Goliath comes after you, drop that damn thing and run like hell," I whispered.

"What're you two *doin'* out here?" Melanie the waitress said in a voice loud enough to wake Jimmy Hoffa.

I almost yelped. Lucy let out a terrified little chirp and junk banged against the side of the shed. My heart tried to pound its way out of my chest.

"Well, jeez, I'm sorry," Melanie said. "I didn't mean to scare you guys."

"Quiet!"

"I couldn't sleep," she said.

Well, shit. I might have to deck her to shut her up.

Too late.

A pair of floodlights came on behind the diner, blasting the backyard with light. It wasn't the big spotlight, but it lit the place up. Bigfoot came charging out with a towel around his waist and what might've been a billy club in one hand. His hair was wet, water running in his eyes. He saw me looking at him from be-hind the shed and headed my way, fast.

"Run," I yelled to Lucy. I gave her a little push, then ran in the opposite direction to keep Buddie away from her. No way to avoid the light once I was out from behind the shed.

Buddie came after me.

So did Lucy.

Sonofabitch.

I whirled, backpedaled, dodged sideways. Buddie scrambled after me making a kind of insane growling, roaring sound. The towel came loose and suddenly Buddie was stark naked. I tried to lead him away from Lucy since she was behind him, not backing off. I yelled for her to run, goddamnit, but she hopped around in the yard with that stupid tree saw in her hands, getting close to him. Too damn close.

Buddie tore after me. I kept out of his reach, barely. It wasn't something I could keep up for long. He was big, not very fast, but I wouldn't be able to trade blows with him—him with that billy club, me with a jack handle. Judo sure as hell wasn't an option. I hadn't learned enough judo to trade punches with Ma. Maybe the best I could do was run, try to keep him away from Lucy.

I was about to turn and run but Lucy was only five or six feet behind him. If he turned fast enough, he'd have her. I drew my .357 and aimed it at his chest. He pulled up short. Then Lucy swung that saw between Bigfoot's legs from behind with its teeth pointed upward. She lifted the teeth up into his groin, hard, and pushed the blade forward, sawing testicles. Buddie screamed, then did exactly the wrong thing. He tried to turn as Lucy yanked the blade back toward herself, lifting and sawing, and Buddie used his stupidity and strength to rip out the femoral artery in his right leg.

Lucy fell on her back. Buddie let out another roar of pain and fury, tried to lunge at her, discovered that she was quick as a lynx, so he turned around and came back toward me, spurting blood like a fire hose. He took eight or ten half-staggering steps with one pink-white testicle dangling out of his torn scrotum, a sight that would haunt my dreams, then fell to his knees, flopped to one side, and stared up at me.

"Aw, fuck," he said.

"Yup," I said, then a shot rang out. Arlene was out the back door, revolver aimed in my general direction, a whiff of smoke spiraling from the barrel. She took aim again.

I dropped. A bullet tore over my head. I don't know where the first one had gone. I rolled, scrambled to one side, dodged another bullet, then zigzagged out into the night, a procedure I'd more or less perfected playing football a lifetime ago and used last October when Julia Reinhart was blasting away at me with a Glock only seconds after she'd murdered Jeri.

Another shot rang out behind me and Lucy let out a cry.

Oh, no.

I turned around, came zigzagging back. Arlene screamed at me. She was in a bathrobe that was flapping open, gun in hand. I didn't see Lucy. I ran at Arlene, threw the jack handle, missed her by half a foot, jumped sideways. She fired off another round that didn't come very close, then ducked back into the diner.

Stalemate.

I'd counted five shots. She had at least one more, and could be reloading in there.

"Lucy," I yelled.

"Over here."

She was in relative darkness behind the shed. When I got to her, she was looking at a furrow in her upper left arm. Blood was flowing, but it was a groove, not an artery opener.

"That . . . that bitch *shot* me."

"Wow," Melanie said. "I never seen anyone shot before."

"Go back to your trailer," I told her. "Call the police."

"Don't got no phone in there. We want to phone, we got to go over to the diner."

Perfect.

"Take off your shirt," I told her.

She took a step back. "What for?"

"I need a bandage." I didn't give her time to back farther away. I got hold of her shirt.

"Okay, *okay*," she said. She took it off. Her bra was pale white in the light reflecting off the backyard.

"Now get back in your trailer and stay there. Where's your husband?"

"Kirby? He's sleepin'. He kin sleep through anything."

"What a guy. Keep him inside if he wakes up. Now go."

She went.

I tore Melanie's shirt into one long strip, folded it, tied it tight around Lucy's arm.

"Hurts," she said.

"Bullet wounds are like that."

"My very first one," she said, and there was a proud note in her voice.

"How about you make it your very last one, too?"

"I'll try. This'll probably leave a pretty good scar."

"Count on it."

I looked around the corner of the shed. Buddie was out in the yard, still on his side. Not moving. He'd probably bled out by now. The dangling nut was probably annoying at the time, but a shredded femoral artery tends to kill quickly.

"Nice work with the saw," I said. "I wouldn't have thought to do that between the legs thing."

"Thanks. Now what? She's still got a gun."

Going after Arlene under these conditions was something a fool might do. Not me.

"Now we get out of here," I said. "Buddie's dead. We won. Let the law handle it. She won't make it far even if she runs."

Right then, headlights pulled off the highway in front of the motel. Life is all about timing. With floodlights blazing in the backyard, I hadn't seen the headlights as they drew near. Peeking around the shed, I saw Ma pull up in that old brown 1963 Cadillac Eldorado of hers. Maude Clary, my boss. She got out of the Caddy and looked around, but the lights behind the diner got her attention and she headed my way.

Not good. Arlene was still inside with a gun.

"Stay put," I said to Lucy.

I ran out from behind the shed, zigging, yelled, "Stay back, Ma!" and Arlene came out the back door and shot the top quarter inch off my right ear as I was passing Goliath who was sprawled in an Olympic-size pool of his own blood.

I dropped, rolled, got up, and Arlene shot me in the shoulder, which dropped me in the dirt. She came across the yard, revolver in her fist. She walked up, taking her time, aimed it at my head, and from the corner of the diner Ma shot Arlene in the right temple with a .45 Sig and blew out the left side of her head.

CHAPTER TWENTY-SEVEN

"Nice shot, Ma," I said, grimacing. I pressed a hand to my shoulder as I sat up on the ground. I had the feeling that standing wouldn't be a good idea. "What the *hell* are you doing here?"

Officer Day walked up beside her. The behemoth had been riding shotgun. Interesting. He had a big service automatic in one hand. Ma had beaten him to the corner of the diner and taken Arlene down ten seconds before he got there.

"Someone's gotta keep an eye on you," she said. Then a tear leaked out of her left eye, second time I'd seen Ma cry. The first was when I told her Jeri had been murdered. Normally Ma was as tough and dry as a nickel steak.

Lucy dropped down beside me and gave me a hug. "Are you okay? She shot you. You're bleeding. Does it hurt?"

"Slow down, kiddo. I'll live."

"You better."

The bullet had hit me low in the shoulder, hit meat, no bone, and went on through. It hurt like a sonofabitch and the pain was only going to get worse. And soon.

Lucy helped me to my feet. I felt wobbly. "Officer Day," I said. "It's nice to see you again."

"You, too, Angel. Any more hostiles around?"

"Nope. Got a crime scene you could secure though."

"Not my jurisdiction, not my job. And it's ugly, but if no one else is gonna pull a gun, I think it's secure enough." He wasn't in uniform, but he had his on-duty holster on his hip. After one last look around, he holstered his weapon.

Lucy stared at Day. He was huge, only marginally smaller than Buddie, lying ten feet away. Arlene was on her back, eyes staring emptily at the sky, a faint look of surprise on her face, not much remaining of the left side of her head, which is what a .45 Hydra-Shok bullet will do.

"*That's* Officer Day?" Lucy said to me with what sounded like a little snarl in her voice.

"Yes, it is. Just in time, too."

"Not very svelte, is *she*?"

"Nope."

"You poophead. She's a he."

"You noticed. Good job. And *he's* a he. *I* never said he was a she." Day let out a low bass rumble.

"For God's sake," Ma said. "*This* is your assistant?"

"Yep. Lucy. She killed Bigfoot over there. You shoulda seen it. I think he's lying on one of his nuts."

"*One* of his nuts? What's that mean?"

"You really don't want to know."

Then, of course, Russell Fairchild pulled up at the motel in his blue Explorer, two minutes late and a dollar short. He got out and ran over to us on short bandy legs, stopped short, and stared at six feet seven inches of naked Yeti in a gallon or two of blood.

"Holy shit," he said. Then he noticed Arlene, bloody brains glistening in the dirt not far away. "Jesus. What the *hell*—"

"You're late," I told him. I gave him a manly smile, blood on shirt, bullet hole in shoulder, top of right ear missing. Something for him to remember. I was sure he'd never been shot. The wimp. I would be able to lord this over him for years.

The tableau held for a few more seconds. Dead lying in the yard, two of us wounded, floodlights glaring. Justice had been done, no judge or jury needed. I wished it had been done without bullet wounds, but Lucy and I had been damned lucky. My nicked ear was the least of it, but one inch to the left and the bullet would have scrambled my brains.

Then the pain started to get serious and I felt faint again. Casually as possible, I said, "This get-together is great even if no one brought wine, but Lucy and I could use a hospital. Sometime tonight? So if someone could arrange that, maybe we could talk to the police and give statements after we get all this bleeding stopped?"

Manly.

Then I slowly crumpled to the ground and passed out.

Shit. Ruined it.

*　*　*

The media circus got fired up about the time the sun poked above the hills east of Vegas, fading the miles and megawatts of neon. I didn't see that. I was in surgery, so the calliope played its cotton-candy music and clowns lit exploding cigars without me. But I heard about it from Ma, later, upstairs in recovery, groggy from the anesthetic—Mortimer Angel, PI extraordinaire, was in the news again, having not only located the missing Jo-X the previous week, but was instrumental in busting up what appeared to be a mother-son family enterprise engaged in mass murder for profit. Maybe O'Roarke would give me more free-drink coupons.

I was starting to hate hospitals, but they're a lot like enemas. When you need 'em, you need 'em, so you grit your teeth and take it and try not to let the whining leak out to where people can hear it and fuck with your gravitas.

"How'd you get there, Ma?" I asked her. My mouth had that gummy, after-surgery medicinal aftertaste that comes up from the lungs. I was in bed in a room that was costing between two and three dollars a minute. I had an IV in one arm and a drain in my shoulder with stuff I didn't want to look at collecting in a bag attached to the side of the bed. Later I found out the bullet had hit a fair-sized blood vessel and Day had compressed the wound all the way to the hospital and possibly saved my life. I would never hear the end of that. And, shit, now I owed him one.

"Get where?" Ma asked.

"To that diner last night. You and Officer Day."

"Drove my Caddy."

"No shit, Shirleylock." I tried to follow up that beauty of a comeback with a fierce look, but it was too soon after surgery and I looked, Ma told me later, like Winston Churchill after three pints too many. So . . . probably not fierce.

"I owe you one, Ma," I said. I would never tell her I'd been shot trying to keep her away from Arlene, or that Lucy and I had been about to escape unscathed and Ma showing up right then was what got me shot. Ma is tough, but not that tough.

"Yes, you do."

"Now that that's out of the way, let's try this again. *Why* are you here? You were in Memphis, which, in case you didn't know, is in Tennessee."

"What I do," she said, "is listen between the lines. You found that subhuman, Jo-X, then got yourself an unauthorized assistant, you were on TV damn near every time the news came on, next thing you're down in southern Nevada acting coy on the phone, not wanting to tell me what you were up to—"

"Well, shit. Between those lines you probably didn't have to listen very hard."

"Not very. And to top it off, you're a world-class flake."

"You knew I was a flake before you left Reno."

"Which is why I shouldn't have gone, so here I am. Just in time, too."

"None of which explains exactly how you ended up at that diner-motel in time to put a bullet in that poor woman's head."

"Poor woman?"

"Kidding."

"With you, I never know. Cliff and me—that's Day's first name in case you didn't know—drove down from Reno, got to Caliente at two in the morning and woke up Detective Fairchild, who said something about wishing he hadn't given Cliff his motel and room number. He said you'd gone back to that motel where shit apparently happens. That seemed ominous, knowing you, so Cliff and I drove over to see what was what."

"You and 'Cliff,' driving around together. Cool."

Her eyes got sly. "He and I have . . . traveled together. It's not our first rodeo."

"Rodeo, Ma. I like that."

"Thought you might."

"So you hustled on over to the Midnight Rider Motel in the Chariot of Fire."

Ma's Cadillac was good for about fifty miles an hour before it started to float and wander on the road, a weird combination of good shocks and soft springs. I'd dubbed it the Chariot of Fire last October when it took forever to get back to Reno from Bend, Oregon. But the seats are comfortable, so there's that.

"It rides better with Cliff in it," Ma said. "He weighs three-thirty. I got it all the way up to sixty and kept it there."

"You could've done seventy with Buddie in the trunk."

"Who's Buddie?"

"Dead guy at the diner lying in two gallons of blood."

"Oh, him. Exsanguinated."

Sounded like a sneeze so I said, "Bless you."

Then Lucy wandered into the room in her hospital gown, the one with backdoor ventilation that allows everyone to see your bum if you don't hold the drapes shut.

She bent down and gave me a gentle lingering kiss. "How you doin', big guy?"

"I chortle in the face of death."

"Good. You're practically normal already."

She backed up a step and looked at my shoulder. "Spiffy bandage, Mort. Lookit mine." She held out her arm and pulled her sleeve up to the shoulder.

"Spiffy. But take note—I've got a drain and *two* bandages." I touched my ear, felt the adhesive.

For the rest of my life, unless I had plastic surgery, which I'm not inclined to do except for possible augmentations, a bit of the top of my right ear would be missing where Arlene had come within an inch of turning out my lights. And she'd done it with a piece-of-shit snub-nose revolver at nearly thirty feet, too, which was a lucky damn shot, getting that close, so it's all a crap-shoot and God doesn't play favorites.

"Show-off," she said.

"And they gave me a pint of blood."

"Yeah? How'd it taste?"

"We ain't been introduced yet," Ma said to her, "and Mort's social skills are in the toilet because he was with the IRS, so I'm Ma. Maude Clary, but only my enemies call me Maude."

"If Arlene is any indication, your enemies end up dead, so they don't call you Maude for long," said my spiffy assistant.

Ma gave me a big smile. "She'll do." Then she gave Lucy a hug, something she'd never done to me. "Mort tells me you want to be a private investigator."

"If I don't have to get shot very often, sure. Last week has been fun. Lot more fun than the crap jobs I've had lately. Except when we were buried alive, that is."

"Big problem though—you have to be at least twenty-one to get a license, so you'll have to wait a while. Mort said you were thirty-one, but he obviously lied."

"I *am* thirty-one. Since April."

Ma stared at her, then at me.

"Yep," I said. "She checks out. And it's been useful to have an assistant with one foot in the grave who looks nineteen."

Ma stared at Lucy again, then shook her head. "Jesus."

The TV was on, sound turned down low. I looked up and there was a big Case backhoe, Department of Transportation on the side, working on a hole in the desert heat. A huge tow truck was standing by, a bunch of guys in orange vests looking on, holding shovels, police cars scattered around in the background. I turned up the volume. A talking head I didn't recognize, Ginny Fernandez out of Vegas, was fifty yards from the action, telling the story of bodies in cars being dug out of the desert behind a place called Arlene's Diner on Highway 93, seventy miles north of Vegas. Three cars had been recovered so far. The most recent appeared to have cleared up the eight-year disappearance of one Lawrence Emory from Tulsa, although the body found in the trunk of Emory's Mercedes had yet to be positively identified, which would have to be done via dental records. Earlier finds were those of Peter Windham, missing for ten years, and Vincent Ignacio, a journalist out of Chicago.

"Journalist," Ma said. "That was magnanimous of them."

"At least they didn't call him the Wharf Rat," Lucy said.

"Wharf Rat?"

"Long story, Ma," I said, yawning, then my eyelids turned to lead plates. It happened suddenly, which was startling. I tried to keep them from banging shut, but they got too heavy and I slipped away.

* * *

When I awoke, Ma and Lucy were gone. Russell Fairchild and a pair of Clark County detectives were in the room, talking quietly. Finally, Russ noticed that I was awake, so then I got all the attention. Which was only as it should be.

The smile muscles of the two Clark plainclothes guys had atrophied, a medical condition that no doubt served them as well in their professional lives as it did mine in my IRS days, back when I was rounding up tax dodgers who thought, oh so wrongly, that the money they had earned was rightfully their own. People who actually work for a living have funny ideas.

I had a hospital lunch of fruit cocktail fresh out of the can, and lime Jell-O, while Detective Bache and Detective Webber, both with that same unusual first name, asked their questions and listened with job-related expert skepticism to answers.

Russ mopped his forehead several times during this initial Q&A session, but I managed to keep Danya and Shanna out of it, which left the story rather unlikely and a bit thin—but like I told Detective and Detective, luck happens—like the time I opened the trunk of my ex-wife's Mercedes and found the decapitated head of Reno's mayor. Pure dumb luck. So—Lucy and I were at the motel a few days ago when a Lexus left late at night—same night a backhoe was digging out in the desert not long after. That of course piqued our interest—the backhoe, not the Lexus. Then we were out there looking at the Milky Way when a searchlight over by the diner came on and scanned the desert, which piqued our interest even further. So Lucy and I went out there in daylight and Bigfoot rolled up in a pickup truck wondering what we were doing out there and, yes, that did nothing to keep our interest from piquing even further—which, as this continuing saga of dumb luck would have it, evidently piqued the interest of Buddie and Arlene to the point that they smoked us out of our motel room and tried to kill us.

"Talk about luck," I said.

"Talk about a lot of piquing," Webber said laconically. I'd finally identified him as the younger of the two, the one with the Groucho moustache and the overlapping incisors.

"Sure was," I responded laconically.

"So you found that Jonnie Xenon character up in Reno," he said. "What brought you down to these parts?"

"These parts?"

His eyes narrowed. "Vegas, Caliente, that motel, diner."

"Vacation."

"Vacation." His voice was as flat as a slab of concrete.

I looked around. "This room has a hell of an echo."

"You find that fuckin' Xenon, get on national TV all over the country, then take a vacation."

"A very concise summation. Good job. After all that success, I was pooped. You would be, too." Back in your court, Detective.

I've been told that talking with me is like talking with your average tree stump. Speaking of stumped, Webber just stared at me for a while after my last comment.

"Huh," he said finally.

"Then," I elaborated, "we got caught up in all that piquing of interest stuff, which turned out badly, since, look, I've got a drain in my shoulder, except that it probably saved taxpayers a million dollars since no trial is needed, so you're welcome."

"By 'we,' you mean"—he checked his notebook—"you and this Lucy Landry, age thirty-one, address in San Francisco?"

"That's her. And I wonder if I could have a brief moment alone with my compadre here," I said, nodding at Russ. "Who is also acting on my behalf as an interim legal advisor."

That earned me a pair of lifted eyebrows and flinty looks, but they stood up, and the older one with the encouraging affable smile and the ball-bearing eyes, Bache, said, "Let's go find some coffee."

They left.

"Legal advisor?" Russ said. "Good one, Mort."

"Notice that they're gone. Is Lucy well enough to travel?"

"Probably. No IVs or drains. What's up?"

"Find Ma—Maude Clary—get Lucy checked out of here and on her way to Reno. My story didn't include Danya and Shanna, but hers might. We need to be on the same page."

"Probably a good idea, but it might not be necessary. That Lucy's a pretty sharp gal."

"Knew that. And it sounds like you're on a first-name basis with her, which is interesting considering that she threatened to throw you out a window a few days ago. What'd she do?"

"Cliff and Maude drove you to the hospital. In my car, since Maude said her Caddy is a ground sloth. Lucy made me hang back. She took me into the diner, into the back rooms where those two murderers lived, and got into their computer. She deleted one of the videos, the one where Shanna is walking with Xenon to that helicopter of his."

"Just that one? Why?"

"Because she's sharper than you, Angel."

"I know that. But I'm at something of a disadvantage right now, wounded like this. Gimme a few minutes."

"Take your time."

Russ looked up at the TV where the sound was off, vehicles being dragged out of holes in the blazing sun. I thought about those videos, what they might mean. Shanna walking with Xenon to the helicopter. That tied her directly to Xenon. The second one didn't, but it put Shanna at Arlene's Diner, which was . . .

"Ah-hah," I said.

Russ turned to me, eyes bright, a half-grin on his face. "So, why'd she do it, hotshot?"

"It explains, sort of, how Xenon got in the girls' garage. Not directly, but it gives the police a way to piece it together, in the absence of other information. Buddie put him there. He'd seen Shanna at the diner. He killed Xenon, must've followed Shanna all the way to Reno since he might've been infatuated with her, the way she was dressed at the diner. Or Arlene told him to do it to get Xenon far away from them. Either way. So Buddie stashes Xenon in her garage, leaves a note demanding money. Records might show that his IQ was in the low teens. No telling what an idiot will do. It isn't as if he's around to tell a different story. Getting rid of that first video unhooks Shanna from Xenon."

"Okay, you're a hotshot."

"Think it'll hold up?"

"Don't know. It's thin, but like you said, those two, Arlene and Buddie, won't be telling any tales. Cops will find that one video on her computer and come up with a story. I've got to talk to Danya and Shanna, get them tuned in. Shanna can say she was at the diner, but that's all she knows. She won't have any idea that that woman made a video of her, or why. Danya could also have been there in the ladies' room when the video was made. They can back each other up. They'll need to act surprised as hell to hear that there's a video. But it explains how two murderers latched onto them and, as weak a link as that is without that first video, it must be how Xenon ended up in their garage. End of story. Which also means none of us knows anything about any video of Shanna. Not until we're told, at least."

"Lucy wants to be a private investigator."

"She's definitely got the smarts for it. But she'll be another fuckin' maverick, I can tell."

"No doubt. But you should still have Ma get her out of here. The fewer stories the cops hear, the better. And get Ma thinking about all of this, figuring out what to say, what not to say. She'll be real good at that."

He stared at me for a moment, maybe wondering about why I thought Ma should chew on this, then he took off.

Bache and Webber returned with coffee and more questions, which I answered—truthfully whenever possible, evasively when evasion was necessary, and I tossed out a lot of "I don't knows," which would be impossible to disprove.

Russ returned, gave me a wink, which put a final seal on our buddyship, and I said to Clark County's finest, "I can barely keep my eyes open, guys. How about coming back when I'm awake and feeling more like myself."

"More like yourself, meaning what? Finding bodies?" Bache said.

"That's good. If I use that in a TV interview, I'll give you the credit, Detective."

Apparently that reminded them they might be walking on eggshells here, career-wise. One wrong move and they could end up as IRS agents, which was the kiss of death if you were human. They closed their notebooks and stood up. Bache turned at the door and fed me Schwarzenegger's line, complete with accent and dead-fish eyes: "I'll be back."

Funny guy.

* * *

Three days later, I left Vegas in the Chariot of Fire. Ma had stashed Lucy in her house in Reno and then came back to pick me up. We went north on US 95, so I'd seen the last of Arlene's Diner and the Midnight Rider Motel. I never found out what happened to Melanie and Kirby, but cooking, room cleaning, and waitressing are transportable life skills so I didn't worry.

Russ told me Arlene's safe deposit box had been opened and they'd found forty-four ten-ounce gold bars. With the ones Lucy and I found in the storage shed, and a spot price of $1,205.66 per ounce, that came to a little over five hundred seventy thousand dollars, which would eventually be distributed among surviving family members of those who'd been murdered by the Hickses.

We'd lost the suite at the Luxor—inactivity—but we got the roulette money, so financially the entire southern Nevada venture turned out great. Medically, not so great. I paid the taxes on the winnings using the Stephen Brewer ID. I'd been with the IRS not long ago and still remembered some of the better dodges, but most active IRS agents don't attempt an end run around the IRS because that bunch of folks would eat their own young.

For a while, television was interesting but depressing. They eventually dug fourteen bodies out of the desert, identified every one of them. Arlene and Buddie Hicks, mother and son *serial* murderers—not mass; glad they got *that* straightened out—were right up there with Bundy and Dahmer. If I'd been able to travel, I would've attended the Wharf Rat's—okay, Ignacio's—funeral service. I'd sort of liked the guy at the end. He didn't deserve what he got. *Celebrity News* played it up big, of course, losing one of their own. Never let a story get away. So there I was with Vince, front page as people went through checkout lines. I sold two million copies and got a check from the *News* for $6,500 so they could use my picture. Worth it to them, too, now that I was once again a household name. Like Ty-D-Bol.

CHAPTER TWENTY-EIGHT

I WAS IN the Green Room at the Golden Goose Casino with Ma and Lucy when Holiday walked in. I was slowly working my way through my first Pete's Wicked Ale since I'd been shot. The barkeep, Patrick O'Roarke, had given me a fistful of free-drink coupons. Lucy got the same. She and I were comparing gunshot wounds, but the poor girl was outclassed. Her scar wasn't going to compare to my chunk of missing ear, even though she said not that much was missing and her scar was going to be bigger. I said mine would be more interesting and was likely to generate more comments. We could've played ping-pong with that all night long and gotten drunk, but the shoulder wound was my ace in the hole. In and out, two scars. She'd only been grazed. She'd had an IV for a few hours, no drain, no surgery with anesthesia, no extra pint of blood, and I had that sword wound from last year that had damn near killed me, so she was out of the running, scarwise.

But . . . Holiday. And Lucy. In the same room. They had spoken on the phone two weeks ago when we were on our way to Vegas, and while I was in the hospital I'd told Holiday that Lucy and I had gotten "close" and things might be serious—however I still thought a Kevlar vest and helmet would be useful clothing accessories when those two met.

But I'm never right about that. They hugged. They always do—women who have slept with me, or at least seen me naked. Maybe there's something cosmic about that, something about having shared or survived a life-altering event.

I got Holiday's next hug. I always get sloppy seconds when the girls I know get to hugging.

"Go easy on the grip, kiddo," I told her as she reached for me. "Shoulder's still getting fed OxyContin."

"I'll be gentle."

She was. The impressive bumpers against my chest helped to mitigate the landing. I thought the hug ran a little long and might cause my new assistant to say something about breaking things up, but she didn't. When Holiday and I parted, Lucy's eyes were bright, happy, unconcerned. So, no Kevlar needed.

Holiday backed off and looked at Lucy and me. Her look got sharper. "You two really *are* sort of an item, aren't you?"

Nothing gets by them.

"If he asks me to marry him, I will," Lucy said matter-of-factly. "Like *today* if he slips up. Not sure yet if he believes it, but, yeah, we're pretty much an item."

"Well, good," Holiday said. "'Cause . . ." She looked at me. "I might've found someone. I mean, maybe I have. When I was in San Francisco. He . . . he's what I guess I've been looking for all this time—since, I don't know, maybe even when I was in high school. But, Mort, I don't want you to think that I—"

I put a finger to her lips. "Shh. It's okay, kiddo. If you found what you need, then stick with it."

She hesitated, then smiled. "Well . . . good."

"If he treats you bad, though, let me know and I'll kill 'im."

"He treats me . . . you know, very good."

"Okay, then. But I'll be watching."

* * *

So I lost a girl, gained a girl, and the PI world kept its books in balance.

"You're not really gonna marry that kid, are you?" Russ asked. It was a week after Holiday met Lucy in the Green Room. He and I were in lawn chairs in my backyard, ten thirty at night, a half-moon flying almost directly overhead, temperature still in the upper seventies. "She looks younger than your daughter." His speech was slightly slurred so I knew the beer was in on the conversation. My daughter, Nicole, was twenty-one years old, in Ithaca, New York, finishing up a degree in dance, which was one step up from a degree in art history—so said Lucy. She should know. Lucy was a PI-in-training at Clary Investigations making fourteen bucks an hour. She had a studio apartment where she actually stayed at times, and drove a recently purchased six-year-old Mustang convertible, paid for in cash. She told me I should drive it out on lonely desert roads while she got a little sun and wind, like before, sans shirt.

Russ had brought over two six-packs of what for him was a very fine brew—Bud Heavy. Love those extra calories. At least it wasn't O'Doul's swamp water, otherwise known as "Why Bother Ale," which I would've quietly set aside and used to kill a tough patch of weeds by the back fence the next day.

"Does look kinda young, doesn't she?" I said comfortably.

"Kinda doesn't cover it, Angel."

"You should call me Mort, now that I've compromised you, got a cop in my back pocket. But, yeah, she does look a little bit young. Thing is, she's getting to be an old maid. I found a gray hair on her head yesterday. Made her look twenty-four."

"Jesus."

"She pulled it out, so she's back to nineteen, but those gray hairs are gonna keep coming."

"Around you, yeah." He tried again: "So, you two gonna get hitched?" He burped, followed that up with, "'Scuse."

"To be determined, Russ. To be determined. Twenty years ago I would've jumped at it. Now . . . I'm practically a grown-up. The world isn't as simple as it once was."

"Yeah. Sucks to get ancient, don't it?"

"Did you ever find out what was in the safe?" I asked.

"Comic books."

"Comic books? That all?"

"That's all, except for a few of his nasty-shit CDs and DVD videos of his concerts. Guy had a solid silver sculpture worth fifty thousand and what's he got in his safe? Fuckin' comics."

"I would've liked to have been there if those two had finally got that safe open."

Another round of silence in the dark. A lot of things had been left unsaid since Vegas. I hadn't told him about Josie, or that Ma had found that Josie signed Xenon's guestbook as *Jo-X, Reno 37-25-36 Remember me?* Measurements, no last name, address, or phone number. Maybe she had the feeling she shouldn't give out too much specific information. She was a cop's daughter so maybe something rubbed off. A million teenagers pronounced Jo-X as "Jo-Z," same as Josie, so, all in all, I thought it had been a close call. I'd spoken with Danya, told her what Josie had done, told her to tell Josie to act dumb and cool if cops came around, and if they brought a tape measure, tell 'em to get a court order.

I was on my fourth Bud and Russ was on his sixth, which was probably why he answered when I said, "Arlene and Buddie Hicks didn't kill Xenon. They were murderers, but they didn't kill him like everyone thinks." Everyone being pretty much the entire country, satisfied that Jo-X's killers died behind Arlene's Diner— satisfaction that did not include the FBI. They'd taken over the investigation based on the theory that Jo-X had gone missing and might've been kidnapped before being murdered, making it a clear-cut case for the FBI. No doubt they had visions of basking in the glory when the bullets in Jo-X's head and chest were matched to those from Arlene's revolver, both of which were .38 caliber. Someone in the upper ranks probably lost his or her job when no such match was found, but they were still sticking to the story that Buddie killed Xenon because it was the only story they had. And, of course, Buddie and Arlene were serial murderers.

Which suited all of us who knew the real story just fine.

"Yeah, I know," Russ said once the silence had gotten a little thick. "I wondered if you knew."

"*She* did it. You and I might not know the reason why, but she killed him."

I emphasized "she" but didn't say who *she* was. And I knew why she'd done it, or I had a pretty good idea. Maybe I shouldn't have said anything, just let it go, but I wondered what he would do with the comment. I also wanted to know how far this cop-PI link-up had gotten us.

He remained silent for over a minute. I could almost hear him over there, neurons grinding away. When he spoke, he didn't sound nearly as drunk. "I know," he said at last. "But how'd you get there? I gotta know if, you know, I'm gonna protect her."

He still hadn't said who "she" was, but I thought it was just as well to leave it like that.

"Timing. Ma found gas receipts in Fallon, Ely, Caliente, Ely again, then Austin. Left a trail from Reno to Caliente and back. Ma's a bloodhound. Gas was purchased using Shanna's father's credit card—don't ask me how Ma found that since I don't know—but at that time, Buddie was following Shanna back to Reno, up 95 through Tonopah, different route, so Shanna wasn't the one using her dad's card. Buddie found out where she lives, then he came back and found Xenon already dead. Xenon had seen a private doctor in Vegas to get himself unglued, then he'd driven back to the diner, flown the helicopter up to his place in the hills. Shanna was nowhere around by then. But . . . gas receipts from Reno to Caliente and back right at that time. Perfect match. Who else could have used that credit card? Caliente isn't very far from Xenon's hideaway. Two and two, Russ. But it's not proof."

He thought about that for a while. "I think that's not gonna be a problem. It's too far out on the edge of it. I mean, Shanna's *father's* credit card? I guess he was letting her use it, her being in college and all. Danya's got one of mine. I'm glad she was smart enough not to use it anywhere."

"How'd you figure things out?" I asked him.

"Jesus, Mort. C'mon."

"Hey, as long as we're talkin', Russ."

He sighed, then dug out his wallet, handed me ten dollars.

"What's this for?" I said.

"I'm hiring you for another ten minutes. You get sixty an hour, right? Now what I say is privileged. And anyway, it's not proof either."

"Okay, no proof is good."

"I've got a gun safe at home. She knows the combination. I was in there a few days ago getting a box of ammo, and I found a Ruger LCR .357 Magnum. Thing is, it used to be a Ruger LCR .38 special plus-P."

"Specials don't often morph into Magnums. Not even plus-P specials."

"No they don't. She didn't know the difference. Guess she knew it was a Ruger LCR, barrel about two inches long, but that's all. It took some doing, but two days ago I found that she bought it at Cabela's. Got the gun registration documents and the background check. She's got a clean record, so buying that gun took roughly an hour. I haven't told her. Not sure what the point would be, so I won't unless it becomes an issue." He looked a question over at me.

"Not me, Russ. I don't have a dog in that fight. It feels like a father-daughter thing. Let's keep it that way."

"Thanks. If the FBI finds that she bought a gun, it'll be after this Xenon business, not before. So she bought it for protection and with my blessing. In fact, now that I think about it, maybe I oughta take her out to a gun range, get her qualified for a carry permit. That'd be good if the FBI comes sniffing around. My dad got that LCR special at a gun show about thirty years ago, when I was still in high school."

"So, no record of you ever owning it."

"Nope. Even if they find the gun somewhere it won't come back to me. But I sure hope she got rid of it someplace where it will never be found."

"She's a cop's daughter."

"Uh-huh. Hope some of that rubbed off." He fell silent, then said, "I still don't know why she'd do something like that. Take out Xenon. Doesn't make any sense."

"You'll have to ask her. I couldn't tell you." Which was true in a sense, but not the way he would take it.

After another minute of silence I said, "Sometimes it doesn't go our way, Russ. Sometimes life is a bitch. We want it tied up in a neat bundle, good guys innocent, bad guys dead or in prison, and sometimes it isn't like that. Xenon in her garage, it makes no sense that she would put him there, and she didn't, so obviously she couldn't have killed him, and then . . . turns out she did. So you end up with an elephant in the refrigerator, not sure what to do about it. Sometimes Occam's Razor doesn't work, which in this case is a good thing."

"Occam's Razor. That's where the simplest explanation is the way it actually happened."

"Yup. Simplest explanation is that Buddie killed Jo-X when he stole stuff from the guy's place, took him up to Reno and hung him in that garage to throw the police off. That particular garage because he liked the way Shanna looked when he saw her at the diner. Something like that, something the FBI will never be able to prove or disprove."

"Jesus, that last part is still goddamn thin."

"But it's where the FBI is at now. I imagine Occam's Razor has 'em scratching their heads. I doubt that it feels right to them but it's all they've got."

He sighed. "Hope that's as far as they ever get."

"Arlene and Buddie aren't gonna put their two cents in. And the Feds will want to close this thing out, go home. They'll take what they can get even if the bullets don't match the gun."

A wet washrag tied in a knot missed me by a foot, landed on the grass beside me with a damp plop. I leaned over and picked it up. Behind me, Lucy called down from the upstairs bedroom window, "That's enough talk, guys. It's late. You should come on up, Mort. I think there's a problem with the shower—the water thingie."

"The *water* thingie?"

"Like the nozzle or the drain or something. You should come up and help me check it out. Like *totally*," she said in her Valley Girl voice.

"Jesus," Russ sighed.

"Be right there, kiddo." My shoulder still wasn't a hundred percent. I levered myself awkwardly out of the lawn chair with one
arm. "Duty calls, Russ."

"I ever tell you I'm in the wrong goddamn line of work?"

"Couple of times. But you probably ought to stick it out on the
force, get the brass-and-walnut 'attaboy' plaque for your wall, and
the damp handshake. Getting shot isn't for wimps."

"Wimps. Screw you, Mort." He got to his feet. "'Night. Oh, the
ten minutes are about up so you're fired again." He headed for the
gate in the fence that would let him out to the street.

"After all this, I think you still owe me, Russ," I called after him.
"So if I ever give you a call, needing some little thing . . ."

"Yeah, yeah, yeah."

The gate clicked shut behind him. I waited a few seconds, then
smiled, listened to the quiet, thought about how good it was to
still be alive and finally off the OxyContin, gave the stars one last
look, then went inside and hiked upstairs to the second floor to
see what I could do about the water thingie.